"I'll turn my back and close my eyes, if you'll do the same."

"Always practical," he grunted, stripping off his shirt, pants and boots, then wrapping the other quilt around himself.

She worked her petticoats off. When she heard him speaking softly, she clutched the quilt tightly around herself and turned.

He had pulled a splintery but sturdy-looking bench up close to the fire and motioned her to join him. "If we huddle together, we'll dry faster."

She turned her face up to his and watched his profile in the dancing firelight, bronzed and beautiful.

Feeling her eyes on him, he looked down into their violet depths. "I was right," he said softly. "Your eyes do darken in passion." Taking her head in his hands, he raised it until her lips met his in a searing kiss.

★ ★ ★

MOON FLOWER

Also by Shirl Henke

Golden Lady
Love Unwilling
Capture the Sun
Cactus Flower
*Night Flower**

**Published by
WARNER BOOKS**

*forthcoming

MOON FLOWER

SHIRL HENKE

WARNER BOOKS

A Warner Communications Company

WARNER BOOKS EDITION

Copyright © 1989 by Shirl Henke
All rights reserved.

Cover design by Barbara Buck
Cover illustration by Max Ginsburg

Warner Books, Inc.
666 Fifth Avenue
New York, N.Y. 10103

A Warner Communications Company

Printed in the United States of America

First Printing: October, 1989

10 9 8 7 6 5 4 3 2 1

For Ken Reynard, who has put up with two "wives" for all these years. "This is for you, Herbie!"

ACKNOWLEDGMENT

As always, I am indebted to my associate Carol V. Reynard for correcting plot and character problems as well as putting my illegible copy on the word processor and editing it afterward.

Once more Carol and I wish to thank Mrs. Hildegard Schnuttgen, Head of Reference at Youngstown State University's Maag Library for her outstanding assistance in securing research materials for us. Mrs. Jessica Travis, Reference Librarian for The Historic New Orleans Collection, was exceedingly helpful in settling a fine point about the Theatre d'Orleans in the 1830s. Mr. John Dibrell of the Sons of the Republic of Texas was kind enough to furnish us with firsthand information about the Jared Groce family.

Texas in the nineteenth century was a violent land where guns were a part of everyday life. For accurate information on the firearms used by Rafe and Joe, as well as those of the Rangers and Comancheros, we are once more indebted to Dr. Carmine V. DelliQuadri, Jr., D.O., weapons collector.

A NOTE FOR MY HUSBAND

After being teased by Carol and me about the lack of romance in the male soul, my husband Jim bet us that he could write a love scene as sensual and as sensitive as one written by a woman, a love scene that would fit the personalities of Rafe and Deborah.

We agreed that if he could write it, we would use it in *Moon Flower*. Well, he did and we have.

A NOTE FOR MY READERS

If you believe you have found Jim's love scene, please write and let us know. Jim, Carol and I are very eager to hear reader opinion regarding his talent as a romance author.

Write to:

Shirl Henke
P.O. Box 72
Adrian, Michigan 49221

Prologue

Boston, 1829

"Deborah Faith Manchester, what are you doing?" Adam Manchester thundered at his thirteen-year-old daughter, who was seated comfortably on the cushions in the library's big bay window, book in hand.

Making no attempt to hide the title, Deborah held the volume securely as she looked at her father. "Why, as you can plainly see, Father, I'm reading."

Adam Manchester was a tall man with iron-gray hair and an austere face that frequently made his subordinates at the bank quake in terror. "I can see that you're reading, but why read that degenerate book?"

Deborah smiled with a serenity that belied her tender years and challenged her father. "You don't object to what Mary Wollstonecraft says, only to the fact that she's related to the scandalous Shelleys."

"And just what does a gently reared young lady know about such libertines as that disgraceful Englishman Shelley?" Adam asked indignantly.

"I know about their free-love notions, and I don't approve of them."

"Well, heavens be praised for that!"

1

She went on calmly, "When I marry a man, I expect it will be as binding on him as on me. A woman can believe in equal rights for her sex, even if she doesn't advocate free love."

"Where have you learned to discuss such unladylike subjects, Miss Manchester?" Adam demanded, admiring her intelligence.

Deborah's lavender eyes danced, reminding him of her mother, dead for over ten years. "You know perfectly well Lisette sends me books. After all, Father, it was you who wanted me to learn French."

"I wanted you to learn to speak French, not to read radical tracts."

"But I read them in French—and understood every word," she added impishly.

"That insane tutor is at fault. I should never have hired a Frenchwoman." Adam inspected the stack of books: some in French, some in English, all dealing with the rights of the lower classes, blacks, and women.

"Don't blame Lisette, Father. She may have brought me the books, but I began thinking for myself at an early age. After all, I'm Adam Manchester's daughter."

Replacing William Godwin's "Political Justice" on the window cushion, Adam put his hands on Deborah's shoulders and looked assessingly into her eyes. "Yes, you undoubtedly are, but I do wish you had inherited your mother's quiet, biddable nature as well as her beauty."

Deborah frowned. Looks were always a sore subject for her. "I'm hardly bound to be a beauty, so I'd best be a bluestocking, don't you think? I'm far too tall and gangly and my hair is lank and colorless. I—"

Adam gave her a gentle shake of reproof. "You are the image of your mother with her beautiful eyes and silver-gilt hair. Just wait until you mature. You'll not be thin and gangly at all. I'm sure I'll be dealing with lovesick young swains by the wagon load."

"I may have Mother's coloring, but I'm afraid I've your considerable height. You should have had a son, not a misfit daughter," she finished forlornly.

"You will be no more than five feet seven inches, I'm certain, and as striking as a platinum Athena."

"Don't you remember, Father, Athena was fated to remain a spinster? And I'm certainly not Aphrodite!" Deborah added with a gentle laugh. "If a man ever appears who would make me a good husband, I'll recognize him and he'll understand he's getting no simpering little puss for a wife."

"All I want is your happiness, Deborah," Adam insisted, "and whether or not you believe it now, it does mean searching for the *right* husband."

New Orleans, 1829

It was Rafael Beaurivage Flamenco's sixteenth birthday and he was very nervous. "I still do not see why this must be arranged now, Papa," the youth protested as he stepped down from their family's gleaming black carriage onto Orleans Street.

His father, already standing on the banquette beneath a flickering gas lamp, stared up at his son. Although he was five foot ten himself, Claude Adrien Flamenco was dwarfed by his boy, and both were much taller than the average Creole gentleman.

"You are a man grown," he rejoined in precise French.

Rafael sighed. He knew what the older man was going to say.

"What do you think will happen if you continue your irresponsible behavior? I will tell you—disgrace!"

The shadowy lights from the street lamp cast the youth's face in sharp relief, coolly haughty and cynically handsome for one of such tender years. "Hardly such disgrace, Papa. After all, Sally Drewery is only an overseer's daughter. You carry on as if I had seduced the daughter of Prospero d'Valmy or Pierre LeJeune."

Claude guided the angry youth toward an arched doorway and into the wide passageway where stairs curved upward. "I realize you are a man now and must indulge the appetites of a man. That is natural. I also realize you know enough not to touch the young women of our class. That is laudable—

and sane," he added with irony. "However, you are too young to marry and too careless in choosing whom you bed."

"So that means I must take on the responsibility of a mistress," Rafael finished his father's speech. "I like variety, Papa. Placing a girl on Rampart Street means almost the same thing as marrying a girl at the cathedral—the same woman, the same boring face, year in and out, not to mention children."

"Yes, we should consider children," Claude interrupted. "A gentleman takes responsibility for his actions, unlike some crass American who breeds indiscriminately and then walks away from his obligations. Consorting with cheap harlots or seducing white trash is not our way, any more than is lying with slaves and having our issue born into perpetual servitude."

"I have never taken advantage of a slave wench, Papa," Rafael replied, stung by the implication.

"I never said you had," the older man replied. "As to the young women you are about to meet," Claude said with a smile, "I do not think you will find them in the least boring. They are educated and charming, yet full of vivacity and fire. Perhaps therein lies the problem, eh? To an impoverished girl like Sally Drewery you are a paragon of a lover and a gentleman. A beautiful octoroon may not be as impressed."

Rafael stiffened. "I shall impress them, Papa," he replied arrogantly. "After all, I am your son."

There could be no doubt of that fact. The two were much alike—only the gray at his temples and a few facial creases marked Claude as twenty-four years the elder. Besides their physical resemblance, they also shared an uncertain temper, fierce Latin pride, and an unflagging interest in the opposite sex. And now, as his own father had once done for him, Claude was taking his son to a Blue Ribbon Ball to choose a quadroon mistress.

"I do not think these belles kissed by the tar brush will find me unappealing," Rafael reassured himself.

Amused by his son's rejoinder, Claude expanded on the etiquette of the business they would transact tonight.

"Remember, after I make the preliminary arrangements with the girl's mother, it will be your responsibility to pay all your mistress's household expenses and, in time, I am confident, see to the children's education."

Rafael grimaced, dropping his mask of sophistication. "It still sounds like marriage to me."

His father laughed tolerantly. "You will have a beautiful, undemanding woman at your command. Caring for the offspring of such a discreet liaison is a small price, believe me. What if you had gotten that Drewery girl with child and had to marry her? That would have been a far worse bargain, I assure you!"

Rafael looked genuinely aghast. "You're actually serious!" He paused to consider, shaking his head to clear it of the horrible vision. "Marry an American? Barbarous! I've always found them overly tall and pale, with appallingly forward ways. No, not for me, Papa." Both men laughed.

They made their way up the wide, curving staircase with its intricately worked, wrought-iron railing. At the top of the steps stood an enormous black man dressed in maroon velvet. He nodded politely to Monsieur Flamenco as he took his tickets and opened the door to the Salle d'Orleans.

The grand ballroom above Toto Davis's gambling establishment was vast, with large double doors opening onto a gallery that circled the building on three sides. The polished hardwood floor and huge crystal chandeliers glowed with the light from thousands of candles. There were brass-railed loges with velvet upholstered seats against the far wall.

Although it was early, the enormous room was already filled with people. Gray-haired Women of Color sat in the loges and watched the scene with pride and predatory interest, while rich white men of all ages laughed and talked in carefree enjoyment. The center of attention was the group of beautiful quadroons and octoroons of pale complexion and midnight tresses who flitted among them like silken butterflies.

Rafael surveyed the dozens of bewitching creatures dressed in Paris gowns as he sipped the finest French champagne, but he was too excited to taste any of the delectable food spread before him. One girl, with an exquisite, tiny face and voluptuous figure, smiled demurely at him, then looked quickly away. She was very young, dressed in a pale rose gown that set off her ivory skin and red lips magnificently. Her features were cameo perfect, and he found himself hypnotized by her enormous golden eyes. Rafael walked unobtrusively over to his father, and soon an elderly Creole gentleman, Armand Ferrier, was making introductions.

"Rafael Flamenco, may I present Lily Duvall."

Chapter 1

Boston, 1835

"Really, Deborah, I don't think you should do it," Lydia Beecher declared. She and her friend had been riding in companionable silence for several minutes on their way to the Bon Marche Modiste.

"Do what?" Deborah pulled herself from her reverie.

"I don't think you should go through with the wedding," Lydia said. For once her bubbling, flighty mein was subdued.

"Not marry Oliver! The engagement party is tomorrow night. We've planned this for months. We are in every way suitable—family backgrounds, religious beliefs, mutual interests and philosophical—"

"Oh, pooh to philosophy," Lydia interrupted her friend's familiar litany. "What about love? Has he ever held you in his arms, ever kissed you?"

Deborah's pale complexion pinkened. She'd already argued with her father on numerous occasions since she had agreed to become Oliver's wife. "Such romantic drivel, Lydia. You read too many novels."

Before she could say anything more, Lydia pounced, "There, you see! You evade the question because you don't

7

even want to think about touching Oliver. I always thought he was a cold fish.''

''That's not fair,'' Deborah defended her fiancé, but she did have some qualms about the nature of their relationship. As if to allay her misgivings, she began to go over her reasons for accepting his suit once more. ''You know how strongly I feel about a woman's position in marriage, Lydia. By law, she loses all rights to her property—even her children are totally under her husband's control. I could never play the simpering, fainting belle to please the vanity of some man. I think women and men should have equal rights. Oliver agrees with me. He respects my mind and will treat me as an adult.''

''I can see it now.'' Lydia rolled her large blue eyes in exasperation. ''There you are, on your honeymoon, all alone on a cozy winter's evening, sitting before a roaring fire. He takes your hand in his and looks deeply into your eyes, sighs, and says, Deborah, my darling, how shall we while away the hours tonight—discussing Mr. Smith's 'Wealth of Nations' or Mr. Malthus's 'Essay on Population'?''

Always lurking beneath the surface of her seriousness, Deborah's sense of humor burst forth as she let out a hearty chuckle. ''Why, Lydia, I never knew you were such a bluestocking! When did you read Adam Smith or Thomas Malthus?''

Lydia shrugged disgustedly. ''I never did, thank God! I just picked up the names from all those boring books you leave lying around. Don't you see, Deborah? You may resent social conventions. Lord knows, Boston is a stuffy, prudish old place, and women's lives are dull and rigid. But that's all the more reason to find an exciting man, one who'll cherish you, dote on you and let you have your way because he loves you, not because of some abstract philosophical ideas. I'd never trust a man who thinks too much, especially if he's not handsome either.''

''Really, Lydia, Oliver may not be the most dashing man in Boston, but he suits me. I don't want to wheedle my way around a husband! I certainly don't want him to dote on me. I can't abide weakness.'' Her eyes were dark with anger now and a bit of ill-concealed hurt.

Lydia was instantly contrite. "Oh, Deborah, I didn't mean to disparage Oliver, or you either. I just wish you'd get over your feelings of inferiority. You are beautiful—why, I'd give anything to have your silvery hair, violet eyes, and statuesque figure."

"You're beginning to sound like Father. Statuesque, indeed! I'm too tall, and men are put off by me. I suspect it's my mind and my manner as much as my looks, but I can't change my ideals any more than I can my height. Be satisfied if I tell you I'm marrying Oliver because he's tall enough for me. Or because he's the only one who has asked me," she finished on a note of grim humor that silenced Lydia's protests.

Just then, they pulled up at Learned Street, which housed the best dressmaker and tailor shops in the city. Deborah's trousseau was being assembled here. She alighted from the carriage with a sigh, thinking of the endless fittings. While Lydia reveled in such frippery, Deborah never had. She had learned the social graces, and how to dress to accent her striking coloring, but she had never exerted any effort to make herself attractive to men.

They spent the next two hours at the dressmaker. By the time they left the shop, Deborah was smarting from pin pricks and stiff from posing. "I positively hate fittings. If only one could walk into a shop and select from large rows of gowns already made up and nicely arranged by size."

"What odd ideas you have, Deborah." Lydia skipped a step as they were strolling down the street, heading toward the milliner's shop in the next block. "It's such a lovely day, let's take a stroll through the park across the way," she said impulsively.

"What are you up to, Lydia? I know you never walk when you can ride. You'll get your curls mussed in the breeze." Deborah looked around as they stepped across the street and began to walk toward the small tree-shaded common, ringed by elegant tradesmen's shops.

Suddenly, her soft lavender eyes locked with a pair of liquid black ones, staring intently at her from a scant fifteen feet away. "Oh," was all she could manage before her throat seemed to collapse on itself and her heart started to thud. Quickly, Deborah looked down at the walk. She forced her feet do her bidding and take her swiftly away from the tall, foreign-looking stranger who was lounging against a light post, watching them—no, watching *her*, she amended. She could still feel the heat of his black eyes scorching her back.

Before they were even out of earshot, Lydia was giggling. "Slow down. We're just out for a stroll in a public park, after all. Now *that* was a specimen I'd think you might consider taking on a honeymoon!"

Deborah gasped and blushed again at her friend's teasing, walking faster as if to escape.

Lydia grabbed Deborah's arm. "He's heading toward the central path. If we walk slowly around the corner at Jacobs Street, he'll cut across our path before he leaves the park. Honestly, Deborah, isn't he the most gorgeous man you've ever seen!" Lydia looked at her friend's flushed face and continued with a superior smirk, "Don't bother to deny it. You thought so, too. Do you suppose he's a foreigner? The clothes, that dark, mysterious air about him. Maybe he's a count or a duke."

"Oh, will you stop it. He's simply some French or Italian dandy, looking for a rich and *foolish* young woman to charm. Anyway, I don't like his forward manner! No gentleman stares at a lady that way!" Deborah could still picture in her mind the sardonic arch of those black brows as the jet eyes bored into her, dancing with mirth at her flushed discomfiture.

"Don't look now, but he's crossing our path again and he really has his eye on you," Lydia hissed, half-amused, half-jealous, for the handsome stranger was indeed strolling across the park on a collision course with them, his gaze fixed unwaveringly on Deborah.

Just as he stepped onto the paved sidewalk in front of them, he stopped and removed the flat-crowned white hat from his head of curly black hair. Making a sweeping bow, he flourished his hat in a courtly manner as he allowed them to pass. He smiled but made no attempt to speak.

Against her will, Deborah found her eyes drawn to him. For several seconds, which seemed like hours, she scanned the classically handsome face, shocked at his boldly admiring gaze. Lewd, that's what it was, absolutely, positively libertine! As if she were some cheaply dressed streetwalker, parading her wares for sale!

Furiously she hissed to Lydia, "Now what do we do? We have to get to the milliner's shop and that means circling all the way around the park or backtracking. Either way he'll know we deliberately cut across to meet him."

"Well, he cut across to see you again, too," Lydia said with a smirk. "Anyway, I'd think an independent woman like you wouldn't care a fig *what* he thought!"

Gritting her teeth, Deborah replied, "You're right," and headed toward the street. "We'll just walk back on the other side of Jacobs Street." So intent was she on escaping the scorching smile of the stranger that she failed to hear the thundering roll of wagon wheels as a huge dray filled with coal careened down the street. Lydia stood rooted to the curb in horror as Deborah stepped abruptly into the path of the onrushing wagon. However, before the mules' sharp hooves could claim their victim, a blur of white intervened. The stranger scooped her into his arms and lifted her back onto the sidewalk as if she were no more than a feather.

Once the overloaded wagon had rumbled past them, he slowly released her, still saying not a word, his night-black eyes mesmerizing her. Deborah could feel the heat of his fingers as they seemed to burn through the thin muslin of her gown. As she reached up to brush her windblown hair from her face, he released her arm. Despite the chill, she felt flushed and weak-kneed but knew it was not from the accident.

Taking a deep breath, she looked up at him and said, "I thank you. You probably saved my life."

"Enchanté, mademoiselle," he replied, dazzling her with a blinding white smile. His complexion was swarthy, and his classically handsome features made him look like some marvelous Greek statue sprung suddenly to life. A lock of ebony hair fell carelessly onto his high forehead as he spoke in a surprisingly soft voice, saying in French, "It was my greatest pleasure to be of assistance. Rafael Beaurivage Flamenco at your command, beautiful Moon Flower."

Raising one delicate silvery brow, Deborah replied in perfect Parisian French, "I'm scarcely a flower, Mr. Flamenco, just a woman who is grateful for your timely help. Now, if you will excuse me . . .''

Deborah saw that he was surprised at her French. Good. Then he smiled insolently and made another flourish with his hat as she turned her back to walk away. Lydia trailed unwillingly after her. If he had only given Mademoiselle Beecher a glance or the slightest encouragement, Deborah knew her friend, in violation of Boston propriety, would have stayed behind to introduce herself. But he had looked at *her*—tall, gawky Deborah. He had not even seemed to notice petite, curvaceous Lydia. Was that why her heart was hammering and her blood racing?

"Do you suppose he's from France? What did he say?" Lydia was as breathless as Deborah, but a great deal less self-conscious about showing it.

"What he said is of no consequence," Deborah replied blithely, attempting to calm her shattered nerves. "He was rather forward and introduced himself. I merely thanked him for his assistance."

Lydia snorted in disbelief at her friend's prim manner.

All afternoon, as they shopped, Lydia chattered about their mysterious Frenchman. Deborah volunteered nothing but became more quiet and withdrawn, pondering her emotions, as runaway as that teamster's dray.

"Only one last stop, Hornby's Merchandisers," Deborah said with a sigh. She did not favor the establishment, for the English merchant who ran it was noted for his sharp business practices. However, Lydia had ordered some oriental brocade from the man. One paid dearly, but the kind of merchandise he offered was available virtually nowhere else in the New World.

They once more climbed aboard the Manchester family carriage and their driver Simms flipped the reins. He had spent many a long day transporting his mistress and her friends on shopping excursions. At least the weather was warm.

For Boston, the April day was unseasonably warm. To Rafael Flamenco it seemed miserably cold. February was spring in New Orleans. Here in this godforsaken Yankee wilderness, it was probably winter until July! His elegantly cut white linen suit, so comfortable when he had left home, was definitely not keeping the chill harbor wind from cutting into his shivering bones. He grinned, remembering the way those Boston misses had stared at his unusual planter's clothing.

"Well, not only my suit," he chuckled, half-aloud. The brunette was flirtatious and open, but the tall one, that lilac-eyed Amazon with the silver-gilt hair, had been fascinated and then angry with herself for her attraction to him—an interesting reaction. She was a cool one and her French was flawless. Perhaps they might meet again, he mused as he paid the hack driver and stepped into the interior of the enormous import house.

By the time Deborah and Lydia arrived at Hornby's, Deborah had a pounding headache. Just nerves, she thought to herself in vexation. As they walked through the crowded emporium to the draper's counter, Deborah heard a familiar voice, cursing stridently in French.

"You dare such an insult, you son of a bitch! If you were a gentleman, I'd call you out." Rafael's face was a thundercloud of furious anger as he threw a bolt of brocade at the Englishman whose narrow eyes were now opened wide in apoplectic anger.

"You see here, you French bastard—"

"Excuse me, Mr. Hornby, Monsieur—Flamenco," Deborah interrupted the tirade, embarrassed at hearing such language and at encountering the Frenchman for the third time in one day. Still, he was a stranger in her country and no doubt spoke little English. It would be like the calculating Hornby to try and fleece a foreigner. At least she owed Monsieur Flamenco her offices as translator after he had saved her life!

Both men turned toward her, surprised as her clear, calm voice intervened in their shouting. "Now, what is the nature of your disagreement, gentlemen?"

"He's a damn froggy thief, that's what he is, Miss Manchester," Ian Hornby said, then muttered a halfhearted apology for his language.

Rafael spoke rapidly in French. "A misunderstanding, I am afraid, Miss Manchester. I agreed to make a most sizable purchase of cloth of gold and brocade, at exorbitant cost. It seems not to be a Yankee custom to bargain over the price as it is where I come from. When I suggested one of those paltry lace handkerchiefs as *lagniappe*, this swine flew into a rage as if I were a common thief bent on slipping it into my pocket!''

"Lagniappe," Deborah said questioningly. Her French was excellent, but she was uncertain of this word.

Rafael smiled and once more her heart seemed to stop. ''Just a colloquial expression, Miss Manchester. It's a custom to throw in some small item when a customer makes a large purchase,'' he said, glowering again in Hornby's direction.

''Look here, Miss Manchester, I don't want no trouble. You vouch for this Frenchy and I'll let it go.''

''Just how much were you charging him for that bolt of brocade?'' She indicated the deep rose cloth lying across the counter.

Hornby seemed to wriggle inside his ill-fitting clothing. ''Well . . .''

''How much were you paying for the brocade?'' she asked Rafael in French.

''One hundred fifty American dollars,'' he replied with one handsome brow arched sardonically, awaiting her reaction.

''One hundred fifty! Why that old robber! My friend ordered the same fabric in yellow only last week and paid seventy-five for it.''

She turned to Hornby and said sweetly in English, ''Surely you want to reconsider and perhaps bargain a bit with Mr. Flamenco over these bolts. And for the price you charge foreigners, I'd add a whole box of lace handkerchiefs.''

Hornby was in a mood to compromise. The youth was tall and dangerous looking, for all his dandified French airs. ''Just explain to him it's all a mistake and I'll write it up as one hundred fifty total, for both bolts.''

Deborah watched the two men complete the transaction and then on impulse she tossed in a lace kerchief while Hornby's clerk was wrapping the package. Rafael smiled. She smiled back saying, *"Lagniappe."*

Deborah felt pleased that she was able to do something to

repay her rescuer. After all, she was only furthering international goodwill. Then why, a small voice nagged, did she wonder who the dress lengths were for? Quickly banishing such thoughts, she responded to Rafael's earnest thanks and blushed like a schoolgirl when he took her hand and saluted it with a gallant kiss. He did not ask where she lived or any other personal questions. Of course, good manners dictated that he not be so forward, but she felt an unexpected stab of disappointment when he turned and walked away with his purchases after bidding her and Lydia good day.

As she woke the next morning, Deborah lay abed for a few minutes. Tonight she would be officially betrothed to Oliver Haversham IV. And she had just spent the whole night dreaming about a dark face with burning black eyes. Throwing off the covers, Deborah sat up abruptly and said, "I can at least control my waking thoughts and I will think only of Oliver today." But she had a difficult time picturing his dark blond hair and light gray eyes, the thin face with its undistinguished features.

Angrily she slipped into a pink linen day dress that her father particularly liked. She would meet him at his bank so they could have lunch together.

Lately, they had not been getting on well and she wanted to do what small things she could to please him. Adam did not approve of her betrothal to Oliver. He didn't prattle of romance like Lydia, but he had made it clear to her that he considered Oliver a snob and an odd sort for agreeing with her ideas on women's rights. He even had hinted that her fiancé might be a bit of a hypocrite, but Deborah had refused to listen.

Adam and Felicia Manchester had been devoted partners in a happy marriage. Deborah desperately longed for that same kind of warmth and security, but every man who had courted her had been unappealing and gauche or insensitive and overbearing. She no more wanted a mewling weakling whom she could dominate than she wanted a pompous ass who would try to direct her life. Then Oliver had come

along just as her twentieth birthday—and spinsterhood—
loomed.

Mr. Bascomb, her father's secretary, was already at lunch.
The heavy walnut door to Adam's office was ajar. She
reached for the knob, then froze as a now familiar voice
caught her ear. The sibilant tones were in English, albeit
spoken with a thick French accent, but fluent colloquial
English!

"I feel my aunt Jolie would want all the family heirlooms
restored to the Beaurivages, Mr. Manchester. As to the
other household furnishings and the home itself, sell them. I
trust your judgment implicitly."

"Are you sure you'll get full value from an American,
Monsieur Flamenco? After all, one of our wily New England
merchants tried to cheat you only yesterday afternoon."
Deborah said as she glided into the office.

Adam noted Rafael's look of recognition. "You've met
Mr. Flamenco?" he asked Deborah.

Before she could reply, Rafael smiled at her and turned to
Adam, explaining smoothly, "Yes, your lovely daughter
was kind enough to rescue me from the clutches of an
unscrupulous import dealer yesterday. I owe her a considerable debt."

"Not nearly so much as I owe you, Monsieur Flamenco." A hint of steel lurked beneath her dulcet tone. "Father,
this gentleman rescued me from a reckless drayman yesterday when Lydia and I were out shopping. I didn't tell you of
the mishap for fear of upsetting you."

"Well, it seems our visitor from New Orleans has had
quite an exciting introduction to our fair city," Adam
replied, curious to hear more about the preceding day.

"New Orleans!" Deborah hated the squeak in her voice.
Gathering her composure, she said, "I understood you were
French, Mr. Flamenco."

His smile was blinding. "I assure you I was born in the
United States, in Louisiana. My mother is of French descent
and my father's mother was also. My father is a Flamenco,
grandson of one of General Alesandro O'Reilly's Spaniards,
who captured New Orleans from the French in 1769 "

"Then you are a Creole," Deborah replied coolly. She knew her history and was determined not to be patronized.

He smiled and nodded, but before he could reply, Adam said, "Well, considering the debt we owe you, Mr. Flamenco, we must extend our hospitality. I am giving a large party this evening to announce my daughter's engagement. You simply must come."

Scorching Deborah with his piercing black eyes, Rafael replied, "Nothing could keep me away, Monsieur Manchester. Absolutely nothing at all." When he smiled, she felt as if he were probing the deepest recesses of her mind, and she blushed.

"Until tonight, Mademoiselle Manchester." He kissed her hand and felt her tremble.

Chapter 2

Rafael shivered in the chill night air as each jounce of the carriage jarred his cold-stiffened bones. Mary and Joseph, how he hated this wretched New England weather! Never in all his life had he been this cold, not even in the north of France when he had gone to the university.

He leaned back against the hard leather seat of the hack and pulled his greatcoat more tightly around him. What was he doing, going to the Manchester miss's engagement party? The Yankee beauty had interested him yesterday as a diversion. Her unsophisticated reaction, then her surprising wit and flawless French were all intriguing, but she was furious with him for his deception at the importers yesterday. He should have declined her father's invitation. He already had enough woman trouble in New Orleans. Still, there was something about the icy-proper Lady Deborah.

Initially, he had attributed the attraction to her exotic coloring. After all, he was used to Creole belles with raven or chestnut hair. Occasionally, a dark blonde appeared, such as his sister. But Deborah's hair was like moonlight, a gleaming meld of silver and palest gold. Her porcelain skin was tinted the most delicate rose hue when she blushed or became angry. He could imagine her enormous lavender eyes darkening to violet in passion. Yes, for all her cool New England propriety, he'd bet that willowy body and silken flesh would quiver under the caress of the right man. He was certain that her fiancé would not be the right man, but some dry intellectual more interested in discussing Plato than in making love. She's picked exactly such a man because she's hiding from herself. Now why did he think that? And why, unbidden, did the thought come to him that he would love to show her what it meant to be a woman?

Rafael swore beneath his breath, realizing the dire complications that could result if he dallied with a proper virgin from a prominent Boston family. If he weren't careful, he could set off a scandal that would follow him all the way back to New Orleans.

He sighed. If only Aunt Jolie had not become involved with Yankees in the first place, he would not be here now, freezing in this miserable place. But she had married a wretched Bostonian. His mother's family had considered it disgraceful to claim a Yankee of uncertain pedigree, a Protestant and a tradesman to boot. Despite the threat of being disowned by her Creole relatives, Jolie had eloped with Graham Warden, a merchant seaman, who had taken her to Boston. At least he did have the good grace to become rich. But now both Graham and Jolie had died without children and it was left to the Beaurivage family to settle the estate. Rafael had been sent north to see to the details.

When he had learned Deborah Manchester's name yesterday, he felt certain she was related to Adam Manchester, the banker who was handling Aunt Jolie's affairs. Of course, he had been surprised to see her descend on Adam's office like one of the furies. He chuckled, recalling her anger. The lady did not like to be deceived.

* * *

"My dear Charles, surely you don't think this is some sort of a love match!" Oliver Haversham uncoiled his long thin frame from the sofa in Adam Manchester's study. He and his cousin Charles were taking a break from the tedium of the engagement party to have a splash of Adam's excellent brandy.

Charles Haversham smiled. "Now Oliver, the chit may be a bit on the tall, thin side, but she is a real beauty and dresses right handsomely, too. Always did favor dark women with big breasts myself, but . . . all that pale silky hair. I say, is it the same color . . ." His voice trailed off delicately as he looked speculatively at his cousin.

If Oliver took offense at the lewd inquiry, he did not show it. "She's a cold fish, I'm afraid. I've never had the interest to pursue, er, divesting her of her clothes or her chastity. That onerous task will fall on our wedding night—that is, if she doesn't engage me in one of her infernal debates about women's rights."

Charles took a quick gulp of his brandy and looked up at his lanky cousin, nearly choking as he said, "Women's rights? Not that rubbish about giving them property rights or the vote? Might as well let one of those black slaves down in Mississippi run Manchester's bank!"

"Quite so, but I'm afraid the success of my suit for Deborah has been predicated upon an ardent espousal of 'her cause.' She thinks me in complete accord with her insane notions and will until I'm firmly and legally in control of her fortune. Then I'll settle matters once and for all."

Deborah stood rooted in the hall, her hand gripping the knob of the study door. She had gone in search of her fiancé, having missed him for the past half hour. Never in her worst nightmare could she have imagined what she had just overheard. Nausea churned in her stomach and bright points of light danced before her eyes. She must collect herself. Then she would face Oliver alone and confront him with his perfidy.

Taking a deep breath, she silently eased the heavy door closed and walked on unsteady legs down the hall. She intended to step into a small sitting room to regain her composure, but her plans were suddenly upset by an unexpected collision.

"Oh, I'm so sorry," she gasped as a pair of strong hands reached out to steady her. Deborah looked at the shiny black boots in front of her own slippered feet, then her gaze traveled up faultlessly tailored gray wool-clad legs to a slim waist encircled by a maroon brocade waistcoat. When her gaze reached the dark, intense face, she gasped, then murmured, "Oh, no!" The last person on earth she wanted to see at this ignominious moment was Rafael Flamenco!

"Are you all right? You look white as porcelain." His hands remained on her pale, trembling shoulders.

"Yes, yes, of course. I just felt a bit warm from the stuffy air in the ballroom. It's quite crowded and I was going to slip into an unheated sitting room for some cool air." She freed herself from his grasp and whirled in a blur of aquamarine silk, vanishing down the hall.

Shrugging, Rafael entered the large ballroom where a lavish buffet table groaned under beef roasts, lobsters in cream sauce, and other sumptuous foods. Next to it stood a bar, complete with champagne fountain and an extensive selection of fine rums and scotch whiskeys. A twelve-piece orchestra played at one end of the room and dozens of couples danced, while even more stood about laughing and talking.

"Quite an impressive turnout for the betrothed," he mused under his breath.

Almost immediately the short, plump wife of Aunt Jolie's attorney recognized him and descended with a homely young girl in tow. He sighed. It was going to be a long evening. After several dances and glasses of Adam's excellent champagne, he glimpsed Deborah out of the corner of his eye. She still seemed a bit wan and subdued, but she looked lovely in a soft blue green gown, cut low off her shoulders, accenting her slim, supple body. Excusing himself from the company of several bankers, Rafael wended his way over to her. As the music resumed, on impulse and without even asking her, he swept her into the waltz, much to the chagrin of the two men with whom she had been conversing.

Once more those enlivening spots of color appeared in her cheeks as he felt her stiffen in anger. "You look more yourself now," he said genially, "all pink and feisty."

"And you're completely in character, as always, Monsieur Flamenco—rude, arrogant and thoroughly insufferable." She prepared to pull free of his embrace, then caught sight of Oliver watching her from the far side of the room, a scowl on his sallow face. Deborah suddenly relaxed into the rhythm of the waltz and let Rafael lead her in an exhilarating exhibition. Seldom had either of them had a partner tall enough to allow them complete freedom to dance in such an unrestrained manner. Matching his graceful, long-legged strides, Deborah quickly found herself floating on a cloud of music, thoroughly enjoying herself as never before.

What had begun as a simple ploy to annoy Oliver suddenly became something alarmingly different. What she saw in Rafael's dark smiling face was smugness and male vanity, but there was something more. Perhaps he was as surprised as she.

"You are an exceptional dancer, Miss Manchester," he said softly in French.

"Thank you. I—I seldom have the opportunity. That is, Oliver doesn't . . ." Her voice trailed off as the blush on her cheeks darkened.

As if reading her thoughts, he said, "A woman who dances so beautifully should never be held back by *little* men. Are all your Yankees so timid?"

She looked up into his eyes, now merry and sparkling like black diamonds. In spite of herself, Deborah returned his smile. "They're not *my* Yankees. Nor are they all timid," she added darkly, seeing Oliver about to cut in on them.

"Your betrothed," Rafael said in French as he relinquished her to Oliver. Then he added, "Well, at least my company was of some profit to you, Moon Flower, for it moved your intended to the dance floor." A smile half quirked at the corners of his mouth.

As Rafael sauntered away, Oliver resumed the dance in

his stiff, uncomfortable way. "What did he say? I detest foreigners speaking a language I cannot understand."

Deborah gave him a wistful smile. "Perhaps neither one of you understands, Oliver."

"Your father will make his announcement soon, my dear," he reminded her. That damn Frenchman must have upset her.

Looking quickly around the floor, Deborah still did not see Adam Manchester. Heavens, she must stop this farce quickly before she was even more humiliated by a public announcement! "I have something to tell you, Oliver. In private. *Now*." She stressed the last word when he looked at her with that unruffled, patronizing air he so often assumed. Why had she never noticed *how* often until now?

He followed her from the floor toward a set of double doors at the far end of the room. She walked resolutely down the back hall, then turned a corner and continued farther on until she came to a small door. "We won't be disturbed in here." As she entered the room, Deborah continued, "Our engagement is ended, Oliver. I won't marry you."

He stood speechless for a moment, then forced an artificial smile and said overbrightly, "Now, my dear, I know you're just a little nervous." He moved forward and tried to embrace her.

Pushing his arms away, she said calmly, "Surely you don't expect a 'cold fish' like me to be capable of bridal nerves, Oliver. After all, with my 'insane ideas' about women's rights, I could forestall the consummation of our marriage by simply engaging you in a discussion about Mary Wollstonecraft." She received some measure of satisfaction when he blanched. "Yes, I overheard you and thank God I did!"

Oliver reached for her again and said angrily, "You can't break our engagement now. All of Boston knows of it. Think of your family honor and mine!"

"Your family honor," she echoed in icy disdain. "The grand Havershams—a pack of fortune-hunting vultures preying on gullible women. You're contemptible!"

"This sudden outburst wouldn't happen to be related to

the attentions of that pretty Frenchman, would it? If you flatter yourself that his type would ever marry you, you are really gullible!'' His eyes were like cold gray slate now as he walked over to the door and slipped the bolt.

"Monsieur Flamenco had nothing to do with my breaking our engagement, be assured. Also, be assured it is broken. Now let me pass." Something in his manner as he calmly began to remove his coat sent a prickle up her spine.

"You little fool," he hissed. "Do you honestly think I'll just let you walk out of here and destroy the planning of over a year? I need your money and I'll do whatever I must to get it, even anticipate the wedding night a wee bit . . ."

As he took his coat off and unbuckled his belt, Deborah was shocked in rigid horror. Then his sallow face loomed over her, contorted in cold, calculating anger. When he reached out and ripped the shoulder of her gown, pulling it down to reveal her small upthrust breast, with its pink nipple rigid in the chill air, she came out of her trancelike state and screamed.

"Carry on all you want. So thoughtful of you to choose such an isolated room. With the orchestra and all that crowd, no one will hear you, my love."

Deborah twisted furiously away from his grasp with a strangled sob and covered her breast. "No matter what you do, I'll never marry you! Never!"

"I think you will. I rather imagine your father will insist." He stalked her then, step by step, until she was backed against a set of double doors that opened onto the back garden.

Frantically, she turned and tried the knob, but it was locked. He smiled. "No escape, Deborah. Just imagine I'm that pretty boy from New Orleans."

He grabbed her once more. She screamed and clawed at his face, raking his left cheek. When he growled in pain and loosened his grip, she lunged past him and reached for a heavy paperweight on the desk, hurling it at him. It missed and went flying through the panes in the door. The shattered shards of glass flew onto the patio bricks like an eruption of diamonds.

Rafael paced on the cold flagstone patio behind the house,

stamping his feet to keep warm as he inhaled a last draught of the fragrant cigar, then tossed it disgustedly into the shrubbery.

"Damn, it's too cold to even enjoy a fine Havana!" Just as he turned to reenter the ballroom, he heard a woman's scream, then the sound of glass breaking. It came from the rear of the house. In a few strides he was at the door with its shattered panes. Looking inside, he was amazed to see Deborah Manchester in Oliver Haversham's none-too-gentle embrace. Her dress was torn and she was obviously struggling. He tried the door. Locked! Two hard lunges sundered the wood and glass; he burst into the room.

By the time he gained entry, Deborah was free of her tormentor, holding the shredded remnants of her gown around her bare shoulders, as regal as Aphrodite stepping from her bath. Her eyes, however, glowed with an unholy fury more reminiscent of Hera ready to reduce an offending mortal to ashes with a glance.

Haversham appeared dazed at the sudden interruption, then sputtered ineffectually as he backed slowly away from the tall, dark man who menaced him. "See here, Flamenco, this is between me and my fiancée—soon to be my wife."

"She's not your wife yet and by the look of things, I don't believe she now plans to be," Rafael said as he placed himself between Deborah and Oliver. "If you intend to challenge me, I would be most obliged to honor your request." The softly spoken words, delivered in a musical French accent, seemed somehow doubly threatening.

Haversham paled and whirled. Hurriedly grabbing his discarded clothing, he slipped the bolt on the door and darted down the hall. Rafael closed the door and walked over to Deborah, who was still standing with her arms wrapped around herself. She began to shiver as the cool night air drifted through the broken patio doors.

"Allow me," Rafael said rapidly in French as he placed his coat gently around her shoulders. Her slender body was lost in the large coat, but it felt warm and comforting, lined with thick satin that smelled faintly of expensive tobacco and a spicy masculine scent she could not identify.

Now the anger had faded, leaving only a profound hurt

and humiliation. She was half-naked, disheveled, and disgraced; her own fiancé had nearly raped her, and she had been rescued yet again by a man who seemed to appear at the most embarrassing times in her life. Suddenly she felt her eyes sting with unshed tears. "What a fool I've been," she said beneath her breath. Rafael took her chin in one hand and gently turned her face up to his. Her enormous lilac eyes brimmed over with jewellike tears.

"Do not, do not, little one," Rafael said as he took her in his arms. Her rocked her gently in his embrace and let her sob out her pain. Then he reached into the pocket of his jacket and extracted a lace kerchief.

"*Lagniappe*, for each beautiful damsel in distress I rescue," he said, presenting it to her with a small flourish when her crying had ceased.

"Why, it's the kerchief from Hornby's!" She could feel the delicate lace pattern as she dabbed it against her hot, wet cheeks. "Why—how?"

He smiled. "I planned to give it to you this evening as a peace offering."

"It seems you're doomed to spend your visit in Boston rescuing me from calamity, Monsieur Flamenco. I do appreciate your help. Oliver is a man of singular purpose, I find." Then recalling what he had said about her pretending that he was Rafael, she blushed scarlet.

"Oliver is a swine and a fool. I assume you broke your engagement and he took it, ah, ungraciously?"

"He was marrying me only for my money. I overheard him tell his cousin earlier in the study." Her voice was steady and cold now, but he could detect the undertone of pain.

"He really is a fool," Rafael breathed, his fingertips lightly grazing her jawline. His other arm reached around her, drawing her into his embrace. As if pulled by a magnet, he lowered his mouth to her upraised, trembling lips. Ever so softly, he brushed them, back and forth as his hand stroked her throat and gently held her head. Then, he deepened the kiss slightly, pressing firmly on her sweet, petal-soft lips before reluctantly releasing her.

Deborah was dizzy and warm, wanting nothing so much

as to cling to this stranger. She had never experienced such a purely physical thrill. When he moved her gently but firmly away from him, she felt a sudden stab of cold. This rejection was more painful than Oliver's perfidy!

Sensing her confusion, and sharing it, Rafael said, "You've been through a terrible ordeal, and I am a man of honor, much to my misfortune. I don't want to take advantage of you, Moon Flower. But I plan to see you again, under less distressing circumstances. That is, if you will permit me?"

At her shy, silent nod of acquiescence, Rafael felt a strange surge of elation. Restraining himself, he asked, "Is there a way to get upstairs to your room so no one will see your torn gown?"

"Yes, I can use the servants' stairs. Please, Rafael, find Father and ask him to come to my room?"

"First I'll see you safely upstairs." He felt an odd warming when she used his given name.

Hearing the noises from the street below, Rafael slowly opened his eyes, then quickly closed them once more. God, the sunlight filtering in through ivory lace curtains was blinding! He rolled over and rubbed his aching head. After his unsettling encounter with Deborah Manchester last evening he had sent her father to her room and then had departed. Rafael suspected the party had quickly deteriorated. Restless and confused, he had frequented a couple of taverns. He had considered taking one yellow-haired barmaid to his bed, but had rejected the idea. The dark roots of her golden locks seemed an inadequate substitute for the silvery enchantment of Deborah.

Disgusted, he drank himself stuporous. Only the honesty of a kind hackey saw him safely to his hotel with money belt and skull intact. On second thought, perhaps his skull was not intact. He groaned and sat up, holding his aching head gingerly between his hands, fearful it might split asunder.

By the time he had secured hot water for a bath and shave, he felt almost human. Still the memory of a lavender-eyed, ethereal blonde would not leave him. What was there about the chit? She was too tall, too thin, too outspoken. She was too American, for heaven's sake! Yet he was fascinated by her.

"The only way to deal with such an absurd fancy is to face it head-on," he gritted out to no one in particular. He would call on Deborah and Adam Manchester. "Perhaps she won't be so enchanting this morning."

Wishing he had Tobias, his manservant, to press and arrange his clothing, he selected a presentable stock of faultless white silk that complemented his tan linen suit. Tobias had taken ill the day they were to embark on the sea voyage and rather than suffer the ministrations of an untrained slave as his valet, he had elected to rough it alone. Rafael whistled as he put the finishing touches to his toilette. Damn, he'd show those gauche Yankees how to dress, even if his light-weight clothes were ill-suited to this barbarous northland. Checking his silk stock and the cut of his jacket in the mirror one last time, he smiled. Now, off to confront his Moon Flower.

Deborah awakened with a sense of dread as she remembered Oliver's treachery. Her engagement had not been announced. A shaken Adam Manchester had told their guests his daughter had been taken ill suddenly. If any of them realized Oliver Haversham had vanished as well, they kept their comments to themselves—for the duration of the party, at least. Deborah was under no illusions about how gossip would treat her in the months to come.

"Better now than after I'd married him," she murmured aloud as she sat in the center of her bed, hugging her knees. She shivered, imagining the horror of waking up the day after her wedding to find what a vicious money grubber he was. Marriage meant total subjugation to one's husband. She had felt herself so smart, so safe, in choosing Oliver. "More fool I!"

Then she pictured another face, an exotic countenance with jet eyes and haughty sculpted features. Pressing her fingertips to her lips, she relived his kiss, so soft and yet so compelling. Oliver had certainly never affected her that way! She put her head down on her knees, feeling lost and forlorn. "He's only a visitor. Soon he'll return to New Orleans, and I'll never see him again."

Feeling foolish for the momentary lapse into an absurd romantic fantasy, she brushed tears from her eyes. "Deborah, you're just in shock. That beautiful, arrogant man is the complete opposite of everything you admire. Forget him."

The future loomed bleakly as she considered her options in proper, staid Boston. "I had few enough suitors before this scandal. Now everyone will be whispering behind my back. Oh, damn!" She threw back the covers and practically leapt from the bed in frustrated anger.

Deborah was still pacing agitatedly in her upstairs parlor, debating how to handle the disastrous situation, when the butler interrupted with a calling card. Monsieur Flamenco had just arrived and requested the honor of seeing her. Feeling her heart accelerate and her cheeks grow pink, she murmured to Ramsey that she would be down shortly. Frantically, she raced to the mirror.

When she entered the parlor several minutes later Deborah appeared the epitome of serenity. She was dressed in a periwinkle blue linen gown that complemented her ivory skin and made her unusual lilac eyes seem enormous and vibrant. Rafael found himself wanting to pull the gleaming silver-gilt hair free from its pins and bury his face in it.

"Good morning, Monsieur Flamenco." She greeted him, her clear musical voice betraying nothing of her inner turmoil. How handsome he was, how dashing, she thought.

He reached for her hands and raised them to his lips, saying, "Last evening you called me Rafael. Please, don't become formal once again."

"I want to thank you once more, Rafael," she emphasized his name, finding the sound of it pleasing on her tongue, "for saving me from Oliver. My father never approved of him, but I was too foolish to listen and I almost paid a terrible price for that stupidity." Her cheeks burned in humiliation.

"That's one reason I am here this morning, that is, if you

do not think it too presumptuous of me." He paused for a beat.

"What do you mean?" Her eyes were wide in puzzlement.

Rafael favored her with a dazzling smile. "Your engagement, I trust, is ended?" At her firm nod, he continued, "Now all of prim, orderly Boston will be waiting to see how you behave. Will you retire under the pressure of gossip, or will you face them down?" He gave her a measuring look. "I think an outing, a very public outing—say a carriage ride and luncheon—would be just the thing, don't you, Mademoiselle Manchester?"

"Deborah, please, Rafael," she said with a hesitant smile. However, her clear violet gaze was steady when she answered him. "I would be delighted to go for a ride and have luncheon with you."

Chapter 3

The day was sunny, the weather so truly springlike that even Rafael was warmed by it. As they rode about in the elegant open carriage he had hired for the day, Deborah gave him a quick tour of the cradle of American democracy, from the Old North Church to Faneuil Hall in which the Sons of Liberty had met during the Revolution.

While they were visiting the harbor, site of the Tea Party, Deborah explained how Boston's patriots had led the protest against tyranny. When she finally paused, he chuckled and said, "Obviously you are very proud of your city, Deborah. All this time I had been led to believe it was Virginia, not Massachusetts, that instigated the American Revolution."

Despite his teasing tone, she felt uncomfortable. Here she was, once more running on like a damned bluestocking when she simply had wanted to enjoy his company and forget her woes. "I didn't mean to sound like a schoolteacher," she murmured. "I'm certain your city rivals any in the United States for history and beauty."

Rafael had a faraway look in his eyes for a moment. "Yes, it is unique. For a French Creole, no place on earth is quite so lovely, but I am enjoying learning about Boston from such a beautiful guide. Perhaps someday you will be in New Orleans and I may be permitted to return the favor?"

Improbable as it sounded, Deborah found herself wishing for just such an opportunity and nodded, feeling the pulse in her throat accelerate under the spell of Rafael's glowing black eyes and blinding white smile. She was saved from making a fool of herself with a vacuous answer when the carriage stopped in front of the familiar four Ionic columns of the Tremont House.

"I've taken the liberty of reserving a table for us since I have eaten here several times and found the fare excellent." He stepped down from the carriage and reached for her hand to assist her.

Tremont House was the last place she would have chosen, although he was right about the food. It was one of the most popular new hotels and restaurants, one frequented by Oliver Haversham and many of their mutual friends. She felt a tight knot of dread forming in her stomach but was unwilling to confess such cowardice to Rafael.

Regal as a queen, she took his arm and they walked into one of the spacious dining rooms. Catching their reflection in the mirrors, Deborah was startled by the striking couple they made: he so dark, she so fair, both of them tall and slim. Heads turned as more patrons noticed the subject of the previous night's debacle, now on the arm of an exotic stranger. Shocking.

While they chatted over their soup course, Deborah was increasingly aware of covert stares and rapidly averted gazes. Judith Lowell and Allison Smythe were seated across the room. Judith, a plain little wren from a distinguished Boston family, had always been enamored of Oliver and spiteful to Deborah. Her ears burned as she imagined what Judith was telling Allison Smythe in stage whispers, doubtless overheard by all at adjoining tables.

Rafael knew they were the subject of much speculation.

"Does it bother an intelligent, strong-willed woman like you to endure their gossip?"

Deborah was so startled by the question she almost dropped her spoon. "No—yes, if I'm honest, it does. I must live here by society's rules even if I disagree with them, for my father's sake at least."

"You weren't marrying Oliver for your father's sake, were you?" He was frankly intrigued.

Looking into Rafael's night-dark eyes, she felt herself hypnotized, drawn to pour out her fears and longings. "I chose Oliver as a compromise, I suppose," she began carefully. "He's from the requisite old Boston family; but more to the point, he seemed to be in sympathy with my ideals."

"Which are?" he prompted.

"You'll be appalled." Suddenly, it became a game to see if she could shock him.

One brow arched, giving his face a sardonic cast. "Mademoiselle, I do not appall easily."

"All right." With that encouragement she launched into a discourse on the inequity with which women were treated under the law. She finished by saying, "A woman is an adult, with an adult's mind, yet when it comes to her own money or land, even her own children, she is treated as a ward of her husband, father, or nearest male relative—in other words, like a child!"

He shrugged. "I'll not debate the accidents of history or the physiological reasons behind the whole course of civilization. Men have always ruled the marketplace, the church, the government. Women have more essential duties in the home, for which they are admirably equipped." At this he couldn't resist reaching across the table to give her hand a gentle squeeze. She blushed and withdrew her fingers quickly, just as he knew she would.

"So, you decided to marry a man who would never rule you or challenge your ideas or inflame your senses?"

Deborah sat up very straight and said in frosty affront, "I scarcely want my senses inflamed if that means losing my capacity to reason."

"Everyone should lose his or her reason once in a

while." His eyes smouldered for a moment, but not wanting to provoke her further, he broke the intensity of their conversation. Smiling he said, "There, you see? For the past hour you've completely forgotten every gossiping tongue in Boston."

She smiled in spite of herself. "Yes. I suppose I have and I do thank you for a most diverting day, but it is late. Father will be home shortly and concerned that I'm still out."

"Then by all means I shall have to accede to the wishes of your 'warden' and see you back under his protection forthwith," he said in good-natured teasing.

Late that evening Deborah sat alone in the parlor, deep in thought, especially about her unexpected, uncharacteristically emotional reaction to Rafael Flamenco. He was the most attractive man she had ever met. But despite his undeniable appeal, he was anathema to everything she held dear. The man was arrogant, patronizing, and downright infuriating. She felt sure he was a womanizer and a rake. Of course he was charming and well educated, as good at witty wordplay as she. In fact, he often bested her, for her prim Boston sensibilities were easily embarrassed by his subtle Latin innuendos.

"Why am I being such a goose over a man to whom I'm only a brief diversion?" She picked up the book she had been trying unsuccessfully to concentrate on for the past hour.

Just then the door opened and Adam came in. Noting her distracted air, he tried to comfort her. "You were quiet all during dinner, Deborah. I realize you're upset, but only thank your lucky stars Haversham revealed himself before it was too late."

She colored in guilt, for in fact, she had not given Oliver a thought all evening. "I am grateful, Father. But my situation is all the more painfully clear to me. No man will accept me for what I am—they want to change me, and failing that, they try to deceive me to get my money. I will never marry. It will be hard to ever trust a man again."

Adam was genuinely alarmed, for he had long feared the stubborn, reclusive nature of his only child. "Deborah, most men are not like Oliver."

She fixed him with a level gaze. "Most men truly think women inferior, though, don't they? Father, I can't live that way. I can't accept being treated as if I were a child with no mind or will of my own."

"How does Rafael Flamenco treat you?" Adam's keen blue eyes never left hers.

"He's every bit as insufferable as you might imagine," she replied without missing a beat. "Is he a fortune hunter like Oliver?"

Adam gave a mirthless chuckle. "Hardly. His aunt Joline Warden left him a tidy sum, and he's already heir to the Flamenco and Beaurivage family wealth. His father controls half the sugar production in Louisiana." He paused and looked sharply at her. "You're not considering anything so insane as marrying a New Orleans Creole, are you?"

Deborah forced a laugh. "Hardly! The last thing either of us contemplates is marriage."

"Father doesn't think Rafael's at all suitable to be squiring me about," Deborah said, popping a fried clam into her mouth and looking over at Lydia for her reaction. They were at Lydia's summer house in the country having a picnic to celebrate the warm weather.

"Posh! He's gorgeous, charming, romantic—ooh, that French accent and those wicked black eyes! He looks like a painting I saw in a museum in London—of a..." Lydia searched her memory—"yes, of a Spanish matador—or was it a conquistador? Well, anyway he was lean and dark and dashing, just like Rafael. You'd be a fool to let him go back to New Orleans alone, you know."

Deborah looked across the field at the subject of their discussion. Rafael was mounted on one of Mr. Beecher's best thoroughbreds, a big gleaming black that he handled with consummate ease. As he cantered up to her, she watched his bold, supple movements. The hawkish features of his face betrayed Iberian bloodlines that went back a millennium. "A conquistador, indeed."

"Want to go for a ride? Mr. Beecher has a pretty little

filly down at his stable." Rafael slid effortlessly from the big black and reached one hand down to pull her up from the picnic cloth where she sat with Lydia.

Before she could reply, Lydia said, "Oh, go ahead. I invited you here for a few days of rustic fun, including romantic trysts on horseback. Of course, Benjamin and I will join you—just to preserve propriety," she added teasingly. Benjamin Landon was her latest beau.

Another young couple who were also Lydia's house guests joined them. Jacob Wyler and Allison Smythe were from old Boston families, both bursting with curiosity about the mysterious Southerner who seemed to be sweeping Deborah Manchester off her feet. They tried to hide their interest behind a veneer of polite small talk, but questions kept popping into the conversation about Rafael's family background, religion, and the property he owned—in general, anything regarding his suitability as a husband.

Finally, mortified and angry, Deborah pleaded a headache and turned her filly quickly away from the group, intent on heading back to the house via a shortcut through a stand of maples. Soon she heard the pounding of hoofbeats and Rafael's big black pulled abreast of her little filly.

"You shouldn't ride alone, little one," he said softly in French. "It is not safe. You also should not let their innocent questions hurt you. It's natural Bostonians are curious about such an oddity as a Creole."

"You know why they're so curious, Rafael. They think you and I are—well, that you . . ." Her sentence suddenly became too awkward to complete.

"That I am going to take Oliver's place," he supplied for her. "Would that be so awful?" There was a teasing tone to his voice now.

"Let's just say we come from such different worlds that it would be unrealistic to consider," she replied very carefully.

He shrugged at the practicality of her answer. "Always so levelheaded, Deborah."

"It's a fault of mine, I fear." She tried to keep the sudden stab of desolation from her voice.

Rafael felt a queer sense of loss at her cool rejoinder. She was right, of course. Nothing could come of these brief weeks together. They disagreed on everything—abolition, religion, the rights of women. Nevertheless, there was this physical spell, an attraction that he kept trying to dismiss as mere sexual frustration. He had simply been too long without a woman. Then why did none of the willing wenches in the public houses appeal to him? He brushed the disquieting thoughts aside and said, "Spring has finally come to New England. I'm glad to see a few green buds on the trees and shrubs. In New Orleans everything is flowering now."

"April is only the beginning of the growing season here, I'm afraid," she said, once more conjuring up visions of a lush subtropical paradise.

"It's also the beginning of the storm season," he added, noticing the suddenly darkening sky.

"These spring squalls often blow inland quickly," Deborah explained. "They don't last long, but they can be fierce. We'd better get back to the house." Her filly was already shying and nervous as the first plump, cold droplets began to pelt them.

When they came to a fork in the overgrown, seldom-used trail, Rafael shouted above the wind, "Which way?"

Deborah shrugged in perplexity. "I don't remember the path splitting here. I haven't ridden at the Beechers in years."

He muttered several French oaths beneath his breath and took the lead, heading in what he hoped was the general direction of the house. Within ten minutes the rain had become a downpour, and he knew they were lost. Being lost in the bayous of Louisiana was one thing, but whoever heard of wilderness in Massachusetts farm country!

The rain was getting colder as the slate skies continued their pitiless downpour. Deborah was having increasing difficulty controlling her mount. Each jagged bolt of lightning and accompanying peal of thunder set the filly to more sidestepping and shying. When Rafael spied a deserted saltbox house, he decided it might be wise to stop before she was thrown and seriously injured.

Once inside the dilapidated structure, he saw to the horses, quartering them in the lean-to where they would be somewhat sheltered. Then he looked around the main room. The sooty remains of a stone fireplace stood against one wall. He had matches on him, if only they had stayed dry. Without hesitation he reached for a dust-covered chair and began to break it in pieces, swearing as splinters embedded themselves in his palms and fingers.

Deborah watched him as she stood shivering with cold in one corner of the room. He heaped the dry rotted wood in a pile on the hearth, then scavenged a few bits of brown, curled paper from the table in the corner. When he carefully positioned them under the wood and lit them, the fire filled the room with a warm orange glow.

Deborah stepped closer to the enticing warmth. He helped her free of her sodden jacket and draped it near the hearth to dry. "You must get out of those soaking clothes and try to dry them by the fire. Let me see what's here for you to cover with."

He rummaged about and finally found two musty quilts stuffed in a wooden crate in the lean-to. When he reentered the main room, Deborah was standing uncertainly in front of the fire, her body silhouetted in its rosy glow. She had taken off her boots and heavy riding skirt, but her thin silk blouse and batiste petticoats clung to her like second skin. Lord, why had he ever thought her too thin? The sleek curves of her hips and buttocks and the startling fullness of her upthrust young breasts made an erotic picture as she turned herself in front of the leaping flames.

Seeing him watch her with such intensity made Deborah even more self-conscious and embarrassed. She stood very still as he walked toward her. Laying one quilt on the table, he took the other and began to wrap it around her, massaging its scratchy surface against her wet clothing and skin. It acted rather like a blotter, taking some of the dampness from her silk shirt. Her petticoats, however, were another matter.

As if reading her mind, he said, "Take your underskirts off and wrap this more tightly around you."

Deborah could hear his teeth chattering as he shivered in his soaking wet clothes. "You'd better follow your own advice," she said, surprising herself. "I'll turn my back and close my eyes, if you do the same," she dared him.

"Always practical," he grunted but did as she had bidden, stripping off his shirt, pants, and boots, then wrapping the other quilt around himself.

She worked her petticoats off, no easy trick with the waist tapes knotted and the long skirts clinging to her legs. When she heard his voice speaking softly, she clutched the quilt tightly around her and turned.

He had pulled a splintery but sturdy-looking bench up close to the fire and was motioning for her to join him on it. "If we huddle together, we'll dry faster." Sweet reasonableness.

As she undressed Deborah's mind raced. Adam's stern warning about Rafael and her own declaration that she would never marry flashed through her memory. *You may never have another chance. You're attracted to one another in a way you and Oliver never were. Just this one time—a memory to last a lifetime.* Her subconscious kept taunting her as she huddled against him and shook, only half from cold now. When his bare arm slipped from his quilt and tightened around her shoulders, she wondered, *How would it feel to have those long, tapered fingers caress your bare skin?* As if mesmerized, she turned her face up to his and watched his profile in the dancing firelight, bronzed and beautiful, like some ancient Latin god.

He looked down into her violet eyes. "I was right," he said softly in French. "Your eyes do darken in passion." With that he pulled her against him and pressed his lips to her eyes, kissing the lids softly, then trailing his mouth down her cheek and burying his face in the damp silken masses of her hair. She smelled of lavender. He groaned as she tipped her head back, eyes closed, lips slightly parted, baring the slender column of her throat. Taking her head in his hands, he raised it until her lips met his in a bruising, searing kiss. As she gasped in surprise at the sudden change from gentleness to passion, his tongue took instant advantage, plunging inside her parted lips. He deepened the kiss as he felt her respond.

He slid one hand inside the quilt and began to do maddening things to her sensitive spine, running strong, cunning fingers up and down. Then his hand trailed around her ribs to cup and lift a breast, which puckered to a hard point at the tip. Once more she gasped, pressing herself against his persuasive palm, wanting to feel him caress all of her throbbing, quivering flesh. By this time both quilts had fallen around their legs and their upper bodies were locked in a fierce embrace. Deborah's own hands were busy, exploring the thick black hair of his chest and the hard flat ridges of muscle across his back. Neither noticed the chill anymore as their pounding blood heated their bodies. Above the soft crackling hiss of the flames, the only sounds were their rough erratic gasps and moans.

When he tried to reach beneath her blouse to the scorching flesh of her breasts, he was thwarted by the damp silk of her camisole. For a moment he fumbled with the fastenings. Then, her trembling hands came down and pushed his aside. She began deftly to unbutton the undergarment. Watching her, so virginal and trembling with passion, he was suddenly struck by the enormity of what he was doing.

Rafael could hear his father's words about self-control and responsibility. This girl was an innocent, from a good family, one who had every right to expect an honorable marriage. He was taking shameless advantage of her inexperience.

Slowly, gently, he pulled her fingers from their task and held her away from him. Taking a deep breath, he forced his passion under control and spoke. "Deborah, we can't do this. It isn't right."

Her eyes flew up to his, filled with surprise, then puzzled hurt. Like him, she had difficulty speaking. "I don't care," she managed as crimson stained her neck and face.

"Soon I'll be leaving Boston, leaving you, forever." His eyes bored into hers, willing her to understand how difficult this was for him.

"I know," was her calm reply.

"You know? You don't expect me to marry you and yet you were willing to have me take your virginity?"

She could no longer meet his eyes, but she had to make him understand. "After long and careful consideration, I've decided that I will never marry. But once, just one time, I wanted to know what it was like to be with someone I was attracted to.'' *With someone I love,* an inner voice amended, surprising and shaking her even further than her appalling behavior already had.

He sat dumbfounded at her revelation. Such audacity, such forthright honesty, and above all, such unstudied passion. "No Creole lady would ever give herself to a man without marriage first."

Deborah's face flamed anew. "I suppose that's a terrible indictment against me, but since I never expected you to marry me, it really doesn't signify whether or not I measure up to your standards, does it?'' She pulled the fallen quilt over her shoulders and rose to reach for her half-dried clothes, spread around the large hearth. She turned her back on him lest he see the glaze of tears in her eyes.

Rafael also stood up. He felt like a heartless fool. He had never meant to make her feel cheap or to hurt her feelings. In fact, when he thought of the Creole girls he knew and compared them with Deborah, he wondered why any man would prefer them. Muttering to himself, "That's what a man has a mistress for," he closed his mind and began to dress.

They rode back to the house in silence. The storm had ended and Rafael quickly found the cutoff that led them out of the woods.

Chapter 4

"You've avoided me ever since you came home, pleading headaches and other vapors, young woman. I think it's time we had a talk." Adam Manchester's eyes were piercing and his voice brooked no opposition.

Deborah sighed and followed him into the study, wondering how much of a confession he would be able to wring from her. Lord, all she wanted was to forget the entire sordid mistake! Sitting stiffly on the sofa, she nervously arranged her skirts. "What do you want me to say, Father? I came home early from the Beechers' because I was not enjoying myself. I was tired and I can't abide Allison Smythe."

"Am I to understand your return had nothing to do with Rafael Flamenco?" he asked as he leaned forward and willed her to meet his eyes.

Feeling the pressure of his insistent stare, Deborah forced herself to look him in the face. "If you must know, Rafael and I quarreled. Oh, Father, we've never agreed on anything. I finally realized just how impossible any relationship between us would be."

"I thought you said you never intended to be serious about him—that he was merely a temporary escort until the gossip over your broken engagement quieted." Adam's eyes were like skewers now, making her squirm like an insect on a board.

Deborah blanched. Observing the set of his jaw and the way his hands were clenched, she knew something was seriously wrong. "What have you heard? More gossip?"

"You tell me. I've always had complete faith in your levelheadedness. Until you met this damn Frenchman." He stood up, looming over her, a tactic he had often found useful in intimidating business adversaries. He loved his only child and did not wish to threaten her, but he had to get this tangle straightened out. "Deborah, exactly what happened when you two were alone in that rainstorm?"

She propelled herself up quickly to stand facing her father. "I am not damaged goods, if that's what you fear. Rafael didn't take advantage of me—not the way you think."

"What the hell does that mean? You're scarcely acting as if nothing happened."

Shame coursed through her in sickening waves. How could she confess to her father that Rafael had controlled his passions far better than she had hers? That he had rejected her? "Let's just say we had a final confrontation and I'll never see him again. I can't tell you any more, father. I have never lied to you and I'm not lying now, but what went on between Rafael and me is too private, too painful to discuss. Ever!'' Her face was chalk white and her eyes were dark violet, brimming with tears as she turned and walked from the room.

Rafael could hardly wait to board the *Sea Mist*. He would sail for New Orleans with the morning tide and it wouldn't be too soon! He strode along the wharf, watching ships from around the world unload their cargoes. For all the bustle and color surrounding him, Rafael was unimpressed. It was cold and gray, bleak as all New England. He was depressed despite the good news he had received this morning from Aunt Jolie's attorney, who had advised him that the estate was finally settled. Everything was done, finished. Then why was he so restless, so desperately unhappy?

Deborah's face, pale and delicate, her lilac eyes glistening with tears, materialized unbidden in his mind. He would never forget her, she of the fiery temperament, sparkling wit, and lush body. But she was American. A tall, blonde Protestant. His family would be aghast. He was aghast. He had come within a whisper of losing himself in her sweet silken flesh, damn her!

Just then he caught sight of the cadaverous figure of Oliver Haversham moving toward him in deliberate haste. Groaning, he considered crossing the street, then decided it was beneath his dignity to allow the fortune-hunting bully that satisfaction.

''Well, Flamenco, I'm surprised you've stayed around, considering the gossip. Old Adam Manchester will deal with you now. It's no longer my concern what anyone says about my *former* fiancée.'' His gray eyes glowed with malice.

He moved to pass Rafael but was able to take only a quick sidestep before a steel-fingered grip stopped him. ''Exactly what do you mean, Adam Manchester will deal with me now?'' Rafael's other hand fastened securely on Haversham's stock and squeezed.

Oliver's sallow complexion darkened several shades to the color of aged newspaper. He choked out, ''You didn't expect your affair with Deborah to go uncommented upon, not after your blatant tryst at the Beechers' summer house!'' He pulled free of Rafael's restraining hands, shrinking from the menacing Creole.

''Who told you we had a tryst?'' Rafael's voice was soft but steely.

Realizing that what had been an irresistible chance to taunt his rival was taking a distinctly dangerous turn, Oliver was immediately at great pains to elucidate. ''Allison Smythe was at the Beechers'. She said the two of you vanished for hours.''

''So, I assume you have spread this tale the length and breadth of Boston.'' Rafael swore softly in French and turned to walk away, then whirled back toward Haversham and said in a deadly calm voice, ''If I hear another word about Deborah Manchester on your lips, I'll thrust a rapier through your skinny gullet.''

Early the next morning he appeared at the Manchesters' house while Adam was still eating his breakfast. The butler announced him in consternation. No one called on Mr. Manchester at the uncivilized hour of seven A.M.!

From her vantage point halfway up the stairs, Deborah heard voices coming from the entry hall, then saw Rafael disappear into the study after her father. *What is he doing here?* Trembling, she picked up the hem of her velvet dressing robe and rushed back upstairs to complete her toilette. She would find out what was going on, at once.

She selected her clothes as if girding herself to do battle. In a way she was, for she sensed the two men downstairs were arrogantly deciding her future. By the time she was satisfied with her appearance, Ramsey had arrived bearing a summons: her father and Mr. Flamenco awaited her in the study.

What does he want? Why is he here? These thoughts had raced through her head all the while she had dressed. Good lord, he might provoke her father into a fight! By the time she reached the study door, she was out of breath and flushed.

When she stepped inside, glacial blue and glowing black eyes stared at her. Her father was very angry but was concealing it from his adversary as he always did. Only she was aware of how tightly he held his temper. Rafael's disposition was much more difficult for her to gauge. Was he, too, angry? His expression held a sensual, heated quality, which made her tremble unaccountably. She nodded uncertainly to both men but volunteered no greeting. In truth, she didn't trust her voice not to squeak.

Without preamble Adam announced, "Mr. Flamenco has asked my permission to marry you, Deborah."

Surprised at the strength of her own voice, she replied, "Well that signifies nothing since he has not asked me!"

"In a proper Creole courtship, Deborah, the man arranges things with the young woman's father," Rafael said as if that explained everything.

"It seems to me, nothing about this 'courtship' has in any way been proper," Adam retorted sourly.

"It hasn't even *been* a courtship!" Deborah glared alternately from her father to her supposed suitor.

Now it was Adam's turn to glare from Deborah to Rafael. "Well, if it wasn't a courtship, then why the hell have the two of you created the scandal of the decade? Would either of you care to enlighten me?"

Deborah's face went from cherry red to blanched white. "What are you talking about—scandal of the decade?"

Rafael replied dryly, "I assume you've spent the past two days without receiving callers. Your 'friend' Allison has been a very busy girl. With some help from her friends Judith and Oliver, she has been spreading the story of how we were caught alone in that rainstorm during the Beechers' party."

"Oh . . . I see," Deborah replied in a hoarse whisper.

"Well, I don't see, but I will and right now. This whole thing has gone far enough." Adam turned to Rafael, but it was Deborah who replied.

"I told you, Father, I am still—intact. We were forced to

seek shelter from the storm in a deserted cabin. Rafael built a fire and we . . . we dried our clothes.''

Rafael smiled thinly. "What Deborah is delicately skirting is that we were forced to take our clothes off and lay them in front of the fire to dry them, and keep ourselves from catching pneumonia.''

"But we had quilts, two quilts," Deborah sputtered. "That is, we each wrapped ourselves in a quilt while our clothes dried." Damn! She was digging herself in deeper.

Adam's shrewd gaze roved measuringly around the room, alighting first on his fidgeting daughter, then on the brooding Creole. "It sounds to me as if the situation would have tested the willpower of a saint!"

Rafael muttered darkly, half to himself, "Believe me, it did, and I'm no saint."

Stiffening her back, Deborah faced Adam Manchester. "Father, do you think I—I slept with this man and then lied to you about it?" Her face flushed beet red in mortification.

Adam shrugged in resignation, then said gently, "No, Deborah, I believe you told me the truth, but it doesn't alter the situation. Yesterday I heard a nasty rumor. From what Mr. Flamenco has told me, a lot worse has been circulating. Soon, everyone in the city will be privy to the scandal. You will be ruined.''

"You must marry me, Deborah. I'm afraid you have no other choice.''

There was a taunting quality to his voice that she could not fathom. What game was he playing? The last thing she expected was a proposal of marriage from Rafael Flamenco!

Adam sensed her hesitation. "There is another possibility, Deborah. Your cousin Marian in Philadelphia would be happy to have you come to live with her.''

"I'm sure she would so I can care for her five small children! I shall simply continue to live here. This is my home and no one will drive me from it." Her eyes blazed violet fire as she stood rigidly with fists clenched.

Rafael walked quickly across the large room and took Deborah's elbow firmly, turning her to face him. Looking intently into her eyes, he said to Adam, "Monsieur Manchester, please allow me to talk with her alone.''

Surprisingly, Adam acquiesced. With a terse nod to his daughter, he strode forcefully from the room saying, "Consider your choices very carefully, Deborah. They do *not* include pretending nothing has happened."

When Adam was gone, Rafael pulled her quickly into his arms and said, "I want to marry you and I think you want to marry me. Why not give in . . . now . . ." He tipped her face up to his, but before he could kiss her, she turned away.

"Until you heard those vicious lies you never intended to see me again," she hissed. "You planned to sail away this morning, forever."

"*Mon cherie*, I might have sailed away"—he shrugged with Gallic nonchalance—"or I might not. Even if I had gone all the way to New Orleans, time would have brought me back—time and you. I replay our passion over and over in my mind."

"*My* passion, don't you mean?" Her voice was choked. "You had little enough difficulty controlling yourself when you decided your 'honor' was involved."

He tightened his arm around her waist and drew her lower body firmly against his. "Does that feel like I am 'controlling' myself? The most difficult thing I have ever done in my life was to stop from taking you that day." She could feel the insistent pressure of his erection, straining into the soft fabric of her skirts.

"I have never wanted a woman as I've wanted you and I am going to marry you." With that his hand fastened in her hair, holding her head as he swooped down to claim a kiss. He ravaged her lips, crushing his own against hers until she gave in, opening to him, tasting him as he tasted her. She was growing dizzy and warm, losing herself in the riotous sensations his touch evoked, feeling his lean hard body crushed so intimately against hers, as if she had been sculpted to fit there forever. Forever. That jolted her back to sanity. Forever meant marriage, and two more unsuited people had never lived.

Rafael felt her stiffen and try to push herself free. Unwillingly, he ended the kiss, but he did not release her. Searching her flushed face, he said, "Are you going to tell me you did not enjoy that?"

"You know I did," she answered guiltily.

"Then you will marry me." It was not a question.

"No! You're only doing this out of a sense of duty. You don't love me. We know nothing about one another except that we disagree on everything."

His eyes took on a devilish light. "Not quite everything. So we disagree about politics, religion, slavery, a woman's position in society, but we have discussed them. We do *understand* one another's feelings. That's a great deal more than I would have been able to do if I'd made the usual Creole marriage."

At her puzzled look, he continued, "It is the Creole custom for parents to arrange marriages when the children are very young. It's often done for economic reasons—two plantations adjoining one another that can be merged, or because families have been friends for generations. I might one day have married a girl right out of convent school, about whom I would have known absolutely nothing. Instead I chose you, all your headstrong Yankee ideas be damned, Deborah. I know what I'm in for and I want to marry you anyway."

"Your parents. What will they say?" She was beginning to want him to win her over. It was crazy, impossible, but maybe he would come to love her as she loved him. Yes, she admitted it finally; she did love Rafael Flamenco.

"My parents will accept you. I've already sent word by the ship I was to sail on, telling them I'll be delayed and that I'm bringing home a bride." He kissed her again suddenly, so that she could not evade his caress. Quickly, she surrendered, melting against him, holding onto him for support.

When he finally released her lips, they curved in an impish smile. "Do you always get your way, Rafael?"

"*Almost* always, *cherie*." He smiled back, kissing the tip of her nose. Then he grew serious. "There is one thing I must ask of you—the marriage must be performed by a Roman priest. Once we've married in church, my parents will be bound to accept you into the family."

Deborah considered how her father, a devout high church Episcopalian, would take that! She looked up into Rafael's eyes, aglow with desire. He drew her into a maelstrom of passion as he held her against his body. Every fiber of her being cried out: *This is where I belong, where I've always longed to be, what I've always longed to feel.*

"Any church, Rafael, I don't care," she said, laughing and reaching up to place her hands on each side of his darkly handsome face. She kissed him quite thoroughly.

"It's impossible! No daughter of mine will set foot in a papist church!" Adam Manchester was beside himself.

Deborah sat calmly across from her father, stirring her coffee. They had been through every argument about the differences between her and Rafael. She had debated him to a standstill until she touched upon the ceremony being held in the Cathedral of the Holy Cross.

"As you pointed out earlier, Father, Rafael's family will be shocked over his sudden marriage to a Yankee. Having the service in their church is the least I can do. Honestly, you sound as bigoted as those rabble who burned the Ursuline Convent last year. The ritual of the Catholics is not so different from our own, it's only chanted in Latin instead of English."

"You seem extraordinarily willing to compromise all your principles just to marry your Frenchman," he snapped, more embarrassed by her reference to bigotry than he wanted to admit.

"He's not a Frenchman, he's Creole." A small smile curved her lips as she recalled Rafael's kisses.

Finally Adam asked, "Deborah, you aren't actually in love with this scoundrel, are you?"

She blushed right up to the roots of her hair. Taking a quick swallow of coffee, she cleared her throat nervously and looked him levelly in the eye. "Yes, I'm afraid I am. Is it so painfully obvious?"

Adam softened. "I thought perhaps you were only willing to go through with this to save your reputation, to escape public censure . . ." His voice faded away. He walked over and put his arm around her. "Has he told you he loves you?'' He could feel her shoulders tense and regretted the question at once.

"He wants to marry me. For now, that will have to suffice," she replied. He desired her, she was certain, but she could never confess such a thing to her father!

Lydia was not so easily put off. When Deborah called on her the next afternoon to ask her to be an attendant in the private ceremony a week hence, her friend went into a romantic tizzy, plying her with endless questions about "that gorgeous Frenchman," as she insisted on calling Rafael. She also tried to squeeze from Deborah every detail of the encounter in the deserted cabin.

"Although I positively hate Allison's tattling gossip, I think it's wonderful that it brought you two to your senses." Lydia paused and cast speculative eyes on her friend. "Deborah, tell me, in strictest confidence, of course, did you . . . did Rafael actually—well, you know? I'm dying to hear what it's really like. Mama has told me the most awful things."

Deborah was shocked at Lydia's audacity, but it was impossible to be angry with her friend's guileless curiosity. "I'll only say don't believe half what your mother has told you, Lydia. Leave it at that."

Sighing, Lydia could tell by the stubborn set of Deborah's chin that her friend would not reveal any intimacies. Changing the subject, she said, "At least you can tell me about your wedding basket. Oh, I think the idea is frightfully romantic!"

Deborah agreed. She had shown Lydia the beautiful engagement ring Rafael had given her. It was a family heirloom, one of the pieces from his aunt's estate. Large and square-cut, the deep blue stone was surrounded by diamonds and set in delicately wrought gold filigree. At Lydia's squeal of delighted awe, Deborah had explained that it was only part of the traditional Creole wedding basket that Rafael had brought her that very morning.

According to an old Creole custom, the bridegroom brought his betrothed a basket of gifts several days before the marriage as a token of his love. It contained gifts of a highly personal nature, including expensive jewelry.

She blushed as she described the lovely items in her basket, not mentioning the way Rafael had presented them to her, slipping the ring on as he kissed a blazing path from her left hand up to her throat where he fastened the matching necklace. "Well, besides the ring, there are several other pieces of exquisite antique jewelry, Chinese jade, rubies, amethysts, and pearls. Also a white cashmere shawl, yards of delicate ivory lace, a silk fan and . . . a few other things."

Lydia cocked her head saucily. "A few other things such as what? Don't you dare keep it from me, Deborah Faith Manchester!"

"Well, a nightrail. It's pale lavender, yards and yards of silk, but so sheer I can see right through it," she confessed.

"Lavender to match your eyes," Lydia exclaimed. And then her own blue eyes filled. "Ooh, I shall miss you so when you leave, Deborah!"

"I'll miss you too, Lydia. You must make plans to visit New Orleans."

Lydia hugged her impulsively and giggled. "I'd love to, after about a year. I expect you'll be terribly occupied for at least that long. I doubt Rafael will give you time to think about me!"

Deborah blushed furiously as she joined her friend in gales of girlish laughter.

If Deborah was excited about her forthcoming marriage and Adam opposed to it, Rafael was ambivalent. After a long and painful night of brooding and drinking, he had acted out of a sense of honor. After all, he was responsible for Deborah's predicament, so he must offer marriage. He had written a carefully edited version of their courtship to his family with the sense of a condemned man writing his will. Marriage was so final, it made his twenty-two-year-old soul shudder.

Then, when Deborah had been summoned into Adam's study, he forgot the animosity radiating from the protective old man, the embarrassment of the social situation, even the anger in which she had parted from him two days earlier. She had stood there so fresh and innocent, all lavender and silver-gilt. He desired her even more in the clear light of morning than he had in the languid glow of firelight. When she had set her delicate jaw and stood rigidly, defying both him and her father, he was amazed at his reaction. Her very spirit pleased him more than if she had been a quaking, acquiescent miss, eager to accept his proposal to save face. He found himself using every taunting, teasing tactic that he had practiced during the past weeks in their verbal battle of wits. To his amazement he discovered that he would not take no for an answer.

Her heated response when she had finally accepted his proposal incited him to such a degree of passion that he had to exert iron willpower not to finish what they had begun in that deserted cabin. Teaching her the pleasures of the flesh would be an incredible delight.

The day of the wedding dawned gray and cloudy, but despite the ride to the church in a chill spring rain, Deborah's spirits were high. She felt giddy and ebullient despite the weather's omen. Only Adam's resigned and withdrawn manner marred the occasion for her.

When they entered the old church on Franklin Street, the flickering uncertain light of the dim candles revealed delicate plaster statuary. The ornate altar and stations of the cross seemed alien and forbidding to Adam Manchester's eyes. Turning to Deborah before he accompanied her down the aisle, he gripped her arm and whispered, "It's not too late to change your mind, daughter."

Her first impulse was to be furiously angry with him for spoiling her day, but when she looked into his eyes, she felt only sorrow for the way in which she must leave him. "I know what I'm doing, Father. It's for the best. You'll see."

The wedding was small, both because of its haste and the circumstances necessitating it. Rafael, of course, had no family attending; Deborah had only Lydia and Adam. She wore a simple day dress of white raw silk. Its high neckline and softly gored skirt were plain, adorned only by seed pearls sewn across the bodice and sleeves. A lace veil covered her silvery hair. Looking down the aisle to the altar she saw Rafael's face light when he caught sight of her. Her groom was resplendent in a snowy white ruffled stock, red brocade waistcoat, and light gray wool suit. The rich clothing emphasized his swarthy coloring and striking handsomeness.

Father Jean performed the ceremony simply and briefly as the groom had requested, accommodating the Episcopalian sensibilities of his new father-in-law. When Rafael slipped the delicate gold filigree wedding band on her finger and looked into her wide lavender eyes, he felt a strong tightening in his throat. He could tell that she shared his feelings as she, too, swallowed with difficulty and pressed her small cool hands tightly inside his large warm ones.

Although they returned to the Manchester house for a light repast, neither bride nor groom noticed what they ate. Adam's taciturn behavior and Lydia's giddy chatter went unnoticed as well. By the time they had reached the wharf where their ship awaited them, Monsieur and Madame Flamenco were simply relieved to take leave of the intrusions of the outside world.

While Deborah and Lydia hugged and exchanged a last girlish confidence, Rafael gravely shook hands with a granite-faced Adam. "I shall take care of her, sir," he said solemnly, attempting to allay his father-in-law's misgivings.

"See that you do," was the terse admonition.

Chapter 5

As they stood watching the bobbing sailboats and tall masts in the Boston Harbor, Rafael wrapped Deborah's white cashmere shawl more securely around her shoulders to ward off the chill. The *Blue Lightning*, the luxury steamship taking them to New Orleans, was heading out to sea and in the brisk April breezes a few strands of Deborah's hair came loose from the pins. Rafael caught a silky curl and ran his lips over it, then bent to place several very warm kisses on her cool neck. When he felt her shiver, he let out a low, wicked chuckle and murmured, "You'll be much warmer below in our cabin, *cherie*."

Nodding silently, Deborah let him guide her down to the spacious quarters. Their stateroom was richly appointed, the best he could reserve on a week's notice. As he had instructed, the galley had sent a bottle of chilled French champagne, an assortment of fine English cheeses, and fresh Caribbean fruit.

Deborah wandered about the room, looking out the small windows, running her hands over the sturdy varnished oak table, chairs, and wardrobe, all the while deliberately avoiding looking at the largest piece of furniture in the room—the wide double bed with its deep plum velvet spread and high mound of fluffy silk bolsters. She slipped off her shawl and folded it precisely, then placed it on top of a chest in one corner.

Rafael opened the champagne and poured two glasses. "This should steady your nerves and give you some sea legs, *amante*." He handed her a glass and she accepted it with a tremulous smile.

"I don't even know if I have sea legs. If the Atlantic is rough, I fear I may disgrace myself." She twisted the stem of the goblet nervously in her fingers.

He touched his glass to hers and the crystal gave off a clear musical peal. "Drink deeply and don't borrow trouble you may never see," he said with a warming smile. He followed his own advice, then laughed when she recoiled from the bubbles tickling her nose as she took a sip. Gamely, she finished the glass and he refilled it.

"I've asked the steward to bring us a very late supper. This should suffice for now." He seated her at the oak table. A single fat candle cast its mellow glow over the exotic fruits and cheeses.

She took another sip of wine and a few tiny bits from an orange segment and papaya slice. "I'm really not hungry, Rafael," she murmured.

"Good." He said the word softly as he reached over and took her half-filled glass. "Then on to more important matters. Come here, silver witch." He pulled her gently from the chair into his embrace. "Since you have no lady's maid, I'll help with the buttons you can't reach. Then I'll allow you privacy to prepare yourself—this time." He kissed her experimentally, running his lips down to her throat; then he turned her in his arms and continued the butterfly soft caressing around her neck as he unhooked the long row of white silk-looped pearl buttons.

When she felt the back of the dress freed, she started to step away, but he stilled her with one arm and then began to unfasten the pins from her hair, skillfully freeing the shimmering silver-gilt mass to tumble below her shoulders. He grabbed fistfuls of it and buried his face in the lavender fragrance. "I've wanted to do that since the first day I laid eyes on you," he breathed through the silken skein.

Deborah turned and placed her arms about his neck, warmed and relaxed by his expert ministrations. She raised her face with lips parted in a smile, and he kissed her, plundering her mouth with his tongue, fiercely fusing their lips and bodies together. She felt a momentary rush of panic at his sudden passion, but before she could react, he released her, taking her hands from his shoulders to plant soft kisses in their palms.

"Change quickly. I must leave you now or I'll be unable to appear in public, *mon coeur,*" he said with a rueful grin, looking down unashamedly at the telltale bulge in his tight gray pants. Flushing, she did not dare to follow his gaze.

When he left the cabin, Deborah undressed and her nervousness grew. Their passion had all been so spontaneous and natural that day in the rainstorm. But now, as she donned the sheer silk peignoir, waiting for him to consummate their marriage, it all seemed so—so premeditated.

"I'm just uncertain that I'll please him," she whispered hoarsely, recalling that he had always been able to control his passions and break free of her when he deemed it appropriate. "If only I knew what to expect, how to respond . . ." Her voice trailed off into silent misery. Deborah had never been told exactly what went on between men and women. No well-bred young girl ever was, but at least most had mothers, older sisters, or some female relatives who could bolster them with some kindly advice, however euphemistically phrased or misleading. Deborah had no woman to help her, and even under more favorable circumstances, Adam would have been unwilling to discuss such a delicate matter with his daughter. Nonetheless, she had a vague idea of what must ultimately occur. She had never been at all sure she would like it, but being practical, she realized that most women married and had children, so it was simply something she must do.

Recalling how good it had felt each time Rafael put his hands and lips on her, how secure and protected his lean powerful body made her feel, she gave herself a mental shake. Soon he would return, expecting to find a wife waiting for him, not some whimpering schoolgirl with the vapors! She ran the hairbrush through her waist-length tresses. Finally, putting the brush down, she inspected herself in the mirror. Too tall, not enough bosom or curve to her hips, she concluded critically.

Rafael lit a cigar, then threw it impatiently over the rail and paced for several minutes, repeatedly checking his gold pocket watch until he decided she had been allowed sufficient time to change. Any more time alone and she'd merely develop a worse case of bridal nerves. And he'd be so overwrought with sexual tension he might well lose control and frighten her.

When he opened the cabin door, Deborah had not heard his soft knock. She stood in front of the beveled-glass mirror in a nightrail so sheer it looked to be spun of gossamer. He could see her long silky flanks and uptilted pink nipples through its illusive veiling. The pale gilt curtain of her hair obscured most of her delectable derriere, but he imagined its firm, satiny roundness.

When she reached for the heavier silk robe that matched the nightrail, he said softly, "Don't."

Hearing the whispered command, she whirled in surprise and dropped the garment. "I didn't hear you come in," she said inanely as he slipped the bolt on the door and then began to walk slowly toward her.

Rafael took her in his arms and then bent down to pick her up with effortless ease. As he carried her to the bed, he kissed her forehead, temples, and fluttering eyelids. Then he slowly slid her down the length of his body, still holding her closely as he reached with one hand to pull down the heavy velvet spread. "Get in and wait for me," he commanded.

Deborah scooted quickly beneath the covers, tucking them modestly up to her chin. She huddled in the center of the large bed, watching as he doused all the lanterns, leaving the dim golden glow of only one candle on the table. Then he began to disrobe, shedding his jacket and waistcoat in a few smooth, swift shrugs. Walking casually over to the bootjack in the corner, he slipped off his boots and peeled off his hose. When he began to unfasten the studs from his shirt, revealing the hard dark expanse of his chest, Deborah remembered the wonderful scent when she had run her fingers through the dense black hair covering it. His silk shirt fluttered to the floor with a barely audible whoosh and then he was reaching for the waistband of his pants. Wide-eyed, she watched the play of lean muscles across his shoulders and chest as he began to unbutton his fly. Suddenly, it dawned on her what he was doing—what *she* was doing!

As if reading her mind, he looked up. Laugh lines crinkled the corners of his eyes and lips as he said, "Do not look away now, *cherie*. I am just getting to the good part." He watched her blush as she closed her eyes and sank beneath the sheets. With a low, hearty chuckle, he quickly stripped off the last of his clothes and strode over to the bed to pull the heavy covers back in one swift motion.

"You've watched me. Now I want to see you, my beautiful wife," he whispered as he knelt on the bed beside her. Turning her averted face toward him, he said in a strangled voice, "You are incredibly beautiful." His hands slid down her throat, grazing the peak of one breast, descending to the hollow of her slim waist, down to trace the curve of her thigh. Rafael's strong warm fingers continued to her ankle, reaching around the slender bones easily. Then he retraced his path up her leg, pausing to caress her inner thigh through the sheer silk of her gown.

Feeling his light touch, Deborah had closed her eyes and drifted like a leaf on a warm summer breeze, reassured by his words of admiration and his gentleness. However, when his hand slid between her legs and began to stroke the sensitive flesh of her thigh, her eyes flew open. Wordlessly, he stopped, sensing her fears, realizing that he must proceed more slowly. He rolled down to lie beside her full length. "Shh, I won't hurt you, *cherie*. Only relax and put your arms around me."

Deborah obliged him instantly, holding tightly as if she were drowning. She wanted to please him, wanted to recapture the rapture she had felt that day of the rainstorm. When he began to run his hands up and down her back and kiss her face and throat, she returned his caresses, marveling at the difference in tone and texture of their skin. He was hard and dark, with crisp black hair across his forearms, chest, and down lower where a steady prodding pressure told her untutored body that he was well prepared to consummate the act. But he held back, instinctively knowing that she needed time to assimilate all these new sensations rioting through her body.

Rafael could feel her gradually accelerating response as she touched and kissed him, tasting and exploring in unpracticed natural curiosity. He rolled over her and lowered his head to capture her lips. Now she eagerly opened to his invading tongue, recognizing and welcoming the pleasure. Slowly he guided her, showing her how to use her lips, teeth, and tongue to tease and arouse him as she kissed him back.

When she was breathless from that exercise, he broke away and lowered his head to her collarbone, running his tongue along the ridge of the delicate bone while he untied the ribbon at the neckline of her gown. She gasped in pleasure when his fingertips circled one upthrust breast, then the other. He could feel her arch her back as the tingling mounds strained against his palm. Her nipples became hard buds beneath his hand and then he caught one in his mouth. The hot wet feeling of his lips enveloping and suckling on the sensitive tip broke down the last of her inhibitions. Deborah let out a low keening moan.

She was breathless now, unthinking, awash in thrilling, new sensations. His questing mouth moved down her belly, trailing after his hands as they peeled the gauzy nightrail down, then slipped it over her hips and finally discarded it.

Rafael levered himself up and admired the view of her alabaster and rose-hued flesh. When he pulled her up to him and kissed her, she responded with a whimpered cry, fastening her fingers in his hair and pulling him back onto the pillows with her.

As they kissed, he ran one hand slowly down between her legs and began to stroke the soft hot core of her body. She opened to him, unconsciously arching against his skillful fingers. When he felt her wet, eager response, he withdrew his hand.

Deborah was afire with hot rippling waves of pleasure. She responded shamelessly. Then when he suddenly pulled away, she let out a low cry of protest, but before she could do more, his hand had grasped her slim wrist and guided her fingers to him.

"Now, touch me," he panted, as he fought to hold himself under control. He placed her hand around his shaft, steeling himself for the raw jolt of ecstasy when she complied. Then he guided her, showing her how to stroke him, but only a few times, fearful he might explode. Once he had caught his breath, he guided her hand, still closed around his pulsing phallus, until it was pressing directly between her legs.

Slowly, he rotated the tip against her wet pink flesh, now hot and eager to receive him. She moaned, calling out his name like a plea. Then he pulled her hand away and entered her, gently, until he felt the barrier of her maidenhead. Pausing to kiss her lips and to murmur an apology, he completed the penetration in one fast, careful stroke.

Deborah felt a sudden, unexpected stab of pain, but it was over quickly and just as quickly forgotten. Rafael set a slow, steady rhythm that she quickly followed until she lost all sense of time. She knew something wondrous was happening to them both, but his reactions were keener, quicker. She could feel him tremble and begin to shudder suddenly; then he gave several hard, long thrusts in rapid succession and collapsed on top of her, gasping in satiation. Radiating waves of pleasure washed over her, paradoxically mixed with want. Unwittingly, she felt her hips still grinding and straining when he slowly withdrew.

Crooning to her in French, he stilled her frantic movements and pulled her close to lie beside him. "I'm sorry, my
love. You see, I've wanted you for so long, I could not
wait, not yet." He caressed her burning flesh and soothed
her, until she began to uncoil, relaxing against the solid
comfort of his body. Finally she slept.

Rafael watched her delicate features, so beautiful and
innocent in sleep. Lord, but she had passion! He could
sense her need and desperately wanted to fill it, to fill her
with all his love, body and soul. *I love her!* He lay very
still, amazed at the sudden flash of insight and more than a
little alarmed at the realization that he would be forever
bound to this slim Yankee girl who slept so securely at his
side. He kissed her softly on the lips and pulled the covers
over them, settling down to drift off himself.

Deborah awakened after a couple of hours, still excited
by all the new experiences the evening had brought. She
could feel the warmth and weight of her husband as he lay
with his hard body pressed full length against hers. One arm
was thrown possessively across her waist and one leg
entwined with her own. He slept on his stomach with his
face turned toward her. She considered the strongly chiseled
features in repose. With those unsettling obsidian eyes
closed, she felt more at ease as she studied him. He was like
some Grandee from a Goya painting. His face was classically perfect, even beautiful, in a virile way. Her eyes traced
the arched brows, thick lashes, and high cheekbones. His
mouth was wide and the jaw cleanly squared. She could see
the beginning shadow of his beard. He must have to shave
often. She fantasized about how it would be to watch him
shave, then reached up to run her fingertips lightly across
his cheek.

Suddenly, his arm tightened and pulled her closer to him.
"Madame Flamenco is no longer sleepy, mmm?" He spoke
in a silky, suggestive whisper, then kissed her languorously
as she melted against him. They rolled across the bed until
he was flat on his back with her lying directly on top of him.

"Like sweet ripe melons," he murmured in French as he
slowly kneaded her buttocks. While his skillful fingers were
busy tracing patterns up and down her spinal column,

teasing a breast, caressing her derriere, his mouth ravaged hers with increasingly fierce and bruising kisses. Where before such harsh caresses had frightened her, now she returned them, matching his passion with her own.

Rafael continued the devouring kiss, feeling her excitement build as they rolled back and forth. Finally, he reached between her legs, stroking the quivering eager flesh until she was on fire, mindless with fierce, hungry wanting.

When he raised over her and spread her legs, she opened eagerly to him, arching up to meet his swift entry with no preliminary testing necessary this time. As if her body knew a secret her mind did not, Deborah found herself straining with every glorious thrust he made. He held her hips to slow their frantic movements and prolong the ecstatic torture until he could sense her cresting. Her eyes, closed in concentration an instant before, flew suddenly open as her nails sank into his back and she emitted a strangled sound of surprise.

"That's it, *ma petite*, just let it happen," he breathed, feeling her body's long, slow release as the velvety walls that sheathed him contracted over and over. When he could hold back no longer, he joined her, pulsing his seed deep inside her in great shuddering waves, then collapsing on top of her.

They lay still, unwilling to break the communion of their joining. Finally, he raised on his elbows to allow her easier breathing. The pale skin across her throat and breasts was delicately stained with rosy splotches and her violet eyes were wide in wonder, open windows to the love that she ached to confess to him.

Deborah looked into his jet eyes, for once not dancing with mirth or accusing in anger, but alight with a tenderness she had never seen in them before. "I love you, Deborah," he said simply.

She kissed him softly. "And I love you, Rafael, more than I ever imagined I could love anyone."

For a moment suspended in time, neither one spoke. Their eyes and their bodies said everything for them. Then a sharp rapping on the door broke the spell. "I believe that's our supper," she said.

Rafael rolled off her with a quick kiss, scooped up his

pants by the bedside and said with a devilish grin, "Are you hungry?" Before she could reply, he added with a wink, "You ought to be. I know I am."

Deborah blushed furiously as Rafael opened the door only wide enough to take the tray from the steward while she remained huddled beneath the covers on the bed. After setting the lavish repast on the table, he walked over to the armoire and ran long dark fingers across the various gowns. Finally he found a robe of deep violet velvet, which he removed.

"Here, this will be warmer than silk. Save that for when we get free of this accursed North Atlantic chill." He held the robe for her to slip into, noting her shyness and hesitation. "You have a lovely body, meant only for me to see, *cherie*. Come," he coaxed softly.

She slipped from the bed and slid into the robe, grateful for its warmth. When he wrapped it around her shoulders, she put her hand over his and drew it to her lips, kissing his fingers. "You don't like our New England cold, do you?"

"No, I don't, but I do like some of your food." A heavenly blend of aromas wafted across the room as he lifted the linen cloth from the tray. With a flourish he seated her and began to dish up the food.

As they ate in companionable silence, she found that she was indeed ravenous and wondered idly if making love always used up so much energy. Madame Flamenco was too embarrassed to ask, however, for fear of her husband's teasing. She decided on a safer topic. "How long will it take us to reach New Orleans?"

"It depends on the weather," he said as he cracked a large, succulent lobster claw. "Several weeks this time of year, I'd estimate. We'll have a real Creole honeymoon."

At her look of puzzlement, he explained. "Traditionally, a Creole couple spends the first five days after the wedding in a private bedroom in her parents' house. They are left completely alone. Not even servants intrude except to leave food trays at the door and bring bathwater."

Deborah was speechless for a moment as the realization sank in—they were virtually in the same situation, alone on the high seas with only the ship's stewards in attendance.

Seeing his devilish pleasure in teasing her, she retorted, "Well, I have a head start in being a proper Creole wife. I suppose the custom was necessary to allow partners in an arranged marriage to become acquainted after rather than before the wedding. A way of making up for lost time."

He reached across the small table and took her hand, then planted a sensuous kiss in the soft palm. "Oh, I plan to have us become very, very well acquainted before we reach New Orleans."

In spite of herself, Deborah could feel her face heating again. Changing the subject she said, "Tell me more about your family. I have so much to learn." *Oh, damnation! There I go again with my silly goose tongue!*

Rafael laughed softly at her unintentional double entendre but answered straightforwardly. "As I already said, I am my father's only heir. That means I have a great deal of responsibility."

"I thought you said you had a sister?"

"Yes, Lenore, a beautiful child. You will like her. She has blue eyes and hair like old Spanish gold. A throwback to Mama's French ancestors, or the Castilian side of Papa's family."

"Won't she be your father's heir, too?"

He smiled dismissively. "No, not in the way you are your father's heir. She will make a good marriage into a proper Creole family and have a large dowry settled on her at the time the wedding contract is written. It has been understood for years that she will marry our third cousin from Mama's side of the family, Georges Beaurivage. But I have no brothers, so I alone must carry on the Flamenco name."

Deborah didn't like his fondly patronizing attitude toward Lenore and she liked the role he intimated for her even less. "And, as your wife, I am to provide you with lots of male children for the next generation of Flamencos."

He noticed her tone and acknowledged it with a question. "You do want children, don't you, Deborah?"

"Of course I do, but I think girls are just as welcome as boys and I'd love to have both." She forced herself to look into those unsettling jet eyes.

His smile would have melted the Arctic wastes. "We

will, *ma petite*. You don't realize we dote upon our daughters. Lenore was always our papa's favorite. But girls cannot carry on the family name or manage business affairs.''

She let the latter remark pass. It was a sore subject since she had often argued with her own father about working in his bank. It seemed he and his son-in-law agreed on at least one matter! "I suppose Creole honeymoon customs do guarantee a head start in producing lots of heirs!"

He threw back his head and laughed as he began to rise from the table. "I never considered it just so, my practical New England wife, but you may well be right. Come here and let us do our proper Creole duty." His eyes were glowing with a different light now and his hands on her shoulders were warm and compelling. She could refuse him nothing.

Their shipboard honeymoon was every bit as cloistered as if they had been a traditional Creole bride and groom. Even more so because they were on neutral territory, so to speak, not in her family's home, nor in his, but in the midst of the ocean. All their fellow travelers were strangers, so the two of them were completely dependent upon each other for company. It was a delightful idyll for Deborah, who found her initiation into the physical pleasures of marriage breathtaking. There was so much to learn and Rafael was a skillful and patient teacher, overcoming her prim Boston inhibitions and convincing her that she was indeed beautiful and desirable. Deborah had always thought of herself as unconventional looking, if not downright unattractive and unappealing. Nonetheless, she obviously appealed to her husband, who made love to her during the scandalous hours of broad daylight, as well as under the respectable veil of night. She found herself more and more drawn into his sensual web. Indeed, when he put his hands on her and kissed her with sweet abandon, she felt herself oblivious to all the principles, ideals, and causes that had heretofore shaped her life.

Since Rafael had been initiated into sexual pleasure at the age of fourteen, he did not find their lovemaking new, but the way he felt toward his wife was disturbingly different from what he had felt toward any other woman. His discovery that he loved her had been a shock, but even more troublesome was the way she filled his thoughts. It was delightful to trade witticisms with her, to debate and enjoy her lightning quick intelligence. Even when he felt her opinions woefully wrongheaded he admired the logical way she could defend them. For the first time in his young life he was intrigued by a woman's complete personality, not just her body.

He was a man most blessed, especially considering that most Creole men married teary-eyed virgins who lay cold and stiff in their marriage beds, merely doing their duty. His own parents had such a relationship. Yet, his intense emotional involvement with Deborah left him distinctly uneasy. No woman should have this much power over his heart and mind. With the careless optimism of spoiled youth, Rafael simply decided to enjoy the delectable honeymoon and face the problem of Deborah's place in his life after they arrived in New Orleans. Once he was back in his own world, surrounded by people and customs he understood, he would be able to put this obsession in perspective.

Rafael looked forward to their arrival in New Orleans, but Deborah dreaded it more as the distance lessened. She feared his parents' reaction to a Yankee. To humor her, Rafael agreed to switch their conversation exclusively to French. Then, she barraged him with questions about the whole social registry of Creole New Orleans. It was a cast of thousands that made her head swim.

"I shall never be able to remember all your relatives," she wailed one morning as he described a boyhood prank he and several of his male cousins had played on their female counterparts. "Was Jean the same one you took fencing lessons with?"

He put down his coffee cup as he answered, "Yes. He and I were often in trouble together. He is my Uncle Francois's eldest son, the oldest of six boys and three girls."

She noted a fleeting expression of regret pass across his face. "All your father's siblings seem to run to large families, especially to boys." Suddenly recalling that Rafael was his father's only son, she wished she had not said that.

However, he shrugged philosophically. "Yes, it would seem my parents were not so blessed as the rest of the

Flamencos and Beaurivages. We shall simply have to remedy the situation in the next generation,'' he added with a grin.

She smiled, conjuring up images of dark cherubic faces with glowing black eyes and bouncing black curls. ''I can picture half a dozen small replicas of you, God help the women of this world,'' she said teasingly.

''Ah, beloved, I'd rather think of tiny gilt-haired daughters, as dainty as porcelain princesses,'' he replied. ''God help the *men* of this world.''

''I do wonder what our children will look like. You said your mother has chestnut hair and your sister is a blonde. You must take after the Spanish branch.'' She blushed, and confessed, ''I first imagined you were some sort of romantic figure from the past, a conquistador riding on a white horse.''

Rafael threw back his head and laughed. ''Well, it's true I do resemble my Spanish forebears. Grandfather Flamenco used to tell me about our illustrious ancestors from Toledo. Our family name and coat of arms was granted to a mercenary who served with the Duke of Alva in the religious wars of the fifteen seventies. Flamenco means Fleming in Spanish.''

Deborah's eyes widened. ''You mean your ancestor served with Ferdinand Alvarez, the 'Bloody Duke,' on his reign of terror in Holland and Flanders?''

He smiled darkly. ''Leave it to you to know every detail of history, even one best forgotten. I suppose Alva was an unpleasant sort, and my ancestor probably was too.''

She sniffed in conciliation. ''Well, it is best forgotten by the Spanish because they lost the war. Anyway, that was over two hundred and fifty years ago.''

With an exaggerated leer, he rose from the breakfast table. ''Still, you never know. I may be a throwback, another bloodthirsty ravisher of women, worse than Alva.''

She chuckled and threw her arms around his neck, happy to forget the tangled web of the past. If they loved each other enough, nothing else would matter, not even those thousands of relatives.

Chapter 6

They would be landing in less than an hour. Rafael had gone above deck to talk to the captain and Deborah was finishing the last of their packing. She scooped up a satin robe and began to fold it, then discovered Rafael's razor strop lying beneath it. He must have forgotten it when he shaved earlier that morning. She picked it up and walked over to the small bag in which he carried his toilet articles. Opening the bag, she placed the strop inside and attempted to refasten it. It would not lock. Puzzled, Deborah reopened it and riffled through its contents. A long velvet case was jammed edgewise in the bottom. She pulled it free and it popped open in her hand, spilling its contents across his shaving gear.

"Scrimshaw," she murmured to herself. It was a beautiful necklace, earring, and comb set of etched ivory whale's teeth. A gift for his mother? Shrugging, she placed the jewelry back in the case and laid it lengthwise in the bottom of the bag, then rearranged everything so the valise would close.

Idly Deborah wondered if Rafael's Creole mother would appreciate such a uniquely New England gift. Or, more to the point, will she appreciate a New England daughter-in-law? She critically studied her outfit, a simple but elegant lilac silk suit and navy blouse. She assured herself Rafael's family would like it; she prayed they would like her.

Looking out the window at the shore, Deborah could see the landscape changing as they moved from the delta upriver. The flat, marshy, coastal plain was giving way to awesome stands of cypress draped with long, airy tentacles of Spanish moss. The dense swamp forest was alien and eerie to her New England eyes, but as they had come closer to the city Rafael identified magnolia and pecan trees for her, exotic and truly beautiful in this subtropical paradise. Southern Louisiana was enchanting. Her adventurous spirit and natural curiosity would have been piqued if she had not felt so much was at stake. As Rafael's wife, she must make this foreign land her home. Her worst fear was adjusting to his family. The exotic environment only added to her sense of apprehension.

Rafael entered their cabin while she was peering out the window. "Why not come above deck and see everything firsthand?"

Surprised out of her reverie, Deborah turned with a small gasp. Before she could speak, he gave her a swift kiss and took her arm, escorting her to the deck to meet the Queen of the South, Belle New Orleans.

Deborah could hear and smell the strange new sounds and odors even before the panorama of the waterfront unfolded. As they climbed the ship's stairs to the main deck, the babble of at least half a dozen languages melded together, some recognizable, others not. Aromas from around the earth mingled with the familiar salt smell of waterfronts everywhere. Heat hung in the humid air like damp clothes stretched on a line, mingling the odors of fermenting molasses with Oriental spices and West Indian rum with overripe fruit. It was perfume; it was pestilence.

Once more in his element, Rafael breathed deeply. He was wearing a lightweight cream linen suit and thin silk shirt, clothes that had marked him as a foreigner in Boston's chill. Now it was Deborah who was dressed inappropriately. She could feel the perspiration seep through the layers of her clothes and dampen the nape of her neck where her heavy hair was pinned in a loose chignon. She hoped she could get used to the heat.

As Rafael helped her take the last step from the gangplank onto solid ground, he squeezed her hand and said, "Welcome to New Orleans, Mrs. Flamenco." He watched her wide lavender eyes gaze around the bustling wharves that were filled with barrels of tobacco from upriver Louisiana, gleaming bins of coal from Pittsburgh, mountains of paving stones from Liverpool, and, most conspicuous of all, bales of cotton and casks of sugar.

As Rafael guided her through the chaos of sights and sounds, Deborah followed like a bewildered child, half-frightened, half-fascinated. She heard several French dialects and the crude English of the mountain men known as Kaintucks, but she could also discern Spanish and Portuguese, even Greek and Italian.

A strange, earringed man dressed in sailor's garb spoke to his companion in a Levantine tongue while both gazed at Deborah's exotic silvery hair with open admiration. A wizened old black man carrying a brilliantly feathered parrot in a cage nearly collided with two Ursuline nuns who were walking lockstep with beads swinging and white headdresses nodding. The parrot squawked in a completely unknown language. Deborah held tightly to her husband's arm as he signaled for an open carriage.

Rafael had already explained to her that although his family knew they were arriving on the *Blue Lightning*, the docking schedule was erratic because of spring storms. They were nearly a week early and no one would be at the wharf to meet them.

"It isn't far from here to our town house," Rafael explained as their hired carriage driver started out slowly.

Deborah watched as two statuesque quadroon women with baskets balanced gracefully on their heads regally ignored the crude patois of an African vendor. The flower stalls took her breath away. Spanish jasmine, violets and pale creamy magnolia blossoms were interspersed with deep crimson roses.

Rafael watched her childlike awe, delighted with the effect his exotic city was having on his Boston lady. "My parents' house is near the old square. The area on the Mississippi bordered by Canal, Rampart, and Esplanade was first called the French Quarter by the Americans, but now even the Creoles use the term. We live on Royal Street. The lower half of the old quarter is the most elegant."

Deborah gazed up at the galleries with their lacy ironwork. "Why are all the living quarters situated on the upper floors with carriage entrances on the ground level?" She could see central courtyards through the narrow gateways that allowed access to the houses.

"The ocean keeps trying to claim us, my love," he

replied. "You see, the original builders of our city didn't consider how low the land here is—the river is higher than the city and drainage must go inland toward Lake Pontchartrain to the northeast. There are no cellars in New Orleans."

Just then, the loud nasal twang of an auctioneer caught Deborah's attention. They were cutting across Chartres Street where a long, open building was packed with people who thronged out onto the sidewalks, called banquettes. Inside, on a raised platform, Deborah could see a long row of black people, several large men in chains, as well as numerous women and children. A young woman, obviously pregnant and gripping a small child by the hand, stood by the auctioneer's side. As he extolled her virtues, several white men came up onto the platform and began to examine her with the crude thoroughness that Deborah could compare only to the way her father's stable man might check a horse.

Their carriage was stalled in the crowd, and their driver swore in an Irish brogue, urging his horses through the press. Oblivious to all else, Deborah stared at the loathsome spectacle of the auction. "Are they selling her in *that* condition?" she whispered.

Noting her pallor and realizing her Northern sensibilities were appalled by the seamier side of the South's "peculiar institution," Rafael uttered a silent oath. "This is the Maspero Exchange, Deborah. It's the largest and best slave auction in the country. Every kind of black is sold here, those wild from Africa, skilled artisans, yes, even pregnant women. It's a fact of life, I'm afraid." He shrugged dismissively as the carriage once more started to move, leaving the disquieting scene behind.

Rafael hoped the more pleasing sights of the city would distract Deborah's attention, but she doggedly pursued the subject. "But—but, they were examining her teeth and touching her belly as if she were a mare about to foal." She was aghast at her own crudity, speaking of things no Boston lady should ever mention aloud, but she was even more aghast at what she had just witnessed. "What must that child think, having his mother humiliated so publicly?"

"The child is a slave, the son of a slave," Rafael answered flatly. "He doesn't think at all."

"How can you know that? He is a human being. Rafael, do you go to those awful things to buy women and children?" Deborah's face had lost its pallor and was taking on the rosy hue of indignation.

"No, of course not. That's what we have hired help for. In the rare instances we need additional people, Kent Austin, our overseer, attends to the purchases."

"How many slaves does the Flamenco family own?" she asked hesitantly.

He shrugged carelessly, having never really had occasion to tally the number. "In town, about a dozen, I suppose. At the plantation, perhaps five hundred. It is one of the largest sugar plantations in Louisiana." Rafael smiled, trying to change the subject. "Wait until you see the town house. I'm sure you'll like it and the summer house on Lake Pontchartrain."

"It must take a lot of servants to keep two homes running," she said uncertainly, once more overwhelmed by the extent of his wealth. Her father had told her the Flamencos were one of the South's richest families. Although the Manchesters were among Boston's monied elite, such conspicuous displays of wealth were unknown in her world.

Trying to soothe her, Rafael said, "Deborah, I know your discomfort with the idea of slavery, but you must remember that the Creoles treat their people with kindness and provide for them in illness and old age a good deal better than your New England mill owners do their paid laborers."

"I've heard that before," she snapped, hating his patronizing tone. "Tell me, when is the last time you heard of a mill owner breaking up a family by selling one of them?"

His face darkened. "The Flamencos don't sell families apart, Deborah. Anyway, there is no legal marriage among the blacks and according to law no child below the age of ten can be separated from his mother."

Her eyes widened. "What makes you think it would hurt a mother less to lose an eleven-year-old than a ten-year-old?"

He shrugged a trifle more uncomfortably now. "I never

thought about it, Deborah, because our blacks have been with us for generations. I'm not responsible for abuses largely perpetrated by American businessmen and plantation owners. You're going to make your home here as my wife, so you must accept our customs." There was a finality in his last words, spoken as they pulled up in front of an elegant three-story building with two tiers of wrought-iron galleries circling it.

Rafael paid the driver and then gave Deborah a reassuring kiss on the cheek, escorting her inside the wide double doors at street level. A large spiral staircase of beautiful wrought iron was situated at the end of the long, narrow hallway. Off to one side, beyond the stairs, the patio was partially visible.

As he helped her negotiate the steep steps, she looked out at the large courtyard where a musical fountain spilled its sparkling water from a jug held by a cherubic Grecian statue. Palm trees shaded the old rust colored bricks from the scorching morning sun. "Oh, it's lovely, Rafael."

Unmindful of the beauty around him, Rafael steered her to a large set of double doors in the center of the gallery. Opening one, he called, "Papa, Mama, the prodigal returns a week early with his lovely bride!"

A tall, gray-haired black man, impeccably dressed in the black broadcloth livery of a butler, appeared in response to his raucous greeting. Upon seeing Rafael, his wizened face creased into a wide grin. "Master Rafael, welcome back and a special welcome to your lady. Congratulations, sir."

Watching the animated exchange carried on in French, Deborah was suddenly struck by the fact that the Creole slaves would speak a French patois, not the strange English dialect she had heard on shipboard and in the North.

"Deborah, this is Antoine. He rules this household with an iron hand," Rafael said fondly.

Deborah nodded, exchanging a warm smile with the old man. Just then a joyous shriek and a string of French endearments rent the air as a tiny plump woman with dark chestnut hair flew into Rafael's arms. Celine Adele Flamenco hugged her tall son who spun her like a doll through the air in a dizzying circle. When her feet finally touched the ground once more, she continued to chatter and hang on to his arm until he gently and laughingly turned her attention to his wife.

Madame Flamenco's dark blue eyes turned cold despite the fixed smile on her pouty red mouth. Deborah felt a ripple of apprehension but forced it aside and smiled her warmest. "I am so pleased to meet you, madame," she said simply, noticing the way the much shorter woman took in her tall, slender figure, as if measuring her womanly attributes and finding them lacking.

"You *do* speak French. Rafael wrote us so, but I feared he exaggerated as he is wont to do, naughty boy," she added aside to him in a coquettish manner. "Of course, this was all so sudden, we were not prepared for our only son to bring a bride home, especially one from so far away."

"Boston was still in the United States last time I checked, Mama," Rafael replied with a smile. "You needn't worry about our living arrangements. We'll just move into my old apartment."

Deborah was certain Madame Flamenco was less concerned with the living arrangements than with having a Yankee daughter-in-law foisted upon her.

"Well, home at last with your new wife," a smooth, well-cultivated baritone voice intoned from the far end of the parlor. Claude Adrien Flamenco strolled across the oak marquetry. His curly black hair was sprinkled with gray and his face creased with fine lines that gave evidence of overindulgence in liquor and late hours. Nevertheless, he was still a handsome man.

His appraisal of Deborah was even more open than his wife's had been. He reached for her hand and saluted it in the French manner. Although his eyes surveyed her with admiration, Deborah could tell he was just as dismayed as Celine about their son's hasty marriage to a Yankee. "What do you think of our city so far?" he queried smoothly.

"It's different from Boston," she replied carefully, "but just as beautiful, in its own distinct fashion."

"Deborah has hardly had time to see enough of New Orleans to appreciate her new home, Papa," Rafael interjected impatiently.

"Perhaps it would be best if she were to take a rest during the mid-afternoon heat, dear heart," his mother said sweetly. "I can see our weather does not agree," she added to Deborah, noting her dampened hairline and flushed face. "Of course, we shall have a whole new wardrobe made for her, befitting our climate. Those fabrics are far too heavy and cut too plainly. Perhaps something with tiered ruffles and some lace, yes, in brighter colors, too." Celine chattered on as she led the way into another sitting room.

When they reached the door, Rafael laughingly took Deborah's arm and said to his mother, "I can show my wife to her new quarters, Mama. Why not send Tonette to unpack for Deborah? By the way, where is Lenore?"

"Off to tea with Anna du May," Celine answered vaguely. "She'll be home for her afternoon rest shortly. She'll be so thrilled to see you, dear heart."

"I'll come back as soon as I get Deborah settled in, Mama." He nodded to his father as well, dreading the grilling he knew would be forthcoming.

The house seemed to go on forever with a long hall and twisting labyrinths of rooms that encircled the patio. Deborah caught glimpses of crystal chandeliers, beveled mirrors set with Louis XIV frames, mahogany furniture, and marble fireplaces. Everywhere the marquetry floors gleamed underfoot, offset with thick imported carpets.

"Where in all this maze is your room, Rafael?" She struggled to keep her bearings.

He laughed. "Not room, darling, rooms—I have had my own separate bachelor quarters at the rear of the house for several years now." With a flourish, he led her outside, onto the gallery and around another corner where an adjacent building was connected to the main dwelling. Opening the door to his apartment, he reached down and scooped her up. "A quaint old Yankee custom, I believe," he breathed into her hair as he carried her over the threshold.

When he set her down, he did not release her, but gathered her close for a lingering kiss. Feeling alone and vulnerable in the large, hostile house, she returned his embrace fiercely. In his arms she was loved and safe.

He gradually broke the sealing kiss. With labored breath

he said, "If we keep this up, I'll not return to report to my father and you'll miss your nap. Now, what do you think of the old place? I know it's in need of a woman's touch, but you can do whatever you like with it."

"It is a bit dark and masculine, but I love the oak furniture," she replied, looking about the spacious parlor furnished with two large leather sofas, a wall of bookshelves, floor to ceiling, and several massive dark oak chests and high-backed chairs. It was actually a combination library, study, and parlor. Adjacent to it was a small sitting room, and across the hall she could see a formal dining room.

Rafael led her into the master bedroom, dominated by a huge four poster bed of black walnut. He took her face in his hands, the dark warm fingers caressing her cheekbones and massaging her temples as he kissed her forehead. "I love you, Deborah. Now, rest while Tonette unpacks some things for us to wear this evening."

"Tonette?"

"Lenore's maid. Until we can find one for you, she'll be glad to help you both," he said blithely as he left the room. When Rafael closed the door, Deborah felt enveloped in the cool darkness. The bedroom had a set of large windows facing onto another open courtyard. A faint breeze blew through them giving some relief from the heat. She slipped off the rest of her outer garments and lay across the big bed in her chemise and pantalettes. Sleep claimed her almost instantly.

When Rafael returned to his parents' quarters, he heard his father's angry voice. "I will have no scandal touch the Flamenco name. Do I make myself clear, young woman?"

"It's no scandal," Lenore protested. "Caleb Armstrong simply offered Anna and me a ride home in his landau. We had been properly introduced, and Mellie was with me after he let Anna off at the du May place, Papa." Listening to the argument Rafael decided there was a mulish note to his sister's voice not unlike Deborah's. Why had he never noticed the similarity before?

"There is no such thing as a proper introduction to an American, Lenore," Celine hissed. "Think of the gossip. He's a land speculator as well. Not our sort at all. What will dear cousin Georges say?"

"For the hundredth time, I am not going to marry my cousin. I can't abide him!" On that tearful note, Lenore fled the room.

"As if Rafael's disastrous marriage isn't bad enough, now Lenore turns on me like a viper! Oh, Claude, what shall we do? My only son's wife—an American and even worse, a Yankee!"

Rafael could hear the grim tightness in his father's voice as he answered her. "I'm afraid there is nothing we can do, my dear. As our son wrote us, they were wed in the church and I am quite certain my son lost no time consummating the marriage."

Celine let out another wail and fled after her distraught daughter.

Quite a homecoming, Rafael thought angrily. *As if I won't have a difficult enough time easing Deborah into my parents' good graces, my silly sister has to go and get herself involved with that Yankee upstart and balk at her sensibly arranged marriage.*

"I applaud your common sense, Papa. Deborah is indeed my wife, and nothing will change that," he said as he stepped into the room.

The older man turned angrily. "So, you've overheard how things go. Good. This is the reward we get from our offspring. Both of you infatuated with foreigners! Your mother was heartsick when she read your letter."

Rafael sighed. "Look, Papa, I am sorry for the shock. We didn't plan to fall in love." He poured himself a glass of cool wine. "In fact, it's a long and complicated story. Simply put, from the moment I saw her, I was lost. Her father is a wealthy banker from a distinguished Boston family. When we decided to wed, we knew it must be done there in his presence. He consented to have a priest perform the ceremony."

"I take it they are not of our faith," Claude observed.

"Deborah will become Catholic, Papa. She'll attend mass with Mama and Lenore. There's no problem with her. It's you who may make things difficult or pleasant. She will be a good wife."

"A proper Creole wife, your Boston Yankee?" Claude's left brow arched in a sardonic gesture of doubt. "She looks as cold as an Atlantic storm."

Rafael's face split in a youthful grin. "There you couldn't be more wrong. I wager you we'll fill this house with babies within the decade."

The old man poured himself some claret and held his glass up with a cynical toast. "To all my grandsons!"

Chapter 7

Deborah awoke from her exhausted slumber and sat up in the middle of the big bed, slowly orienting herself to the large room. Idly, she ran one hand across the silk sheets and imagined how it would feel to be naked on them with Rafael. Her heated thoughts were interrupted by a gentle tapping and a melodic feminine voice. "Hello. Deborah?"

Jumping out of bed, Deborah spied the sheer silk robe to her wedding peignoir. Slipping it on, she walked to the parlor where a small, slim young woman with dark gold hair stood, hesitantly calling her name.

"You must be Lenore," she said, pushing a heavy mass of hair back over her shoulder as she welcomed her new sister-in-law and was rewarded with the first genuine smile she had received from any of her in-laws.

"I know you are Deborah. I've never seen hair so pale and shiny before, or violet eyes. No wonder my heart-breaking brother couldn't leave you behind. I'm so glad to meet you.'' Lenore was open and friendly, the opposite of her mother.

Impulsively, Deborah reached out and hugged her new sister-in-law. ''I can tell already we're going to be friends.'' She could see the quiet beauty of this girl with large china blue eyes—eyes that showed evidence of tears. Hoping she and Rafael were not the cause, Deborah asked, ''Have you seen your brother?''

''No, I arrived home when you and Rafael were settling in here. Then, I'm afraid, I had a disagreement with our parents. By the time I recovered myself, he had gone out; but he'll be back for dinner. That's why I came to see if you were dressing yet. I've been dying to meet the woman who won my brother's heart.''

They chatted like old friends as Deborah selected the coolest dress she owned. While she had been sleeping, the maid had unpacked her clothes and pressed several dresses. Now they all hung neatly in a mirrored armoire in the dressing room. Lenore helped fasten her gown and was amazed when Deborah brushed her own hair and quickly fashioned it into a smooth fat chignon at the nape of her neck.

''I could never do my hair without Tonette, but she can do for you, too, until we find you a maid.''

Deborah smiled. ''I've always done my own hair. In fact, except for occasional help with fastenings and pressing, of course, I never really asked our maid to assist me at all.''

''But every woman of quality must have her own personal maid!''

Deborah chuckled as she replied, ''Well, maybe in New Orleans, but I grew up in pragmatic old Boston. I've never been comfortable with too many servants underfoot. We only had four.''

''But Rafael said your father was a leading banker and you lived in a great, beautiful house—oh, I didn't mean to offend you, Deborah.'' Lenore's face was scarlet.

Deborah laughed. ''No offense taken, Lenore. We did have a large house, but my father and I preferred to live simply. When we entertained, I hired staff temporarily. Free men and women,'' she added softly.

"Are you trying to make an abolitionist out of my sister, too, beloved?"

At the sound of Rafael's voice, Lenore whirled and catapulted herself at him with a squeal of girlish delight, barraging him with questions. How was he? How was married life agreeing with him? What had Boston been like? Did he know how fortunate he was to have found Deborah?

Rafael laughingly replied, "I'll tell you all about how we met. Only wait for dinner when Mama and Papa are present." Lenore's face suddenly became shuttered and her eyes lost their sparkle.

Rafael questioned gently, "Were you quarreling with Mama and Papa when I came downstairs earlier, little one? Perhaps after dinner you and I can talk alone?"

Lenore brightened immediately, then hesitated. "I would love that, only . . ."

"Only . . ." he prodded patiently.

"I'm afraid you won't approve. You've always favored Georges." She stopped short and looked over at Deborah, a silent onlooker at the reunion. "But now that you've broken Creole tradition and chosen such a wonderful *American* wife, perhaps you'll look at Caleb differently than you would have before!"

With that burst of youthful enthusiasm, she gave Deborah a quick peck on the cheek, hugged her brother again, and raced downstairs.

With a look of exaggerated aggravation, he turned to his wife. "She's such a child. Hard to believe she's eighteen, of marriageable age and then some."

"I think she's delightful, only not quite as conventional as a 'proper Creole lady' is supposed to be. What's this about someone named Caleb? Is he American?"

Now Rafael really scowled. "Yes, he's American." He said the word as if it were a malediction, taking her quite aback. "He's also a land speculator. Completely unsuitable for my sister. Georges is our kind. He'll make her a good husband."

Deborah felt oddly hurt by what he said and even more hurt by the logical extension of what he implied. "I, too, am American, Rafael. So are you and all Creoles now. Is this Caleb some kind of fortune hunter?'' She was acutely sensitive about that sort of situation.

He shrugged. "He scarcely needs her dowry, if that's what you mean. He's a self-made millionaire, typical of the crassly ambitious Yankees who are strangling our civilization.''

"If he doesn't need her money, then perhaps he really loves her," she said gently.

Rafael's face became shuttered, much as his sister's had earlier. "Lenore has nothing to say about it. She will marry one of her own kind, a man of breeding, a gentleman, not someone who works in his shirtsleeves and drinks whiskey,'' he said disdainfully.

Remembering the times she had come late to her father's study to find the Boston banker with sleeves rolled up, intent on his ledgers while sipping a tot of rum, Deborah was suddenly very angry. Willing herself to calm down, she took a deep breath and said levelly, "I was under the naive assumption that love had a great deal to do with marriages. Perhaps this American isn't the right man for Lenore, but if she is dead set against your cousin Georges, he is scarcely the right man for her simply because he happens to be a Creole. Oliver Haversham was from a fine old Boston family and you were an outsider. Should I have married him instead of you?'' She held her breath, suddenly afraid of his reply.

Rafael was in a foul humor, pressed on all sides by his parents, his sister, and now his wife, but he could sense the fear and insecurity in her query. Wanting to reassure her, perhaps to reassure himself, he reached out and drew her into his arms. "You must understand the difference it makes when a son marries as opposed to when a daughter marries. A man can take a wife from outside his culture and bring her into it. She can become a part of it because she bears his name and raises his children. When a woman leaves her own people and marries an outsider, she is lost to her family. If Lenore marries Caleb Armstrong, she'll be ostracized from all proper Creole circles here in New Orleans. She's too young and impetuous to see the consequences of the infatuation. She is Creole and she belongs here.''

I am not Creole and I will never belong here. Deborah

took small comfort from his unconsciously patronizing assurances, but squeezed back a sudden rush of tears. She had never had patience with vaporing women. She would simply have to try and help his sister in a less direct way.

Deborah was determined to fit into her new life, but the adjustments were not easy. Early the next morning she arose, eager to begin her household duties only to find she had none. Wilma the cook and Antoine the butler ran the city house like a piece of well-oiled machinery. Even Celine did little more than make up the menus. Everything was left in capable black hands.

Assuming that Creole wives did some useful work outside the home such as charity or educational endeavors, Deborah found that such a thought scandalized her mother-in-law. No proper lady of the upper class would ever dream of doing anything so degrading as tend the sick or teach the poor. Such matters were completely in the hands of the Church. The good sisters were admired for their efforts, but no lady, except in rare instances when one took the veil, ever thought of such a thing!

Even Lenore, an open and generous young woman, was aghast when Deborah explained that society ladies in northern cities volunteered in hospitals, opened schools for the underprivileged, and raised money for all sorts of charities. When she told her sister-in-law about the women's suffrage movement in England and France, which so many of her Boston and New York counterparts were embracing, Lenore paled, fascinated in spite of herself.

"You mean, you actually expect to *vote*?" she fairly croaked as they sat in the parlor one afternoon.

"A woman has a mind capable of thought. If she's responsible for bringing new life into the world, why shouldn't she be guaranteed some say about her children's lives?"

Lenore considered this for a moment, then said hesitantly, "Do you think a man like Caleb might agree with such a radical Yankee idea? Georges certainly wouldn't. Neither would Papa or Rafael," she added sadly.

Deborah responded honestly. "I've never met Mr. Armstrong, so I don't know. Just because he's an American doesn't mean he espouses women's rights. I know Rafael wasn't very supportive the other night when you discussed Mr. Armstrong but perhaps he'll soften in time."

Lenore sighed and nodded. "I hope so, but I have to do what he and Papa say even if they insist I marry Georges."

Recalling her own near miss with Oliver Haversham, Deborah said forcefully, "No one can make you marry against your will. You must face up to them if you find your cousin so unpleasant."

It was like talking into the fog, however. Lenore had been so sheltered, cosseted, and molded into her role that she could not imagine openly defying the men of her family.

If she despaired about Lenore, Deborah found her own situation little better. She hated the boring social whirl of dances, masquerades, horse races, and operas, the trips to the modistes and shoemakers, the endless tittering gossip of the young matrons in tea shops and cafes. Boston was a town with the motto: Business occasionally stops for pleasure. New Orleans seemed to have that concept completely reversed: Pleasure occasionally stops for business.

Most frustrating of all for Deborah was Celine's hostility. First on the agenda had been a trip to the dressmaker. Deborah's clothes were too heavy for the steamy tropical heat, and she did love the gauzy sheer muslins, silks, and organzas the southern women wore. However, when it came to style, she and Celine were doomed to clash. Like most Creole women, the Flamencos were petite. Delicate, frilly clothes with ruffles and bows in frothy, elaborate styles looked attractive on them. Not so their Yankee in-law. Deborah was tall and slim; ruffles and bows made her look gawky.

Madame Manlon, the modiste, was sympathetic to Deborah's tastes but knew where the power lay. Madame Flamenco had been her valued customer for years. She quickly bowed out of what became the ribbon riot of Dumaine Street.

Holding a pale aqua watered-silk dress up with a disdainful sniff Celine said, "We must at least put some color in this gown. I know! Some of that cunning grosgrain." She snatched at the spool of ribbon on the counter. It was a bright rose pink color, heavy and shiny. "Yes, along the shoulders and caught at the hem. Of course, the shoes should have buckles made of it, too." She babbled on, completely ignoring Deborah's blazing violet eyes.

"Mama, perhaps the dress would be more dramatic if it were plainer," Lenore ventured but was quickly waved aside.

After a full morning of arguments over colors and styles, enduring all sorts of sweetly delivered slurs about her taste in clothing, Deborah had had enough.

"Mother Celine"—she hated the title but suspected not half as much as her mother-in-law did—"I will not wear that or any other dress with gewgaws on it. They do not flatter me." Her voice had an edge of steel to it that even Celine could not ignore.

The dressmaker quickly excused herself and fled the crowded fitting room. Lenore was trapped haplessly but backed off into a corner, instinctively reacting like a rabbit in the presence of two airedales.

Celine's eyes snapped. "You know nothing about fashion. Northern women may be plain as posts, but this is New Orleans and women dress as ladies here."

Deborah's expression was surprisingly cool now, although she was seething inside. She stared down her mother-in-law's spiteful glare. "I dress to please my husband, not the Creole ladies of New Orleans."

Celine stamped her foot, shoving the dress at her daughter-in-law and throwing the heavy spool of ribbon on the floor, where it unwound in a splashy pile of rose glitter. "I shall have a talk with my son about your manners." With that she whirled to leave, chin held imperiously high, only to fall face-forward through the door. She had stepped into the entrapping pile of ribbons, which wound around her ankles, tripping her in a tangled web. As she grabbed for the doorframe, she heard the rip of her skirts, which had caught on a protruding bolt. Unable to free her bound feet or her crinolines, she crumpled in a sobbing, ignominious heap on the floor just outside the dressing room.

Hearing the commotion, Madame Manlon came flying

down the hall and knelt to assist her customer. The pink ribbon had entangled Madame Flamenco's stiff red taffeta dress like a fisherman's net. Celine rather closely resembled a pink and red blowfish freshly netted from the Gulf. As her plump body thrashed amid her billowing crinolines, she appeared even more rotund. The thick mass of her glossy chestnut hair had come unceremoniously down and was tangled around her shoulders. Her face was as red as her dress by the time the modiste, Lenore, and Deborah had extricated her.

Biting back her laughter, Deborah nonetheless refused the huffy harridan an apology, merely calling after Celine that she would complete her order and have a hired carriage take her home. She and Madame Manlon finished the day peaceably in complete agreement about pale, cool colors and straight, clean lines.

"I tell you, Claude, you have to do something! She will disgrace us. She talks about nothing but books and philosophy and politics, for heaven's sake! And her clothes. Oh! I can never show my face at Madame Manlon's again." Celine cried and twisted her kerchief in her fingers, daubing delicately at her eyelids as she watched her husband sigh in exasperation.

Just then Rafael sauntered into the parlor in time to see his agitated parents replaying a scene he had often witnessed— his mother tearful and hysterical, his father stern yet placating.

Seeing him, Celine launched into a new fit of weeping, recounting her debacle at the dressmaker's through hiccups of rage and embarrassment. "She is so openly contemptuous of our ways, Rafael. And those horrid washed-out clothes fit only for a governess—it's humiliating."

Used to her tears and pleading, he sighed in resignation, much like his father. "Mama, you have to give Deborah time to adjust. I will speak with her."

As he headed for his quarters, *their* quarters now, he braced himself for another tantrum. What he found instead was a nervous but dry-eyed Deborah, sitting in their parlor, reading. When he entered, she put her book aside and stood up. "I assume your mother told you I tried to strangle her with grosgrain ribbon this morning?"

He smiled thinly. "Something to that general effect. Why can't you let her guide you just a bit, Deborah? She only wants to help you fit in. You really do owe her an apology for your behavior today."

Deborah's temper was coming to a slow boil. Then an idea flashed in her mind. Smiling sweetly, she said, "You're right, my love. I'll go speak with her immediately."

Rafael should have been suspicious of her easy capitulation.

Deborah made a handsome apology to Celine and asked for her help in selecting a gown for the Gautiers' ball. Celine was pleased that her son had at least controlled the hateful chit and vowed to outdo herself selecting style, fabric, and trim. They departed for the modiste once more the next morning. The following week passed with superficial harmony between mother-in-law and daughter-in-law. Father and son were relieved.

When Rafael entered their bedroom on the night of the ball, Deborah was still wearing a silk wrapper. Flushed from a scented bath, she looked delectably ready to be swept off to bed, not to a gala! "Why aren't you dressed, Moon Flower? It's almost time to be fashionably late, as Mama prefers."

Smiling broadly, she replied, "I want to surprise you with the dress. It *is* special. Will you wait for me in the parlor with your parents? I won't be long."

Brushing her nose with a kiss, he complied, whistling jauntily down the hall.

True to her word, Deborah appeared shortly in the doorway to the parlor where Rafael and Claude were engaged in a heated debate over a horse race. Neither saw her as they raised their glasses in a toast. Catching sight of Deborah from the corner of her eye, Celine glided over to her charge and ushered her into the room.

Looking over his son's shoulder, Claude's eyebrows arched, but he said nothing as his wife began to speak. "Well, at last here's your wife, dressed as a pretty Creole belle should be."

Taking a deep draught of cognac, Rafael turned with a smile starting to curve his mobile lips. When he saw his wife, the smug grin froze and the fiery brandy caught in his throat. He nearly scorched his lungs as he choked and gasped, attempting to swallow the liquor and yell at Deborah simultaneously. "What the hell have you done with yourself?"

Poised regally as a queen, Deborah stood silently in the center of the room with all eyes fastened on her. She was swathed in fuchsia satin, yards and yards of it, layered into billowing ruffles, rows and rows of them, falling from her shoulders, her waistline, and her hips, flaring out to three more tiers. Her fuchsia slippers had large gold lace bows that matched the gathered gold lace trim edging every layer of the ruffled dress. Her hair was pulled back at each side by combs with large gold lace bows on them.

"You look like a Spanish galleon under full sail," he hissed when he finally regained his breath. "Change at once! I'll not be seen in public with you in that monstrosity!"

So intent was Rafael on his wife's hideous appearance that he had completely forgotten his mother. Celine's face darkened to the shade of Deborah's dress as she fanned herself with small, jerky sweeps of her lace kerchief. "Is it my fault, darling boy, that your overly tall, overly pale wife can't wear such a beautiful gown? Why, on Minnette Gautier it would look positively delicious."

Deborah said not a word, but looked soberly from one Flamenco to another. Old Claude's eyes betrayed a sort of grudging respect, although he was careful to conceal it. He sipped his cognac, saying nothing.

Rafael looked from his furious mother back to his wife's calm face. *You conniving silver-haired bitch. You arranged this,* he thought.

Then Celine's small plump fingers dug into his jacket sleeve. "Surely you don't fault my taste in fashion, do you, Rafael?" Her voice was tight as a bowstring.

Now, the faintest trace of a smile hovered on Deborah's lips. "Perhaps it is you who owe your mother an apology this time, dear." With that parting sally, she quit the room, five tiers of ruffles and lace swirling about her.

"With all the air that costume stirs up, we'll never need a ceiling fan again," Claude said dryly. When Celine stomped her foot in fury, he raised his glass in mock surrender and subsided.

Celine glared at her husband, then turned her attention back to Rafael. "Well, have you lost your glib tongue? When your sister wears pretty dresses you always compliment her. Why not your wife?"

"Look, Mama, I'm sorry I called it a monstrosity. I'm not blaming you or criticizing your taste. But Deborah is tall and has such different coloring that she must wear different clothes to bring out her beauty—not that the dress wasn't beautiful," he amended quickly. "As you said, it would have been perfect for Minnette Gautier."

"Then you should have married Minnette Gautier, not that gauche foreigner!" Dabbing at her eyes with the kerchief, Celine choked out, "I'll see if Lenore's ready—that is, once I've composed myself."

Claude refilled Rafael's glass, saying ironically, "I do believe, courtesy of your Yankee bride, we shall be more than fashionably late for the soiree."

Rafael's first impulse was to throttle his wife, but observing Claude's calm, cynical air, he decided his father's ability to ride out these teapot tempests was perhaps the best method of dealing with women. He took a good stiff gulp of the brandy.

Within twenty minutes Deborah returned dressed in an elegant gown of aqua watered silk. She looked radiant.

"Pleased with yourself, *cherie*?" he whispered softly in English as she glided over to him.

"I only hope this dress is acceptable, *cheri*," she replied innocently.

Ignoring their exchange in the distasteful foreign language, Claude said resignedly, "I shall go cajole your mother, Rafael. Why don't you escort your bride to the carriage?"

The ride to the Gautiers' was made in strained silence, but mercifully the Flamencos' old friends lived only a short distance away. Jacque Gautier was one of the city's leading bankers and his daughter Minnette was a leading belle. Lenore had already warned Deborah about the beauteous Minnette, who had enlisted Celine in her cause to become Rafael's wife.

As they stepped from the coach, Deborah could feel

Rafael's eyes on her. In spite of his anger, she knew he approved of her pale aqua gown, cut in straight lines and molded to her slender curves. She wore a cluster of fresh jasmine blossoms in her hair, which was knotted on top of her head in a sleek coil with a few tendrils whispering along her temples. Her only jewels were the aquamarine earrings and necklace that had been in her wedding basket.

When Rafael introduced his wife to Minnette Gautier, the spoiled beauty's petulant snappishness was apparent to everyone but Celine. Chattering and hugging Minnette to her, the older woman discussed the upcoming trip to their summer homes on the lake. Standing discreetly to the side, with her hand rather possessively on her husband's arm, Deborah watched Minnette. She was no more than seventeen, petite and black haired, with patrician features and large dark eyes that narrowed whenever she glanced in Deborah's direction. She was beautiful in the same classic Latin way Rafael was. Deborah could understand why Celine had chosen her. Minnette was Creole to her fingertips, coy and flirtatious, a daughter-in-law Celine could understand and control.

By the time Rafael had introduced his Yankee bride to the rest of the assembly, Deborah's fears of being a wallflower were put to rest. The women were mostly cool and standoffish, but the men were gallant to the point of effusion. Her statuesque silvery beauty stood out dramatically in the room full of chattering Creole belles with their darker coloring and gaudy fashions. She danced every dance.

Several of Rafael's cousins were outrageously flirtatious and teasing. They declared they were pleased that their cousin had brought such beauty to grace New Orleans, but distraught that she was already claimed. When Rafael's boyhood companion Jean attempted to dance her out the double doors onto the gallery, Rafael rescued her in the nick of time.

"You're the topic of every man's conversation," Rafael said, when they finally danced a waltz together.

She looked up at his scowling face, and a slow smile began to dimple her cheeks. "Why, Rafael Flamenco, I do believe you're jealous."

He loosened his fierce grip on her and relaxed his frown into a smirk. "Just remember who you belong to, my love."

"I do," she breathed softly against his neck, pulling him closer until she could feel a small ripple of tension and pleasure go through his body.

"Witch," he replied. Then, looking over her shoulder, he saw a cluster of people at the refreshment tables and stiffened in anger. "How the hell did *he* get an invitation?"

"Who?" Deborah's eyes followed her husband's gaze to where Lenore was chatting animatedly with a tall, well-dressed man with russet hair and rough-hewn, handsome features. His size and speech gave him away as an American in the room full of fine-boned, aquiline Creole men with their dandyish attire. Indeed, Rafael was the only man present who was as tall as the American.

"That is Caleb Armstrong, and I may well have to call him out," Rafael muttered in muted fury. He quickly escorted her to the side of the dance floor. But as he stalked toward Armstrong and Lenore, Deborah resolutely followed, catching his arm and whispering fiercely, "Don't be rude! At least find out who invited him and meet the man before you ruin your sister's evening." Maybe ruin her life, too, she thought.

Unable to rid himself of his tenacious wife, Rafael gritted his teeth and continued across the room. When they approached Lenore and Caleb, Jacque Gautier suddenly materialized from behind the big American.

"Rafael Flamenco, Madame Flamenco, may I present Caleb Armstrong, a business associate of mine," the old man said smoothly in his heavily accented English. Noting the agitated manner in which Rafael had strode toward the American, he continued, "I found Mademoiselle Flamenco already had been introduced to Monsieur Armstrong. My Minnette met him at the same time."

Without the slightest hint of a smile, Rafael offered his hand to Caleb who returned the gesture and bowed politely to Deborah. It was the least effusive greeting she'd had since arriving in this city of Latin excesses. She liked him instantly. The American was indeed handsome, with bright blue eyes and a square-jawed strength to his features.

His smile for Deborah was open and friendly. "I understand from Mademoiselle Flamenco that you're a fellow New Englander, madame?"

Deborah's smile broadened. "From Boston. I thought I detected a bit of 'down east' in your accent. Maine?"

"Portland," he replied. "Although I must confess to liking the tropical Gulf more than the chill Atlantic. After seven years in New Orleans, I'd hate to contemplate a winter in New England. This place will spoil you."

She, Caleb, and Lenore made small talk while Jacque Gautier drew Rafael into a discussion about a cockfight to be held on the morrow. Outside of a few scowling looks toward the trio, Rafael did nothing more overt to show his displeasure at the American's presence, although he did speak French when addressing his host.

"Why, Papa, there you are with Rafael . . . and his charming new bride," Minnette added as an afterthought in thickly accented English. "Perhaps Monsieur Armstrong might favor his host's daughter with a dance?" It was an obvious ploy to make Rafael jealous, but Jacque seemed pleased with his daughter's boldness and smiled when Caleb escorted her to the dance floor after making his excuses to Lenore and Deborah. Rafael ignored Minnette's wiles and asked to speak with Gautier in private.

On the way home, the carriage ride was again strained. After saying good night to the rest of the family, Rafael and Deborah retired to their quarters. She was fairly bursting to find out what had happened between old man Gautier and her husband. They were no more than in the door of their sitting room when she spoke.

"Tell me what you learned."

He arched one brow in that infuriatingly condescending manner she was coming to detest and said, "Learned about what, love?"

She almost stamped her foot. "I know you talked to Jacque Gautier about Caleb Armstrong. Obviously the gentleman has gained widespread acceptance in Creole social circles."

He scoffed. "He's hardly a gentleman. Gautier and du May are partners in a bank, which is in trouble. They've been 'sponsoring' Armstrong in the best circles in hopes of getting him to invest in their floundering enterprises. And, although he didn't say so, I'm sure Gautier hopes to snare a rich husband for his dear Minnette to cement the deal."

"Now that dear Minnette has lost her heart's choice to a usurping Yankee," she said archly.

"Now who's jealous?" he teased, his mood suddenly lightening as he scooped her up and strode purposefully to the bedroom.

Chapter 8

Deborah awoke with the lethargic satiety she had come to associate with Rafael's drugging passion. He had made love to her with fierce possessiveness last night and they had slept late. Feeling the warmth and weight next to her removed, she sat up and looked across the room. Rafael was donning a thin white cotton robe over that magnificent dark physique. She watched him ring for a houseboy. "Where are you going?"

Turning to see his sleepy-eyed wife, he smiled and walked over to the bed. "I have a date with Jacque and my cousin Jean to see a cockfight in an hour. But I'll be home after we meet at the café for an aperitif and luncheon." He kissed her nose. Even this small gesture, so naturally casual, seemed sensuous.

"We've been home for two weeks and you've not yet gone back to work. You've been to your tailor, horse races, cockfights, out shooting alligators on the river with your cousin Martin. Don't you have to see about the plantation or the shipping business or . . . or something?" Deborah couldn't imagine a wealthy gentleman in Boston circles who didn't have an office and work at least some regular hours.

Rafael smiled tolerantly as if reassuring an inquisitive child. "Of course I do not work. I need not bother with things like crops or ships. We hire an overseer like Kent Austin to run the sugar plantation. Our factor, James Rafferty, handles the shipping and brokerage. Oh, from time to time Papa or I must sit down with them to check their reports and make decisions, but the day-to-day running of commerce is left in their hands. A Creole gentleman doesn't grub after money. He enjoys it." He grinned broadly at her look of faint dismay, ignoring its implications.

"I see. You hire American overseers to 'grub after money' for you, and you have your slaves to do the work." As soon as she said it, it sounded mean-spirited and ungrateful, not to mention disloyal.

Rafael crossed his arms over that magnificent expanse of hairy chest and stood with legs braced apart, rigid in anger. "Mama's been telling me about your irritating penchant for manual labor, mucking about with the servants at the market and complaining that you have nothing to do but enjoy life. An unthinkable sin for a Puritan, I fancy."

"I'm used to working, Rafael. My whole family always had productive things to do. To help the less fortunate is part of that."

"Get one thing straight." He spoke as he strode back to the bed and took her chin roughly in his strong dark fingers. "You are the wife of a gentleman. You will behave as a proper lady and accept our way of life. If that means bearing up under the hardship of parties, balls, operas, and trips to the dressmaker, I have every confidence you can withstand the rigors. As to 'productive things' to do..." His gaze softened finally as he saw the tears she forced back. "We can work on starting that brood of Flamenco children right now. That should keep you quite occupied."

His hand stole down her neck, his fingers gentling as they slipped softly beneath her gauzy nightrail to tease and heft a breast. He kissed her opened lips, deepening the caress and probing with his tongue, tasting her cheeks, tracing over her teeth. As she responded, reaching up to grasp his shoulders, he eased her back on the bed and covered her slim body with his own. His loose cotton robe fell open and he shrugged it off, then reached for the hem of her nightrail, lifting the sheer fabric and caressing her sleek, long legs as he inched it higher and higher.

"You'll be late for the cockfight," she breathed, getting the words out between small pants of desire.

"Let them go on without me," he ground out as he ripped the gown over her head and threw it across the floor.

Warm naked flesh pressing warm naked flesh, they rolled to the center of the big bed, arms and legs entwined. Soon their sensuous caresses were slicked by their perspiration, which added to the exotic sensations rioting through their bodies. She reached up to brush a damp curling lock of black hair from his forehead, then buried her fingers in the crisp thick hair of his head, holding it to her as he licked and bit her throat. Her moist palms moved down his back until she reached the swell of his small, hard buttocks. She sank her fingers into them, attemping to imitate the rough caress he had used on her so often, but his muscles were like iron. She could not knead them, but she could dig in her nails, which elicited a gasp of pleasure from him.

"Greedy little Silver Hair," he gasped, raising up over her and reaching between her legs, now eagerly spread for him. He watched with satisfaction when her eyes closed and her head thrashed from side to side in ecstasy as he slid his skillful fingers into the wet hot core of her, stroking gently, persistently. When he withdrew his hand from the silver curls and prepared to enter her, Deborah's eyes opened, and she boldly grasped his hot hard shaft, guiding it to her, watching him as he drove into her full length. She grasped his shoulders, arching up to meet his thrusts.

"After that, I don't think I can wait long, love," he whispered frantically.

"You won't have to," she panted in return, feeling the onrush of those now familiar dizzying contractions that signaled her release. When she felt him stiffen and pulse his seed deeply inside her, she held him in a fierce embrace, her knees clamped tightly to his narrow hips, imprisoning him in her flesh.

Slowly recovering himself, Rafael was the first to move, gently disengaging her arms and rolling to lie on his back. She followed him, curling against his side like a snuggly kitten, not wanting to lose the feel of his body joining hers.

Thoughts rioting through his head, Rafael stared at the ceiling. Never, with any woman, had it been this good, but more than that—and that was what worried him—she controlled his mind, his very soul, not just his body. He could be murderously angry at her one minute, then pull her to him in tender passion the next. Once settled into his routine here in New Orleans, he had hoped to quickly put his obsession for his wife into perspective. She should have taken her place as a proper Creole lady: shopping, attending teas and balls, socializing with his mother's and sister's friends. But he knew now that Deborah would never be a dutiful Creole wife.

What had begun as a surprisingly wonderful discovery of shared passion was rapidly turning into a threat for Rafael. No woman should ever have so large a place in a man's life. Certainly his mother did not have such a hold over his father. Creole women were cosseted and loved, but shelved when it suited the men's convenience.

Still, he and Deborah had only been married a little over a month. Time would solve the problem. Time and, in due course, motherhood.

Suddenly, his thoughts turned to Lily. Perhaps a visit to Rampart Street might be a good idea, too. When Deborah stirred and spoke, he was angry at his sudden rush of guilt. "What?" he queried more sharply than he intended.

Deborah's hand stilled on his chest and she repeated softly, "I only asked what you were thinking. You seemed a million miles away."

He chuckled darkly. "All too close to home, *cherie*," he said, switching to English, "all too close to you."

Saturday evening, Rafael announced at the dinner table that he was joining his father for a turn at the gaming tables. Deborah had already heard stories about the fabled twenty-four-hour, seven-day-a-week casinos so infamous in the Sin City of New Orleans. Every kind of card game was offered: *ecarte*, vingt-et-un, poker, faro, and roulette. Often, as much as twenty-five thousand dollars passed from one gentleman's hands to another's in a night. She had also heard about the other amusements offered above stairs in such establishments, but when her mother-in-law took the announcement with such disinterested calm, she could see no reason to protest. Surely if the men had planned anything more than playing cards, they would not be so casually open about going to "Toto" Davis's famous establishment.

When she asked Rafael what time he would be home, Claude gave her a disdainful look. Celine appeared in shock at her audacity. Her husband merely shrugged and told her not to expect the Flaménco men to accompany their women to mass the following morning. After they left, Deborah threw her napkin down on the table and rose to leave the room.

Celine's voice stopped her with its frosty venom. "Rafael will not long humor your incredible presumptuousness. You'd best learn to guard your tongue and not question when you should not like the answers."

Glaring unrepentently at Celine, Deborah let her seething anger burst forth. "All I did was make a reasonable inquiry. Rafael has gone out the past three evenings for gentlemen's amusements, leaving me alone. I'm used to a bit more consideration."

"I've invited you to join me for dominoes at the du Mayses' and to see the La Rues' newly redecorated home, but you have declined. You don't want to fit in. You certainly cannot expect your husband to dance attendance on you full time. We don't do things that way here." Celine's voice was flat with contempt.

"You don't do most things here the way I'm accustomed to," Deborah shot back.

"But you married into a Creole family and it's a wife's duty to adapt, isn't it, my dear," Celine said with oversweet reasonableness, now gloating over this first obvious rift between her son and his hateful wife.

"So it's been explained to me before," Deborah said with a sigh, turning to leave the room.

Rafael came home around four A.M. He smelled faintly of cigar smoke and Madeira but had not been drinking much.

It was a strict rule of Creole propriety never to be drunk in public. He had carefully undressed and then collapsed across the bed after cheerfully announcing that he had won twenty-two thousand dollars. "But what if you had *lost* that much!" She was aghast at his profligacy.

"I frequently have," he calmly announced. "We can easily afford it, Deborah. Now go to sleep. I'm exhausted." He was asleep within seconds, leaving her fuming and wide awake.

When she arose the next morning she was angry at Rafael's refusal to accompany her to mass. He rolled over, urged her to join his mother and sister, then fell immediately back to sleep.

Deborah dressed and headed toward the family dining room. As she passed Celine's sitting room, she heard a sharp smack and a muffled sob. Tonette ran from the room with tears glistening in her big brown eyes. From what Deborah had overheard, it was apparent she had not pressed Celine's dress to her mistress's satisfaction.

"Creole Christian charity," Deborah muttered to herself and went to comfort the girl who had fled to the kitchen. Although uneasy over the idea of commanding and owning slaves, Deborah had gradually formed a good relationship with most of the family's "people," as they were called. Antoine the butler and Wilma the cook were warm and gracious, but it was the young girl Tonette, Lenore's companion and personal maid, to whom Deborah was closest.

Once Tonette had overcome her natural suspicion of the "Yankee foreigner," the girl had become a source of gossip and information. On several occasions, Deborah had witnessed Celine's cruelty to the younger servants, although the clever woman never attempted to interfere with Antoine or Wilma. A seventeen-year-old girl, however, was a different matter.

Deborah sat at the kitchen table with Tonette, whose pale tan shoulders shook. She was so pretty, Deborah thought, with her light coffee-and-cream complexion, golden brown eyes, and tall, elegant figure.

"Don't cry, Tonette." She patted the girl's back and looked helplessly over at Wilma, whose ample girth blocked out half the enormous fireplace where she was stirring a pot of gumbo.

Wilma was from Virginia, a skilled cook and housekeeper, purchased twenty years ago. "Doan nevah mind Miz Celine, chile. She fly off one minute, be givin' you sweet treats th' next. She be chang'ble as wind in a hurricane."

The Frenchwoman was incredibly volatile. In Boston she'd never keep servants with her bizarre outbursts and effusive turnabouts. Of course, when someone owns you, you can't quit no matter how frightening or insufferable the mistress, Deborah thought bitterly.

Swallowing her outrage over Celine's behavior, Deborah accompanied her mother-in-law and Lenore to mass. She still felt like an intruder in the beautiful old St. Louis Cathedral. Rafael had attended church with her only once. When she asked Lenore why there were so few men at mass, her sister-in-law answered her whispered inquiry with puzzlement. Most men made their Easter duty and went on Christmas Eve, but otherwise, with the exception of special occasions such as marriages and christenings, they seldom set foot in church. Having grown up in staid, straightlaced Boston, where most folks were at least outwardly conformant, such cavalier religious sentiments shocked her. Adam Manchester was a stout Episcopalian who had attended church with his daughter every Sunday. Now, she needed the comfort of her husband's presence. Kneeling beside Celine Flamenco gave her distinctly un-Christian feelings.

After mass, Celine went off to visit with some of her friends, leaving Lenore and Deborah alone in the sitting room. Attempting to ease her sister-in-law's despondency over Celine's behavior, Lenore said, "Tonette will soon forget Mama's anger. Don't worry, Deborah. This afternoon is free time and the Congos will be dancing in the square."

"Congos?" Deborah's face was puzzled.

Lenore laughed. "I keep forgetting you're a newcomer to New Orleans. 'Congo' just means African. Everyone calls the open field above Rampart Street Congo Square. Most Creoles give their slaves Sunday afternoon off to dance until sundown. It's the real Africans, those who remember the old tribal dances, who put on the best show.'' She gave a delicate shudder and said quickly, "Or so I've heard.''

Deborah was intrigued. She had heard the soulful, poignant music of the "coloreds," both the slaves and those existing in the twilight world of "Free People of Color." There was such haunting beauty and primitive power in it that she had been fascinated. Her first week in New Orleans, she'd heard a black slave poling a ferry and singing a mournful dirge that had echoed in her dreams ever since:

> De night is dark, de day is long
> An we are far from home
> Weep, my brodders, weep.

Lenore watched Deborah's reverie, once more puzzled. Like her brother, she had grown up surrounded by the black subculture and thought little about it, negatively or positively. It simply existed. "What are you thinking about now?" Lenore waited a beat, half-afraid of the answer.

"How would you like to take a little excursion this afternoon, Lenore?" Deborah could see a mixture of incredulity, fear, and curiosity written on her sister-in-law's face.

When the big, open park unfolded before Deborah and Lenore, they could see hundreds of people massed in groups of varying sizes, dancing beneath enormous spreading sycamore trees. The Congos or pure Africans were kinky haired and very dark. A liberal mixture of brown, tan, and golden skin was visible as well, more of the latter among the spectators than the dancers, however. Also ringing the leaping, swaying, undulating men and women were numerous whites—Creoles and Americans, rich and poor. Some were fascinated, others repelled. The spectators were almost as numerous as the participants.

Deborah quickly alighted from the carriage under the impassive stare of their black driver, Guy. Lenore was a bit more reticent but doggedly followed Deborah as she wended her way through the crowd.

There was a great deal of variety in the dancing. Some groups moved slowly in highly stylized, repetitive steps. Others were wild and raucous, but all were graceful. The music was created by primitive instruments, drums of all sizes and shapes, reed pipes and flutes, and oddly shaped stringed instruments. The sounds were a bizarre blend of eerie loveliness and cacophonous racket.

Deborah's eye was caught by a man and woman off to one side who were engaged in a most sensual, erotic ballet that shockingly imitated the motions of lovemaking. She blushed furiously at the undulating gyrations, wondering if Lenore knew what they symbolized. Judging from her sister-in-law's flushed face and averted eyes, she did.

Deborah was standing entranced by the performance, when the noise of arguing voices brought her from her reverie. Lenore's hissed whisper was unintelligible, but the cold, clipped male voice that replied was distinct. "You are disgracing me and the whole family. You will come home this instant. I'll have that boy whipped for bringing you to this place."

The speaker was a striking-looking man of medium height, fine-boned and dark. When he turned to Deborah, she was amazed by his resemblance to Rafael. The same haughty, classically perfect Latin features, but more delicately drawn, colder, almost effete. His beautiful face and elegant body seemed to her the end result of too much inbreeding. Observing his proprietary grip on Lenore's arm, she knew at once that he was Georges Beaurivage.

"Georges, please. I came with Deborah." Lenore reached for her sister-in-law's hand, needing reassurance. She shook, whether from fear or from anger, Deborah could not tell.

The look Georges turned on her would have frozen wood alcohol. With a stiff bow his glacial black eyes raked over her insolently. "Ah yes, your brother's *northern* wife," he said in English. His inflection on the word "northern" might well have equated it with "ax murderess" if not merely streetwalker, Deborah decided grimly. If Lenore had ever needed an ally to oppose this marriage, she had one now.

"Good afternoon, Monsieur Beaurivage," she said in English. "I have heard so much about you from the family." She was rewarded for her deceit when he began to speak rapidly to Lenore in French.

"Aunt Celine has told me about this disastrous marriage. Poor Rafael must have been insane. Small wonder Uncle Claude is so upset. You are not to associate with this hoyden again and certainly never to be seen in such a place as this, ever!" Then, switching to heavily accented English, he reached for both women's arms, saying, "Ladies, allow me to escort you home."

"I would be desolate to put you to so much trouble, cousin, especially considering how your reputation might suffer, being seen with such a hoyden." Deborah's French was flawless and her smile withering. Georges Beaurivage paled and dropped his hand from her elbow.

Deborah seized Lenore's arm and began to stalk off when another voice interrupted. "I didn't believe Wilma when she told me!" Rafael's face was as stormy as a hurricane. Looking from his wife to Lenore and her fiancé, he said incredulously, "Surely, you didn't suggest this charming excursion, Cousin Georges?"

At once the shorter man drew himself up to his full five feet nine inches. Indignantly, he replied, "Never think it! I was on my way to—to meet a friend, when I saw Guy and the Flamenco carriage over on Rampart. I stopped at once to question him. When I learned my fiancée was witnessing this disgustingly barbaric spectacle, I came to escort her safely home."

"It was my idea to see the dancing, Rafael," Deborah said with a steady, cutting glare in Georges's direction. "But I don't consider it disgusting or barbaric. Actually, it's quite fascinating. I want to learn all I can of New Orleans culture and—"

"This could hardly be called culture, dear cousin," Georges interrupted with a patronizing air, now sure it was Deborah and not he who would bear the brunt of Rafael's famous temper.

Deborah opened her mouth to respond, but Rafael cut her short, holding her arm in a painful grip as he addressed Georges. "Please do me the great courtesy of seeing Lenore home, cousin. I have some matters to explain to my wife."

With a martyred look, Lenore followed an overly solicitous Georges Beaurivage to where his carriage was waiting at the edge of the crowd.

Rafael felt Deborah trying to strain free of his painful grip and said softly, "If you make a scene in front of this riffraff, it won't be any more of a disgrace than you've already created for me to pick you up bodily and carry you away kicking and screaming."

One look at his slitted eyes convinced her that he meant it. Unlike the effete, petty possessiveness of Georges, Rafael's manner was almost savage in intensity. She walked with him in silence to where he had the closed carriage waiting.

"I've tried to be patient, Deborah. I know this is a life different from yours in Boston, but you refuse to be guided by Mama or me or anyone else. Now you've even involved Lenore in one of your escapades. She's an unmarried girl, for God's sake! An innocent. Her reputation would be ruined if any of Mama's friends saw her in such a place."

"How could they see her unless they were here watching the dancing themselves?" she snapped with infuriating logic.

"Servants' gossip! The slaves' grapevine is almost supernatural in its effectiveness. Honestly, Deborah, there's so much you don't understand. A proper Creole wife would—"

She whirled on him in murderous fury. "If I hear that expression one more time I think I'll vomit! 'A proper Creole wife' is a mindless, simpering ninny who never does anything without consulting her male relatives! You knew I wasn't like that before you married me and I'll never change."

"As a man of honor, I had little enough choice in the matter of marrying you, madame," he said coldly.

Her first impulse was to slap his face, that beautiful aristocratic face she loved so, but tears suddenly blurred her vision. She turned and stepped into the carriage before he could assist her.

Rafael saw her stiffen in pain at his cruel remark. Why did she always make him so blindly furious that he said things he did not mean? He climbed inside after her, expecting to be subjected to a sea of weeping. Once more he had underestimated her. Unlike his mother and sister, unlike most all "proper Creole women," Deborah did not weep. She sat rigidly still, forcing back the tears and staring out the opposite window, chin held proudly high.

She was different and impossible, and he had never desired her as much as he did at that moment. However, he fought the surge of irrational emotion with pride and anger of his own. No woman would rule his life and humiliate him in front of his friends.

The short carriage ride to Royal Street seemed an eternity as the silence thickened.

Chapter 9

Dinner Sunday evening was subdued. Lenore had been thoroughly chastised by her parents for accompanying Deborah that afternoon. Georges Beaurivage had made certain Claude and Celine heard about how he had snatched his fiancée from the jaws of social disgrace. As for Rafael and Deborah, their silence at the table told all wordlessly.

After dinner father and son shared cigars and Madeira in the study. Observing Rafael's bleak countenance, Claude took a long pull on his cigar and exhaled, then spoke in measured tones. "I think, my dear boy, the honeymoon is over. You've made a bad bargain, but, alas, one you must live with. If you get her breeding, she will at least have something to occupy herself with besides creating scandals." He paused and looked levelly at his son.

"No, she's not pregnant," Rafael replied with an aggravated sigh. "But I'm certain she soon will be."

The older man gave a characteristically Gallic snort of derision. "So was I assured with your mother. A lot of good it did me. One miscarriage after the other. In thirty years of marriage, it's a miracle I have one son."

Rafael ground out his cigar and replied angrily, "I realize

that now it's up to me to carry on the Flamenco name, at least on this side of the color line.''

''Speaking of our other families, have you visited Lily since your return?'' Claude interjected smoothly. ''It might prove quite therapeutic for you to do so.''

Rafael's face did not lose its scowl, but he did shrug with ironic resignation. ''No, I have been putting off that diversion in favor of doing my duty, Papa. I've slept with my wife every night.''

Once more Claude barked a snort of derisive laughter, then fixed his son with keen black eyes. ''I think if you stop trying so hard and 'divert' yourself instead, it might just mend the situation all the way around.''

''Perhaps you're right,'' Rafael replied quietly, ''perhaps you're right . . .''

Deborah spent a miserable evening, waiting for Rafael to come to their quarters, wanting to mend the ugly rift between them. She had been grievously hurt when he had said he was forced into the marriage, but they were married and she loved him desperately. For the first time, she considered the possibility that he might not really love her at all, but it was simply too much for her to bear. Temper and Creole pride had led him to say those hurtful things to her this afternoon. He did not—*could* not have meant that he regretted their marriage.

She laid out a beautiful gray silk peignoir with black lace trim and took a long, scented bath. However, after several hours of restless waiting in her seductive finery, it became apparent that her husband had gone out for the evening. But where? To Davis's casino again? Perhaps it was another father and son debauch. She decided to search out Lenore and see what she knew.

''Didn't Rafael say anything to you before he left?'' Lenore asked. Her blue eyes were veiled, as she attempted to hide her discomfort. At Deborah's negative reply, Lenore added, ''Well, Papa's still here, but that doesn't mean my brother couldn't have gone to a card room or to play billiards by himself. He often does—or down to the river to shoot with some of his friends.''

Deborah gave a disbelieving look. "In the dark? It's past ten, Lenore. No, he's probably at that accursed casino."

"Yes, I'm sure that's it," Lenore agreed a bit too readily.

Deborah looked at her sister-in-law and had the uneasy feeling that she knew something more than she was telling. Had he gone to a bordello? Surely a gently reared girl like Lenore wouldn't know about such a thing, but then in this alien culture, who knew what went on! Celine certainly seemed willing to ignore a great deal where Claude was concerned. Deborah, however, was prepared to ignore nothing.

Lily watched the carriage pull up and recognized the tall figure who descended. He had sent her a note hours ago and she had been eagerly awaiting him. *Thank heaven he has finally come to me.* Lily had heard through the servants' grapevine that Rafael had a wife, a silver blond Yankee with an icy Boston demeanor. She had been instantly thrown into a panic for he had always said he was in no hurry to marry. Indeed, since the age of nineteen, he had put off his mother's matchmaking with dismissive good humor.

Now, unexpectedly, he was wed. Too proud to go and look for herself, Lily nevertheless listened when the servants gossiped about the young Madame Flamenco's exotic coloring. They assured her that Deborah was skinny and plain, but she feared the worst. Rafael must have been besotted to defy his family for her. Sometimes, after he married, a Creole man gave up his mistress and pensioned her off to satisfy the demands of his wife, especially if it was a love match.

For days Lily waited fearfully for a dismissal. Then when none came and her regular allowance did, she waited joyously for her lover to return to their house on Rampart Street. After a few weeks, anticipation and disappointment turned her mercurial temperament waspish. Then, early that evening a message had finally arrived. Lily checked her appearance in the mirror again. Sleek pompadour faultlessly coiffed, huge dark gold eyes fringed with thick black lashes, small, exquisite features set serenely. She ran a hand down the rose satin peignoir, pleased at her still-tiny waist after two birthings.

The small, elegantly furnished living room was prepared for him with his favorite cigars and a fine white bordeaux laid out, along with a late night supper of iced shellfish, cold roast squab, and crusty bread with assorted cheeses. The covers had been turned down on the big bed in the next room where a scented candle flickered enticingly.

"Cheri," she whispered, as he opened the door and stepped inside. Standing on tiptoe she pulled him down into a languorous, slow kiss.

I'd forgotten how tiny she is, he thought to himself as he bent down to embrace her. "You still smell of jasmine," he said, nibbling her ear.

"Have you missed me, darling?" She took his hands and drew him into the living room. "Sit and I'll pour you some wine."

As he reclined on the large overstuffed sofa cushions, she placed his feet on a velvet ottoman and pulled his shoes off, then lit his cigar. He let his eyes trail over the rich interior of Lily's small house, noting that she had purchased a new silver tea service, gleaming dully on the mahogany table in the corner. The rich maroon and deep blues of the Turkey carpet and velvet upholstered furniture created an atmosphere of darkness and languor. There was too much furniture and bric-a-brac, but then Lily had always been a collector. He smiled in tolerant amusement as she fussed over him. "I have something for you," he said, pulling a case from his jacket pocket.

She let out a small squeal of delight and opened the case. The gleaming ivory took her breath away. It was a necklace, heavy and intricate, made of a series of whale's teeth, each etched beautifully. Besides the necklace there were several exquisite combs with the same delicate ivory carving on them and a pair of long whale's tooth earrings that matched the other pieces.

"Oh, Rafael, it's magnificent, like nothing I've ever seen," she breathed, reaching over to kiss him.

"The New England whalers call it scrimshaw." He watched her preen before the mirror, trying the earrings and necklace on, fitting the combs into her midnight tresses. When she finished her delighted inspection, she placed the heavy jewelry back into its case and came over to kiss him like a child who had won a long absent parent's attention.

She was afraid I'd leave her when she heard about Deborah, he thought suddenly. Until now, he'd never bothered to consider her reaction to his marriage. He'd sent her allowance as usual, but the thought had never entered his mind to send her word explaining his plans. In fact, he had never planned ahead at all. He had always assumed that marriage would not impinge on keeping a mistress. With a Creole wife there would have been no question of it. He thought fleetingly of Deborah's reaction and dismissed the idea from his mind. She and Lily scarcely ran in the same social circles! Rafael stubbed out his cigar and emptied his wineglass. "Come here."

She obeyed with alacrity, like an obedient puppy, but her soft, skillful body reminded him more of a sinuous little cat. She slithered up alongside him and began to run her small pink tongue and lips across his jawline, then down his neck, while her busy fingers unfastened his shirt studs and pulled the front open. Then her hands and mouth caressed his chest. As she kissed and nipped, she slipped off his jacket and shirt. Slowly, savoringly, she leaned back and began to unfasten her robe, letting the hissing satin slip down around her hips. He reached over and slid the thin straps of her gown from her shoulders. She helped him, twisting free of its confines until her large, rounded breasts spilled out so he could grasp them in his hands.

He teased and kneaded her ripe flesh until she moaned as her brown nipples hardened. At his smile of satisfaction, she moved her hands to the waistband of his trousers, releasing the belt and then unbuttoning his fly. "Now, lie back, Rafael," she whispered, pushing him to a reclining position on the sofa. Her small fingers eased his swollen shaft from the imprisonment of the tight pants. She felt his body stiffen and heard his soft gasp of pleasure as she took the hardened member in her hot little mouth. He forced the tension from his body and relaxed, letting her pleasure him, clearing his mind of all thought, all women but this one. His release was sudden and swift under her practiced ministrations, but the night was young and they had time for much, much more in the big soft bed in the next room.

Lily lifted herself triumphantly, like a small, regal cat, preening before her master. "Your pale Yankee wife could never please you like that!"

His face, which had been softened in satiation, turned instantly harsh and shuttered. "I am not in the habit of discussing my wife with my mistress, Lily," he said coldly.

Eyes downcast and mouth midway between trembling and pouting, she stood up and slipped the peignoir back on, then went to have the houseboy bring water for him.

While he cleansed himself quickly in the basin of warm water, Lily brought him a black silk robe from the armoire and helped him into the comfortable garment. As she reached around his narrow waist for the belt, he ran his fingers through her hair. It was straight and thick, blue-black and glossy. He often looked at her slightly slanted eyes and high cheekbones wondering if some Cherokee princess were not one of her ancestors. There was a faint golden glow to her skin, but with seven-eighths of her blood being white, her complexion was, in fact, paler than his own.

They shared some wine and ate the light repast as he answered her questions about Boston and his journey on the *Blue Lightning*, omitting, of course, any mention of Deborah. Finally, he said, "Enough of my trip. Now tell me about Melanie." His black eyes scanned her face for some signs of maternal affection. "Does she do well with her school-work?"

Lily waved the question aside carelessly, saying, "Of course, she is quite bright. What would you expect? She *is* your daughter."

"Why don't you let her stay here, Lily? I could hire a tutor and have a chance to see her more often."

Lily's face froze and she seized Rafael's hands, beseeching him. "No, she is far happier in St. Louis with my mother. She has the finest tutors." Her huge gold eyes filled with tears and her tiny hands tightened over his larger ones.

"I—I cannot have her here since my Francois died. I cannot, Rafael! I wanted to give you sons, not daughters."

"We could have another son, Lily," he said patiently.

She shook her head frantically. "No! No, I could not bear it, to have another little boy and hold him while he dies of the accursed fever, no! No more children, Rafael, please. I will do anything for you—anything to please you. I love you, but do not ask for more children!"

He took her in his arms and stroked her much like a father calming a child. She was the same age as he, but since their son had died two years ago in a yellow fever epidemic, Lily had changed. She had never been happy that her first child was a female. When Francois was born, she was overjoyed. Melanie was a precious, beautiful little girl, but for the most part it had been Lily's maid Morine who had cared for her.

After Melanie's brother had died and she had survived the decimating epidemic of 1833, Lily couldn't bear to look at Melanie. She had insisted on sending her to live in St. Louis where the child's grandmother and aunt had moved. Unwilling to keep Melanie in a household where she was not loved, and unable to find any other place for her, Rafael had finally agreed. She was almost six now, a proper young lady with bright golden eyes and jet black hair, her Spanish, French, and African heritage beautifully blended together. He had her Aunt Therese bring her downriver for visits several times a year, but other than that he did not see her, only paid for her support and education.

"Don't cry, Lily," he sighed. "I won't tell you to stop taking your potions."

At once, she brightened and stopped her heartrending sobbing. "Thank you, beloved. I am so grateful you understand."

"I don't keep you here to provide me with offspring, but with divertissement, little cat," he replied with a lopsided smile. *Anyway, soon I'll have legitimate heirs with Deborah.* The thought came unbidden, but he did not want to consider it. Angry at himself as well as at his neurotic mistress, he reached over and scooped her off the sofa in one rough, abrupt movement. He carried her into the bedroom and tossed her onto the bed.

He quickly stripped away his robe, then knelt on the edge of the mattress. Lily pulled him down and wrapped her small voluptuous body around his. They caressed with languorous practice, knowing one another's most sensitive secret places. Finally he rolled her on top of him and impaled her wet eager flesh on his phallus. When she could feel him beginning to swell and explode, she arched her back and made one last gyrating descent, collapsing on his chest, feeling her own deep radiating waves of climax joining his. They panted in the warm dark night for several minutes, then fell asleep, still locked together. It was always good with Lily.

When he first came to her she had been but a sixteen-year-old virgin, he a sixteen-year-old boy. However, despite his lusty romps with a variety of experienced lower-class girls, he had been the innocent. Lily had been explicitly instructed from childhood in all the ways of pleasing a man. She could excite and tantalize like the most experienced courtesan. She had been taught by her own mother and aunt, both *placées* themselves in their youths. For a beautiful woman of color, it was by far the most practical way to assure her future.

Rafael had been Lily's first lover. Together they quickly learned how to give one another exquisite pleasure. Six years later, Rafael still enjoyed the relationship. It had never occurred to him to end it when he married. Now, threatened by his feelings for Deborah, he was more determined than ever to keep Lily as a counterbalance against the disturbing influence of his wife.

Early the next morning Lily rose and instructed the kitchen maid about breakfast, then bathed, made her toilette, and had a hot bath brought for Rafael. By the time he was finished, she carried a breakfast tray in and they ate together in bed.

"I really must get home, Lily. It's nearly noon," he said, wiping his mouth and tossing a snowy linen napkin onto the tray.

"Morine is going to the market for some fresh crayfish,

Rafael. Perhaps while there she'll see Wilma with your wife." She casually picked up a delicate china cup and took a sip of the thick café noir, waiting to gauge his reaction.

"Deborah shops with the servants on occasion. It occupies her time," he replied casually as he slipped on his freshly pressed jacket.

"It seems odd for a lady to muck through the public markets with black slaves, but then I suppose Yankees are different from Creole women." She could see he was growing angry. Unable to stop herself, Lily catapulted into his arms. "Oh, Rafael, she'll never please you! She could never do what I did last night." Her busy little hands insinuated themselves inside his jacket as she pressed her lower body closely to his.

He reached down and unwound her arms, pushing her away as he held her wrists. "I told you last night, I don't discuss one of my women with the other, *ever*! You have your place in my life, Lily. Be satisfied with that." His black eyes were hard as obsidian.

Lowering her head, she murmured, *"Oui, cheri,"* but her thick lashes veiled the wounded fury in her eyes.

Feeling strangely disturbed, Deborah awoke. The bedroom was cold and lonely despite the warmth of May. Deborah had become used to lying by Rafael's side and feeling the beat of his heart when he held her in sleep. With a sick sense of dread she arose and rang for Tonette. Knowing what she knew about all the diversions of Creole men, it was just as likely he had spent the night betting on a cockfight or playing cards as sleeping with another woman. The thought of her husband lying in some whore's cheap, soiled bed made her ill. Forcing the sickening thought aside, she resolved to face the day.

She knew Wilma was going to the public market that morning to buy fresh shellfish and produce. Deborah loved the noise and international flavor of the city's shopping center. Indeed, when Wilma found the new mistress could speak halting German and even some Spanish, the old cook was delighted. Deborah could bargain with those merchants far more effectively than could she, whose French was barely intelligible and who could speak not a word of any other language but English.

Wending her way through the crowds in the fierce noon-day heat, Deborah watched the kaleidoscope of the market. Free Women of Color with huge baskets balanced on their turbaned heads walked regally past, selling rice cakes. A swarthy Spaniard hawked salt fish. As she wiped a trickle of perspiration from her temple, Deborah wondered why Celine had looked so pleased when her errant daughter-in-law departed that morning. Usually Madame made deprecating remarks when Deborah accompanied Wilma. But today Celine had been uncharacteristically gracious, asking Deborah to select the oysters for tonight's dinner. Willing to make any reasonable attempt to placate her in-laws, Deborah had agreed, although after she had dug through the seaweed-coated, odoriferous oyster barrels, she felt as smelly and slimy as the unwashed shellfish. Oh to get home and sink into a tub of fresh cool water!

Wilma was barking her usual fierce orders to Guy about taking care in loading the fresh fruit and vegetables onto the wagon when Deborah approached them. Just then she caught sight of a carriage turning onto Dumaine Street. Inside sat Caleb Armstrong and Lenore! It was a closed carriage and Deborah recognized her sister-in-law only because of the hat and heavy veil she'd seen her wearing when she had left the house that morning. Small wonder she wished to disguise herself! She was trysting with the Yankee banker! She felt a surge of increasing anger at the injustice of it all. Claude and Rafael were able to come and go, do anything immoral or scandalous with no one thinking less of them, while a good young woman like Lenore, who only wanted to have a normal courtship with a fine young man, would be castigat-ed and condemned.

Damn Rafael, where was he? She vowed to confront him when he returned and also to try to counsel her sister-in-law. It was too dangerous to be seen so openly with her Yankee. If *she* recognized Lenore, so might other less sympathetic people. Perspiring and fuming, she climbed aboard the wagon with Wilma and sat back. She tried to fan herself with her skirts. Would she ever get used to the heat and humidity of New Orleans? It was only May!

When they returned home, Deborah helped Wilma unload and arrange the foodstuffs in the kitchen, then trudged across the courtyard, intent on reaching her quarters where Tonette could draw her a bath. Over the musical tinkle of the central courtyard fountain, she heard the murmur of female voices. Not wanting to be seen, she decided to slip quietly up the back stairs. However, she had not reckoned on her mother-in-law's watchful eyes.

"Oh, Deborah, there you are, just in time for luncheon." Celine's greeting was oversweet and bubbling. "Do come down and join me."

Observing her daughter-in-law's perspiration-drenched clothes and stringy, half-fallen knot of damp hair, she smiled archly. Yes, she even smelled of oyster barrels. Perfect! She walked quickly to the stairs and took Deborah's hand, drawing her around the shield of the fountain and shrubbery to where Minnette Gautier sat in dainty cool perfection beneath the canopy of an ornamental fig tree. Next to her sat her mother, her aunt, and several other of Celine's friends, all dressed and coiffed immaculately. Minnette's eyes widened in delight as she compared her crisp yellow gown to Deborah's limp, seaweed soaked rag. *Why, she looks a positive fright!*

"Oh, my, you seem to have been caught in the sun without a parasol," she cooed viciously. Her aunt simply gaped and several of the other women whispered behind their fans.

Deborah was rooted to the ground in horror, stunned at her mother-in-law's cunning. *I'll grind up those oysters, shells and all, and put them in her facial cream,* she thought vengefully. Composing herself, she ignored the simpering Minnette and tittering matrons. Instead she concentrated on the formidable Celine.

"You planned this flawlessly, Mother Celine," she said evenly. "I must compliment you. Too bad Rafael isn't here to witness my public humiliation, but I'm certain Miss Gautier will have described my discomfort to half of New

Orleans by nightfall—right down to the stench of seaweed,''
she added, noting the way Minnette's dainty nose wrinkled.
The little Creole swished her skirt carefully away from
Deborah's and gasped in outrage at the insult.

"Minnette doesn't need to tell me, Deborah. I'm here to
see for myself." Rafael's tone was as deadly as his murderous facial expression. He strode swiftly across the courtyard
from the stairs he had just descended. His eyes swept
disgustedly from her stringy hair down to her filthy sweat-
soaked skirts, then back up to her face, glistening with
perspiration and smudged with dirt. Glaring at her he said,
"If you ladies will excuse us, my wife and I have things to
discuss upstairs."

Too shocked to protest more, Deborah watched him bow
and kiss Minnette's fingers, nod tersely to Celine and the rest
of the entourage, and then take her elbow in a bone-crushing
grip, ushering her toward the stairs to their quarters. He
did not speak until they were in their apartment. "If you
ever again appear before my mother's friends in this condition, I swear I'll take you to the plantation upriver and lock
you away for a year!"

"I didn't appear before them—I was entrapped. She
asked me to select oysters at the market and then sent off
those invitations deliberately—even dragged me into the
courtyard to confront her guests!" What had begun in anger
ended in sorrow. She was just too humiliated to be angry.
"Your mother despises me, Rafael." Her eyes made an
unspoken plea for his support.

"Small wonder if she didn't! You've done nothing but
give her embarrassment and aggravation. If you stayed
home and dressed as a lady instead of traipsing around with
the servants, this whole thing would never have happened,"
he finished coldly. Damn, he was mightily fed up with
women—Lily, Celine, and Deborah!

"I suppose if I were picture-perfect like Minnette you'd
be pleased with me?" She hadn't meant it to sound so
jealous.

He threw up his hands in a Gallic gesture of disgust, then
paced furiously over to the cabinet where crystal glasses and
cool water were kept. "Devil take that prissy little flirt.

Mother favored her, I certainly never did. Forget Minnette Gautier and think of me. You're my wife and you have certain duties and obligations to me. You—"

"Yes, and what about your duties and obligations to me, *husband*?" she interrupted him acidly, stung beyond words that he would always side with his parents against her. "You were gone all night without even the courtesy of a note to explain where you'd be. Since you always place the worst construction on my actions, maybe I should do the same with yours." She held her breath, horrified at what anger had goaded her into blurting out, but even more afraid of what he might confess.

He poured a glass of water and took a drink, his back to her. Then he turned and smiled, but the warmth of his lips never reached the chilly depths of his eyes. "Perhaps if I had a sweet-smelling, beautifully dressed wife to come home to, I might be more tempted."

Deborah fought down the urge to start ripping books from the shelves behind her and hurling them at the scoundrel. She had bathed and dressed in lace and silk for him, waiting all night in their bed alone, but she would never give him the satisfaction of knowing that now. Wordlessly, she turned and walked toward the bedroom.

Chapter 10

For the next three days the Flamenco household was in chaos as the servants packed and prepared for the annual move to the lake house. Deborah was so busy with preparations that she fell into bed each night too exhausted to cry. Her estrangement from her husband continued.

He and Deborah spoke only when necessary and her sense of isolation within the family increased. Celine snubbed her, Claude disdained her, and Rafael ignored her. Only Lenore was sympathetic.

However, Lenore had her own difficulties, as Deborah was well aware. Celine hounded her daughter incessantly about an official betrothal announcement and marriage plans with Georges Beaurivage. So far, her father was disposed to heed her tearful pleas to wait, but Deborah knew he and Rafael would force the issue sooner or later. If they discovered her trysts with Caleb Armstrong, it would be sooner. Deborah resolved to broach the subject and find out just what was going on between her sister-in-law and the charming Yankee.

An opportunity to talk in private with Lenore did not present itself for several days, but when she saw Lenore return from one of her outings, supposedly to the shoemaker, Deborah decided to act. Celine was in the dining room supervising the packing and the men had gone for a meeting with their factor. Intercepting Lenore on the gallery, Deborah invited her to her quarters for lemonade.

Once Tonette had brought the refreshment and was dismissed, Deborah fixed Lenore with a level gaze and said, "How is Caleb, Lenore?"

In shock, Lenore splashed lemonade on her dress. "How did you—we were so careful . . ." Her voice was a whisper and she could not meet Deborah's eyes.

Sitting down beside her, Deborah took the glass from her hands and placed it on a small table, then grasped Lenore's cold fingers in her own and gently squeezed them. "Look at me, Lenore. I'm your friend. I want to be certain you don't get hurt, that this man isn't taking advantage of a gently reared girl."

Lenore's blue eyes widened and flew to meet Deborah's. "Oh, no. You don't think that we—that he—oh, Deborah, he's been a perfect gentleman! Of course, I know we didn't have a chaperon, but how could we—with my family so set against him?"

"How long have you known him?" Deborah's heart went out to the sad, gentle young woman.

"We met last fall when he first went into business with Mister Gautier and Mister du May. We accidentally collided on the stairs. Oh, Deborah, he was so charming and handsome. Nothing like Creole suitors who are vain and dress like peacocks!''

Lenore launched into a long description of how that first innocent encounter blossomed into a secret romance. At first they met at the opera, the market, several cafés popular with the young people of New Orleans. Then one evening at a dance he asked her to take a carriage ride with him the following day. She had been daring and accepted. After that they met in private every week. When he wanted to approach her parents, she confessed the betrothal agreement between her and Cousin Georges. Caleb railed against something so medieval in the nineteenth century.

"Do you love Caleb, Lenore? Enough to defy your family and marry him?" Deborah asked gently.

"I'm not like Mama, Deborah. I don't want to live the kind of life she does. Since I've met Caleb, I've learned so much. He's traveled to St. Petersburg and Rome and London—even to Africa." Her face reflected confusion and embarrassment as she hesitated, then plunged on with, "I know you don't hold with slavery and neither does Caleb. Oh, Deborah, he told me some sickening things about how they capture and ship the Congos to the New World. I never thought about that part of it—how they got here. They were once free in their own land."

"All the more reason for your family to dislike Caleb," Deborah said dryly, amazed at how Armstrong had changed Lenore's outlook. "Are you sure this doesn't make you a bit of a bluestocking instead of a Creole belle, Lenore?" she teased, then asked seriously, "Has Caleb asked you to marry him?"

"Oh yes, of course, but . . ." Lenore's face flamed and she went on in a low murmur, "there is one thing . . ." In a misery of embarrassment, she stood up and walked over to the window. With her back turned she said, "I'm afraid—oh, not of Caleb. He's always been gentle and he's so very handsome, but after we're married, I'm afraid it'll be different. Mama has told me it's awful but women have to endure it. I don't feel that way when he kisses me—oh!" She reddened even more at her slip. "Deborah, all he's done is kiss me a few times."

If Deborah's dislike of her mother-in-law needed any further fueling, that was being provided now. She walked over and put her hand gently on Lenore's shoulder. "Don't listen to your mother, Lenore. She's wrong, so wrong. If you love a man and he loves you, it can be beautiful, even breathtakingly pleasurable. If you liked a few simple kisses, let me assure you what follows is a thousand times more wonderful."

Lenore's blush didn't lessen as she turned and looked Deborah in the eye. "I—I thought you and Rafael weren't like Mama and Papa. I've watched you dance and exchange glances and touch. Oh, Deborah, I hope it will be that way for Caleb and me!"

Deborah silently hoped for a very different relationship for Lenore and her American. There was far more to a successful marriage than pleasure in bed. She certainly had that with Rafael, but now she was coming to realize that she possessed little else besides her husband's body.

Deborah sat in the open carriage with her parasol defiantly tipped back so the sun hit her face fully. Every irritated glare shot her way from Celine was matched by a carefully concealed but impish smile of conspiracy from Lenore. Creole ladies were deathly afraid of having their skin sun-darkened. It was not fashionable. Besides, there was the ever-hovering threat of being "kissed by the tar brush," a southern euphemism for a family's having any faint strain of African blood in their ancestry. Deborah felt all the more incentive to sun herself because it irked her mother-in-law and defied Creole bigotry.

The baleful pall of New Orleans humidity lifted as they neared Lake Pontchartrain. The spicy scent of pines was in the air and a slight breeze carried the fragrance gently toward the women in the carriage and the men on horseback.

As they rode, Rafael watched the interplay between his wife, mother and sister. He was becoming increasingly alarmed at how readily Lenore adopted Deborah's ideas and outspoken manner. If the foolish child was not careful, she could ruin her reputation. He watched the way Deborah and Celine fenced with words and Lenore's attempts to intercede on her sister-in-law's behalf. Tonight he would confront his father and urge him to end the women's squabble once and for all. Lenore would marry Georges and be safely removed from his wife's influence.

Even as Deborah angered him, he felt himself drawn to her moonlight-delicate beauty in the midday heat. He had not touched her in nearly two weeks. In town he had Lily to assuage his needs, but once at the lake house, he would claim his conjugal rights again. *Damn, just looking at her makes me want to ravish her,* he thought in irritation. Months of marriage had not cooled his ardor for her. Fearfully, he wondered if years would.

Lake Pontchartrain materialized in front of them like a rippling aqua carpet, brilliant in the noonday sun. In front of them was one of the most imposing houses Deborah had ever seen, two stories high with a spacious porch circling around it. Both stories were set with wide double doors to catch every hint of lake breeze. The house was painted a pastel green, lush and cool, shaded by tall live oaks towering over it. It was situated on a slight rise, which fell off about one hundred yards to the water. Ornamental and vegetable gardens spread around the lake side of the house, and off to the northwest, a large brick dairy room sat beneath a cluster of live oaks.

As Deborah took in the panorama, Lenore told her about all the comforts in this vast domain that the Flamenco family had built in order to escape summers on the sugar plantation much farther upriver. "Why, we even have an underground ice house just out back. All our punch and lemonade will be cold," Lenore bubbled.

"I can't wait to see the inside. It looks so cool and inviting." After the cloying heat of New Orleans Deborah longed to sit on the upstairs veranda and feel the fresh lake breeze.

"You and Deborah will have the quarters on the north side," Celine said to Rafael. There was only one bedroom in the suite, but the sitting room could easily be refurbished into a second one if he so desired.

As if reading her mind, Rafael answered. "My old room will suit us fine, Mama."

Rafael's "old room" was magnificent with a splendid view of the lake, polished cypress floors, and comfortable leather furniture. The large four-poster bed was positioned directly across from the open double doors.

Watching Deborah eye the bed as she stood in the center of the large room, Rafael walked up behind her and placed his hands possessively on her shoulders. "Tonight"—he punctuated his speech with a brief nuzzling kiss to her neck—"we'll put this bed to good use."

Deborah stiffened at the unexpected embrace, even more at his words. "I was under the impression you found our 'forced' marriage so unpleasant that you no longer wanted to share a bed with me," she snapped.

He laughed softly and turned her in his arms, ignoring her resistance. "Ah, so you've missed my nightly attentions, have you?"

She colored in mortification, hating herself because it was true. "I'm sure you found other amusements with which to replace me," she said, struggling to sound detached.

"Perhaps," he replied in that low silky voice she both loved and resented for its hypnotic effect on her, "but I can't produce any legal Flamenco heirs that way."

Rafael could not have elicited a more pained reaction if he had struck her. He felt her stiffen and push him away, turning her face to hide the tears forming in her eyes. *Why did I say that?* he raged to himself, recalling his earlier words about being forced to marry her. That had begun this estrangement and now he had just made it worse. *Damn! I'm a blundering ass!*

She broke free of his hold and fled across the room to stand silhouetted in the doorway to the porch. Her face was chalky pale. "I might have known your only motives for coming near me were related to family duty—proper Creole duty!" Her voice dripped with scorn. "Why don't you apply for an annulment, Rafael? After all, you married me against your will and I'll never be a proper Creole wife. Your father, your mother, and you be damned if you think you'll make me over into something I'm not!"

His first impulse was to throw her on the bed, rip off her clothes, and make love to her. He took several menacing steps toward her before his sanity reasserted itself. His parents and sister were in adjacent rooms. Everyone would hear the ensuing battle, and one look at Deborah's mutinously set chin convinced him that it would indeed be a battle royal.

He stopped and said coldly, "I wouldn't dream of forcing you to do something so distasteful as endure my touch, madame. As to an annulment, I'll give it serious consideration." With that he turned sharply on his heel and stormed from the room.

That night they lay stiffly in the dark, side by side in the big bed. Both were grateful that it was large enough that they did not have to touch. Their mutual misery hung in the warm summer air.

The next morning when Lenore offered to show her the lake area, Deborah quickly agreed. She desperately needed some physical activity to occupy her mind and body. They rode accompanied by Gaspar, one of the black stable hands. Lenore pointed out various elegant summer houses. Most belonged to friends of the family, but a few on the outlying north end of the lake road had been built by Americans.

One, a lovely Greek revival house of small, exquisite proportions, was set back in a secluded area surrounded by pines. "That house is lovely, Lenore."

Lenore flushed and fidgeted with the reins of her small tan filly. "It belongs to Caleb."

Deborah smiled and said gently, "And that's why you rode in this direction?"

"Oh, he's not here now. He only comes to the lake at the end of the week when he has time free from his work."

"At least he works," Deborah said acerbically. "Were you able to talk with him before we left the city?"

Lenore looked away once more and answered in a whisper, "Yes, but we quarreled. He insists on confronting Papa and asking for permission to court me."

Deborah scowled. "I can just imagine how much good that would do!"

"Exactly, but I fear I didn't convince him. He hates seeing me in secret."

"You'll have to make a choice soon, Lenore." Deborah knew how difficult it would be for her young sister-in-law to break her ties with mother, father, brother, and all Creole society. She might well conclude that Caleb was not worth the sacrifice. A small voice niggled in the back of her mind, *Was Rafael worth the sacrifice for you?*

They rode back in subdued silence, each lost in unhappy thoughts. After Gaspar led the horses off for a rubdown, they entered the house from the side door. Loud, angry voices greeted them—men's voices speaking in English—Claude Flamenco's thick accent and Caleb Armstrong's clipped New England tones.

"I have done nothing dishonorable, sir. I love your daughter and I want to marry her."

"She is already betrothed. It is settled. Now, will you leave my property or shall I set our hounds on you?" Claude's voice was growing more strident with every word.

"With or without your blessing, I will marry Lenore. Rest assured of it, sir." Caleb's voice was suddenly louder as he burst through the study door into the hall where he almost collided with Lenore and Deborah.

Lenore clutched Deborah's sleeve, then took a halting step toward Caleb. He reached out to take her in his arms, but her father's voice stopped her the instant before she stepped into Caleb's comforting embrace.

Claude's normally swarthy complexion was mottled dark red as he hissed in French, "Lenore, go at once to your room lest I have your brother call this barbaric intruder onto the field of honor—if he possesses any honor, which I doubt!"

She hesitated for only a second, considering her father's threat. Rafael was deadly with rapier or pistol. With a heart-wrenching sob she whirled and fled upstairs.

Caleb clenched his hands impotently at his sides. "This is not the time or place to continue this discussion, but the matter is *not* closed," he said rigidly to Claude. Turning to Deborah, he nodded politely. "Good day, Mrs. Flamenco."

As she watched his retreating back, she heard Celine call to Claude, "Has he gone, dearest?"

While looking at Deborah, Claude replied to his wife, who was now standing in the parlor door, "The *American* will never set foot in this house again."

Recognizing the slur implied against her in his epithet, Deborah walked calmly up the steps without a backward glance.

"Oh, Deborah, what will I do?" Lenore was lying on her bed, her eyes red from weeping. "Caleb's no duelist. Rafael will kill him!"

"Perhaps not. If you were already married and there was nothing more to be gained, I doubt even Rafael would want to make his only sister a widow," Deborah said quietly.

Lenore turned on the bed and rolled into a sitting position, hope lighting her face. "But you heard Papa. He can't ever come here again and if I try to leave, they'll stop me . . ." She hesitated, waiting for Deborah to continue.

"No one will think it odd if I go riding on Saturday morning. You said Caleb often spends his free time at his lake house in the summer. I can give him a message from you, saying you accept his proposal—you do still want to marry him, knowing it means cutting all ties to your family?"

Lenore looked determinedly at Deborah. "You did it, didn't you? If a woman loves a man enough, she has to make the sacrifice."

But what about the man? Doesn't it cost him anything? Deborah thought. Aloud she replied, "Yes, Lenore, I did it, and I'll help you and your Yankee."

Claude and Celine were watching Lenore as if she were a wild thing ready to bolt, but slipping out for a ride alone the following morning was not difficult for Deborah. Rafael, who had spent yesterday upriver carousing with friends, was still abed in exhausted slumber. He had returned late last night, long after everyone else had retired.

The ground was still cool and damp from a late night rain and the rich moldy earth smelled pungent and refreshing. It was a cloudy morning with a brisk breeze stirring. Deborah urged her mount on, eager to get the deed done and return undetected to the house.

It took nearly an hour to reach the back entry to Caleb's property and another to discuss Lenore's note and their elopement. Caleb was overjoyed that Lenore wanted to marry him, but pridefully resistant at stealing her away from the haughty Flamencos.

"What would you rather do—kill Lenore's brother or have him kill you? Claude wasn't making an idle threat, Caleb. I know him and I know my husband. They'll never give in. Right now Lenore is listening as Celine and Claude plan a big betrothal party. Georges Beaurivage will arrive on Friday and the engagement will be announced that night."

Caleb's big body was tense with anxiety and anger. "Why? Why in hell are they so dead set against me? The du Mays and Gautiers have sponsored me into their rarefied Creole circles. I'm certainly wealthy enough to provide for Lenore."

Deborah smiled sadly. "That's exactly the point, I'm afraid. You *are* rich. Your Creole business partners wanted your money and skills for their failing bank. But the Flamencos are as rich as you. They don't need your money and they don't want their precious blue blood diluted any more than it already has been by unsuitable marriages."

He looked at her with compassion written across his face. "You know who'll pay the highest price of all for this subterfuge, don't you?"

She shrugged in resignation. "Considering the state of grace I find myself in now, there's little I can do to worsen my image in the Flamencos' estimation."

"Even Rafael's?"

She sighed. "Especially Rafael's."

By the time she left Caleb, it was nearly eleven. If she were not home for luncheon, she'd be missed. The sun was high now, having emerged from behind the clouds to cast its brilliant rays in a patchwork of gold over the secluded woods. It was so cool and peaceful that she hated to break away from the forest's spell.

Then she heard the underbrush snapping and muffled hoofbeats approaching. Panic seized her as she recalled

Rafael's warnings about the riffraff who occasionally inhabited the deserted backwoods areas around the lake houses of the rich. She had taken a very out-of-the-way route so no one would see her. Now the danger of discovery paled in comparison to this unknown menace.

She tried to head her mount off the trail into the dense foliage, but she had never been an accomplished horsewoman and could not manage it before the rider saw her and called out.

"What in hell are you doing riding alone in the middle of nowhere!" Rafael pulled his big black alongside her smaller chestnut and grabbed the reins.

Wanting to divert him from her secret mission, Deborah asked, "Why are you speaking English?" Seldom since they had left Boston did he do so.

"Your native tongue is so admirably equipped for swearing, which is exactly what I feel like doing now, *cherie.*" He proceeded to demonstrate with startling fluency.

"Damn you, Rafael, let me go." She tried to twist away from his bruising grip, but he held fast to her wrist.

"I awoke an hour ago and was told my wife had ridden out at daybreak, heading into a trackless bayou area. You could have been alligator meat by now if not worse—raped and killed by the trash that happens through here!" His eyes were glowing with black fire. He had been terrified that she was injured or lost in the woods. Now to find her calmly cantering back home infuriated him beyond reason.

Deborah recoiled from his wrath, half-angry with him, half-afraid of him. "How convenient for you if I broke my neck," she spat. "It'd save you the trouble of an annulment!"

"Don't tempt me," he ground out. When she tried to pull free again, he reached across the saddle and hauled her, kicking and screaming, off her horse onto his.

Now, she really was frightened. His grip was viselike, squeezing the breath from her as he attempted to subdue her. Deborah was a strong woman for all her slimness. In vain she thrashed and writhed, refusing to give in to the pain he was inflicting.

The more he felt her body pressed against his and smelled the sweet lavender fragrance of her moonlight hair, the more he wanted her. It had been all he could do to lie in that big bed with empty space between them, forcing himself not to touch her. "Well, it had to end sometime," he muttered beneath his breath as he dropped her to the moss-covered earth beside his horse and swiftly dismounted.

She turned and tried to run, but he was on her in a few pantherlike strides. "Let me go!" She raised her hand and slapped him a stinging blow across the cheek.

"You're repeating yourself, *cherie*," he responded as he grasped the offending hand by the wrist, pulling it behind her with a hard twist. Quickly he imprisoned the other with it and held both slender wrists behind her back in one of his large strong hands. He pressed her breathless body against him and then tangled his free hand in the silvery skein of her hair.

At what point her furious struggle turned to breathless trembling, she was not certain. All at once they were staring into each other's eyes, black and violet locked in a silent duel. Neither wanted to expose what each knew the windows of the soul revealed.

They were both breathing raggedly and trembling, both silent and desperate. Very slowly, he lowered his mouth to hers and she raised her lips to him. It was an oddly gentle kiss at first, experimental, hesitant. Then, with a groan he tightened his hold on her thick hair and pressed her face to his, deepening the kiss.

Deborah opened to him, accepting the offer of his tongue with a soft cry of surrender. She arched her whole body against him. When he released her wrists, she wrapped her arms tightly around his waist. Slowly they sank to the soft mossy ground. Side by side, locked in the intensity of the kiss, their arms and legs entwined as their passions grew.

She could feel his skillful fingers inside the jacket of her riding habit, quickly and deftly unfastening buttons, then cupping and teasing her breasts through the thin silk of her camisole. The soft pale tips hardened to points instantly and hot flashes of pleasure shot through her.

He wore only a thin white lawn shirt and tan trousers. Following his lead, she quickly pulled the shirt open and buried her palm in the thick black hair on his chest. She could feel the furious thrum of his heartbeat.

With a few swift yanking movements he freed her of the jacket and skirt, then shed his shirt in one fluid movement. He ran his hands down her lacy sheer undergarments, unfastening the tapes to her petticoats and swishing them off her legs. When he had undressed her, he kissed a wet hot trail over her slim ankles and up her delicate calves. She lay breathless and trembling, her hands tangled in the curly black hair of his head.

One of his hands slipped higher, between her thighs to stroke the ache that was growing there. He could feel the wetness through her sheer pantalets. She gasped and arched as he applied massaging pressure. When she whimpered, he raised his head and pulled her face to his for another sealing kiss. All the while his hand continued to stoke the frantic need at her core.

The world receded in a whirling vortex of pleasure and hunger. Deborah held onto Rafael, so afire nothing else mattered but that he join his body to hers.

Then he rolled abruptly into a sitting position. She watched him strip off boots and pants in a few swift ripping movements. When he turned to her again she reached up to embrace him feverishly as he peeled off her pantalets.

He took her small pale hand and lowered it between their bodies to grasp his phallus. The hot hard flesh sent a thrill of need shooting through her entire body. She could hear his sharp intake of breath as she stroked him and guided the tip of his shaft into her.

The heat and hunger were unbearable now. In unison he thrust in her and she raised up to envelop him. They were lost in one another, joined and unified in mindless spiraling pleasure, panting and thrusting toward a hard swift release that came to both of them with electrifying force.

He rolled her over so she lay on top of him. Then he raised her upper body and slowly suckled her breasts as they hung suspended before him like pearly melons. She clamped her thighs tightly around his hips and closed her eyes, throwing her head back to revel in the renewal of spent passion. Long moments later he lowered her down on his hardness. She quickly caught the rhythm, controlling their movements, rolling, undulating, twisting until she felt she would go mad with the pleasure. He laid his head against the ground and arched up, thrusting into her as she rode him.

This time they went slowly, neither wanting it to end. His hands slid from her hips, up her spine, then around to tease her swaying breasts. She raked her nails down his chest, felt the flexing hard tension in his shoulders and biceps, then caressed his swarthy, sculpted jawline and brow. Finally, when she could hold back no longer, he seemed to sense it and tangled his hands in her hair, pulling her down to him for a hard deep kiss as she stiffened in climax. In rhythmic pulsing bursts, he released his seed deep within her.

Neither could have said how long they lay, sweat-soaked and exhausted, tightly fused together, each unwilling to break the joining. Finally, he stroked her cheek softly and felt the wetness of tears. At his gentle caress, she raised her face from the curve of his shoulder and their eyes locked.

"Oh, Rafael, what do we do now?" she asked brokenly.

"I don't know, Moon Flower, I don't know," he whispered in reply.

Chapter 11

"Do you think it will work?" Lenore's face was taut as she surveyed her sister-in-law.

Deborah was dressed in Lenore's costume for the masked ball. Lenore had convinced her parents that if she were to announce her betrothal to Georges that night, the festivities must be of her choosing. She wanted a masquerade. Creoles loved such costume affairs, and her father, delighted that she was finally willing to comply with their plans, quickly endorsed the idea.

The plan was Deborah's, not Lenore's. Now Deborah stood dressed in Lenore's elaborate shepherdess costume with its frilly, flowing overskirts, long lacy gloves, and huge wide-brimmed bonnet. She wore a wig of long yellow curls and a mask. The costume was chosen with care so as to conceal every distinguishing feature of either woman.

"Be sure you don't let anyone see your feet," Lenore admonished. She was a good four or five inches shorter than her sister-in-law. However, if Deborah wore flat-heeled slippers instead of the very high-heeled clogged shoes that Lenore had chosen, the height difference might go unnoticed. Deborah had always observed that people see what they expect to see. Celine and Claude had watched Lenore twirl and mince all week during fittings for the frothy costume. In secret Deborah had practiced the same flirtatious movements.

"I do declare, you can use your fan as adroitly as any Creole belle, Deborah," Lenore said in amazement as she watched her double practice a coy gesture.

"Well, let's hope I can get by with your 'sore throat' voice as well," Deborah said darkly. That morning Lenore had feigned a sudden cold, but insisted the ball must go on as planned despite a problem with her voice. "If I only can keep Georges talking, he shouldn't notice the substitution until it's too late."

"Just let him talk about himself. He'll be amused for hours," Lenore replied acidly, then begged reassurance. "You're positive Caleb will be out behind the dairy house?"

"Sure as you're in love with him, and he's in love with you," Deborah said soothingly.

That afternoon when Georges arrived, Lenore had pleaded her nervousness over the night's festivities as an excuse not to greet him. Deborah had stayed upstairs, as well, sending word that she, too, had caught Lenore's ailment and would not attend the gala. If Rafael was irritated with her refusal to participate, his parents were relieved.

"You're sure Rafael won't come up to see that you're all right?" Lenore still saw all manner of pitfalls to their scheme.

"Just before he went downstairs, I provoked a bit of a tiff," she replied grimly. *As if I needed to make him angrier,* she thought desolately. "He won't be concerned about me. All his friends and cousins are downstairs reveling with him. I'm sure Minnette Gautier has wasted no time batting her eyelashes at him either."

Lenore put her arm around Deborah's slim shoulders. "Minnette doesn't mean a thing to Rafael."

Deborah swallowed and said with false brightness, "Oh, bother the silly twit. I have to remember to hide my feet and keep my eyelashes lowered so my eyes don't show violet."

Lenore dimpled. "Just stay away from the chandeliers. Let Georges think you enjoy huddling in romantic dark corners with him." She paused and said thoughtfully, "Strange, now that I think of it, he never seemed to want to—well, you know, get close to me that way. Only when he wanted to control me would he really touch me—" She dismissed the distasteful memory and said "Caleb and I will never forget what you're doing for us, Deborah. If there's anything we can ever do to help you, you know to come at once."

The two women hugged fiercely. Then Deborah gave Lenore a quick shove toward the open doors facing the rear of the house. "I must face the lion's den downstairs and you must slip through the kitchen and out to Caleb. Now, go."

The room was crowded with richly costumed men and women. Greek muses simpered in silver and white robes, outlandish pirates dripped with gold chains, sporting gleaming sabers. Deborah saw Rafael at once, standing across the room, a head taller than the men and women who surrounded him. He was resplendent in the burnished breastplate and leather breeches of a Spanish conquistador. Idly she wondered if he had chosen the costume to remind her of his ruthless ancestry, or if he had done it only because it became his bold, swarthy looks so well.

Minnette Gautier wasn't the only one hanging on him, Deborah thought acidly. All the women seemed to appreciate the Spanish mercenary in their midst. Well and good that he was occupied. In her disguise she must avoid him at all costs. She might fool Georges and her in-laws, but she could never deceive her husband.

Almost at once Celine swept across the floor, with Georges

in tow behind her. Because of the crowd, the noise, and the flickering lights, Celine did not penetrate Deborah's disguise. She gushed when Lenore placed her gloved hand timidly in Georges's and curtsied.

Georges held her stiffly, not at all the way Deborah would have thought an eager fiancé would hold his beloved. Even Oliver Haversham was a far better actor than this, she thought as her irritation changed to a prickling uneasiness. However, her subterfuge was working, for he talked of his plans for the tour of Europe they would take after their marriage.

Deborah tried in vain to reassure herself that it was only his resemblance to Rafael that bothered her. She cast quick appraising glances at his face through her mask, careful to hide her eyes. His picture-perfect features were too pretty, his gestures too precise. There was none of the bold virility she had always felt tenuously leashed in Rafael, although the same arrogance and haughtiness were certainly present in Georges's manner. Something was wrong. Lenore must be married before this night was over, safe from this enigma!

Deborah was relieved when Monsieur Gautier cut in on Georges but not as grateful, she suspected, as was Georges. He fled toward the punch bowl and a group of his friends while she made hoarse, desultory small talk with the kindly old man.

"How does your fiancé find New Orleans after spending two years in Paris?" He inclined his head to hear her raspy voice.

"I suspect he misses Europe. We're to take a grand tour on our honeymoon." *Georges will have to tour alone, which I suspect will be more to his liking anyway.*

For the next two hours, Deborah danced, flirted, and talked as little as possible. She avoided Rafael and his parents, spending a great deal of time with casual acquaintances who were unlikely to notice the subterfuge. As for Georges, he danced with her only as often as it seemed he must for appearances. The rest of the time he spent in conversation with his friend Paul Ravat, a fellow student from his university days in France. If she were uneasy over Georges, she was outright repelled when Paul's chilly gray eyes followed her across the dance floor. It was as if he knew some secret Lenore didn't.

Scolding herself for being fanciful, she checked the clock on the mantel once more. Nearly time to make her exit. She had bought Lenore and Caleb three hours, more than ample time for the lovers to be married and to consummate their marriage before the Flamenco family could intervene.

The unmasking and official betrothal announcement were to take place at midnight with a lavish banquet to follow. However, when she made her excuse at a quarter to twelve and did not reappear, there would be no announcement, nor likely any celebration supper. Deborah would be found sleeping in her room and Lenore would have vanished without a trace. A note on her dressing table would tell the tale. *If only I can slip by undetected.* She watched the minute hand inch toward the nine with agonizing slowness.

It was nearing midnight as Rafael watched Lenore dance a slow quadrille with Georges, then excuse herself and turn to leave the press. Suddenly, he felt a need to be assured of her happiness before the irreversible announcement took place. She was going upstairs to freshen up for the big moment, no doubt.

"Lenore, wait, little one," he called out at her retreating back as he followed her into the front hall.

She turned and caught sight of him. Gasping, she murmured hoarsely, "I must repair my toilette before the unmasking, Rafael. Tell Papa and Georges I'll meet them by the south door." With that she picked up her skirts and scampered up the wide low stairs to the second floor.

His immediate impulse was to follow her. But he quickly stifled the urge. What was done was done. Still, something nagged at the back of his mind—what was it? He mulled distractedly as he searched for his father and soon-to-be brother-in-law.

When Lenore did not come down at midnight, Celine quickly went up to see what was detaining her. She returned ashen and pulled Rafael and Claude into the hallway. "She is not in the retiring room. None of the ladies who are there have seen her. I've sent the servants to search her room and the grounds discreetly."

Claude let out an impatient sigh. "She cannot have gone far. Rafael saw her go upstairs a scant ten minutes ago."

Rafael suddenly ripped off his mask and swore, then automatically apologized to his shocked mother. "The shoes, that's it!" With that he was gone, sprinting toward the rear stairs and his room, where he knew Deborah would be waiting.

"Did you return the dress and wig to her room and put them next to the unused clogs?" His voice sliced through the warm night air as he ripped the sheet from her still form.

Deborah had heard him enter and prayed that if she feigned sleep he would leave her. But he did not. Reluctantly, she sat up in bed. One look into his blazing black eyes told her all. "How did you know?"

"Your flat-heeled shoes. When you ran so precipitously up the steps, you raised your skirts too high, *cherie*. I should have recognized my wife's beautiful ankles." He slid one strong hand around a slim ankle and squeezed cruelly. "Where is Lenore?"

She shivered despite the heat as he held her fast.

"Well, I'm waiting. So are my parents, her fiancé, and over one hundred people." He increased the pressure.

Tears swam in her eyes, but she blinked them back. "It's too late, Rafael. She and Caleb were married hours ago."

He swore at her, even more virulently than he had the morning in the woods, but this time he used French, as if to emphasize the distance between them. With a disgusted grunt, he released her ankle, shoving her away from him.

"Where are you going? Rafael, let them have peace. There's nothing you can do now. She loves Caleb, not Georges!" But she was crying to an empty room.

After dressing in haste, she slipped quietly down the hall to where she heard the low murmurs of Rafael and Claude interspersed with Celine's shrill denunciation. They were in the elder Flamenco's private sitting room and Rafael was standing at Claude's desk, calmly loading a pistol.

"What will we tell Georges? Our guests?" Celine's voice wailed in anguish.

"I shall announce that Lenore was taken suddenly quite ill. After all she did have a 'sore throat' tonight. The betrothal is merely postponed. Rafael will bring her home. You must go to her room and wait. People will expect that you are attending her.'' Claude's voice was calm, but his face was gray.

"She and that skulking wolf may be at his lake house, but I doubt it. They've probably used this time to flee to New Orleans and search for a priest. I'll go to the cottage and then head to his city house.'' Rafael slipped the pistol into his belt with deadly ease.

"You're admirably dressed for the role you plan to play,'' Deborah said from the doorway. Celine gasped and made a lunge toward her daughter-in-law with claws out, but Claude restrained her. Deborah ignored the woman and turned her attention to Rafael. "If you kill him you'll break her heart. She is married to him now.''

"No priest in New Orleans would marry a Creole girl of good family to an American—in the dead of night with no family in attendance,'' Celine spat venomously.

"An Episcopal priest would. Caleb is a good parishioner. He made the arrangements days ago,'' Deborah's voice sounded lifeless. What was the use hiding her role in the charade? She must keep Rafael from doing something terrible, even if it meant turning all the family's wrath on herself.

"She would not marry outside the Church.'' In a voice filled with impatience, Claude dismissed the idea.

Celine's eyes narrowed as she stared at Deborah's straight back and assured stance. "You concocted this scheme with Armstrong, didn't you? You've led her immortal soul astray.'' In truth, Celine was as little concerned with religion as were her husband and son. What would their friends think? The scandal of the elopement loomed far larger than the threat of perdition.

Understanding what was going on in her mother-in-law's mind, Deborah retorted, "I only helped your daughter marry the right man.'' She put her hand hesitantly on Rafael's arm, but he withdrew as if stung, before she could speak.

"None of this signifies. I'm going after them. Deborah,

if you value your neck, get back to bed and stay there!'' He stalked from the room and slammed the door.

When Caleb responded to the butler's summons, Lenore knew it was her brother or her father. She had heard only one set of hoofbeats pounding up to Caleb's Garden District home in the stillness of the early morning hours. Likely it was her brother. With numb fingers she struggled to pull on her dressing gown.

This was her wedding night. Why must something so beautiful and private be marred by confrontation and violence? As she ran her fingers through her tousled gold ringlets, she looked quickly into the mirror. *Do I look any different? Will Rafael be able to tell?* She colored as she recalled the gentleness of her new husband's touch and the sweet, breathless pleasure she had found in his arms only a few hours earlier. She must never lose him, never lose his love. Quickly she headed downstairs toward the sound of angry male voices.

Caleb stood in the center of the richly paneled hallway facing a coldly furious Rafael. The American was of a height with his new brother-in-law but heavy-boned next to Rafael's leanness. A bigger target beneath the Dueling Oaks, Caleb thought with grim humor as he looked into those cold, black eyes.

''I don't want to fight you, Rafael, your Creole honor be damned. A practical Yankee like me doesn't set much stock by it.'' He waited, poised tautly on the balls of his feet, knowing that he could not live up to his resolution if the dangerous young Creole attacked him.

''You'd let a challenge go unanswered?'' Rafael responded scornfully. ''No one in New Orleans would do business with you again.''

''My Creole partners at the bank have done business with me until now. I imagine they'll have to decide for themselves if this breach of your etiquette casts me outside the pale,'' Caleb said almost gently.

''We have a proverb in New Orleans,'' Rafael replied

icily. "Cutting off a mule's ears will never make him a horse. Neither will an American gain acceptance hiding behind the skirts of an innocent girl. I've come to take my sister home, Armstrong, whether or not you honor my challenge!" He moved forward as if to bypass the larger man, but Armstrong was quick. He blocked Rafael's path and stood still, hands clenched into fists, yet making no move to strike the first blow.

"Flamenco, I'm not hiding behind Lenore or anywhere else."

Rafael took another step toward Caleb and reached to his sash for the pistol.

Before he could draw it free, Lenore's voice carried down from the top of the curved mahogany staircase. "If you harm him, Rafael, I'll kill myself. I swear it!" She ran down the stairs, her face ashen and her blue eyes enormous.

Lenore placed one arm around Caleb's sturdy waist, but before she could say any more, he gently pushed her behind him. "My *wife* is not going anywhere with you. You're right about one thing, though—I am a Yankee mule and I won't budge."

Rafael looked at Armstrong's regretful but firm expression and realized that short of shooting him in cold blood, he could exact no further punishment from him now. He turned to Lenore, who once more stepped beside her husband. Her robe was askew and her face flushed. One look at her told the story. The marriage had indeed been consummated. He felt his vision go dark as a sickening rage filled him. "Why have you done this to Mama and Papa? To Georges? You've disgraced the Flamenco name."

"I'm sorry I hurt you and our parents, but no one would listen to me. I loathe Georges Beaurivage!" Her face paled as she ground out the words. "He makes my skin crawl. He never wanted me for who I am. He merely wanted a suitable match, and our families agreed."

"You're too young to understand why marriage arrangements are made," Rafael interjected disgustedly.

"And I suppose at the great age of twenty-two you know far more," Caleb said softly.

"Let's just say I'm learning from my mistakes," Rafael responded, grim resignation replacing his killing anger.

"Rafael, I love Caleb. That's the best reason of all for marriage—that and children." She paused and blushed, then placed her hand on Caleb's arm. "I could already be carrying a child. I want my husband to live to see it, Rafael. And you, too. Don't do this. Don't let hate destroy you— *either* of you. If you love me, don't force this fight."

Defeated, Rafael sighed and released the hold on his gun, letting his hand drop, empty, to his side. "I withdraw my challenge, Armstrong." He stared coldly at Caleb and measured each word. "You don't know what you've begun this night. My sister has lost her parents, her friends, the life she's always known. Take care of her." He turned to leave, but Lenore slipped from Caleb's embrace and placed one hand on his arm to stop him. "Rafael, I know Mama and Papa won't forgive me, but Deborah . . ." She felt him stiffen at the mention of his wife's name. "Deborah is my friend and I want her to visit me. Would you permit that?"

He turned slowly, and the look of leashed fury in his eyes struck her like a blow. Her hand dropped from his arm. "Why ever should she need my permission? She'll do as she pleases, as she always has. Do you think I don't know who thought up this elaborate scheme? You're not nearly devious enough, little sister. And your stalwart Yankee here probably had to be cajoled into letting my wife betray me!"

"Rafael, that's not fair! She only did it out of love for me—she didn't betray you." Lenore could see by the look on his face that nothing she could say would have the slightest effect.

Caleb walked up and put his arm around his wife's dejected shoulders. Together they stood in the doorway, watching the proud young Creole walk stiffly across the lawn toward his waiting horse.

Chapter 12

Rafael came home at three A.M., grim and silent, saying only that he had promised his sister he would not challenge her husband. The marriage was in fact accomplished. He did not speak to Deborah all week, going out of his way to avoid her, as if he feared what he might do to her. A few nights he slept in their sitting room on a small bed he had a servant set up. Other nights, including the last one, he spent in the city. Deborah did not want to think where.

For the first time since her marriage she considered writing the truth to her father about her deteriorating relationship with Rafael. She had made three futile attempts and then abandoned the idea. It was too painful. She left her writing desk to lie on a chaise longue on the gallery outside their rooms, too exhausted and depressed to move. Then she heard Celine and Claude begin to argue in a room below.

"I tell you, Claude, I shall never live it down. People are too embarrassed to meet my eyes. Yesterday at the Lacroix luncheon I was virtually ostracized."

"My dear, only wait until fall. Half a dozen other scandals will break by the time we return to the city and the winter season begins." Claude's voice was smooth.

"Nothing this horrible! Our daughter has left the Church. How can I even hold my head up at mass?"

Claude chuckled tolerantly. "Darling, I thought the idea was to *bow* one's head at mass."

"Don't trifle with me, Claude! I've lost my baby and it's all that accursed Yankee's fault. Oh, why did Rafael bring her here? If only he had married Minnette Gautier."

"But he did not. What is done is done." Claude's voice was steely and bitter now. "Lenore was my only daughter

135

and I adored her. I grieve for her loss, but we still have Rafael, and his wife is now our only hope for grandchildren. Our son assures me she'll produce a child within the year. Hope for that.''

"And what of the added scandal of the duel?'' Celine seemed determined to ignore Claude's attempts to end the conversation.

Deborah's reaction shifted from humiliation to fear. Now, she leaned forward to catch every word.

"Since our son was so foolishly swayed by Lenore to spare that cur's life, it was Georges's right to meet him on the field of honor. He was most clever, too. He provoked Armstrong into making the challenge so he had the choice of weapons. The ignorant American is a good shot but a poor swordsman.''

"I certainly hope our Georges can defeat that—that seducer! What will happen if Lenore's left a widow?'' Celine's voice took on a surprised note, as if the thought had just occurred to her.

"I trust her merchant husband will provide well for her. She is no longer a Flamenco. We cannot take her back after she disgraced our name.'' His voice was cold and final.

Deborah was shaking as she stood and walked woodenly inside. She must speak to Rafael. No matter how much he hated her, he must stop Georges from killing Lenore's husband. Pacing, she practiced a speech, dreading the late afternoon when he would return from upriver to bathe and prepare for his evening's amusements.

The interview proved even more difficult than she had anticipated. Having ridden in a horse race, he came home dusty and sweat soaked, calling curtly for bathwater.

When she knocked on the door to the sitting room, which now doubled as his bedroom, Deborah received a sharp command to enter. Obviously he had thought her a slave, for he was in the process of shedding his clothing, clad only in a pair of riding breeches. He stood in the center of the room, barefooted, unbuttoning his trousers.

"Hurry up, Guy. Pour the—'' He stopped abruptly. "What the hell do you want?'' He didn't move but stared with furious black eyes at her.

"I have to speak to you, Rafael, no matter how angry you are with me." She paused and gathered courage, then stepped inside and closed the door, leaning against it to hide her trembling. "I just heard Georges Beaurivage is going to fight a duel with Caleb using swords. Caleb is no swordsman. He'll be killed, Rafael! You must stop them!"

He scowled and shrugged disgustedly. "I might have known you'd come begging for your countryman's life. I can't interfere in a matter of honor. Georges has the right—"

"To kill a man who has never learned to fence?" she interrupted furiously. "Rafael, you promised Lenore Caleb would be safe."

"I promised I wouldn't kill him, which I could easily have done with sword or pistol," he said arrogantly. "But I won't stop the duel. If I did, Armstrong would be disgraced. He's a grown man and he has to face the consequences of his filthy behavior. It's out of my hands." He turned and resumed his undressing. "Now, you can let me have my bath in peace—or stay and scrub my back if you wish, *cherie*," he added tauntingly in English. She fled.

Early the next morning Deborah rode out, supposedly for a morning's canter along the lake. In fact, she headed as quickly as she could toward the city, to the Armstrongs' Garden District home.

Deborah could sense something was dreadfully amiss as soon as she was admitted to the front foyer by a poker-faced maid. A moment later when Lenore rushed down the spiral staircase to greet her, Deborah knew by her sister-in-law's ashen face that the duel had taken place.

Lenore's blue eyes were dark with fright as she took her taller friend into a trembling embrace. "Oh, Deborah, I'm so glad you've come!"

"As soon as I heard I tried to get Rafael to stop it, but—"

Lenore interrupted, "He couldn't—Caleb wouldn't have listened to anyone, not even my brother. I'm only grateful that Beaurivage jackal thought him dead and left quickly." Her beautiful face, always so youthful and soft, looked startlingly hard and filled with loathing.

Hesitantly, Deborah asked, "How badly did Georges injure him?"

Lenore's pain overshadowed her anger. "The doctor is with him now. He says Caleb is lucky to be alive. The final thrust just missed his heart and lung. He's lost so much blood! Oh, Deborah, if he dies . . ."

"We Yankees are a tough lot, Lenore," Deborah said soothingly. "Hush now, you need to save your strength so you can take care of him. What can I do to help? I've had excellent training as a nurse."

"Does Rafael know you're here?" Almost unconsciously Lenore looked around the foyer and out the door.

"No, I came alone." The quelling look in those lavender eyes put an end to that subject.

Lenore recounted the events leading up to the duel and its shattering aftermath. When a servant came down and told the mistress her husband was asking for her, Lenore flew upstairs with Deborah quickly following.

Although weak and pale, the big Yankee was lucid and smiling when the women entered the room. "I ache like hell, but I'm ravenously hungry. Damn stupid customs you Creoles have, my love, dueling at daybreak on an empty stomach."

The physician, Dr. Lambert, gave a snort of approval. "I don't think a poleax between the ears could kill you, Caleb, but take it easy and stick to light, easily digestible foods for the next few days." Looking over at Lenore, the doctor said, "Keep him quiet so the wounds can knit. I don't relish having to put any more stitches in his tough hide!"

"All of your patients should have such thick skin, Harry," Caleb responded goodnaturedly, "Think of the reputation you'd gain as a healer if everyone was as hard to kill as me!"

The jaunty exchange between Caleb and his friend did not fool Deborah who could see by the strain on his face how much her brother-in-law had suffered. To distract Lenore she said, "Why don't you see to some nice consomme and stewed fruit for our patient."

The patient groaned in disgust. "Broth and mush are for babies and old men. What I really want is a steak!"

By the time Deborah rode away from the Garden District it was late afternoon. Caleb was restive, but the seriousness of his injuries quickly quelled his protests for more solid food. He slept while Lenore lovingly sat at his bedside.

Deborah prayed that he would recover. If he died, Lenore, now completely cut off from her family, would be totally alone.

Preoccupied, Deborah cantered her horse through the deepening shadows on the deserted road. She had stayed longer in town than she had intended and now realized it would mean another ugly scene when she returned to the lake house.

What's the use? I can't please Celine and Claude no matter what I do anyway. Of Rafael's brooding reaction to her lately, she thought not at all.

Just then her horse whickered and began to favor its right foreleg. "What is it, Chamette?" Deborah quickly dismounted and checked the limping filly.

Hoofbeats sounded on the road coming from the lake. Someone to help, or some riffraff who might pose a threat to a woman alone? Before she could even attempt to hide behind the dense roadside vegetation, the rider saw her.

In a lisping, insinuating voice Georges Beaurivage said, "Well, imagine the coincidence. I just paid my respects to your husband and his parents, but you were mysteriously absent, little cousin. And here you are, unattended on the road like a common streetwalker." His·face twisted into cruel lines, distorting the pretty features.

She scarcely flinched at his crude insult, expecting no better from Celine's vicious cousin, but when he dismounted, a real tremor of fear coursed through her. They were alone on a deserted road at dusk and she was the person responsible for helping Lenore escape his clutches. *What might he do to me?*

In answer to her unspoken question, he sneered, "Since you insist on acting like a harlot, perhaps I should treat you like one." With that he reached for her with one slim, pale hand, yanking her brutally by her wrist.

Deborah grabbed for the pommel of her saddle to keep her balance as she twisted away from his icy, repellent touch. As soon as her hand was free, she raised it and delivered a smashing backhand across the side of his face. As he staggered, she clawed at the sidesaddle, reaching across it for the quirt, which she never used on the gentle filly. She would have no compunction about using it on Beaurivage.

Recovering from the blow, Georges muttered several curses in French and lunged for her with both hands. "You will pay for that, you American slut!"

He ripped her riding jacket and blouse exposing a pale gleam of collarbone and breast, but before he could further undress her, Deborah freed the quirt and began to wield it in a stinging frenzy. Georges released her instantly to protect his face from the razor-edged cut of the little whip.

Chamette whickered and reared up in fright as they fought. Deborah was able to throw herself clear, but Georges, busy covering his face, did not see the flashing hooves until it was almost too late. The filly narrowly missed him as he lunged sideways and tripped.

Quickly rolling up from the dusty ground, she grabbed frantically for the reins of his gelding, which stood patiently alongside the road. As she pulled herself into the saddle, Georges yanked a fistful of coiled hair free from its pins but was unable to get a firm grip. She urged the horse forward, clinging to the animal as it galloped toward the lake house.

It was almost dark when she trotted the gelding up the drive. As stealthily as possible she rode to the stable, where a wide-eyed slave took in her appearance with mute amazement as she handed him the reins.

After negotiating the path to the rear door, Deborah began to hope she could get to their quarters undetected. She made it as far as the back stairs when her husband's furious voice cut through the silence. "Where the hell have you been?" he hissed. "I just saw you ride up on Georges's horse. Why in hell would he let you have his best racer?"

Her eyes darkened in fury as she held the torn remnants of her jacket across her shoulder. "He didn't exactly 'let me have' the horse. More like I stole it from the depraved bastard!"

His eyes took in her tangled hair and dirt-smeared face, then fastened accusingly on the torn clothing. As he pulled her hands away the material parted, revealing the swell of her shoulder and breast. In a cold, deadly voice he asked, "Are you telling me Georges did this?"

Outraged, she jerked away from his touch. "Do you think I attacked him to steal his horse? I was riding back from Lenore's when my filly pulled up lame. Georges came along and would have raped me if I hadn't used a riding quirt on that pretty face of his!''

Rafael's swarthy skin whitened visibly. "Go to your room and stay there," was all he said, then turned and stalked down the hall to the study.

Too angry and frightened from the whole horrifying day to fight him anymore, Deborah trudged upstairs and rang for Tonette. After a long soak in warm water, she ate a small portion of the cold supper the maid brought to her room and then fell into a restless, exhausted sleep.

When Deborah awakened the next morning, she looked through the door to the adjoining room. Rafael had not returned to his bed last night. With a mounting sense of apprehension, she dressed in haste and went downstairs toward the parlor where Celine and Claude were arguing.

"But Georges is my cousin's only son! Rafael can't do this, Claude."

Her husband made a snort of disgust. "You seem to take it for granted Rafael will win. What if your precious Georges kills *your* only son, madame?"

Celine whitened and gasped. "No, it's not possible! Rafael has always won."

"So has Georges—until now," Claude replied acerbically.

Deborah's heart stopped. *Dear God, he's challenged Georges Beaurivage to a duel because of me!* She stood frozen in the wide cypress door frame of the parlor.

Celine finally saw her and whirled on her stricken daughter-in-law in fury. "This is all your doing, you Yankee whore—my son and his own cousin about to kill each other over you!"

Determinedly, Deborah asked in a clear voice, "Where are they? I must stop it. Enough blood has been spilled already."

Claude surprised her by grasping her arm roughly and spinning her around to face him. "It is already taking place, this morning—as if you *could* stop it. Not that I doubt you would try," he added in disgust.

"You've done enough already to disgrace our name, pitting the men of our family against one another," Celine spat.

"I did nothing! That swine attacked me and I defended myself," Deborah cried.

"You were riding alone on a deserted road." Claude roared at her. "Small wonder Georges took you for what you are. The pity of it is that Rafael must fight him over one such as you."

Seeing the implacable hatred of her in-laws, Deborah turned to leave. She had heard stories about the infamous Dueling Oaks on the Allard Plantation just outside the city. Her heart hammered furiously in her breast as she raced down to the stables with Celine's shrill cries and Claude's angry threats ringing in her ears.

By the time Deborah reached the plantation, she was windblown and soaked with perspiration. Heedless of amazed stares from the servants, she pushed the exhausted horse toward the tall stand of live oaks that draped their long, gnarled branches earthward as if to conceal the deadly violence that routinely took place beneath them.

When she saw Rafael and Georges, Deborah pulled her horse up and slid to the ground a distance away. She walked with a determined stride toward the two men locked in mortal combat.

Deborah did not see Rafael's cousin, Jean Pierre, who was acting as his second, until his firm grip on her arm stopped her. "No, madame, you cannot interfere. This is a matter of honor," he said stiffly, his hold on her remaining obdurate.

"I won't let them kill each other over me!" She struggled to get free as she stared at the two slim figures whose deadly ballet continued despite her arrival.

The doctor earnestly interceded. "Please, Madame Flamenco, you might cause your husband's death if you distract him."

Realizing the truth of his entreaty, she subsided between the two men to watch the outcome. Deborah realized with sick dread that Claude had been right. Rafael and Georges were evenly matched. Both were slim with the supple grace and lightning reflexes of born fencers, experts taught by the same New Orleans fencing master, Charles Bertin. She could see the sweat beading their faces and running in rivulets down their chests, soaking the thin lawn shirts to their chests in the cool morning air. They were both marked, bleeding freely from a number of superficial nicks.

Rafael concentrated on Georges's face, watching for that telltale nuance in expression that gave away a man's actions before he moved his blade. His present adversary was cooler and more skilled than most, holding his own against Flamenco's deadly rapier.

However, Georges was tiring, although he hid it well. But then, he had dissembled many things in his life. Now sheer desperation led him to goad his cousin. "I see your American wench has not even the decorum of your octoroon. At least Lily knows more than to appear under the oaks to disrupt an affair of honor."

He expected the taunt to distract Rafael, but it did not work. Without taking his eyes off Beaurivage, Rafael replied through clenched teeth, "I'll deal with her after I finish with you, cousin."

Then, Georges did precisely what Rafael hoped he would do. Feinting low he moved in for the kill, aiming at Rafael's heart, but his eyes gave him away. Rafael deflected the blade and slipped past Georges's guard to slide his own rapier cleanly into his opponent's throat. "Bertin always told us not to move our eyes ahead of our blade, Georges," he said with cool detachment as Beaurivage crumpled to the dew-drenched grass.

Rafael had heard Deborah's gasp of horror as he narrowly missed being skewered on Georges's blade. Her face was chalky and her lavender eyes were wide with fright as his cousin Jean Pierre released her. She stood trembling as he advanced toward her in ruthless strides, looking like a Satanic angel. One lock of curly dark hair fell onto his brow and sweat beaded his face. He handed the bloodied rapier to Jean Pierre. His cousin had the good grace to take it and leave quickly.

Tension crackled between them. "I just killed a man because you went out unescorted yesterday. And here you are today, improperly dressed, alone, and in a place no lady would ever set foot."

"You killed a man because your absurd Creole code

demanded it, not to save my life *or* my honor. I thrashed him and saved myself! And I'll come and go as I want, chaperones be damned!''

She was filled with rage, but it was rage oddly mixed with fright that he might have been killed. Rafael sensed only her willful anger, which fueled his own. Taking a deep breath, he said, ''Either you walk quietly with me to my horse and allow me to carry you home with your legs decently covered or I'll throw you over my shoulder and slam you across the saddle like a sack of rice. Take your choice.''

Head held defiantly high, she spun and walked toward his big black stallion without a backward glance at the physician kneeling over Georges's body while the two seconds looked on.

On the long ride back to the lake they spoke not a word. When they arrived, she quickly retreated to the sanctuary of her room, leaving him to give his parents an account of the duel. Deborah was soaked with Rafael's sweat and smeared with his blood after their close contact riding home. Wanting to scrub the violent and disturbing male scent from her body, she rang for a bath.

As she sat in the soothing warm water, Deborah reviewed the shambles of her marriage. Celine and Claude's thinly veiled contempt had now blossomed into open hate. Rafael had not touched her in the weeks since that unplanned, desperate encounter in the woods. Perhaps he never would again. But then that would mean no Flamenco heirs, she thought bitterly. *I can't live this way!*

Refusing the summons to luncheon, Deborah flew into a frenzy of packing, sending Tonette away and selecting only what she could carry herself in two light valises: mostly they were the old clothes she had brought with her from Boston. She had some money, enough to book passage on a steamer. Dreading the disappointment she knew she'd see on Adam Manchester's face, she forced herself to consider only how good it would feel to be consoled by someone who really loved and understood her.

As she removed her heavy wedding band, she trembled and fought back the tears, then resolutely picked up her bags and headed for the stairs. *I can imagine how relieved Claude and Celine will be. What will Rafael say?* Deborah hoped she could slip out without the agony of a final confrontation. The wedding ring left sitting on the top of her jewel case would say it all.

Rafael was just coming from another miserable dinner-table battle with his teary mother and tight-lipped father, both insisting that he do something about Deborah. On several occasions he and Claude had discussed the possibility of an annulment, a drastic recourse that earlier would have shocked Celine. Now even she saw it as a lesser evil than continuing his marriage. He had let them talk, neither agreeing nor disagreeing, confused over his own feelings and most uncertain about his wife's.

Just then he looked up and saw her coming down the stairs, dressed in a traveling costume of rose silk, carrying two suitcases. Placing one booted foot firmly on the bottom step to block her path, he asked, "Just what in the hell do you think you're doing?"

"That should be obvious, Rafael. I'm leaving you." *Don't cry, damn you. Stay in control.*

He quirked one brow in mock amazement. "And just where will you go? Back to your beloved father?"

"Yes." *He loves me. You don't.*

"Like hell!" Her cool self-possessed answer sent ripples of fury coursing through him. And to think only moments ago he was debating ending the marriage! *Fool. As if I could ever let her go, no matter what she does!* He reached up and yanked the bags from her, tossing them carelessly to the floor.

"You can't make me stay, Rafael," she said mutinously. "You don't want me."

"You're *my* wife and I always keep what's mine, Deborah." With that he drew her roughly into his arms and ground his mouth down over hers in a fierce, possessive kiss. He could feel her resistance, stiff and unyielding, her lips pursed closed. He continued to savage them as he held her tightly pressed against his chest while his hands roamed with insistent familiarity across her back, down her buttocks, around to cup and massage her breasts. When she gasped for breath in his bruising hold, he plunged his tongue inside her mouth to tease and tantalize.

She began to weaken, first trembling with the urgent need to salvage her wounded pride, then gradually as desire overrode shame, she opened to him with a small moan of surrender. He could feel her response as her arms slipped around his shoulders and her tongue entwined with his. Once sure of his hold on her, he gentled the kisses and caresses, slowly, savoringly making love to her with his mouth and hands.

When he could hold off no longer, he scooped her into his arms and carried her back upstairs, taking the long, steep steps quickly in his haste to reach their bed. "Let me show you how much I want you," he whispered. *Let me show you how much I love you,* he thought.

Chapter 13

It was the opening night of the opera and Deborah was late. She hated to go, but it was expected that the Flamenco family put in an appearance, especially Rafael and his notorious Yankee wife. *We must put on the facade of a happily married couple to quell the gossip,* she thought bitterly as Tonette fussed with her hair.

Deborah sat disconsolately before the large mirror in her room, staring at her reflection. She had used creams and even powder, but the deep purple smudges beneath her enormous eyes would not go away. She looked haunted. *It's because I am haunted by the nightmare my life's become in the past six months.*

"Monsieur Flamenco will find you most beautiful, madame," Tonette said as she let the last springy coil of silver-gilt hair fall artfully to Deborah's shoulder. The elaborate style was set with pearls twined through it to match the seed pearls on the neckline and sleeves of her soft rose silk gown. Despite the pallor of her cheeks, she looked ethereally lovely.

"I hope so, Tonette," she replied levelly. *I am beautiful to him—a beautiful thing, a mindless ornament for his pleasure. I must only do my duty and breed for him, that's all.* She rose and picked up her fan and wrap, then headed with leaden feet to join the rest of the family in the parlor.

Ever since she had tried to leave him at the lake house last summer, Rafael had resumed his attentions to her in bed. They slept together, but if they were passion-enslaved lovers by night, they were distant strangers by day. An uneasy truce had been gradually established in the Flamenco household. Claude and Celine were icily civil to her in return for her acquiescence as Rafael's wife.

She never again attempted to leave her husband after he informed her precisely of his legal rights. He could drag her out of Adam Manchester's very house—in the unlikely event she got that far. No one could shelter a runaway wife if her husband wanted her back. And Rafael had made it clear that he did want her, at least physically. Under the law, she had no more say in her life than did a Congo slave.

In spite of her hurt and resentment at Rafael's high-handedness, Deborah desperately wanted her relationship with her husband to return to what it had been when they were first married. They must find a way to recapture the magic, the love.

A child might bring us close, she thought wistfully. However, even in that most basic duty Deborah was proving an unsatisfactory Creole wife. Rafael made love to her every night, yet she did not quicken. *Perhaps I'm barren,* she thought sadly, then forced the disquieting thought from her mind as she walked down the long hall.

When she entered the parlor, Rafael saluted her coolly by raising his crystal glass of sherry the tiniest bit, then sipping it as he watched her with brooding midnight eyes. "Your gown is superb," he said with the voice of a connoisseur. A small smile tipped his lips as he watched her flush at his inspection, which lingered overlong on her décolletage. He took her arm proprietarily and said, "Shall we go, my love?"

When they arrived at the opera house, Orleans Street between Bourbon and Royal was jammed with vehicles and pedestrians, everyone splendidly attired in their finery for the beginning of the New Orleans social season. Because of the press of carriages, the Flamencos had to wait their turn to pull up the short block in front of the theater.

Since it had been a dry fall, the streets were mercifully free of mud and easily traversable. A number of elegantly dressed Free People of Color were making their way along the street to the special theater entrance reserved for them. The second tier of the Orleans had been their exclusive domain for many years and no white would ever have intruded. The separation of colored and white by floors comprised a racial layer cake with many a wealthy Creole gentleman seated on the first floor with his white family, while his quadroon or octoroon family sat directly above him.

It was a warm evening and the Flamencos had taken an open carriage, affording them an excellent view of the kaleidoscope of humanity on its way to the gala. Looking out over the press of pedestrians, Celine said, "Some of the costumes for tonight's performance came directly from Paris, so Madame du May says. The lead soprano—" She stopped in mid-sentence and emitted a small, quickly stifled gasp as she turned her head and fanned herself furiously. Claude coughed and initiated a rather inane discussion with Rafael about the sugar harvest.

Sensing the undercurrent, Deborah's eyes scanned the crowd her mother-in-law had been surveying. The sight of two young men, elegantly dressed and startlingly handsome, riveted her to the carriage seat. If she had thought Georges Beaurivage resembled her husband, the two tall, slim men passing on the opposite site of the narrow street were his doubles—and they were most obviously Free Men of Color! With a sinking sensation, Deborah realized that the older woman they escorted was the source of Celine's upset. The quadroon was tall and slim, youthful looking but probably past forty. Her tawny skin was clear, her aquiline features strong and flawless. Beautiful gold coin eyes flashed as she laughed lightly at a riposte from one of the young men. The trio swept inside the theater, oblivious to the Flamenco carriage.

Intuition told Deborah that the sophisticated woman was the mother of those two young men; obviously Claude Flamenco was their father. *Why am I so shocked*, she thought to herself, feeling Rafael's eyes on her.

She had not lived in New Orleans for nearly eight months without learning about the demimonde and the shadow world of second families fathered by wealthy Creole gentlemen. A seasoned roué such as Claude Flamenco would certainly partake of such fleshly pleasures. Rafael had half brothers, the additional sons that Celine had been unable to give Claude. But they were sons who could not carry on the Flamenco name. A great many things were now beginning to make sense to Deborah—the underlying tension between Claude and Celine and the way Lenore had aways avoided the subject of her father's overnight absences. Deborah tried to stop the logical progression of her thoughts, which moved from Claude to Rafael.

He must not have a beautiful young quadroon. I'm not an unresponsive, frivolous wife like Celine. I must hold his interest! Surely all he had done since they were married was visit some of the elegant bordellos in the city when he was displeased with her, nothing more binding—certainly not another family. After all, he was only twenty-two years old!

Numbly, she took her husband's hand and allowed him to assist her down from the carriage at the front door of the theater. Celine's chatter resumed with forced brightness. For the first time, Deborah felt a stirring of pity for her mother-in-law.

Rafael swore to himself as he watched Deborah's face pale and freeze when she saw Damon and Paul, then their mother. She knows, damn! He cursed Flamenco heredity that always seemed to make the males in the mirror image of their fathers, regardless of who the mothers might be. If only she understood Creole social conventions. He laughed bitterly to himself. If only she were a proper Creole wife.

When he felt her trembling, he wished that he did not love her so obsessively.

"All right, out with it—what's upset you so, Deborah? You're pale and jumpy as a cat." Lenore sat pouring tea in her parlor while her sister-in-law fidgeted. They spoke English, as they did on all Deborah's visits, since Lenore insisted on perfecting her fluency in her husband's native tongue.

"I have a question to ask you, Lenore. One no proper Creole lady would ever ask." Deborah took a cup from Lenore and downed several sips of the hot, spicy beverage to fortify her courage.

A warning look came into Lenore's calm blue eyes. "Why is it I feel this might be a question better left unanswered?"

"I have to know. I haven't been able to sleep since I saw them three nights ago at the opera. Oh, Lenore, they look exactly like Rafael, both of them!"

Lenore set her cup down. "I take it you saw two of Rafael's half brothers," she said gently.

"Two? You mean there are more?"

"Four. Sophie gave Papa all the sons Mama could not."

Deborah almost dropped her cup. "How can you be so—so calm about it? How can you accept such behavior from your own father?"

"I grew up with it, Deborah. Although it's never spoken of, we know. We overhear servants' gossip, whispers at the opera, we see. We're just supposed to *pretend* we don't know—or care," she finished bitterly. "I love my father, but . . ."

Deborah picked up her sister-in-law's unfinished thought. "You would never want to marry a man like him—or like your brother."

Placing her arm around Deborah's shoulder, Lenore said, "I only meant that I can love Papa without excusing his behavior. And I know that Mama never . . ." She flushed and continued. "Well, she never enjoyed his attentions. I actually think she was glad when he went elsewhere."

"How can any woman want her husband to give another woman children? To have another family—a divided loyalty?"

Lenore took a deep breath, realizing she must prepare her vulnerable sister-in-law for the inevitable. "I remember when I first found out about our half brothers—I was twelve years old. I went to the market with Wilma and several other servants. Tonette and I were just children, more ignored than anything else. We slipped off to watch the glass blowers while the older servants made their purchases. I came back sooner than expected, I guess. Strange, how a child can sense when to keep silent, knowing she's hearing something forbidden. Wilma and the stall-keepers were speculating as to whether Sophie or Mama would sooner have another of Papa's babies. I'd grown up knowing about the *placées*, but I'd never connected such a practice with my papa. When I got home, I ran sobbing to find Mama and begged her to tell me they were lying. I'll never forget her face. For the first time I could remember, she didn't cosset me. She took me into her sitting room and closed the door. Then she began to explain some things to me, things she coldly told me would never be mentioned again. And, she was right. She never again spoke of Sophie and I certainly never tried to bring up the subject!"

"But you've heard other gossip?" Deborah asked. "Some of it more recent?"

Lenore sighed, "I suppose you'll pursue this until you have all the answers, won't you? No matter how painful."

"No matter how painful," Deborah echoed, bracing herself. "Like father, like son. Perhaps I always knew, ever since the first time we quarreled and he spent the night away from me. Who is she, Lenore?"

"Her name is Lily Duvall, an octoroon. Papa made the arrangement for Rafael when he was sixteen."

"Sixteen! He was only a boy!" Deborah cried in outrage, infuriated with her depraved father-in-law.

Lenore smiled sadly. "The same age at which *Granpere* Flamenco made a similar arrangement for his son."

Deborah felt herself growing dizzy and struggled to regain her calm. "Are there any children?" Her voice sounded flat and dead.

Lenore shrugged helplessly. "I don't know."

"Have you ever seen her?" Why this self-torturing need to know everything? She couldn't seem to stop herself.

Lenore said firmly, "Deborah, nothing's to be gained by ripping yourself apart this way. The arrangement was made over seven years ago, but Rafael still resisted marrying a Creole girl despite our parents' pressure. He married you. He loves you. Build on that. Forget Lily—make *him* forget Lily. It's not unheard of for a Creole man to pension off his mistress after making a happy marriage. Only..." She paused here and placed a hand over Deborah's cold clenched fist. "Don't force the issue and confront him. I know his Flamenco pride. He won't stand for that."

Deborah's eyes darkened in anguish. "Pride, it seems, is a luxury reserved only for the male of the species." She rose and reached for her reticule. "Thank you, Lenore, for telling me the truth and for being my friend."

"Only remember, my brother does love you."

My brother does love you. The words echoed over and over in Deborah's mind. Creole men sometimes pensioned off mistresses. It was possible that if Rafael loved her enough, he would do so, too. She must win him in the oldest way a woman ever won a man, with her body, using the same sensual skills that his beautiful mistress used.

Deborah soaked in a violet scented bath while Tonette rinsed her hair with rainwater and toweled it dry. If I've gotten used to the constant ministrations of slaves, I must be adapting to Creole life, she mused as she eyed the black silk peignoir laid out across the bed.

Rafael was home from his evening of shooting at the river, even now bathing in preparation for going to bed. *Bed.* She could hear the splashing of water next door and knew he would enter in a few moments with his late-night cognac in hand. He would expect to find her trembling on her side of their big bed, feigning sleep, hoping he would leave her in peace for one night. That was how it had been these past months. But it would be different tonight.

Slipping from the silken embrace of the oiled water, she let Tonette wrap a towel around her slim body and dismissed the girl with thanks. Then she brushed her hair to crackling splendor. When she slid the silky gown over her shoulders, she felt her pulse begin to race.

My God, it shows everything, she thought with a small gasp as she ran her hands down her body's curves and hollows. Quickly she pulled on the matching black robe, tied the belt, then arranged the lacy ruffles around her throat.

A touch of violet perfume and—the door opened. Rafael stood very still, silhouetted in the dim light from his dressing room. He was wearing only a blue velvet robe, carelessly belted at his narrow waist. His face was shadowed, but his black eyes glowed like coals.

Boldly walking across the floor to him, she reached up and took the snifter of cognac from his hand. She deliberately turned it to place her mouth where his had been and then took a sip of the fiery liquor. When she handed it back to him, she looked into his face but could not read it except for the blaze of desire so obviously written across it. Taking his hand, she led him to the bed.

Nervously, Deborah reached up and slipped her arms around his neck. "Am I too bold for a proper Creole wife?"

"No more than I want you to be," he murmured just before he devoured her lips in a searing kiss.

She returned his fire with her own, opening to him, entwining her tongue with his as he had taught her, doing everything he had taught her, pressing her body closer to his and undulating her hips against his. When she slipped her hands inside his robe and ran the palms down his shoulders, sliding the robe off them, he groaned and reached up to unfasten the lace covering her breasts.

"Let me," she whispered and slowly slipped off the frilly outer layer of the peignoir.

He reached up and touched her proudly upthrust breasts as she unfastened his belt and pulled the robe completely off him, then stepped back to admire his dark male beauty as he stood naked, his skin still warm and damp from his bath. Her palms were irresistibly drawn to rub soft, caressing patterns in the thick hair on his chest and follow it downward until she reached his pulsing shaft. When she took it boldly in her hands, he groaned again.

"Better slow down, *cherie*, or I won't be able to wait for you." He knelt and lifted the hem of the sheer gown. Its whispering black silk rippled softly as he peeled it slowly upward, revealing her long, sleek legs and softly rounded hips, gleaming like cream in the dim light.

"The gown is beautiful, but not nearly as beautiful as the woman under it," he breathed as he tossed the filmy garment on the floor. "All silver and ivory, my pale, perfect Moon Flower."

Deborah pulled him with her onto the bed, her hands busily caressing while her lips sought his. Breathlessly, she broke the kiss at last and rained swift, sweet nibbles and bites over the hard muscles of his neck and shoulder, then down his chest and lower. When she neared his pulsing shaft, she slowed, feeling it must be natural to kiss him there, too, but her courage failed her.

Sensing her reticence, Rafael whispered, "Let me show you, *cherie*." With that he sat up and pressed her down onto the sheets. When his hands pushed her thighs apart and held her firmly spread-eagled, she stiffened in alarm. But when the warmth of his mouth moved across her belly and then began to caress around the pale, silvery curls between her legs, she discovered that her body had a will of its own. She arched up and cried out in shocked pleasure as he continued, licking and suckling ever so softly. Slowly and evenly he plied his caresses, tasting the heady essence of her, feeling the delicate tissues swell and pulse in ecstasy.

Deborah writhed in a haze of passion, unconsciously digging her fingers into the curly black hair of his head, until a series of exquisite, blinding contractions released her from sweet, sweet torment. She lay replete, panting softly to catch her breath.

Rafael raised his head and placed several soft, quick kisses on her inner thighs and belly, then levered himself up to lie alongside her and hold her in his arms. His breath was warm on her face as he whispered, "That is how it's done, Deborah." He kissed her lips softly.

"You taste of me," she said in a breathless voice. "Now let me taste you." He rolled onto his back, allowing her to trail soft kisses down his chest and belly. This time she did not hesitate as her lips approached his staff, which was rigidly hard with unspent passion. As her long, silver hair fell like a waterfall between his legs, she slowly took him in her mouth and began to emulate the soft, suckling pressure on him that he had used with such devastatingly delightful effect on her. He thrust his hips up and tangled his hands in her hair as he guided her to rougher, longer strokes. She gladly accommodated him, feeling a primitive thrill of power from knowing she could please him this way, as he had pleased her. Suddenly, his fists clenched and his whole body shuddered in a swift, beautiful explosion.

Rafael lay dazed with pleasure and amazement as he felt his wife's lithe silky body slide up to lie beside him. Remembering Lily's question about whether his wife could do what she did for him, he almost chuckled aloud. Instead, he said, "Deborah, *cherie*, you are a continuous surprise . . . and delight." He punctuated his words with kisses to her nose and eyes, then her mouth.

"I—I wanted to please you," she said hesitantly.

"Do you think, after that, that you failed?" he asked with mock severity.

"I was awfully bold for a proper Creole wife," she replied.

He laughed then, a rich, deep rumble, and said, "Or for a proper *Boston* wife, either, but I want you like this, Deborah. Don't let us lose this closeness, *mon coeur*, not ever."

"Not ever," she echoed.

Chapter 14

January 1836 arrived with rain and fog, but it was mild and warm even as New Orleans winters went. The weather was the least of Lily Duvall's concerns. Rafael had sent a note in mid-December requesting to see Melanie for Christmas. When he visited Lily a week later she had informed him that she did not want the child traveling in winter and had not sent word to her mother to bring Melanie. Rafael had coldly informed her that he would send his daughter's presents to St. Louis by post. Hers had arrived the same way. For the first time in seven years, Rafael had not visited her over the holiday. She was bereft and angry.

"As if he has come that often in the past months anyway," she muttered as she paced in the empty parlor. In truth, since he had returned home last spring with that damnable Yankee bride, he had neglected Lily. For a while through the summer he had resumed his attentions to her, but since October he had made scarcely half a dozen visits. *And none at Christmas!* Lavish gifts, yes, but he gave nothing of himself. Would he pension her off? She shuddered. She must recapture his interest. No other mistress or illicit amour held his fancy. Her servants had carefully checked this on the slaves' grapevine, which was infallible when it came to such matters. Her enemy was clearly Deborah Flamenco, no other.

But what could she do? How could she fight a white woman who had position, wealth, power—her lover's name? On the few occasions he had deigned to visit her lately, Rafael had seemed more interested in reports of Melanie's schooling than in bedding his seductive mistress. How could a white lady hold him in that way—compete with Lily and all her carefully nurtured courtesan's skills?

When Lily had first sent her servants to spy on Rafael's bride, they had said she was thin and tall, purple-eyed and silver-haired, with skin as white as a fish. Deborah had sounded unattractive and strange. The unflattering description had satisfied Lily's vanity at the time, which was exactly what her slaves had intended. Now, with Rafael's interest so obviously held by this unlikely seductress from Boston, Lily wanted to see her rival firsthand. But how? She might go to the opera and watch for Deborah, but Rafael would be furious if he caught her. No, it must be somewhere when he would not be present. But where?

Then she remembered the scandalously juicy gossip about Madame Flamenco's penchant for accompanying the household slaves to the public market, actually grubbing about in the oyster bins. Rafael had purchased Lily ample domestic help so that she need not bother with the mundane chores of marketing. Now, however, she suddenly found herself desirous of making a personal selection of Adolfo's shrimp.

Melanie must also be brought home. Their child was one way to bring Rafael to her. She sat down at her escritoire to compose a letter to her mother.

Deborah felt the cold morning air hit her as she threw back the covers on their warm bed. Rafael rolled over and grasped a slim wrist and planted a kiss on the inside of it. With a sleepy, languorous expression on his face, he said, "Why arise so early, *cherie*? We were awake late last night."

She pinkened at his subtle reference to their lovemaking the preceding evening. "It's marketing day and I promised Wilma I'd help her haggle with the German sausage maker."

He rolled his eyes in mock exasperation, and lay back on the bed. "Well, good luck, foolish wife. *I* plan to sleep another hour, then attend a most diverting horse race, if the weather holds. There will be ladies present. Want to join me?"

She still found it difficult to accept his indolent life-style but was slowly becoming resigned to it. Grateful for his invitation, she replied, "I'm sorry, darling, but I already promised the du Mays that I'd have luncheon with them." It was tacitly understood by both of them that Mrs. Armstrong would also be a guest of Anna du May. Her eyes pleaded understanding for her covert friendship with the disowned Flamenco daughter.

He shrugged philosophically and said, "If you've already given your word, you cannot break it." It was as near as Rafael could go to giving permission for his wife's and sister's friendship.

As she and Wilma rode in the back of the large wagon to the bustling market, Deborah mulled over her ever-shifting relationship with Rafael. Her attempt to win him away from his mistress seemed to be working. He was seldom gone overnight anymore and his attentions to her were almost the same as they had been on their honeymoon. Although he spent fewer nights away from her bed, he still did so on occasion, and he still refused to explain his absence. Just like Claude, she thought bitterly. But I'm not like Celine. It isn't fair!

"Whut yo frettin' 'bout, Miz Debra?" Wilma's round black face creased in a frown. "Not still worryin' 'bout babies, is yo? Be happenin' by 'n by. Doan be givin' up, thas all."

Deborah replied in a flustered voice, "No, Wilma, I'm not worried about that. I know it takes time." She looked up at Guy, who was driving the wagon, but quickly realized that like all the other Flamenco slaves, he spoke only French. She and Wilma could have a private conversation. There was a question she wanted to ask of the kindly older woman, who was the only other person in the Flamenco household not born into Creole culture. "Wilma, do you think—that is . . ." She stuttered to a halt, mortified at how to ask such an indelicate thing.

"Whut yo be wantin' ta know? 'Bout birthin' babies?" Her face split in a broad grin now. "Doan be listenin' ta Miz Celine. It be easy."

"Oh, it's not that, Wilma. I just wondered when a woman gets pregnant"—she paused and reddened again—"well, she gets fat and unattractive . . . I don't even know if she can . . . I mean, would it hurt the baby if . . ."

Wilma nodded in dawning understanding. Small wonder the mistress feared, with a handsome devil of a husband who had half the women in New Orleans at his beck and call. Smiling, she reassured the young woman. "No, Miz Debra. It be fine foah ever'one—mama, papa, 'n baby. Doan fret. Ya jist gits yoself in a family way 'n keeps on doin' it!" She stopped for a minute and then asked, "Be thinkin' yo might have somethin' ta tell Massah Rafael?"

"I—I'm not sure yet. I've only missed once, and I want to be positive." *I also want him to desire me while I'm pregnant.*

With these thoughts whirling around in her mind, Deborah bargained half-heartedly with the German butcher. She could see Wilma watching her speculatively as she paid too much for the spicy sausage. Flustered, she said, "Here, you take these and then go down to the vegetable stalls. I'll get the oysters from Adolfo and meet you there."

Ordinarily, Deborah loved the sights and smells of the market. Its cosmopolitan bustle was balm to her soul, hearing German, Italian and English spoken. At times she thought if she heard one more word of French she'd scream. At least she had persuaded Rafael to use English when they were alone together, a major concession to her, she had to admit. "Everything in my life centers around Rafael, damn him! If only I didn't love him so much," she muttered.

As she perused the shrimp and oyster bins, Deborah became uncomfortably aware that she was being watched. Perhaps she should not have sent Guy with Wilma, she thought in annoyance, turning to give a cold, withering stare to another insolent Creole roué as she had to do so frequently. When she saw who was staring at her, she froze.

The most beautiful Woman of Color she had ever seen stood not twenty feet from her. She was tiny and voluptuous with delicate bone structure and regal bearing. Lustrous raven hair was swept high into a magnificent coil on top of her head. The fathomless gold eyes were enormous, fringed with thick lashes. They radiated hate.

Deborah almost recoiled from the venomous look Lily Duvall gave her, but her shock at the woman's nerve was compounded when her eyes caught and held at Lily's throat. Her long, lacquered nails stroked the gleaming patina of an ivory necklace—a unique, heavy piece of scrimshaw that Deborah instantly recognized. The matching earrings swayed gently from her tiny earlobes. *It's the necklace and earring set I found in Rafael's valise on shipboard!* At last the mystery of what he'd done with it was solved.

Lily had watched the beautiful silver blonde walking through the market stalls. She was tall for a woman, but then Rafael was tall for a man. Although she refused to admit it, Lily knew her slaves had lied. The Yankee's large violet eyes were thickly fringed with dark gold lashes and her patrician bone structure was exquisite. A gently curving figure was concealed in the rather plain cotton dress, but Lily knew it was a good one. Nothing, however, compared with the hair—like sun and moon blazing and shimmering as she moved. Lily had never seen hair that color. Here was a far more dangerous rival than she could have ever conjured up in her worst nightmare.

When she noted the way Deborah's face paled as her eyes traveled from the necklace to the earrings, Lily suddenly realized that Deborah must recognized the set. Yes! Rafael had said it was made by Boston whalers. His bride must have known he bought it. Now she knew for whom he bought it! Lily glided toward the statuesque form frozen at the oyster bin, saying nothing but daring much. As she strolled ever so slowly past her taller adversary, she stared at Deborah, taking in her uncoiffed hair and drab day dress with insolent assessment written plainly across her face.

Addressing her houseboy in a clear voice that carried back to Deborah, she said, ''Come along, Jules, I have better things to do than spend my day in the market.''

She knew the message she had sent to Rafael would bring him to Rampart Street that evening. Melanie would arrive from St. Louis today.

Rafael swore as he scanned the note, then tore it up and tossed it carelessly into the fireplace. ''Bad enough Deborah's acting wounded and morose all afternoon, refusing to tell me what's wrong, now this!''

Claude watched his long-legged son eat up the carpet with his agitated pacing. He knew the note must be from

Lily. "After a brief truce, it seems you and your 'bride' have once more drawn the battle lines," he said with his usual sarcasm. "I had hoped before she once more drove you to quit her bed you might at least get her breeding."

Rafael looked distractedly at his father, lounging with indolent ease in his favorite chair. "Papa, I have to go out tonight. Let matters between Deborah and me remain private."

"You go to Lily." The old man said it without inflecting a question. He knew how a man could need solace from a cold wife.

"I go to see my daughter." He swore and finished off his brandy, preparing to leave the room.

"Better look to legal heirs, not those kissed by the tar brush, Rafael," the old man said dryly.

Pausing with his hand on the door, his son quirked one brow and said, "I may already have taken care of that matter, too. I suspect my wife's ill humor and recent bouts of morning indisposition may indicate she has news for us—in her own good time." With that surprising announcement he left the old man to nurse his brandy alone.

In fact, Rafael only hoped that what he had said was true. Deborah had been moody for the past several weeks and he knew that she had been sick yesterday morning, but he was far from certain she was *enciente*. He had planned to wait her out instead of questioning her directly, not wanting to make her feel she was only a brood mare. He had hurt her grievously last summer, telling her she had a duty to give his family heirs. As much as he did want children with her, he had not really meant it the way anger had made it come out.

After she had tried to leave him, he had admitted to himself that he could not imagine life without her. *I love her too much ever to give her up*, he thought grimly as he swung onto his big black stallion at the rear entrance of their quarters. *Annulment, indeed*, he snorted to himself, arrogantly assured he'd keep what was his.

Deborah sat pressed against the side of the coach with her heart in her throat. Huddled in the shadows, her bright hair hidden beneath a dark veil, she watched Rafael ride away from the house, then leaned out and instructed the hackman, "That's the man. Follow him and I'll pay you as we agreed."

* * *

The following morning, Deborah arose leaden-eyed and aching but determined to look her best for the forthcoming confrontation. She rang for Tonette and had a hot bath drawn. All had gone smoothly last night. She knew where Lily lived.

When the carriage pulled up in front of the small white house on Rampart Street, it was nearly noon. Deborah checked her appearance once more, smoothing her carefully coiled hair with one gloved hand. She had dressed in her best new suit of deep violet velvet and wore her amethyst jewelry. The necklace and earrings were ornately elegant and would put the scrimshaw set to shame. *Let me look every inch the part of a Flamenco lady*, she thought grimly. After all, she was the wife, the one with legal rights as well as moral ones!

"Good day, *Mademoiselle* Duvall," Deborah stressed the unmarried title with cool disdain, then swept past Rafael's petite mistress into the expensively cluttered parlor. Lily stared at her in round-eyed wonder.

Her huge gold eyes quickly slitted, shifting from shock to fury. With one hand on her fuchsia silk robe, Lily returned Deborah's assessing air. Her robe was carelessly belted with an expanse of tawny cleavage spilling bountifully from its confines. Her hair was spread around her shoulders like a tangled mantle of blue black satin.

Artlessly, she pushed the dark mass from her eyes and flung it backward. "You have dared too much, Yankee. This is my home. You have no business here," she snapped.

"No, you're the one who has the 'business' here," Deborah returned. "But that's going to change—or at least your customer is going to change." She stopped and looked down at the tiny woman in morning dishabille, trying not to think of how her hair had become so mussed and her eyes had received their heavy-lidded look of satiety.

"And just how do you plan to accomplish this feat?" Lily taunted scornfully. "Forbid Rafael my bed? Or deny him yours if he refuses? I'd fear to push it, Yankee. You're no match for me when it comes to pleasuring a man." Lily looked like a cream-fed cat, and Deborah wanted to claw her eyes out.

Instead the "Yankee" hid her balled up fists in the heavy folds of her dress and said, "I didn't come to trade bedroom recipes. My husband is well enough pleased with me that way, and, Lily, he is *my* husband, the father of my child."

At Lily's sharp intake of breath, Deborah paused to look directly into her fathomless eyes. "I know Claude Flamenco made an arrangement with you long before Rafael and I married. Now I'm willing to make a generous settlement on you. I can send you to the Caribbean . . . or France if you wish. You can love and marry there with no color bar to stigmatize you. But I want you out of my husband's life and his child's life."

Lily let her finish her speech, half-curious to know how much the brazen foreigner might offer her. She'd heard the Yankee's father was rich. Still, it would never be enough. With a cunning smile, she walked over to the escritoire and picked up a daguerreotype. "*Your* child's life is not the only one to be considered," she said cryptically. "There is also the matter of Rafael's other children—my children."

Deborah felt her heart freeze in her breast as Lily thrust the portrait of a beautiful little girl and baby boy into her nerveless fingers. Their luminous eyes stared out, set in classically sculpted Flamenco faces.

"Melanie will be six in the spring," she said triumphantly, watching the color drain from Deborah's face.

Six. He fathered a child when he was only sixteen! Swallowing, Deborah said with amazing steadiness, "I will, of course, provide the best education available on the Continent for your children." One look at Lily's implacable face banished all her hopes.

"Melanie's father has already provided handsomely for her education. In fact, he—"

Suddenly, the backdoor burst open and a small girl with bouncing black curls darted into the room. Her piquant face was wreathed in smiles and she was expensively dressed in a red velvet coat and gleaming black patent shoes. The rosy glow of outdoor chill still blushed her cheeks as she stopped short and curtsied at the strange lady in her mother's parlor,

"Excuse me, Mother. Papa wanted to know—"

"Melanie, please leave us!" Lily snapped, then looked past the child nervously. "Where is Morine? Go find her and have her take you to the market."

Melanie bobbed another uncertain curtsy and started to back out of the room, nearly colliding with her father.

"Lily, why aren't you dressed yet?" Rafael's voice was annoyed as he caught sight of his mistress standing near the bedroom door, still clad in her robe. Then, when he stepped into the parlor, his gaze instantly shifted from Lily to Deborah—and froze in incredulity. "What in the name of all reason and sanity are you doing here?"

"Morine, take Mellie for a walk," he commanded the young servant girl standing in the door. He scooped up his frightened daughter and gave her a quick hug of reassurance, then transferred her into the arms of the slave.

Deborah watched the child's sad little face vanish as Morine whisked her away. The pain tore at her, clawing her insides apart. Why had she ever come? What madness to presume she could beat this insidious system. She felt the room whirling and struggled to breathe.

Lily was screaming something and Deborah forced herself to listen, not daring to face the black fury on her husband's face. All traces of love and gentleness had vanished from its austere planes when his daughter had left the room.

"She threatened me! She told me she was going to make you give me up, Rafael. Just because she's pregnant doesn't mean you will desert us, does it?" Lily was certain his Creole arrogance would never stand such a blow.

"That's a lie," Deborah gasped weakly, but her husband whirled on her with such fury that his look silenced her.

"So, you *are enciente*," he said. "I suspected as much, but it does *not* give you license for this disgusting behavior. If you ever again dare interfere in matters that don't concern you, I'll lock you in your apartment under guard."

"Matters that don't concern me!" Deborah cried. Pain at seeing his daughter gave way to rage over his betrayal.

"You keep a complete, separate family like a—a Muslim pasha and expect me to pretend they don't exist!"

"Madame, either control yourself and leave here like a lady—on second thought, that's not possible. No lady would ever create this situation. Just walk out that door, get in the carriage, and wait for me."

"Wait for you! It seems to me, *cheri*, I spend a great deal of my life waiting for you, while you're out philandering." Scathing sarcasm hid her anguish. "Your mother may take it—and *she* may too"—Deborah turned a contemptuous glare on Lily—"but *I will not!*"

With an obscene oath Rafael reached out and seized Deborah's wrist, intent on dragging her to the front door.

"Don't you ever again put your filthy adulterous hands on me!" She wrenched free, unable to bear his touch.

"I'll do whatever I wish with you—touch you, bed you, plant my seed in you. You're my wife, God help us both!" With that he threw her over his shoulder like a sack of rice, just as he had threatened to do that day at the Dueling Oaks.

As she kicked and writhed, he marched stiffly to the door, treating his thrashing burden as if she weighed nothing. Lily quickly opened the door and let them out. Her head was bowed in silence but her downcast eyes glowed with triumph.

Around the corner of the house, Melanie hid, listening to the exchange and watching her papa carrying the beautiful lady to the waiting carriage. If she was his wife, then what was her mother?

Chapter 15

"I helped you once. Now I'm asking you to help me," Deborah said simply to Caleb Armstrong as she sat across from him in his parlor.

Lenore stood behind Deborah, her hand resting supportively

on her friend's shoulder. Looking at the two women, Caleb smiled despite the sadness of the situation. "And I suppose she's persuaded you to help her?" he asked his wife.

"I tried to dissuade her, Caleb. It's dangerous and I know she'll be lonely, but I can understand how she feels. I'd never share you with another woman." She reddened at her bold statement.

"My mind is made up, Caleb. With or without your help, I'm leaving Rafael." Deborah fought her urge to cry.

Caleb said in amazement, "I can't believe the man would choose to destroy a loving marriage over a mistress. He should provide for her children, of course, but end it with Lily Duvall."

"Child," Lenore corrected softly. "Only the girl is left alive. The boy died in the yellow fever epidemic three years ago."

"You knew about them all along," Deborah accused.

Lenore's eyes softened. "What was to be gained by telling you? I never dreamed you'd confront her. What made you do something so reckless?"

Deborah fidgeted and looked down. She had not told Lenore and Caleb that she was pregnant, although in the past weeks since her confrontation with Lily, she had missed her second monthly. There was no doubt now; but if they knew of her condition, they would never help her escape. "I asked her to leave New Orleans—I offered to pay her way to France and settle some money on her. My father . . ." she paused in mortification, remembering how Adam Manchester had warned her about marrying Rafael, "my father placed a great deal of money in my name in a bank here when we married. Rafael doesn't know about it."

"I take it Lily refused your offer," Caleb said grimly.

Wordlessly she nodded. "The marriage is over, Caleb." She cringed, remembering the cold, shuttered look on Rafael's face when he answered her tearful pleas to pension off the beautiful octoroon.

"She has her place in my life and you have yours. Your position is certainly better," he had said with finality.

"Rafael plans to keep her as he always has and I'm to pretend his other family doesn't exist. I won't share him!" She stood up abruptly. "The emigrant party leaves March first. I plan to be with them even if I have to make the arrangements myself."

"But, Deborah, Texas! It's so wild and dangerous. Why can't you return to Boston instead? I know your father would take you in." Lenore shuddered at the thought of the violent land across the Sabine River.

"My father couldn't stop Rafael if he came and dragged me out of his own home," Deborah replied bleakly. "I know the law and I know what my husband is capable of. If my father tried to stop him—oh, Lenore, Rafael might hurt him."

Caleb cleared his throat as he watched Lenore blanch. Her brother was as violent as she was gentle. "Deborah's right, darling. The law is on Rafael's side. If he wants to, he can force her to live with him."

"Only if he can find me," Deborah said grimly.

"But then, why not some other eastern city—or Europe?" Lenore was horrified at Deborah's scheme to lose herself in the throngs of people emigrating to Texas.

"You could be caught in the middle of a war, Deborah," Caleb said. "I know General Cos surrendered in December and the Texians think they'll win autonomy, but they're a long way from being free of Santa Anna. Sam Houston knows El Presidente won't give up."

"I read that *General* Houston will whip Santa Anna the minute he dares show his face in Texas," Deborah responded. In fact, she could not wait for the dust to clear in Texas any more than she could wait to take a ship for Europe. By the time anything like that could be arranged, her pregnancy would be obvious and she wouldn't be able to travel. Then Rafael would have control of their child and he would never give it up. No, she must vanish now, before he could raise another generation of selfish Flamenco men or doomed Flamenco women. "I want to go with the Pettyjohn party to Texas, Caleb. Will you arrange it or not?"

With a sigh, Caleb relented.

Rafael stood in the bedroom, beside Deborah's dressing table, anger and fright suffusing his whole body. He trembled as he read Deborah's carefully worded letter.

Rafael:
When you find this I shall be gone. I ask nothing from our ill-fated marriage, neither your name nor your wealth, since you could not give me your love. Follow your parents' wishes and find a proper Creole girl to marry after you have secured an annulment. Everyone will be happier for it.

With regret,
Deborah Manchester

Cursing, he balled up the missive and began to throw it into the fire, then stopped. It might well contain the last words he would ever hear from her. He smoothed out the crumpled note and folded it, placing it in his coat pocket with trembling hands.

No. I swear I'll find you, Deborah Flamenco. No annulment, no other wife. Deborah Manchester, indeed!

"I can have this house searched, you know." The light in Rafael's eyes glowed like a cold black flame.

Caleb shrugged and waved his arm around the large entry hall. "Search. You need no warrant. Your wife isn't here, Rafael."

Lenore stood beside her tall Yankee, gazing at her brother with anguish written on her face, but Rafael realized with a sinking heart that it was the anguish of broken family ties, not fear of Deborah's discovery. His wife was not here. He knew it with a sudden gut intuition that both infuriated him and made him despair.

"You only win a round. I know you helped her book passage to Boston, but it won't do her or Adam Manchester any good. I'll drag her back!"

Lenore watched his retreating figure, feeling the pain of this parting even more than when he had left this house the night of her marriage.

"Well, this will buy Deborah some time to cover her trail," Caleb said.

"I only pray we did the right thing," his wife replied in a tear-choked voice.

The journey to Boston seemed so much longer than it had the preceding year. In the weeks since Deborah's disappearance, time had cooled Rafael's wrath. He considered how he would win her back. Despite his threat to the Armstrongs, he did not relish dragging an unwilling wife from her father's house and holding her virtual prisoner for the duration of her pregnancy. She might lose the child under such duress.

Rafael pondered his options. Perhaps the best thing was to stay in Boston for the duration of her confinement. She might be more secure in familiar surroundings. While dreading the idea of a New England winter, he had decided that might indeed be the way to prove his love for her. *Once she has a child to occupy her, she won't have time for worrying about Lily or Melanie.*

Adam Manchester had read his daughter's letter a hundred times, reliving her pain. All the worst he had feared and predicted had come to pass. Resting his head in his hands, he considered once more how he would deal with her husband. He knew, even if Deborah had not warned him, that a man like Rafael Flamenco would not be inclined to give up his wife and his heir without a fight.

Yet how to fight? Certainly the law would be on Rafael's side. More than anything, he longed to bring his daughter home, to see her safe and loved, her child loved and protected from the perfidy of the Flamenco family. But that was not to be. She was gone, off into the western wilderness, to Texas. Beyond that, she had told him nothing more specific for fear the information might somehow fall into Rafael's hands. *Thank God I was able to provide her with sufficient money to see her through, but in time that will be exhausted.*

His bitter musings were interrupted by a commotion in the hall. Hearing the strident voice of his butler and another with a thick French accent, Adam stiffened. "So, already he's arrived," he muttered grimly.

"You've wasted no time getting here. May I take it as a token of your concern for my daughter?" Adam's voice was laced with irony but surprisingly level.

Rafael turned his attention from the stiff butler to his father-in-law. He bowed formally.

"I've come to talk with my wife."

"Only talk with her, not bundle her off to your ancestral home forthwith?" Adam asked with one shaggy white brow arched.

Rafael smiled thinly. "In spite of what she may have told you, I do love my wife, monsieur, and I will not endanger either her or my child." He waited, poised like a fencer on the balls of his feet.

When Adam hesitated, he added softly, "You know I have the proper documents from your courts to see her by force if necessary. Which is it to be?"

The big Yankee seemed to wither before Rafael's cold black gaze. He looked suddenly old as he replied in a flat voice, "Neither." He motioned for his son-in-law to follow him into his study. Sitting down wearily, Adam slid Deborah's letter across the desk to Rafael and leaned back.

"It arrived two weeks ago, and I've been expecting you ever since. Do your worst, monsieur. I cannot produce your wife." Manchester's eyes narrowed as he watched Rafael's swarthy face pale.

The young man sat down suddenly in a large leather chair behind him and read his wife's long, pain-filled letter to her father.

He really is shaken, Adam thought. Finally, he said softly, "Search the house if it will make you rest easier. I've already dispatched operatives to search for her—checking every means of transportation out of New Orleans. Ocean-going vessels, upriver boats, emigrant parties, any and every way a woman could hope to lose herself heading west . . . but it's a big frontier . . .'' His words trailed off into hopeless silence.

"How could she do something so dangerous?'' Rafael's voice sounded more bewildered than angry now, all the silky assurance of earlier evaporated.

"She was desperate—desperate to free her son or daughter from your way of life, from the taint of corruption.'' Adama impaled Rafael with accusing blue eyes. "Go home to your mistress and tend to her children. I'll see to my daughter and my grandchild.''

Rafael stood up slowly. The rekindled anger coursing through him brought color back to his face. "You Yankee Puritans are always quick to cast the first stone. Or, more facile at covering your own vices.'' He turned and began to leave, pausing at the door only long enough to say quietly, "If she comes here my own operatives shall inform me. If I find her first, I'll inform you, a courtesy I somehow doubt you would reciprocate.''

The haggard, exhausted man who debarked in New Orleans harbor was a far cry from the self-assured youth who had set out a scant six weeks earlier in search of his wayward wife.

"I never believed I'd lose her, I guess,'' he said to Claude that night at dinner.

Celine scarcely looked up from her plate but said between dainty bites, "I could discuss with the bishop—''

"No!'' Rafael jumped up from the table and threw his napkin down. "When will you get it through your head! I will not dissolve my marriage. Deborah is my wife. She's carrying my child. There will be no annulment!''

Celine dropped her fork. "You never told me she was with child,'' his mother accused.

"All things considered, there was scarcely time,'' Rafael replied darkly. "I've wasted weeks while her trail grows cold. I think it's time to wring some truth out of my sister and her husband.''

Claude responded, "Nothing's to be gained by this, Rafael. That American will tell you nothing.''

"He may not, but my sister will. I don't believe Lenore would let my wife go through the dangers of a frontier emigration if she knew Deborah was pregnant.'' The more he had turned that thought over in his mind, the more convinced of it he became. He would learn the truth!

Texas! Deborah was finally here, although her first sight of land was less than promising. At the mouth of the Brazos River, the Gulf plain was marshy and flat, seeming to stretch into the skyline. The overcrowded schooner that brought the Pettyjohn party of settlers to the banks of the Brazos had been becalmed for over a week. The water supply had run low and the humid heat had made Deborah's head ache. She was seasick despite the stillness of the ocean.

Exhausted, Deborah trudged up the muddy riverbank, dragging her trunk behind her with minimal help from Mr. Pettyjohn's surly son Thad.

"You got books 'n sech in this here box? It sure weighs 'nough," he complained. Ever since she had rebuffed the lanky youth's unwelcome attentions on board ship, he had sulked.

"A few books, Mr. Pettyjohn, but mostly clothing," she replied wearily.

"I told ya ta call me Thad, *Deborah*," he said angrily, setting the trunk down abruptly in the mud.

"And I told you to call me Widow Kensington, *Mr.* Pettyjohn," she answered waspishly.

"Jist cuz you got learnin' 'n plan ta be a schoolmarm in San Felipe don't give ya th' right ta look down yer nose at me, Mrs. Boston Prim!" His florid face was flushed with anger despite the drizzly weather.

Deborah had a backache, an upset stomach, and was thoroughly out of patience with the twenty-year-old lout. "Your manners match your grammar, Mr. Pettyjohn."

"Well, ya cud learn me what's proper if ya wuz ta try," he said, glancing around to make sure his father and the other men weren't within earshot.

When he put one grimy hand on her arm, Deborah flung it away furiously. "What do I have to do to make it clear to you that your attentions are inappropriate and unwelcome?"

Ignoring her question, he grabbed a handful of silvery hair and pulled her suddenly into his arms. "If I was ta tell my pa ya made up ta me, ya bein' a lonely widder woman 'n all, he'd believe me. Put ya off th' train quick as ya cud blink."

"Why, you cheap blackmailer," Deborah hissed, twisting in an attempt to get free of his noisome breath as he tried to kiss her.

Their struggle was suddenly interrupted when a large, reddened hand yanked at Thad's collar roughly. "Mebbe yew should larn some manners afore yew go 'a courtin', youngun." The loud voice belonged to a woman as sturdy and rough as a Texas sycamore. She was dressed in plain black homespun and wore her graying brown hair in a snarled knot of braids across the top of her head.

"Why don't ya mind yer own business. Deborah here's my sweetheart 'n I'll tend ta her," Thad said peevishly, shrugging off the woman's hand and turning to pull Deborah to him once more.

The woman's wide face creased in a fearsome scowl as she fixed the offending youth with a fierce, brown-eyed glare. "Jeehosaphet! Ain't they any boys with manners in this land th' Lord niver knowed?" With that, she hoisted the thin youth by his armpits and sat him down several feet from Deborah. When he took a menacing step toward her, she stood her ground. "I'd do me a pretty considerable o' thinkin' afore I'd come closer, tadpole," she said as one hand produced a wicked-looking hunting knife from the voluminous folds of her wrinkled dress.

With a muttered oath the youth took a step backward and tripped over Deborah's trunk. While he lay sprawled in the mud, Deborah's rescuer reached down and plucked up the heavy luggage as if it weighed nothing.

"Name's Obedience Jones 'n I be a widder woman, too. Yew with th' Pettyjohn bunch?"

"Not anymore, I'm afraid," Deborah replied as she followed the Widow Jones up the slippery bank. "My name is Deborah Kensington and I do thank you for your help, Mrs. Jones."

"Jeehosaphet! Call me Obedience 'n don't fret none 'bout

thet boy. I seen his kind afore. All bluff 'n no guts. Where yew stayin'?''

Deborah shrugged helplessly. "Mrs. Pettyjohn had asked me to spend the night with their family, but after this, I suspect I might not be welcome.''

"Yew be welcome ta share my tent. Right this away,'' she said, never breaking stride or pausing to inquire if Deborah agreed to her offer of hospitality.

"You're very kind, M—Obedience,'' Deborah replied, following the big woman through the ooze to a crude shelter constructed of log poles and canvas.

"Ain't nothin' fancy, but it's dry,'' Obedience said as she ushered Deborah inside and deposited her trunk on the earthen floor. "Heerd th' commotion 'n thought yew might cud use a hand. I wuz fixin' ta eat afore thet. Pull up a crate 'n join in. Not as good as I kin cook with a proper oven, but it's hot.''

Obedience was better than her word. She served up crisp, steaming cornbread and sizzling smoked bacon chopped into a plate of savory beans. They sat amid a scattering of crates and boxes, which Obedience explained were supplies for her brother's boarding house in San Antonio.

"His wife 'n my husband, God rest their souls, both passed ta their reward 'bout th' same time. Seth needed a woman ta cook 'n clean 'n I needed a place ta hang my hat. Whut yew fixin' on doin' in Mr. Austin's colony?''

Deborah took a sip of fragrant black coffee as she framed her answer. When Caleb had signed her up for the journey to San Felipe, he had assured Mrs. Pettyjohn that she would be a welcome addition to the settlement as a schoolteacher. Of course, he did not know that in a few months her pregnancy would keep her from fulfilling her duties. Assuming her mother's maiden name, Deborah had also added the fabrication about being a widow to explain her condition when it became apparent to the rest of the settlers.

Uncertainly, she replied to Obedience, "I had planned to teach school. The settlers need teachers and I had a good education in Boston. Now, with all the trouble Thad Pettyjohn has made, well, they may not want me to continue on. I wish I had some other skills besides lettering and ciphering.

Here on the frontier, I'm afraid I'm pretty useless. Why, I can't even cook.''

Obedience's face creased in a gap-toothed grin. ''Jeehosaphet! Thet's easy 'nough fixed. I'll larn yew ta cook if'n yew show me how ta write my name. Niver had no chance fer larnin' in th' hill country—east Tennessee, thet is. How'd yew git so fer from Boston? Yer man bring ya West ta stake a claim on free land?''

Having made up her story before she left New Orleans, Deborah considered retelling it once more, but something in Obedience's shrewd, kindly face stopped her. ''Everyone here thinks my husbnad was a New England seaman who drowned when we came to Mobile, but . . .''

''But he warn't,'' Obedience supplied. ''If yew don't want ta talk 'bout it, shore 'nough ain't my way ta pry. Lots o' folks in Texas got them plenty more ta hide 'n yew'll ever have. Don't fret.'' With that she rose and began to clear off the dishes.

As she helped Obedience wash and dry the simple utensils, Deborah listened in fascination to the older woman's hair-raising tales about crossing the Tennessee wilderness in a wagon.

''Roughest part wuz when we tuk thet flatboat down th' Mississip. River pirates done fer Mr. Ryan.''

''Mr. Ryan?'' Deborah questioned.

''My second husband. That's five years ago. Met up with Mr. Jones in Arkansas three years back. We's on our way ta Texas when he up 'n tuk a fever. Always wuz a puny man.'' She shook her head. ''Neither o' em worth a hair on my first man's head—Jeb Freeman. Now there wuz a man. Jeehosaphet!''

Deborah was flabbergasted. ''You've had three husbands!'' *And I couldn't even manage one!*

''An' fixin' on findin' me a fourth,'' Obedience responded, unabashed. ''One with a strong back. A woman my size tends ta kinda overpower most men. Mr. Jones used ta say, Lord rest him, 'Obedience', says he, 'Niver was a woman so misnamed!' Jeehosaphet, I reckon it's true. I kin out-lift, out-plant, out-dig, outtalk, out-cuss, 'n outdrink most any man alive since 't Mr. Freeman wuz kilt.''

"Then why look for a fourth husband?" Deborah was overwhelmed.

"Men is purely th' most worthless creatures God ever put on this earth—'cept fer one thing, if'n ya take my meanin'." She gave Deborah as assessing gaze, then said, "Yep, I reckon yew do," as she observed the younger woman's heated blush. "Ain't nuthin' ta get flustered 'bout. Yew niver fixin' on remarryin'? Lots o' men in Texas lookin' fer a good woman."

Deborah studied her hands, then looked up into Obedience's clear brown eyes. "I can't remarry, Obedience. My husband isn't dead. I left him."

Obedience considered that for a moment, then said, "Figgered somethin' like thet. Still, if'n yew meet up with a likely gent whut'll treat yew better'n yore first man did, marry him! No one'll know th' difference."

The rains intensified over the next several days, confining the immigrants to their temporary lodgings while they waited for the Brazos River to be safe for their northward journey to San Felipe. Good as her word, Obedience gave Deborah some rudimentary instructions in cooking and Deborah showed her how to write her name—Obedience Leona Morton Freeman Ryan Jones. Considering all Obedience's surnames by marriage, Deborah did not expect her friend to master them before they had to part ways.

Thinking of saying good-bye saddened Deborah, for she had become very fond of the outspoken older woman. Many of the prim ladies in the Pettyjohn party shunned the loud Amazon, but Deborah found her honesty and friendliness refreshing.

After her brushes with Thad Pettyjohn, Thad's mother was incensed, believing her son's tale about how Deborah had led him on. A week later matters came to a head. Obedience could tell by Deborah's dejected walk that something was wrong when she returned from a meeting of the settlers. "Yew look like a wooden-legged man jist let out o' a room full o' termites. Whut happened?"

"The Pettyjohns have asked me to remain here when they leave for San Felipe next week. I'm trouble, it seems. A veritable Jezebel who tempts men to perdition." She sat down shakily on a barrel. "Where will I go? I can't return to New Orleans."

"Jeehosaphet! Thet's easy 'nough! My brother Seth's got him a big boardin' house 'n no women folk ta do fer it. Yew'll come ta Santone with me."

Chapter 16

By the time they arrived in the small town of Gonzales, Deborah was almost ready to flee to Boston and take her chances confronting Rafael. She had endured incessant bone-chilling rains and crude camps made by the trailside. She had slept on wet, rocky ground beneath Obedience's wagon and eaten the meager trail fare prepared hastily over sputtering fires. The fatigue and nausea that had plagued her since leaving New Orleans refused to abate.

Along the trail they enountered a trickle of emigrants who had heard rumors about a Mexican invasion in the west and had decided to flee east to safety. Just south of Gonzales they encountered a sprawling, unruly army camp, consisting of nearly four hundred men and a motley assortment of wives, children, and other civilians. They looked ragged, ill-fed, and poorly disciplined.

"This is the army that's going to defend Texas?" Deborah asked incredulously.

"Uniforms don't always make fer th' fightenest soldiers," was all Obedience replied.

In an attempt to cheer Deborah when they arrived in Gonzales, Obedience said, "Hot vittles'll shore taste fine after weevily hardtack. Ugh!" She made a grimace of disgust. Eyeing the jerry-built frame structure that served as a wayfarer's inn, she was not assured that her assessment of the place's food was accurate.

"It looks as if the roof leaks," Deborah said, echoing

Obedience's thoughts as she climbed down the wagon. "Forget the hot food—I want a hot bath!" She rubbed her aching rump with one hand and massaged her protesting stomach with the other.

"Thet disagreement o' th' bowels still troublin' yew?" Obedience's shrewd gaze took in her friend's actions as well as her pallor.

"Just too many hard biscuits," Deborah replied.

"Say, yore tender stomach 'n tuckered out feelins might'nt be cuz o' somethin' else, sides yore bein' a greenhorn?"

Deborah flushed and fidgeted, trying to decide if she should reveal her pregnancy to Obedience. "I—I don't want to be a burden, Obedience. I can do my share of the work—"

"Bein' in a family way ain't cause fer a woman ta be turned out ta pasture, Deborah," Obedience interrupted. "Yew git kinda cranky 'n all cuz yew cain't handle food so good 'n yore played out tired, but it passes in a few months. Leastways it did fer me, ever' time."

Deborah was taken aback. "Obedience, you never told me you had children! Oh! I hope I didn't bring up painful memories." She knew well the fearful infant mortality that claimed so many children on the frontier.

"Not so's I can complain, honey." Obedience's brown eyes softened. "Birthed three younguns ta Mr. Freeman. Got me two fine sons, all growed 'n married back in Tennessee. Might even be a grandma by now, but, 'course when I remarried 'n left, they wuz no way ta keep in touch. Always figgered on goin' back someday after I done good in Texas. Visit my daughter's grave 'n mebbe bring th' boys 'n their families back here. Now, with yew havin' a youngun, well I got me one o' them grandchildren fer sure here 'n now!"

All thoughts of ever leaving Texas and this gruff, dear woman were forgotten as Deborah hugged Obedience fiercely.

They had a passably decent meal at the inn. Deborah retired to the corn husk mattress she was to share with Obedience, while her friend braved the rain to see to their wagon. The two men they had hired in Brazoria to accompany them to San Antonio were rubbing down the team of mules.

Everyone is doing their share but me, she thought bleakly as she dropped off into an exhausted sleep. In fact that was far from true. She had insisted on paying Zebulon Moore and Ira Shroeder for acting as trail helpers and stock handlers. Both men carried Kentucky long rifles and were excellent shots, which afforded the women protection and assured them of fresh game on the seemingly endless trail.

If Deborah was "green from the States," she was a quick learner, insisting Zeb give her lessons loading and firing a rifle. She became almost as adept at that as she had in her culinary endeavors. Obedience promised as soon as they were settled in San Antonio that she would teach Deborah how to bake the lightest, most toothsome crusty bread west of the Mississippi River. Even now, Deborah's biscuits were fluffy and her cornbread crunchy. She dreamed of a vegetable garden.

The next evening their supper was interrupted suddenly when Zeb rushed in with some startling news.

"We got us company, folks," he announced to the group seated around the table. "General Houston hisself with Colonel Hockley 'n three men from Washington-on-the-Brazos. He's come to lead our militia. We got us a genuine declaration of independence!"

Marsh Plunket, owner of the inn, jumped up from the table, splashing a spoon in his corn mush. "Glory be, we're finally free o' them greaser sidewinders down south."

"Pears ta me," Obedience said shrewdly, "thet we'll be free only if'n General Houston can whup Santy Anny 'n save all them men at th' Alamo."

Deborah knew Obedience was thinking of her brother who was doubtless among the Alamo's defenders. He had long been a staunch Texas patriot.

"If'n thet fool Fannin'd get his fancy tail here like th' General ordered, they could march tomorrow," Zeb put in. "Yew shoulda heerd th' General cuss when he heerd Fannin 'n his men wuz still sittin in Goliad."

Everyone around the table chuckled, for Houston's colorful swearing was legendary. Deborah had read about the exploits of the brilliant politician who had been elected Governor of Tennessee before his thirty-fifth birthday, Andrew Jackson's hand-picked successor for the American presidency. Then after a marriage scandal he had quit politics to live among the Cherokee in the Mississippi wilderness. Houston resurfaced in Texas three years later where he became embroiled in the long constitutional battle that ultimately led to the Texian break with Mexico. Now he was taking command of the militia, including the ragtag volunteers milling about outside Gonzales.

After supper, Obedience and Deborah joined Marsh and Fannie Plunket, and Zeb and Ira on the front porch of the inn. Up and down the street people were beginning to filter out of their houses to listen for news from the council of war that Houston was holding just outside town. Some men milled about the muddy streets talking while others displayed rifles and handguns. A few women in damp calico huddled in small groups around the houses. An air of expectancy hovered over the small town as dusk settled gently and a light drizzle arrived with it.

"They been palaverin' a pretty considerable o' time, it seems ta me," Marsh Plunket said.

"From what I heerd 'bout General Houston," Obedience guffawed, "they been listenin' while he done th' palaverin'!"

" 'Bout time someone took charge o' them damn militia—beggin' your pardon, ladies," Zeb said with a flush.

Obedience snorted. "Jeehosaphet, we all got sense ta know whut needs doin'. Git all th' men with guns 'n guts an' head fer Santone, pronto!"

"General Sam'll do it!" Fannie Plunket said, with vehemence.

Down the street two men, muddy and trail-stained, were talking with one of Houston's men, who then mounted up and escorted them in the direction of the army camp. "Whut yew s'pose them Mex's is doin', goin' in ta see th' general?" Marsh speculated.

"Ain't thet Deaf Smith?" Zeb asked. They all watched the buckskin-clad scout with his companion Henry Karnes ride toward the camp. In less than five minutes they raced back through town headed directly to San Antonio, heedless of the darkening skies and the increasingly heavy rain.

Rumors were rife over the next two days, but Houston and the other military men were keeping their own counsel. Some folks said the Alamo had fallen, some that Santa Anna had been driven over the Nueces River with his tail between his legs. No one knew for sure.

Obedience and Deborah, like many travelers in Texas that spring, were stranded far from their destination. The fortunes of war would decide the fate of everyone. At twilight on March 13, Houston's scouts returned to Gonzales. Riding with them was a young woman carrying a baby. As Deaf Smith helped her dismount, she clutched the crying child to her bosom, almost collapsing when her injured leg buckled. Her face was gray with pain and her appearance was disheveled and filthy. But it was the dazed look of incredulous horror in her eyes that held everyone spellbound.

"I know I don't want ta hear whut thet poor gal has ta say." Obedience sat on the mattress in their room, rubbing her big hands over her wrinkled cotton skirt. The townspeople had been hastily summoned by Houston to a clearing outside town. With leaden feet she and Deborah trudged to the meeting.

An uneasy pall hung over the crowd. Just then a graying giant of a man gently ushered a small woman into the midst of the people. Sam Houston was always courtly and considerate of women, but never more than of this young girl who must tell such a tale of savagery.

Deborah held Obedience's arm as Suzannah Dickerson described the fall of the Alamo. She had been within the walls on March 6, just before daybreak when the final bloody assault had begun. In less than ninety minutes, one hundred eighty-three Texians had died. The bodies had been stacked like cordwood in pyres and burned. Only the newly widowed Mrs. Dickerson and her child had been spared by the dictator and given instructions to carry word to the rest of Texas: No quarter.

Deborah felt a shudder go through Obedience, but the big woman remained steady after that, her blunt features impassive while many of the other women shrieked and cried, knowing they would never again see husbands, brothers, sons. In fascinated horror, Deborah watched the gentle lion Houston place his arm protectively around the young Widow Dickerson, comforting her when she paused, overcome with grief and exhaustion.

But Suzannah Dickerson was made of the same stuff as Obedience Jones. Squaring her shoulders, and forcing down her tears, she gave the assembled multitude even more frightening news. The dictator had told her that he was marching directly to Gonzales with General Sesma. Over seven hundred of their elite vanguard were already on the road, surely by now not more than a few days away!

Gonzales was in imminent danger! A few hotheads were urging the armed men to stand and fight, others fled in panic, but most milled about waiting for someone to take charge. They did not have long to wait. Sam Houston, a head taller than anyone in the crowd, with a voice to match his size, bellowed out a command for silence.

"I want every man, woman, and child in this camp to attend me!" Hysterical women and shamefaced men shuffled quietly, awaiting the general's orders.

"I have less than four hundred men here, but others shall rally to the standard of Texas. We must stay alive so we can fight *when the time is right*. Until then, our families must be evacuated to safety. Then we shall mass an army to deal Santa Anna a killing blow! Go to your homes and pack quickly. Take only what you can carry. We leave tonight."

The general's sonorous, clear voice rang with purpose and calm. People responded to it. Deborah and Obedience headed toward the Plunkets' place with Zeb and Ira to get their wagon. Instead of heading west on the San Antonio road, they were striking out in the opposite direction toward Burnham's Crossing. Houston felt that having a few rivers between the Texians and the Mexicans would be a good delaying tactic, allowing him to regroup his scattered forces.

At eleven that night a long, meandering caravan straggled out of Gonzales. The drizzle had stopped sufficiently for all stores that could not be taken to be burned. A few explosions ripped through the still night air. Someone said it was whiskey barrels blowing up in the flames. "I'd a loved a snort o' thet stuff!" Obedience averred.

Obedience's large wagon, one of the few available, would have been commandeered by the army for the transportation of civilians, but the Widow Jones offered it gladly. Wet and miserable, Deborah sat on the front seat between Obedience and Fannie Plunket. Half a dozen other women and three small children were huddled haphazardly between boxes and bundles of food and supplies in the wagon bed. The rain began again in full force after midnight.

In the weeks that followed, the ranks of Houston's ragtag army swelled gradually. But the volunteers were outnumbered by terrified, fleeing civilians and many men desirous of fighting felt their first loyalty was to see their families to safety if the general would not stand and fight at once.

What had begun in Gonzales as an orderly retreat under army protection rapidly deteriorated into a rout. Farmers threw down plows in their fields, blacksmiths left forges glowing red-hot, shopkeepers tossed aside aprons and leapt over their store counters. Food and coffee were left to cool on the dinner table while cream curdled in the churn. All of Anglo Texas was in the throes of the "runaway scrape," a headlong rush to the east to escape the invading Mexican army.

By the time Houston's army had reached Burnham's Crossing on the Colorado, the straggling civilian horde created chaos. It took two days for Houston's men to assist the civilians in crossing before the main force of the army could follow it on March 19.

Deborah and Obedience were among the first to cross the swirling red water, raised to flood level by the fierce spring rains. "Hold onta th' ropes 'n don't look back," was all the big woman said as she stepped onto the crude, log raft after Deborah, who huddled near the middle with their belongings, praying. Driftwood bobbed and swayed with deadly menace all around the raft. Men on horseback were swimming unwilling mules, oxen, and horses across the river. Deborah closed her eyes. She wanted to stop up her ears and close out the sound of men's furious curses, horses' terrified neighs, and oxen's enraged bellows, but she could not. Her hands were fully occupied holding on to the ropes as the raft was buffeted across the river. Why couldn't Boston girls learn to swim like boys? *I'll drown in this wilderness.*

Just then their raft hit an uprooted tree. A small boy standing near the edge tumbled between Ira's legs as he poled with all his strength, attempting to free them. The child was caught half-on, half-off the raft. Instinctively, Deborah leapt toward him and shoved him into his mother's outreaching arms, but suddenly the tree broke free of the raft, entangling her skirts in its limbs. She was pulled into the water, away from the bobbing raft. The more she struggled, the more she was drawn beneath the water as her hair tangled in the branches along with her clothing. The weight bore her down as she coughed and screamed. ''Help me! Oh, please, God!'' *Oh, Rafael, I don't want our child to die!*

Out of nowhere an arm welded itself around her, hauling her free of certain death in the branches of the tree limb. ''Easy, ma'am. Polvo's a strong swimmer. He'll have us on the bank quickly if you don't fight us.'' The voice was gravelly and hoarse, young but authoritative. Despite the stinging pain as her hair ripped free of the branches, Deborah calmed and clung to her rescuer's saddle. He was right. The big buckskin stallion hit bottom near the east bank and surefootedly scrambled out of the icy currents of the Colorado in a few minutes.

As the rider let her carefully slide from the side of his big horse to stand shakily on solid ground, Deborah took several deep breaths and then looked up at the youth who was dismounting. He was tall and slim with deep gold hair and finely chiseled features set in a darkly tanned face, handsome and hard looking for his years. Dressed in buckskins and heavily armed, he was one of Houston's volunteers.

''I want to thank you. You saved my life, Mr.—?'' She looked into his amber cougar's eyes.

''Slade, James August Slade, ma'am.'' As he tipped his hat, the hard, unshaven face split into a beautiful smile, and he looked more like his eighteen or so years.

''I'm Deborah Fla—Kensington.'' She caught herself and

coughed to hide the mistake. Hardly surprising what a brush with death could do to one's presence of mind!

The strained moment was interrupted by a bellowed "Jeehosaphet! Yew like ta near scared a score o' years off'n my life, Deborah! Yew near drowned!" Obedience leapt from the beached raft with startling agility for one so large and bounded up the muddy shore to embrace her drenched friend. Turning her attention to Jim Slade, she said, "Much obliged, son, for savin' her life. Saved two. She's a widder woman in a family way. Don't know whut I'd a done if'n she up 'n died on me."

"Then I'm doubly glad I could be of service, ma'am," the youth replied to Obedience but smiled warmly once more at Deborah. "You're quite a brave woman. I saw how you risked your own life to save that boy."

"Yep, Texas needs women like Deborah," Obedience agreed. "We'll be campin' down stream apiece. Yore right welcome ta take dinner with us, son."

"Yes, Mr. Slade, please do. We'd be honored," Deborah seconded.

That evening Obedience muttered curses at the sputtering fire but served up surprisingly crisp cornbread from her blackened iron skillet, along with savory beans. She had gone all out to serve a passable meal to Deborah's handsome young rescuer.

As Deborah poured thick black coffee in his mug, Jim said, "This is the best food I've eaten since I left Bluebonnet, Mrs. Jones, Mrs. Kensington."

"Bluebonnet?" Deborah questioned.

"My ranch, mine and my pa's. When I got word of Santa Anna's invasion, I went to San Antonio to join the army there."

Obedience looked up suddenly and set the skillet on the ground. "My brother, Seth Morton, was with Colonel Bowie at th' Alamo. You seen him, mebbe?"

"I knew Mr. Morton, yes, ma'am. I didn't see him while I was in the fort, but I remember him and his wife from town. I'm sorry for your loss, Mrs. Jones."

"Ever' one left there wuz kilt, they say." Obedience left the question unasked. Surely a boy with courage enough to drag a flailing woman from the Colorado River was no coward.

Slade understood the direction of her thoughts. "I left the fort with Captain Seguin on February 25. We carried messages from Colonel Travis asking for reinforcements."

"They never got there," Obedience said quietly.

"Forgive me, Mrs. Jones," Slade said, choosing his words carefully, "I know those men who perished were brave patriots, your brother among them, but if Travis and Bowie hadn't disobeyed orders, likely none of them would have died."

Obedience's eyes narrowed. "Whut yew mean, son?"

"I saw the orders they received from General Houston. They were told to raze the walls and abandon the place. It was a deathtrap. Houston knew they'd be hopelessly outnumbered and surrounded."

"Just as our army is now. That's why the general is marching east and calling for more volunteers, isn't he, Lieutenant Slade?" Deborah's eyes were filled with sudden understanding.

"Yes, ma'am. This isn't the place to make a stand. Houston'll know when the time is right. He'll choose."

"When the time is right," Obedience echoed. "That's whut he said when we left Gonzales. Some folks is gettin' real eager ta stand 'n fight right now."

A long retreat into victory did seem an unlikely solution to many, but Houston issued orders. Once more the army would pull back, covering the retreat of the civilians who were scattering for points east across the trackless prairie.

March 21 Deborah and Obedience headed northeast with a small party of others toward Groce's Plantation, a wayside inn where shelter and food could be secured for a price. Situated in the rich bottomlands of the Brazos basin, the plantation was famous for its wealth and for the exorbitant rates charged wayfarers.

Deborah wanted nothing so much as to sleep under a dry quilt in a real bed. Obedience itched to cook and bake some palatable food after their weeks on the wet, miserable march. Jared Groce welcomed the group and took immediate note of Deborah's willingness to pay for shelter with

American banknotes. When her companion expressed a desire to take charge of the kitchen, he agreed at once.

The plantation was overcrowded with refugees and stranded wayfarers and the overburdened slaves were grateful for Obedience's help. They learned the first night that the provisional government had spent four days under Jared Groce's roof. They had narrowly missed meeting President Burnet and his cabinet, before they fled toward the Gulf.

"Jeehosaphet! Thet so-called goverment's got greased wheels, if'n yew ask me. Plumb undermines a body's faith in Texas," Obedience said the next morning as she beat biscuit batter with fierce, rapid thumps.

"Ole Sam'll hold onta things," Zeb averred as he piled kindling beside the fireplace.

"Humph," Obedience snorted, "if'n he kin hold onta his army."

During the next week, Deborah ate and slept, feeling at last a slight abatement in her bone-weary, nauseated condition. But if her body was restored, her spirits were flagging. Every day more settlers poured into the bottomland, some begging, a few able to buy supplies from Groce. Deborah, seeing the gaunt hunger in dirty faces of rag-clad children, could do nothing but buy corn and beans for the families, many of whom had fled with only the clothes on their backs.

"But when will the army stand and fight? Where the hell are they?" Ira demanded.

"Old Sam won't let a passel of Mex's run him out of Texas. We'll win," Plunket avowed.

Zeb considered. "If yew feel so all fired sure o' winnin', Marsh, why don't yew go 'n find ole Sam's army 'n join in th' fight?"

Plunket reddened but was saved from replying by the clatter of hooves. Jim Slade had arrived and all gathered on the front porch to hear his news. Houston's army was encamped across the river from the plantation and the general had just received word that Colonel Fannin's command at Goliad had been massacred under direct orders from Santa Anna.

"That's why the general left off the fight with Sesma on the Colorado. He'd received word even then that Fannin was surrounded and would likely be cut to pieces. He knew his six hundred men were all that was left between three invading Mexican armies and the population of Texas." The young lieutenant finished his grim report, saying, "If Fannin had obeyed orders and retreated to Victoria like General Houston told him, he wouldn't have been trapped."

"Jeehosaphet!" Obedience exploded. "Don't nobody have th' sense God gave geese! How many good men gotta die afore th' fools learn?"

When Mr. Groce extended hospitality to Jim Slade and offered him dinner, Slade gave a wide, white grin and thanked the planter but then said apologetically, "Mr. Groce, er, the general's going to need some supplies—beef and corn, to be exact, maybe some tobacco. I expect he'll be requisitioning them."

"What choice do I have, Lieutenant Slade? If Santa Anna wins, I'll be executed. If the Texian army wins, I'll merely be destitute." Shrugging, he added, "Take what you need."

For the next two weeks Houston attempted to forge an unruly horde of volunteers into an army. The men were rugged frontier individualists who were used to electing their own officers and dismissing them at whim. Mutiny was constantly in the air and reports filtered across to the plantation house from the camp. Jim Slade was often sent as requisition officer from Houston to Groce. On one such supply mission, he dined with Obedience and Deborah while recounting the general's woes.

"That Georgia poet Lamar fancied himself able to lead the men in a headlong rush to whip Santa Anna. Had the support of Lieutenant Perry and some other officers. Lots of the men were yelling to go, too," Slade said disgustedly.

"What happened?" Deborah asked.

Slade grinned like a shark and replied, "Houston had half a dozen graves dug and told Lamar he'd get to occupy the first one if he yammered anymore about 'sounding the trumpet for glory'!"

Obedience snorted in laughter. " 'N thet settled thet, I betcha."

"The gentleman is now a colonel in Houston's cavalry, drilling his men and awaiting orders," Slade added levelly.

The following evening, a weary General Houston, along with a number of his staff, took a rare dinner with the Groces and their guests. Deborah and Obedience were included in the motley assortment. Obedience did what she could with dwindling supplies to supervise a palatable feast. Houston gallantly complimented her.

Fixing her with his riveting blue eyes, he said, "After weeks of half-raw beef and corn mush cooked over smoldering campfires, I vow I've answered my summons and gone to heaven, dining on such a splendid repast, madam. Of course," he added with a twinkle to Deborah, "there are those, including President Burnet, who are assured I'll be summoned the opposite direction!"

Everyone laughed as Deborah protested such an unlikely event.

When the conversation turned to the war, everyone became grave and none more so than Houston. Yet the brooding giant seemed to lend a calmness and strength to the gathering. He exchanged ideas on strategy with other men at the table, inclining his large, shaggy head to consider a point made by Jared Groce or Anson Jones, then gave a measured reply.

No wonder he's held that band of mutinous volunteers together, Deborah thought. His towering size and compelling voice were matched by a shrewd intelligence. He was a man who listened yet kept his own counsel. When the final decision is made, it will be his alone. Somehow, this thought reassured Deborah. *When the time is right* echoed through her mind.

While Houston enjoyed his first hot meal at a table in nearly a month, his men encamped three miles downriver on the farmlands of another wealthy planter named Thomas Donahoe. As the general was departing after supper, he related a story about Farmer Donahoe. "Donahoe came up to me most upset because Lieutenant Slade had a detail of men chopping his scrap pines for firewood. I cast my eyes about"—he gestured broadly to the company standing on the porch—"and what met my line of vision but a split rail fence. Must have been a mile long, all prime hardwood. I ventured the opinion to the lieutenant that the good farmer was quite correct. Why should soldiers marching in the cause of liberty labor to cut timber? Here was all that fine fence wood just ripe for the taking. The fires should be blazing bright to guide me into camp tonight! Ladies, gentlemen, I bid you *adieu*.'' With a gallant bow to Mrs. Groce, Obedience, Deborah, and the other women, he vanished into the darkness.

The next morning word came from Houston that General Sesma's army had crossed the Brazos below them at Ft. Bend. To protect their southern flank, Houston's army must move from the open bottomlands and march southeast, maneuvering for a favorable position from which to fight.

His retreat-and-skirmish policy had gained Houston many detractors, but Deborah agreed with Obedience's assessment of the general. Obedience Jones had known him when he was a backwoods schoolteacher and later a Tennessee congressman. "He'll do whut he has ta when th' time is right," was her final word on the subject.

Late in the afternoon of April 21, the time was finally right. The place was a boggy open stretch of land beside Buffalo Bayou called the Plain of San Jacinto. The battle took eighteen minutes. It was a complete rout of Santa Anna's army, which was having an afternoon siesta. Not quite eight hundred enraged Texians stormed the fortifications and fell upon over twelve hundred fifty of Santa Anna's best troops, massacring six hundred of them and taking six hundred fifty prisoner.

The self-styled "Napoleon of the West" had fled the scene of the debacle, only to be ignominiously captured, camouflaged in a private's uniform. Santa Anna's diamond-studded silk undershirt gave him away. With the dictator in his hands, Houston was assured of the withdrawal of all the invading armies.

Word of the glorious deliverance spread like prairie grassfire across Texas. While the refugees at Groce's Plantation rejoiced and prepared to return to their homes, Obedience and Deborah were thoughtful. Obedience remembered her brother, fallen at the Alamo.

"Shore hope thet nice young Lieutenant Slade warn't one o' them kilt at San Jacinto," she ventured aloud, echoing

Deborah's thoughts. The two women packed their belongings and once more headed west toward San Antonio. Now they would make their home in the Republic of Texas.

Chapter 17

The trip to San Antonio was made under far more pleasant conditions than the runaway flight east had been. The weather turned warm and sunny, the raw, miserable drizzle ended, and a late, lush spring finally arrived. Deborah welcomed their steady progress along the San Antonio Road.

The scenery was as glorious as the dry, clean air. At night the sky was filled with brilliant stars, each blazing forth as if claiming the right to be the one on the Texas flag. During the day they rode over gently swelling hills, past burbling, clear springs that magically appeared from underground sources, leaving the land ablaze with riotous carpets of wildflowers: bluebonnets, buttercups, and Indian paintbrush. Their glorious colors and pungent perfume were balm to Deborah's weary soul and body.

She stretched and rubbed her aching back. Her stomach was noticeably protuberant now and she had taken to wearing high waisted skirts with pleats in front to allow her freedom of movement.

"Yew feelin' poorly?" Obedience asked solicitously, noting her young friend's stiff movements as she climbed off the wagon seat.

Deborah smiled. "No, just a little tired and sore from all this kicking." She grinned as she rubbed her belly. "She's going to be a regular Texas hellion."

Obedience harrumphed. "Or *he's* gonna be. Yew settle on names yet?"

"I'm still tending toward Katherine, but perhaps Lenore.

She is a very dear friend I shall never see again. How does Lenore Obedience sound to you?'' She cocked her head, a gamin grin on her lips.

Obedience threw up her hands, soup ladle and all, and rocked back on her heels. ''Jeehosaphet! What a mouthful! I'd bet me half this wagonload 'o goods that it'll be yer pa's namesake 'n save th' pore critter from bein' cursed with my ugly handle.''

Suppressing a chuckle, Deborah replied, ''Why only *half* the wagonload, Obedience?''

The older woman looked disgustedly at her greenhorn charge. ''I got ta teach yew how ta play poker. Odds is only half thet yew'll git yore girl, so I'll only bet half I git my boy.''

''Well, if he turns out like your sons, I'll not be sorry,'' Deborah equivocated, refusing to think about the child turning out like Rafael.

Sensing the direction of Deborah's thoughts, Obedience changed the subject. ''We should git inta Santone tomorrow. Cain't rightly wait ta see it, after hearin' all Seth's stories.''

''Is it really very Spanish-looking? I hope the Mexican townspeople won't resent us.''

Obedience gestured dismissively and said, ''Yew mean the *Tejano* townsfolk? Why, Jeehosaphet! Ain't yew niver heerd o' Texas's Vice President Lorenzo Zavala er Colonel Juan Seguin in General Sam's army? The *Tejanos* wuz as afeard o' Santy Anny as anyone. Lots o' them folks sent food 'n supplies ta th' men inside th' Alamo, some even fought 'n died with 'em. Nah, we ain't got nothin' ta fear from *Tejanos*—thet's whut the Mexican Texians is called.''

''*Tejanos*,'' Deborah rolled the unfamiliar word around on her tongue. ''Jim Slade, the young lieutenant who saved my life, is a *Tejano* or sort of. His mother was a Sandoval who married a Virginian. I do hope he's all right.''

''So do I. Nice lookin young gent. Say, don't he have a spread hereabouts—outside Santone?'' Obedience remembered the blond youth's striking looks and educated manner. A likely suitor for Deborah!

Reading her friend's mind, Deborah said, ''Yes, his

father owns a ranch 'hereabouts' and no, I am not interested in him that way. I've already told you my husband is alive back in New Orleans. Anyway, Jim Slade is two years younger than I am—a boy!''

Obedience threw back her head and roared. ''Jeehosaphet! That don't count fer nothin' in Texas! 'N thet *boy* as yew call 'em has seen more fightin' 'n done more work 'n most grandpas back east! Yew could do a lot worse.''

''I already have. At least I won't repeat my first mistake and fall for a handsome face,'' she replied darkly.

''I don't 'spect, considerin' how yew look, thet yew'd ever hafta settle fer a plug ugly toadyfrog.''

In spite of herself, Deborah laughed, holding her belly.

When the caravan arrived in San Antonio the next afternoon, Deborah exclaimed, ''Oh, Obedience, it's so beautiful!'' She could see the spires of an old Spanish cathedral peeking above lush stands of cypress trees. The warm June sun beat down on thick-walled, low buildings. They were whitewashed and many had red tile roofs and iron grillwork balconies. Broad, clean streets lined with oak and cottonwood trees were filled with all manner of traffic as they neared the Main Plaza. Several peasant women dressed in white blouses and bright cotton skirts carried big clay pots of water on their shoulders. A *caballero* in a tight-fitting silver-trimmed jacket and pants rode a magnificently outfitted black horse. A teamster cursed and flogged his long train of mules as they pulled a heavy load of dry goods. Here and there Anglo women in calico dresses and sunbonnets made their way across the thoroughfare, as did farmers in rough homespun and hard-looking mountain men dressed in buckskins, weighed down with knives and guns.

The city included a motley assortment of humanity, Hispanic and Anglo, rich and poor, desperate and dangerous. Deborah drank it in, as colorful and exotic in its way as New Orleans had been. *Please let this be home for me and my child*.

Obedience stopped and asked directions at the Main Plaza while Deborah admired the spacious tree-lined square. She heard a mixture of English and Spanish, with occasional dialects unfamiliar to her, perhaps Indian language. But she heard no one speak French. She was grateful and oddly sad at the same time.

"Jist up a couple o' blocks thataways," Obedience instructed Zeb who gave their mules a sharp slap of the reins, "'n we'll be home."

"I can hardly wait to see the house," Deborah said with a grin.

"Now, I warned yew, don't go a gettin' yer hopes up fer a fancy place like back east. My brother, God rest his soul, tended ta put a leetle stretch on th' truth now 'n then."

Even so, Deborah was not prepared for the dilapidated wooden structure at the end of Commerce Street. It had two stories and a wide front porch. Seth had not lied about that, but the bare boards were crudely fitted and the windows innocent of glass. The doors hung crookedly on their hinges and the porch rail was half-finished. Indeed, the whole place looked half-finished.

"Why, Obedience, it's—it's got lots of potential," Deborah managed as they pulled up.

"Jeehosaphet! If'n thet means it's a dump, then I reckon yore right," Obedience said as she jumped down from the wagon and forged across the dusty front yard toward the door.

In her condition Deborah could only follow slowly. Obedience's call at the front door was met by a small, crablike black woman wearing a fierce scowl that matched the tall Tennesseean's.

"You be wantin' rooms? Mr. Seth he doan rents ta females." The black woman spoke in a no-nonsense voice.

"I ain't rentin'. I'm ownin'. Obedience Jones is my name 'n I'm Seth Morton's sister. He wuz expectin' me afore th' war. Who are yew?"

"I be Sadie 'n I runs this here house fer Mr. Seth since Miz Mathilda die."

"I don't hold with slavery, even if my sister-in-law did. I'll see ta yore bein' freed—"

"Yo cain't free me!" Sadie interrupted with a triumphant gleam in her eye, her stooped body still blocking the door. "I already is free. Got me papers to prove it. I *works* fer Mr. Seth!"

"Jeehosaphet! Yew cud'a jist said so," Obedience replied in a huff.

"Maybe you never gave her a chance," Deborah said softly, trying to ease the confrontation. Feeling the black woman's eyes shift to her, Deborah smiled and introduced herself. "I'm Deborah Kensington. Mrs. Jones is the new owner, truly. I know she does appreciate your keeping the boardinghouse operating while we were detained by the war."

Sadie smiled. "Come in and set. It be hot outside." She ushered them inside with a flourish of her arthritic arm and then scrabbled down the long, wide central hall to a room on the right. "This be th' parlor. I'll bring lemonade. Set yoself." She indicated a large leather chair to Deborah and made a gesture toward her belly. Pregnant women should rest was the obvious implication.

Reddening, Deborah sat down while Obedience made a quick inspection of the large, scantily furnished room. Sadie went after the promised refreshment.

"Well, it is big and roomy," Deborah ventured.

"Filthy as a hawg pen. They ain't hardly no furniture!" Obedience responded.

There were two crude leather chairs and an ugly horsehair sofa. One small, rickety table sat beside it with a lard wick stuck into a saucer that served as the room's only apparent lamp.

"We might see if Zeb and Ira would consider hiring on to do some chores for a while," Deborah suggested, then added, "I have plenty of money to pay them and I want to do my share, Obedience."

The old woman grinned. "Right stubborn fer sech a skinny leetle thing, aintcha?"

By the next day, Obedience had all her questions answered. Seth had built his large house and had made plans to finish it, ordering the furniture from New Orleans and hiring workmen to paint walls and put glass in the windows. However, he had scarcely begun when Mathilda had become gravely ill. She had been the planner, the one responsible for choosing colors, furniture, wallpaper, everything for the interior decoration.

After she died, Seth Morton had written to ask his sister to come to San Antonio, but he had lost interest in his wife's dream. He had thrown himself into the revolution with the fervor of a rootless man and had left the house, with six, old male boarders, under the care of Mathilda's servant, Sadie.

In the months that followed, Deborah joined Obedience in a whirlwind of activity, converting the half-finished boardinghouse into a comfortably furnished home.

As Obedience had predicted, Deborah's lethargy, nausea, and other discomforts of pregnancy abated, leaving her feeling surprising healthy and energetic during the dry sunny days of San Antonio's summer. Her appetite was voracious, but her diligence in working alongside Obedience kept her from gaining much weight. Recalling the odious tales of "confinement" Celine and her friends whispered about, Deborah often laughed as she traveled about the city and worked in the boardinghouse, heedless of her ripening figure.

A thin, nervous man of indeterminate years named Chester Granger appeared the second day they had set to work. Hat in hand, Adam's apple bobbing and feet shuffling, he inquired if the new owners wanted a general handyman. He could drive a team, work livestock, prune the orchards, and do anything else they needed.

Realizing Zeb and Ira planned to homestead their own land the following spring, Deborah was inclined to hire Chester.

"We need someone who can be a jack-of-all-trades for us," Deborah said to Obedience as she and the older woman talked in the kitchen while the applicant waited nervously on the side porch.

"Jeehosaphet! He's too puny 'n too twitchy ta lift a flour sack without spillin' it," Obedience replied, giving the encrusted pot she was scrubbing a masterful scrape to free a hunk of baked-on food.

"He's had experience working in orchards and growing things. I really want to reclaim the fruit trees out back and grow a large garden to supplement our table." Deborah's voice was beseeching. "I'm sure he'll be helpful."

"Harrumph, like thet crippled ole Sadie's helpful! I declare, we're runnin' a orphanage fer growed-up misfits whut cain't do fer themselves." Her tone was brusque, but Deborah could see she was coming around.

"For all your bluff and bluster, Obedience Jones, you've taken in more than your share of misfits along the way, including one scared, pregnant runaway," she replied, tiptoeing up to kiss the leathery cheek of the big Tennesseean. "I'll tell Chester he can start right away!"

While Chester sawed, spliced, and put mud plasters on tree wounds in the orchard, Deborah sweated in the garden, planting sweet potatoes and corn as well as a large assortment of beans, carrots, broccoli, and cabbages. They would have a bountiful harvest of wholesome fresh vegetables this fall. "I can grow anything in his rich warm earth that they can in sticky old Louisiana," she promised herself as she wiped the sweat from her brow, applying herself to the seeding once more.

"Yore overdoin', mark me," Obedience scolded, kneeling alongside Deborah with a grunt.

"Zeb turned the ground for me and prepared it. All I'm doing is patting seeds into it. No heavy lifting. Anyway, I've heard you say you plowed and milked cows when you were pregnant," Deborah rejoined, ignoring the ache in her back.

"Jeehosaphet! Look at yew 'n me. I'm jist a tech bigger 'n sturdier. Kinda like thet little bitty fig tree over there standin' up ta th' cypress tree by San Fernando Church!"

Even Deborah had to giggle at the comparison. The cypress trees around the cathedral towered over all the surrounding buildings while her fig tree was small and delicate. "I guess I am like the fig tree after all—ready to bear fruit this fall."

As the big Fourth of July celebration neared, Obedience had to credit Deborah's grit. The thin, harried young woman she had met in the cold rains of spring had blossomed under the summer sun. Her porcelain white skin was now tinged a delicate incandescent gold and her hair was even more silvery white. Still slender but for her growing belly, Deborah was no longer hollow-eyed and gaunt but firmly fleshed from exercise in the open air and a good, hearty appetite. Above all, she was gaining a sense of accomplishment in her work.

The boardinghouse now had ten boarders, three of the four new additions being women, two widow ladies and one spinster. The fine table set by Obedience and Deborah won praise from everyone.

Deborah's Boston refinement seemed to impart respect for her rules to all the boarders, even the tough old mountain man, Racine Schwartz. He loved to frighten the women with grisly tales of scalpings, horse stealing, and knife fights, but now he watched his language as he did so. She allowed no chewing or spitting of tobacco in Jones's Boardinghouse, an incredible injunction in Texas where six year old boys often indulged in the vice. Gentlemen wore shirts and jackets to the dinner table and everyone followed Deborah's lead in using appropriate utensils and observing table manners.

"We got us three more men waitin' ta move in, Deborah. Seems word o' yore clean sheets 'n fancy menus been gettin' 'round," Obedience said as they prepared to leave for the July Fourth dance and celebration in the Main Plaza.

"You can't give me the credit for your splendid cooking, Obedience," her friend rejoined.

"Jeehosaphet! I'd a been feedin' them sweet taters 'n meat 'n biscuits. Yew was th' one growin' all them fancy greens. I learned me ta cook stuff I never heerd o' afore I met yew. Cain't believe how good them broccoli things taste."

"You, Chester and Sadie have all helped," Deborah replied.

"Who got the crazy idea o' dealin' with them Tonks, huh?"

Deborah had made an exceptional arrangement. When several friendly Tonkawa Indians had come to their kitchen door with a brace of quail to barter, Sadie had run screaming she was about to be scalped by Comanche. Deborah reasoned that hostile raiders would scarcely knock and bring foodstuffs, after riding openly through the center of town. Chester, who had lived in central Texas all his life, assured her these were remnants of a small, decimated tribe who subsisted on the periphery of white society.

Wanting fresh game for their table to supplement the endlessly boring pork and beef menus, Deborah had enlisted Chester as an interpreter. She bartered salt and cornmeal for the quail, then reached an agreement with them for more fresh meat. Turkey, rabbit, and venison now varied their main courses, as did the chickens she was raising for eggs and for the cookpot.

"I suppose we have much to celebrate this July Fourth, don't we?" she said with a warm smile for Obedience. Things were prospering.

"Yup, thet we do. Let's go tie one on. Seems almost like bein' back in the good ole United States whut with th' way folks hereabouts carry on."

Texians always took advantage of any excuse to celebrate—American holidays, Mexican saints' fiestas—any day they could stage horse races, set off fireworks, hold a dance, drink, and feast. People who worked hard played hard as well—nowhere more so than in Texas.

"Yew expect ta see Jim Slade at th' fandango?" Obedience asked as the two women strolled toward the Main Plaza.

"Only if he's squiring about his fianceé, Señorita Aguilar," Deborah replied.

Jim Slade had returned to his ranch just in time to see his father die of a heart condition. Although Obedience fostered the friendship between the youthful owner of Bluebonnet Ranch and her friend, nothing came of it. Within a couple of months Jim was engaged to Tomasina Aguilar, whose father Don Simon was an old friend of the Slades. The best *Tejano* and Texian families in San Antonio clucked their approval of the impending marriage.

"Speakin' o' them two, here they come," Obedience said as she scanned the crowd thronging the plaza. Jim Slade, dressed in an elegant suit of brown homespun, looked adoringly down at the tiny, black-haired girl on his arm.

Seeing Obedience bearing down on them with Deborah in tow, he smiled warmly. "Hello, Mrs. Jones, Mrs. Kensington."

"Howdy, Jimmy. Figgered yew'd be out ta take in th'

sights. Afternoon, Miz Aguilar.'' Obedience nodded at his beautiful companion.

Although Tomasina smiled at the big woman, when her jet eyes caught Deborah's lavender gaze, her expression suddenly cooled. She nodded to the ''boardinghouse widows'' as many San Antonians called them.

Forcing a smile at Tomasina, Deborah said, ''We haven't seen you in town in a while, Mr. Slade. I hope things are going well at Bluebonnet.''

They chatted a bit about the cattle business and how Jim was faring as he took over the big operation.

After a few minutes Tomasina said in her precisely accented English, ''If you will be so kind as to excuse us, señoras, I see some old friends we must greet across the plaza.''

Watching them depart, Obedience said shrewdly, ''He fair follers her like a pup now, but I got me a feelin' it cain't last, even if'n she is purty as one o' them Madonnas in San Fernando Church.''

Deborah gave a snort of derision. ''Some Madonna! She heartily disapproves of me showing myself in this disgraceful condition. Couldn't you see how she stared?''

Obedience laughed out loud. ''Might cud be yew fancy havin' her man fer yerself. Yew'd suit him much better 'n her. She's a snooty one, thet'n.''

Deborah's cheeks flamed. ''Honestly, Obedience, how often must I remind you Jim Slade is only a friend—and one who is two years younger than me to boot!''

''Yep,'' Obedience replied, having heard it all before. ''Yore purely witherin' on the vine o' old age! But a great-lookin' stud bull like thet yeller-haired young devil'd fix yew up jist fine.''

Now it was Deborah's turn to laugh, holding her distended abdomen. ''I can scarcely summon up any base physical cravings at the moment, Obedience. Look at me, waddling along, seven months pregnant.''

''Harrumph! Thet's only temporary. Believe me, I oughta know,'' the undaunted Amazon replied.

Deborah silently prayed it would not be, wanting no return of tortuous, bittersweet dreams of her Creole lover.

To Obedience she said only, "I'm still a married woman and that's the end of it."

Summer spent itself into a long, golden fall, full of the rich promise of a bountiful harvest. Deborah worked along-side Obedience and Sadie in the boardinghouse backyard, stirring the steaming cauldrons of apple butter. The spicy sweet perfume wafted on the warm September air.

"We're going to have the best table ever set in San Antonio this winter, mark me," Deborah said proudly to Obedience as they stood on the boardinghouse porch, looking out on their domain. She had just commissioned the digging of a real ice cellar on the back of the property, deep beneath a rocky hill. Once sealed off and filled with ice during the winter, the storage cave would guarantee cool drinks for everyone the following summer.

"Sinful luxury, that's whut a Baptist preacher back in Tennessee would call all this here high livin'," Obedience said with a glow of unrepentant pride.

Deborah laughed. "Well, this is Texas and I'm Episcopalian, not Baptist. We don't fret over sin. We just enjoy luxury."

"Yew worked ta earn it, I reckon. In fact, I think yore plumb peaked today," Obedience said, inspecting Deborah's face.

"Oh, it's just this backache I woke up with this morning, that's all. I'll be fine. In fact, I wish I could walk to town and vote. It's the Texas Republic's first election day and women are just as excluded here as they were in Boston or New Orleans."

"I think General Sam'll get hisself elected president without our votes," Obedience said dryly, knowing another of Deborah's soapbox speeches was imminent.

Just then her friend winced and emitted a small, surprised gasp. "Oh, you rascal, what a kick," she exclaimed as she leaned against the porch banister.

"How long yew been havin' them 'kicks'?" Obedience asked casually.

"One every fifteen minutes or so since lunch. They're nothing compared to this accursed backache, though . . ." Deborah's words faded as she looked up at Obedience with dawning comprehension. Spluttering, she stood up. "You mean I've been having a baby and I didn't even know it!"

"Jeehosaphet!" Obedience laughed. "It shore 'pears that way, but if 'n yew never done it afore, how kin yew know what it's supposed ta feel like?"

Recalling Celine's horror stories of travail, Deborah gave a hearty chuckle and said, "I think you might send Chester to fetch Dr. Weidermann. Tell him I'll be out back checking the progress on the icehouse!"

By the time the young physician had been located outside of town where he was collecting medicinal herbs, Deborah had begun to experience hard labor pains and had finally agreed to go upstairs to her room and rest.

Smiling, the doctor reassured Deborah in his precisely accented English, "Your contractions are only four minutes apart now. It should not take much longer."

"I'm glad to hear it, since it's been getting rather uncomfortable the past hour or so," Deborah replied.

Obedience came in with a pitcher of spring water and began to bathe Deborah's brow. "A woman works up a bigger sweat birthin' a youngun than a man does bustin' a mustang!"

"All the men in this world who never worked this hard get to vote and we don't," Deborah gritted as she felt a particularly hard contraction begin. "I'm entitled to cast my vote for Sam Houston, too!"

"Yew got yew more important bizness ta take keer o'," Obedience replied.

And she did. At seven fifteen that evening, September 5, 1836, Adam Samuel Kensington was born, a lusty, squalling seven pounds of black-haired, black-eyed boy. He was the image of the father whose name he could never bear.

Within the month Adam Manchester received another letter from his daughter, which both gladdened and saddened him.

Dear Father:
    You are a grandpa. His name is Adam Samuel, named for you and for the first president of the Republic of Texas, who was elected on the day of his birth. We are

fine and flourishing. Your namesake weighs seven pounds, has a voracious appetite, and a set of lungs to do any New England whaler proud.

As he continued reading her description of his grandson, Adam could picture the boy with his jet hair and eyes, chiseled features, and proud Flamenco jawline. He could also read between the lines how much his daughter ached for her absent husband and longed to show him his son. But she was independent and successful, running a business with another widow, making a comfortable living. If only her lonely proud spirit could triumph as well.

Chapter 18

When Rafael Flamenco stepped off the small boat at San Felipe, the Brazos River air was sunny and warm with the spring smells of May. It was a welcome relief after the bitterly cold rains of April.

Amazing. I'm in a foreign country. The Republic of Texas. Worriedly he speculated about the legal ramifications of reclaiming a runaway wife in this wild land. "First I'd better find her," he muttered aloud as he scanned the bleak-looking settlement, or what remained of it after Santa Anna's armies burned their way through the abandoned village.

So much had changed in less than a month. While he had lost precious time on a false trail to Boston, Texas had thrown off the yoke of Santa Anna's dictatorship. But the cost had been dear. The countryside was in chaos. The runaway scrape had left thousands of homeless wanderers on the roads, many returning to find what the Austin Colony settlers had: cabins burned, crops trampled, and livestock run off or confiscated.

It'll be a miracle if I can find her in all this wreckage. He had tracked the Pettyjohn settlers this far. Now if only he could find his wife among them.

The colony, once the cultivated and prosperous showplace of Texas, was now a welter of burned-out homes and doggedly stubborn people. The settlers had returned from exile with renewed determination to begin again. An afternoon of questioning proved fruitless.

"Pettyjohn family. Nope. Never heerd o' 'em."

"Tall gal with silver hair. Mister, I wish I'd a seen her afore yew!"

"Everyone's so scattered in the runaway. Some folks crossed the Sabine and never come back. Hard ta say. Sorry."

The next morning, Rafael purchased a small, rangy mustang. He rode inland, away from the river. For three days the disheartening news was the same, but the hospitality of the people amazed him. With barely enough to feed themselves, farmers and stockmen offered him bed and food. Hardly the luxurious fare he was accustomed to, but nonetheless welcome.

On the fourth day, he stopped in front of a newly constructed cabin. With guarded hopefulness, he doffed his hat and trudged up the dusty path. A tall, gangly youth with light, stringy hair sat whittling on the porch.

"Afternoon. I'm Rafael Flamenco from New Orleans," he said in precise, accented English.

"What kin I do fer yew?"

"I'm looking for the settlers in the Pettyjohn party who arrived in Texas early in March."

"Yeah. Whut ya want with 'em?"

"One of the women in the party is my wife, Deborah Flamenco, although I doubt she's using that name. A tall woman with violet eyes. Her hair is thick and silver colored. She's very beautiful." Rafael held his breath as the boy dropped his stick and sheathed his knife, then stood up.

"Yer wife, ya say? Hell, she told us she was a widder woman. I'm Thad Pettyjohn and she wuz with my pa's party. Why'd she run away from yew?"

Thinking the boy was protecting Deborah, Rafael chose

his words carefully. "We had a lover's quarrel back in New Orleans. She's pregnant and not herself."

Thad's sallow skin reddened. Carrying this Frenchy's brat was she, and to think he would have married her! Now her rich husband wanted to make up and take her back. Well, 'Lady Deborah,' we'll jist see 'bout thet, he thought vengefully. "I'm powerful sorry she ain't here now, mister. She decided not ta stay with us. Guess th' work wuz too hard here."

Watching the shiftless youth who had sat whittling, Rafael was given to wonder about that. "Where did she go?"

"She met up with another woman, real prim 'n proper old lady, spinster schoolmarm from back east named Marshall, yeah, Rose Marshall. The two o' them headed northeast. She had kin somewheres 'round Nacogdoches, I think. 'Course, whut with th' war 'n all, lots o' folks kinda moved 'round a lot. I spect they cud be anywheres. Texas is a big place." Watching the handsome Frenchy's face turn bleak, Thad Pettyjohn felt a surge of exhilaration. Yep, let her rot in Texas, her 'n thet fat, loud mouthed old cow Obedience Jones!

"Lord, Jules, fan faster. I am burning up. This is the hottest August I can remember," Lily said to her houseboy as he waved a large plumed fan.

It was oppressively sultry and quiet in the late afternoon. Melanie had just returned to St. Louis with her aunt and grandmother, for which Lily was grateful, but she was unhappy to be alone. *Bored. I'm bored and I miss Rafael so desperately.*

After that dreadful confrontation with his wife, Lily had felt triumphantly assured of her place in Rafael's life. Of course, Melanie had cried and carried on, confused about the white "lady". When the child was a bit older she would explain to her, or better yet, she'd have *maman* do it. Rafael had returned the next night, only to cosset the child. He had virtually ignored Lily once he found out Melanie had overheard the angry exchange between the adults. What he had told his daughter, Lily had no idea nor did she care, but she did care that he had been preoccupied in the following weeks.

Once more jealous fears had invaded her mind as she imagined Rafael turning her out to humor his pregnant wife. He had visited her twice in the following month, making love to her fiercely and roughly, seeming to use her without enjoyment. That had never been his way before and she hated the Yankee for it.

Then a note had arrived saying he would be gone for four to six weeks. Her servants brought her word that he had traveled to Boston in search of his runaway wife, only to return in April, alone. Within a week he left again, this time headed to Texas.

Lily had waited and seethed for the first two months. By July, her fury had turned to fear. Texas was a savage wilderness full of deadly snakes and mountain lions, deserts and flash floods, not to mention all sorts of dangerous criminals. What if he were killed? All over that crazy, silver-haired bitch!

Finally, last week she had received word that he was back in Louisiana. He had returned empty-handed again. Good riddance, she had thought, but still he did not come to see her. Then this afternoon he had sent a message saying he would visit her tomorrow. The hours had been endless ever since.

Bathed and perfumed, dressed in her best red silk peignoir, Lily ran a brush over her hair one last time, as the front door opened and closed. It was Rafael, early for a change. Nervously, she stood up, feeling a sudden foreboding. Something terrible was about to happen. Forcing her most seductive smile, she walked to the bedroom door and caught her first glimpse of him as he poured a brandy at the bar. He looks haggard, she thought.

Rafael's face had been darkened by the merciless Texas sun and his hair was long and shaggy. He had not even bothered to have it trimmed! The look in his eyes stopped her headlong rush to throw herself into his arms. "*Cheri*, you grieve for her," she said quietly as she walked over and placed her hand on his linen coat.

He made no move to touch her and her heart skipped a

beat. Reaching up, she pulled his head down for a light, experimental kiss. "I am so glad you have returned to me, my darling."

When he gently pulled away from her and took another drink of the brandy, her heart sank. Holding her breath, she waited for him to speak, her soul awash in misery.

Rafael could see love and fear—and yes, jealousy and anger—burning in her beautiful gold eyes. He felt a sharp stab of guilt and pity, oddly mixed, as he took her hand and ushered her to the sofa. "We have a great many things to talk about, Lily. You are right. I grieve for Deborah. I love her. These past months since she left have shown me how deep my feelings are. Far more, I'm afraid, than I ever allowed myself to admit. I've been a fool, a provincial Creole who wanted her to fit into my world, live by my rules. I gave no thought to her hurts or''—he shrugged with a sad little smile—"to her rights."

"Rights? What rights have you denied her—she has your name, your family wealth and position, everything any white lady could ever ask," Lily argued, an edge of bitterness in her voice.

Rafael sighed. "Everything but what I gave her my oath to do. Forsake all others and be faithful to her."

Lily's eyes widened in disbelief. "But no man does that! Oh, some give up their mistresses or hide them. Some visit brothels discreetly, but all men are the same. What could a wife expect when she is fat and ugly in pregnancy? Or after birthing?"

"If a woman is great with her husband's child, he should love her all the more. As to the other, it's only for a month or so. I think I could endure such abstinence. In fact, for nearly five months now, I've not been with a woman."

Lily could scarcely believe any of the incredible things he was saying. "Sacred blood! That Texas sun must have baked your brains, Rafael."

For the first time he laughed, seeming a bit more like her old Rafael. "Oh, Lily, maybe it did! Or, it beat some sense into my thick skull, I don't know which. I only know my life's been changed. I'm returning to Texas."

"But, for how long?" she added with dread in her voice.

"I don't ever plan to return," he replied grimly, remembering his furious, bitter argument with his father. "I came back only to settle things with my family and to take care of you and Melanie. I've made a settlement with my attorney, Louis Ducet. You own this house and will have a monthly income for as long as you live. Melanie will have the finest education France can offer her when she's old enough, and a sizable dowry. I'll keep in touch with her always, Lily.

"You are young and beautiful. Find a good man to marry you. There are educated men of your race who could offer you much, businessmen, physicians."

"No, no, I love you, Rafael!" Sobbing, she flung herself into his arms.

He held her and crooned soothing words softly, calming her hysterical outburst. "Oh, Lily, after all we've been through together, perhaps I've been the most unfair of all to you. Forgive me, love. I do care for you, but I cannot go on as we were. I must make a new life in Texas and you must make one here—or, if you wish, you could go to France."

"I don't want to live anywhere without you," she hiccuped.

"Lily, Lily," he sighed. He had known this was going to be difficult, but it was even worse than he'd imagined.

She snuggled in his arms, pressing her breasts against his chest, stroking her sleek little hands down his arms and working them up beneath his jacket.

As if reading her thoughts, he gave a mirthless chuckle and restrained her busy fingers. "No, Lily, it won't work. I'm leaving for good within a week. Nothing you can do will change my mind."

She sat very still for a moment, letting the finality of his words sink in. Then she looked up into his face, her eyes lustrous with tears. "If I am never to see you again, Rafael, this one last time, please, make love to me."

The wistfulness in her voice reached out to him and he understood what she meant. He had used Lily ever since he had married Deborah, refusing to face his love for his wife. Lily had been his counterbalance, a distraction, a crutch. She deserved better. Perhaps all the women on Rampart Street did. He could not change what was past, but he could make love to her in the old way for one last bittersweet night.

"For our youth, sweetheart, for old times," he breathed as he kissed her gently, reclining back against the sofa and drawing her with him.

Rafael left the small white house early the next morning. "At least the city place will be deserted with my parents at Lake Pontchartrain," he muttered as he mounted up and headed south. Upon arriving, he sprinted up the stairs and opened the door. The dark interior was inviting in its cool stillness. He stepped inside and stiffened when he heard Claude's mocking voice.

"I imagined you'd go to see Lily. After all the crudities of Texas whores, it must have been exquisite to have a woman of refinement." He sauntered into the parlor, expecting his son to follow.

Rafael stood in the door and scowled down at the indolent figure settled in the large velvet chair. "We've said it all, Papa. Why did you come back to the city?"

"My brokenhearted, lovesick swain who cannot be parted from his wife—you deny you've spent the night with Lily Duvall?" He cocked one elegant brow, waiting.

"Yes, I spent the night and I also told her I was leaving for good. She understands, something you refuse to do."

Claude shot up from the chair. "I am not some high yellow you dismiss from services with a bonus! I am your father! You have a name, a family tradition to honor. You cannot simply turn your back on your duty." His face was dark with rage. "I left your mother prostrate in tears at the lake. She still cannot believe you'll go through with this insane scheme."

"It's hardly insane. Thousands of people have gone to Texas before me. The political situation is stable now, I have a land grant, and adequate money to build a home."

"A home! Pah! Your grandfather's unproven tract of wilderness. I only wish he hadn't been so foolish as to leave your inheritance to you directly."

"Even if you could cut me off without a cent, I'd leave, Papa," Rafael said wearily. "I've used most of the money to take care of Lily and Melanie, anyway. I will be a pioneer in Texas."

"So, you'll work, grow calluses on your hands, grovel in the dirt like an American?" Claude said with a sneer. "And who is to give me grandchildren? Comfort your mother in her old age?" His eyes burned into Rafael's.

"You have a daughter, Papa. And her child will be born right here in New Orleans in a few months."

Claude's nostrils flared in contempt. "An American child. I'll never accept that riffraff into my home."

Something in Rafael snapped, seeing the same provincial disdain his family had always displayed. He turned on Claude with eyes blazing. "At least be grateful your daughter has married a man who's capable of giving her children!"

"What is that supposed to mean?" Claude asked guardedly.

"My cousin, Jean Pierre, met me at the dock with some juicy gossip. The family tried to hush it up, of course, but I was so aghast I did some checking and verified it. It seems that Georges Beaurivage's university companion, Paul Ravat, killed himself in St. Louis. He was prostrate over the death of his lover. . . ."

"I refuse to listen to such cesspool talk!" Claude's face was white. He had heard rumors before Georges was sent to Paris but had dismissed them. "Your cousin had an impeccable reputation and wanted to marry Lenore."

"You mean he was a Beaurivage, from such an illustrious family that his parents threatened him if he didn't marry to hide his sickness! My sister could have been tied to that perverted creature, used as a cover, while he paraded men—even boys—in front of her!" Rafael turned from his father with a sickened look on his face. "And all of us, Jean Pierre, you, Mama, and me—we were all going to see Lenore married to a man who despised her, despised all women, simply because he was a Creole gentleman, a Beaurivage. Thank God my wife saved her. If it were possible to love Deborah more than I do, I would, just for that!

"Maybe you can live with what we've done, Papa, but I

can't.'' He stopped, too weary to go on, as he looked at the set, frozen lines of the older man's face. ''You don't believe me, do you? Or, at least you'll pretend not to.'' He shrugged, knowing it was useless, yet feeling a profound sense of regret.

Taking a deep, steadying breath, he felt something else—freedom from the rigid life he had lived in this closed society. *I'm free from all the old hates and hurts so long festering here. Texas can offer me a second chance. But Deborah gave me my first one.*

''Rafael, I can hardly believe it's you!'' Lenore hugged her brother in amazement, taking in his rough, homespun clothing, shaggy hair, and sun-darkened face.

''I leave for Texas with the morning tide, Lenore. I wanted to say good-bye first.''

Her face creased in a puzzled frown. ''You sound as if you're going to *move* there.''

''I am. Remember the old land grant Grandfather left me as part of my inheritance? Well, it's in northern Texas, in the general area where I lost Deborah's trail. I'm going to use it as a base, build it up as a working ranch while I search for her. I can't stay here.''

Lenore could see the pain and regret etched deeply in his face and imagined well the reaction of their parents. ''So now you've been disowned, too,'' she said sadly.

''Let's just say I've learned to make some hard choices, just as you did,'' he replied softly.

''You're sure she's still there? She might have gone to Boston when the war began.''

''I have agents in Boston, but even without their report, I'm sure she's still in Texas. She and another woman were headed north to Nacogdoches. The chaos and dislocation during the Mexican invasion would have made it almost impossible to get out.''

''Oh, Rafael, I feel so guilty, so stupid for sending her into danger, especially when she was pregnant,'' Lenore sobbed, her hands clutching at her own distended abdomen in unconscious empathy.

He patted her arm affectionately. "Don't blame yourself. Deborah would have gone with or without you. Anyway, my wife is an amazingly strong and resourceful woman. She'll survive. And I *will* find her."

"I'll pray for you every day." Her china blue eyes were crystalline with tears.

"Don't cry, little sister. I have a feeling about all this, about Texas, I guess. Deborah chose it, but after I spent those months searching for her, well, I chose it, too. It's hard to put into words, the feeling of newness, of beginning again. When I find her, we'll stay there and make a new start. If she made a poor Creole, I'd make a dreadful Bostonian, but I think we'll make two fine Texians." He gave his sister a lopsided smile that started her tears anew.

She hugged him awkwardly, her belly getting in the way. "Oh, Rafael, I feel as if we're children again! You're the best big brother any girl could have. Take care of yourself."

"Hardly a girl anymore," he teased, eyeing her belly, "but I am so glad we've discovered each other again, even if we've lost our parents."

"I don't think Deborah will chance writing to us, but if she does, we'll tell you as soon as we can reach you. My word on it," Caleb said as he stood in the door, taking in the tender scene between his wife and her brother.

Rafael turned and faced his brother-in-law. "Caleb, I've said and done some things I regret—"

Armstrong stretched out his hand. "I didn't exactly play by the rules, courting Lenore, either. That's over and best forgotten."

Rafael shook the big American's hand, saying, "I expect to hear if I have a niece or nephew shortly. I'll send an address for you to post to in Nacogdoches."

"This calls for a drink," Caleb said.

When he had poured Lenore a thin-stemmed glass of sherry and each of them a generous snifter of brandy, they all three raised their drinks in salute.

"To Deborah and Texas," Caleb said. "May you find her there."

* * *

Swatting at the incessant torture of mosquitoes, Rafael squatted before the campfire. He poured himself a cup of coffee, took a swallow of the gallishly bitter brew and poured the rest of it out with an oath. When he rose, he winced in pain. *I hope my companions don't notice how sore the "dude" is.* Even Micah Brandish, a tough old smith well past sixty, rode from dawn to dark without any seeming discomfort. Lord, Rafael had thought a lifetime of fencing and riding had toned his muscles superbly, but after a week of traveling overland with this immigrant party from Louisiana he was ready to drop. Reluctantly, he admitted that he was not prepared to keep up with a group of lower class men who were used to the backbreaking labor his field slaves did.

Remembering his father's admonition about groveling in the dirt and growing calluses on his hands, he grimaced thinking about the irony of it. His smooth elegantly sculpted fingers were indeed blistered and filthy. God, he stank of sweat and horse and greasy pork! Fingering a two-week growth of black beard, he promised himself a bath and a barber as soon as they reached a town.

By the time they reached Nacogdoches, Rafael was too saddle sore and tired to care about the poor accommodations and crude populace. The town was an odd mixture, an early eighteenth-century Spanish settlement, overrun in the nineteenth century by Anglo colonists. Mexican and Yankee populations did not mix overmuch and the place was filled with crude, dog-trot cabins scattered around a central core of older Spanish-style adobes.

Rafael bid farewell to his traveling companions with little regret. Always aloof with Americans, his Creole pride and their lower-class manners made him even more reserved, especially considering how poorly he compared with them in frontier survival skills. But he reminded himself grimly that he had learned to build fires, shoot, clean, and cook squirrels and rabbits, feed and care for his own mount, and stay in the saddle for twelve hours at a crack without complaint. If they saw nothing to admire in his fortitude, he congratulated himself on it.

It was wonderful to soak the filth from his body. The tavern he was lodged in was scarcely more than a shanty by New Orleans standards, but in Texas it was a haven of luxury.

"More hot water, señor?" A buxom young maid stood poised in the door with a steaming bucket in her hands. Her large brown eyes assessed him openly as she swished in and poured more water into the large wooden tub.

"Would there by any chance be a barber available?" he asked in Spanish.

"Yes, but his shop is closed for the night," she replied, surprised to find he spoke her language fluently.

He sighed. The idea that a barber might come to attend a gentleman in his lodgings was, of course, absurd in Texas. Giving the maid a dazzling smile, he requested a shaving mug and some soap, thinking, *I'll probably learn to braid my hair like an Indian before I find someone to give me a decent haircut!*

After a simple meal in the tavern, Rafael decided to stretch his legs and see the burgeoning town. As he wandered down a small lane, the raucous laughter of a tavern beckoned him. Looking inside he could see several tables of men playing cards and dice. A long bar of crude planking stretched along one wall and a motley assortment of border ruffians clad in buckskins and homespun stood drinking corn whiskey.

Rafael sauntered in and headed to the bar. Brandy or even rum were doubtless unheard of. He ordered a whiskey. As he grimaced at its fiery trail burning down his throat, he noticed several customers staring at him. Dressed as he was in a clean white linen shirt, cord breeches, and polished riding boots, he realized he did look out of place. But he had been so damn sick of the scratchy, coarse homespun he'd worn on the trail that he had eagerly donned these simple but expensive eastern clothes.

"Lookee thar, whut a pretty feller. Looks like a greaser, but he dresses like a dandyman." A burly fellow with stringy reddish hair spoke as he ran his bleary gray eyes up and down Flamenco.

"Yer jist jealous, Lew," a young female voice said in a coarse, jesting, border-state accent. She was tall like Deborah, but there the resemblance ended. Her brownish hair was lusterless and frizzy and her face was painted. Smoothing her cheap yellow satin dress, she edged toward Rafael. "Yew be new ta these here parts, I kin tell. Yew a planter er somethin'?"

"Or something," he replied levelly.

"Where from?" She was not to be deterred.

"New Orleans, mademoiselle." He was definitely not interested in her, but she seemed oblivious of that fact.

"One 'o them Creole fellers, all lace hankies 'n limp wrists," the bellicose redhead rejoined in an ugly tone of voice.

Never possessing an even temper, Rafael turned slowly and faced his antagonist with black eyes slitted dangerously. "At home, I would never soil my honor dealing with a man of your crudity, monsieur. Even now I find it distasteful," he said as he touched the elaborate dueling pistol at his belt. "But if you would be so kind as to meet me outside and bring your pistol? I have no doubt you require no second. I shall do without one as well."

Rafael got no farther than the door before he was hit from behind with a thudding tackle that brought him crashing to the earthen floor. Lew Grazer was on top of him, crushing the air from his lungs.

"Out here we don't fight us duels like fool dandymen, Frenchy. We fight with knives 'n fists." One of Grazer's huge paws grabbed the white linen shirt and yanked its tall, slim owner up as he lurched to his own feet.

Fighting waves of blackness from the loss of breath, Rafael shook his head. Before he could do more than back free of Grazer's grasp, two other buckskin-clad figures grabbed him. One held his arms while the other pulled his gun free and tossed it to a third man across the room.

"Lookee th' handle—pearl er some sech! If'n Lew beats him daid, I git ta keep this," the small, scraggly man said.

Just then Lew pulled a big, ugly-looking knife from his

belt and stood, feet braced apart in front of Rafael. "Yew ever use one o' Mr. Bowie's knives, dandyman? Mebbe I cud teach ya." He advanced a step while Rafael, eyes now clearly focused on the evil silvery gleam of the knife, backed away a step.

Cursing beneath his breath, Rafael searched the clearing circle of men for a weapon. Just as the brute lunged with his knife, the lightning-fast Creole kicked a chair in his path. The rough frontiersmen obviously disliked the foreigner and wanted him taught a lesson, perhaps a permanent one. He looked for no help from the crowd. He had never fought with knives or his hands. Now he was fighting for his life. Once more cursing his stupidity for blundering into this den of cutthroats, Rafael dodged as Lew rolled up from his sprawl and lunged again.

"If'n it wuz me, I'd o' knocked me cold whilst I wuz on the floor, dandyman. But yew bein' a gentleman 'n all, hah!" He guffawed at the stupidity of fighting by rules.

At the moment Rafael Flamenco agreed with him. He must get that knife away from the brute. But how? One rickety chair held together with hemp sat half-shoved beneath the planking of the bar. He dove for it and came up holding it in one hand. Several men vocalized their approval.

"Dude's quick."

"Frenchy's got guts, Lew."

"Lambast him, honey," yelled the tart.

That cheer for the Frenchman seemed to galvanize Grazer who struck out in a slashing arc with his big knife. Rafael danced out of reach again. Instead of using the chair as a shield, he quickly swung it across the stout plank bar top with all his strength. It flew apart with a loud clatter, leaving a long sturdy leg clenched in his fist. Not losing the momentum from his surprise move, he brought the chair leg around and up toward Grazer's knife hand. It was crude compared to a fencing foil, but his aim and agility had always been good. The chair leg connected with Lew's hand, sending the blade flying. As it arced into the air, men scrambled to avoid its descent.

In the melee, one of Grazer's friends swept Rafael's feet

from under him. Lew threw his two-hundred-twenty-pound body toward his fallen enemy, but Rafael rolled free.

Both men rose, panting and covered with sawdust and mud from the floor. Rafael had lost his club. Grazer's hands clenched into enormous fists as he advanced with murderous intent. Rafael knew he must avoid those fists, but that was not so easily done. He dodged with the practiced instinct of a fencer, looking for an opening. There were vital points that caused pain with a rapier; so, too, they must hurt if hit with fists. Grazer caught him a wicked blow to his midsection, luckily just missing the solar plexus. Nonetheless, he was in agony as he struggled to stay on his feet and avoid another roundhouse swing at the same time. Gritting his teeth, he took a breath and ducked Grazer's next punch, at the same time landing one of his own on the big man's temple. His knuckles throbbed wickedly, but the blow staggered Grazer for a few seconds. Not wanting to lose the initiative, Rafael followed through with another solid body punch.

Grazer let out a whoosh and a muffled oath as the air left his lungs, but he stayed on his feet and recovered in time to land a telling blow to Rafael's left eye. Both antagonists were well bloodied.

By sheer dint of will, Rafael stayed on his feet and kept returning the punishing blows of Grazer, but he was growing too groggy and exhausted to dodge and feint. The sheer size and bulk of his enemy was beginning to tell. *I can't fall. Once I'm down, he'll trample me like a wild boar.*

Quite a few of the onlookers were impressed with the slim young Creole's tenacity. When Grazer made a final lunge and carried them both to the floor once more, several men yelled for the dude. This time, however, his roll to the side did not work. Lew kept his hold on Rafael and began to rain punishing blows to his face, holding the limp figure up by his shirtfront. Rafael was out cold.

When one of Grazer's friends, the small weasely man called Acuff, tossed him his knife, a low voice, punctuated by the clicking hammer of a blunderbuss, interrupted the action. "The dude fought ya fair, which is more'n I kin say fer you 'n yer pals helpin' ya, Grazer. Ya beat him. Now leave it be."

Chapter 19

The room quieted suddenly as men cleared a path for Cherokee Joe De Villiers. The small, wiry man's British blunderbuss was a lethal weapon. The men in the bar knew Joe kept its flaring muzzle loaded with rusty nail heads. His eyes shifted from Grazer to his two friends Acuff and Ryan.

Slowly, feeling the crowd's sentiment shifting to join De Villiers in his support of the unconscious Creole, Lew Grazer let him drop onto the dirt floor and rose to sheathe the knife.

"I got no quarrel with yew, Joe. Dandyman here's been taught a lesson in frontier fightin', I reckon." He grimaced at his own split lip, throbbing skull, and aching gut.

" 'Pears ta me, fer someone half yer weight, the kid did a pretty considerable o' damage, Lew," Joe said genially. He motioned to two men standing near the Creole, who was beginning to stir. "You boys haul him out ta my horse." Turning his attention back to Grazer, he spat a wad of tobacco on the floor and said, "Give th' dude a few more lessons 'n he jist might beat ya, Lew. 'Specially if'n ya git caught without yer *compañeros* here ta back ya."

The laughter from the tavern faded as Joe moved silently up the street with the semiconscious form of Rafael Flamenco draped over his horse.

Rafael could smell coffee and something else cooking, pungent and strong. When he struggled to sit up, pain shot through his midsection. "Aaugh!" With a muffled moan through bloodied, cracked lips, he collapsed again.

Footsteps crunched softly across the dry grass and a low voice spoke in strangely accented English. "Didn't figger ya'd be awake so quick. Better if'n ya sleep. Here, drink this."

218

Something bitter tasting was forced between his parched lips and he slipped once more into unconsciousness, knowing he'd heard the voice before, unable to remember where.

Joe De Villiers looked at the young man. Both eyes were swollen shut, most of his teeth were loose, a nasty gash ran down his jawline, and several ribs were probably broken. Knowing the healing power of sleep and some efficacious Cherokee herbal remedies, Joe hoped the kid would rest easy until nightfall, and let the poultices do a little toward taking out the pain and swelling.

"How long have I been out?" Rafael squinted to see through the narrow slits of his swollen eyes. A campfire danced orange and yellow in front of him and a man sat on the other side of it.

"Near a day, I reckon," Joe replied as he reached to pour a cup of coffee. When he rose and walked over to Rafael's pallet to give it to him, the younger man let out a painful oath as he tried to sit up too fast.

"Watch them ribs. I wrapped 'em, but I spect they's broke. Cuda been worse. You wuz plumb lucky. Got real *puha*, yessir." He chuckled at some private joke and handed the cup to the young Creole. He grinned when Rafael almost dropped it because of the stiffness in his knuckles. Doggedly he held on and began to sip.

"I certainly do not feel lucky," he said gingerly, feeling to see if any teeth were missing. Sacred Blood! Not an inch of him was undamaged!

"You'll mend right 'nough. Fer a New Orleans fancypants, ya got grit, boy. Stood up ta Lew better 'n I seen many a old hand do."

Rafael looked at his benefactor. He was medium height, rather more wiry than slim with very dark skin and shoulder-length straight black hair held back with a calico headband. "Who are you and why did you save me?" He rubbed his head. "At least I think I remember that you did."

Joe laughed. "Yep, reckon I dragged ya outta there. Fool thing fer a feller dressed like you ta do—go inta the Rattler 'n order a drink, 'specially in a ferrin accent. I'm Joe De Villiers, Cherokee Joe De Villiers. Another Louisiana Frenchy, only not like you. Guess I helped ya out cuz I liked yer spunk er mebbe I don't like Lew Grazer.''

Rafael smiled painfully. "I am in your debt in any case, Monsieur De Villiers. Rafael Flamenco is my name. Why do they call you Cherokee?''

"Cuz I'm a breed. Know thet might not set too good with most Creoles, but now thet ya come ta Texas, I reckon ya'll have ta make do. My ma was Cherokee 'n my pa was a French trapper.''

Rafael nodded. He noted the man's hawkish features and the reddish cast to his complexion. Joe wore greasy buckskins and a beaded rawhide necklace. "As you said, this is Texas and I can make do. However, if you hadn't stopped Grazer, I wouldn't be making do at all. If your father was French, you should speak his language. Do you?" he asked, openly curious. De Villiers's accent puzzled him.

"*Oui*. I also speak Cherokee, English, Snake, 'n pretty passable border Spanish. Fer an uneducated feller, I'm a wonder,'' he answered guilelessly.

Rafael burst out laughing, then quickly subsided as his cracked ribs and split lips protested. "I too speak Spanish, French, and English. What is Snake?''

Joe grunted. "Snake's lingo is th' most useful one fer tradin' 'mongst all plains Indians. Snakes is really two tribes, leastways fer th' last hunnert years er so since they split. Up north they's called Shoshones. Their enemies th' Utes give 'em another name when the southern bands wuz first movin' onta th' plains after buffalo—*Koh-mahts*. Means enemy. Kinda stuck. Only now everyone jist says Comanche.''

Rafael grunted. "*Them* I've heard of.''

De Villiers laughed. "Ain't everybody. Fiercer, more cunnin' horse Indians never lived.''

"I take it you've traveled among them,'' Rafael said, fascinated, for he'd heard horror stories about the Comanche on his first visit to Texas last spring.

"I traded some horses with 'em. They ain't like my ma's people, er most others. They don't let outsiders live with 'em, nor use their women neither. Ya interested in tradin' with th' Comanche?''

"I doubt it, but I've heard they roam on my land. When I

begin to reclaim it, I may need to deal with them—peacefully, I hope," Rafael replied.

"Comanche don't do much o' nothin' peaceful," Joe scoffed. "They don't reckon anyone owns land neither."

"That's not what my Great Grandfather Flamenco's land grant from the king of Spain says," Rafael replied with a superior grin.

"Anyone been livin' on it lately—like in th' past fifty years er so?"

"No. My grandfather went to New Orleans in 1779 to seek a bride. He married Louise Beaurivage, who convinced him she would languish in a strange land. He never returned," Rafael said. "I imagine there's little left of the stone house his father built, but the land has a good water supply, and abundant wild horses and longhorn cattle roaming free. I intend to rebuild it."

Joe scratched his chin thoughtfully. "Since th' People— Comanche—moved onta th' Texas plains, they kinda spread out—beat th' other Indian groups 'n drove the Mexicans out. Ain't been no white settlers able ta stand up ta 'em in my lifetime. Whereabouts is yer place?"

Rafael grimaced in embarrassment. "I have maps, but I'm not certain. I need a guide who's familiar with the land northwest of the Brazos River."

De Villiers whistled low. "Could be smack in th' middle o' th' plains where th' People roam free. Say, ya got a map?"

"Back in my room at the tavern."

Joe grunted. "When yer movin' easier we'll take us a look-see."

"Could you guide me there? I now realize I'm a 'greenhorn,'" Rafael said with chagrin, recalling his stupidity on the previous night.

Joe gave him a measuring look. "Yep. Might could be. I been mustangin' on th' plains fer years. Got me no long-thought-out plans."

Over the next several days Joe and Rafael formed the unlikeliest of friendships. The tough half-breed was quick and shrewd, possessing a subtle sense of humor and great empathy. Rafael knew he had a great deal to learn about his adopted land, and a man like De Villiers could teach him, as well as guide him to his property.

Joe described Texas weather and the lands to the west inhabited only by migrating bands of Indians; he explained how he captured wild horses and broke them to saddle. De Villiers demonstrated more of practical healing skills than most physicians in New Orleans and understood Texas history better than Rafael's university professors. Joe knew weapons and survival. Realizing dueling pistols and rapiers would not be useful in Texas, Rafael wanted to learn how to use fists, knives, and long rifles.

"First ya gotta leave yer broke bones ta heal," was Joe's reply to the request. "Then we'll see. I 'spect ya got it in ya ta fight ta win. You ever kill a man?"

"Yes," was the terse reply.

"Thought so."

Joe watched in approval while Rafael squatted at the campfire and ate spitted rabbit roasted whole over the coals. By the end of the week he was able to ride to town with Joe.

He paid his room bill at the tavern, collected his gear, and brought it to Joe's camp. They examined his old maps that night by firelight.

Joe spat a wad of tobacco from his mouth and considered the map. "Yep, pretty country. Yer right 'bout th' water, mustangs, 'n longhorns."

"You've been there—seen it?" Rafael's interest was excited. At first the landgrant had been only a base from which to search for Deborah. Gradually it had become more. It would be a home to bring her to, a new start for them both.

"I know the land. Kinda isolated. Not many Comanche cause there ain't many buffalo. Thet's not ta say it'll be easy pickins. You know thet?"

"Let's just say I'm beginning to learn," Rafael said, stroking the scar forming over his left eyebrow.

Inside three weeks they had crossed the Trinity and the Brazos Rivers, which were at low water in the dry, fall weather. The pine and hardwood forested land around Nacogdoches gradually gave way to rich blackland soil and oak savannah. They passed by stands of giant cottonwoods in river basins. Interspersed between the lush woodlands were vast stretches of rolling plains where the kaleidoscopic herds of wild horses and longhorn cattle ran free, legacies left centuries earlier by ill-fated Spanish explorers.

"You could ride all the way across Europe and not see as varied a landscape as we've passed through," Rafael said as they stopped to rest their horses in a lush canyon.

"An' this is only halfway across Texas," Joe replied laughingly. "Farther west it gets real flat, hot 'n dry. Lots more cactus 'n strange-shaped mountains. Bleak but sorta beautiful, too, with all them bright red 'n purple colored rocks."

"Are there springs like this everywhere—even in the desert?" Rafael bent over painfully, favoring his aching ribs, to cup his hand and drink the clear sparkling water rushing down the canyon.

"Ones in th' desert go underground a lot more, 'specially in dry seasons like this, but they is a lot o' 'em."

Joe watched as his young companion mounted his horse, doing his best to mask the pain his cracked ribs and bruised hands were giving him. Rafael slept on the hard ground, helped with camp chores, and even fired a .45 caliber Kentucky long rifle. Two days earlier he had brought down a deer, providing them with an abundant supply of meat, but at fearful cost. The recoil had jarred his broken body so painfully Joe expected him to faint. Rafael had whitened and held his breath but recovered and insisted on helping dress the deer. Never seen a blueblood with *cojones* like him, he thought.

Late that afternoon they crested a rise and looked down on a gently sloping valley with a meandering stream nestled deep in the rich bottomland. Joe could sense Rafael's excitement.

"This is it, isn't it, Joe?"

"See over there where the creek forks—look real close," the half-breed instructed.

"The house! I can see the house!" With a whoop of jubilation he spurred his wiry little mustang into a headlong gallop.

When they reached the house, the close-up view was no

surprise to De Villiers, but he feared it might be to Flamenco. The thick stone walls were crumbled in several places and the roof was completely caved in. Vines of mustang grape grew wild across the doors and windows.

Measuring his young companion, who had endured so much to get here, Joe said, "I warned you it would be this way."

Rafael's eyes glowed as he envisioned the house with a stout roof, its thick walls keeping the inside cool in summer heat, warm against winter chill. "It can be rebuilt. The basic structure seems sound. And look at the site—the trees, the water. It's magnificent, Joe!" He dismounted and began to tear away the vines blocking the front door.

Joe helped him and they entered the large front room. Even in the August heat, it was cool, just as Rafael knew it would be.

"This will be my home, Joe," he said reverently.

"The home you'll bring yer woman to? Deborah?"

Rafael whirled. "How did you know—"

"You were out fer a day 'n night. Even after thet I gave ya medicine ta let ya sleep. Ya talked—shit, raved in yer sleep, Rafael. I know yer lookin' fer a silver-haired woman who ran off from New Orleans carryin' yer youngun. Ya'll find 'er—if anyone can. Got a feelin'. You know Cherokee have a sixth sense. Believe in it. Believe in yerself."

Rafael felt a solid sense of kinship, a bond forged in the wilderness with this older man of mixed race. How remarkable that he should feel closer to Cherokee Joe than he ever had to his own father.

"I believe, Joe, I believe. I'll call this place Renacimiento—Rebirth. It'll be a new home, a new beginning for Deborah and me and our children." He reached out and clasped the callused red hand firmly.

They made a careful inventory of the supplies they'd need to begin restoring the buildings and starting a working ranch. Several months capturing and breaking wild horses would mean basic work stock for the ranch and also a sizable profit if they sold the excess to the hordes of settlers pouring into Texas. Now that the war was over, the new Republic was offering homestead grants of two square miles to a family. It might take years, but with this rich, hidden valley full of lush vegetation and wild livestock, Rafael knew he could build a home for his family.

His family: Deborah and their child. Her time was near. Would it be a girl or boy? He prayed she was safe and that he would find her soon.

On the ride back to Nacogdoches, Joe told him about his time among the various tribes of red men in Texas, especially the dominant ones—the Comanche or Nerms, who called themselves the People.

"They paint theirselves black fer war, 'n start a mission only at night. Move quick 'n quiet. Slip in 'n kill fast. Live ta enjoy the spoils of victory. No dumb stand up 'n shoot in straight lines like whites do. Stupid waste o' lives."

"Like dueling?" Rafael asked with a grin.

"Yep, like duelin'. Don't never fight by rules, boy. Only fight when yer back's ta the wall. Then, fight ta kill. Use yer head 'n make th' other feller lose his. 'N never show fear. I 'spect ever' man's afraid, only a fool wouldn't be afraid ta die, but they's a mind set ta fear 'n it eats at ya. Yer enemy kin sense it 'n it gives him th' edge. Makes better *puha* ta bury fear."

"You said once I had strong *puha*," Rafael mused. "What is it?"

"Nerm's word fer magic, er power. Kinda medicine that makes a man believe in hisself."

"And then other men believe in him too," Rafael said.

Joe nodded. The greenhorn was learning fast. Very fast.

When they arrived back in Nacogdoches they headed first to Brown's Tavern for a drink.

"Joe! Damn, I been lookin' fer yew fer weeks. Where'd yew git to so quick?" The speaker was a big frontiersman with a curly red beard.

"Sabine!" Joe turned to Rafael as he pumped the big man's hand. "Rafael Flamenco, meet Sabine Mike Forkness. Good man."

They exchanged a hearty handshake. Rafael was glad his bruised and blistered hands had healed and strengthened in the past month.

"Joe, I got word fer ya from Louisiana. Yer sister's man

is real bad 'n she asks ya to come 'n help her. Here—she sent me with this.'' He took a badly crumpled and water-stained packet from inside his odoriferous buckskins.

Joe read the Cherokee script slowly and carefully, his face grave. ''I gotta go, Rafael. Felice needs my help. She's my baby sister 'n I hafta take care o' her.''

''When will you return?'' Rafael asked, thinking of Lenore and knowing he'd do the same.

''I 'spect in a month er so. Git yer supplies ordered 'n see 'bout some men. Sabine here'll help ya.''

The burly redhead nodded immediately. ''Yep. We kin do 'er, Rafael.'' He stumbled over the foreign name, then amended, ''Rafe. Yep—Rafe—that suits better, huh?''

Looking from one buckskin-clad figure to the other, Rafael Flamenco let out a hearty laugh. ''How about making me all Texian—Rafe Fleming? From now on, that's my name.''

Sabine slapped the younger man's back, jarring his almost healed ribs. ''Welcome ta Texas, Rafe Fleming.''

Joe had departed for Louisiana two days ago, telling Rafe to expect him at the ranch in four to six weeks. Sabine and Rafe were just about ready to depart, but they lacked enough men to begin the arduous task of reclaiming the land.

He and Sabine were sitting down to dinner in Brown's Tavern with that weighty issue hanging over their heads when a smooth, low voice said in Spanish-accented English, ''*Pardón*, señors, but I understand you look for *mesteñeros*?''

Rafe looked up at the hard-faced, swarthy man dressed in simple vaquero's clothes. He looked like hundreds of other *Tejanos* at first glance, but there was a feral watchfulness in his eyes that struck a spark of uneasiness in Rafe. He has eyes like Georges Beaurivage, Rafe thought.

Dismissing the idea as fanciful, he asked, ''Have you ever captured mustangs on the plains west of here?''

''Permit me to introduce myself. I am Enrique Flores and this''—he paused to allow a squat, heavy man with a bristling beard to materialize from behind him—"is Ray Garter. We have captured, broken, and sold many herds from here to Santa Fe."

"Lots of comancheros use Santa Fe as a base," Sabine said quietly.

Flores looked at Rafe's companion gravely but steadily. "*Sí*, I've met a few, but who has lived in Texas and not seen them? I understood you were looking for good men and we are the best, Señor Fleming."

"You're right. I need experienced men," Rafe said with finality. "We leave in two days. You can get whatever gear you need from Gareson's General Store tomorrow."

A week of retracing their route to Renacimiento brought them to their first dry camp. After all the spring rains that had so plagued both Mexican and Texian armies in the revolution, the late summer weather was dry in the extreme.

"Feast er famine in Texas," Sabine said, as several men carped about the dried-up spring where they camped. "Wait'll ya see th' springs at th' ranch. Ole Joe said they wuz so deep they went clear ta China. Always have water there."

Mort Soller spat a stream of tobacco juice and nodded. "Wish we cud git cross this dry stretch quicker. I'd rest easier knowin' I's near water."

"Where'd Enrique go, Ray?" Sabine asked, wanting to take the men's minds off the hard, dangerous trip ahead.

Garter looked from Sabine to Fleming. "He's scouting a shortcut. There's water south of here. A small settlement of Anglo farmers lives there."

"Joe never mentioned it to me," Rafe said, looking at Ray guardedly.

Garter shrugged. "Even Cherokee Joe De Villiers may not know everything."

"I don't like it, Rafe," Sabine said in a low voice as he squatted by the fire to pour coffee into a tin cup.

"Post an extra guard tonight. I'll wait up for Enrique myself," Rafe responded.

Aching and tired, Rafe sat staring into the leaping flames of the campfire, waiting for Flores to return. He dreamed of a woman with long silver hair and violet eyes.

Suddenly the whole campsite erupted in chaos. Shots

were fired, and men cursed and yelled as blood-chilling, savage war cries sounded. Rafe leapt to his feet, but spots and blackness were all he could see. He was blinded in the dark after staring into the bright flames of the fire, something Joe had cautioned him never to do! When he felt a sinewy hand grasp at his shirt, he instinctively warded off the blow with his right arm, only to feel the sharp slash of a knife penetrate his jacket and cut his forearm.

A sharp scream of *"Aaa-hey"* rent the air as he sent one man flying, only to have another pounce from the other side and grab his hair with brutal strength. Certain he was about to be scalped, Rafe twisted and dropped into a roll, thinking to dislodge his attacker, but he had not counted on the first one coming back so quickly. Both were on him, wrestling with him as he tried to pull his knife free from its sheath. Then one of the savages struck him a sharp blow to the temple and he slipped into inky oblivion.

All around the unconscious man his companions were falling, swarmed over in their sleep by the stealthy raiders who now systematically finished off all who resisted. Sabine was sprawled facedown across the fire from Rafe, with a red stain widening across his back. Mort Soller and Jose Ramirez were lying faceup with their eyes wide open in death. Felix Solidad was scarcely alive, with a war lance run through his abdomen, pinning him to the ground. The screams of the dying blended with the screams of the triumphant Comanche.

"Wake up, amigo. Iron Hand's men went to a great deal of trouble to keep you alive. You can't disappoint them," Ray Garter's voice rasped in Rafe's ear.

Bastards set us up. Sabine was right! Rafe thought bitterly. Why hadn't he followed his instincts about Garter and Flores? Pretending to be unconscious, he let Garter haul him up from his prone position on the ground. He wasn't tied. Good. He knew well from Joe's description what happened to captives among the Comanche!

With a pantherlike lunge he sprang to life, toppling Garter

backward. In a blur, Rafe ripped the knife from the comanchero's belt and plunged it into his enemy's throat. Expecting to feel the impact of a bullet or lance any instant, Rafe crouched, knife arching back and forth as he gazed at the evil assemblage.

"I told you he had *puha*," a low voice said in Spanish. Rafe whirled to confront Enrique Flores who stood next to a barrel-chested Comanche wearing a demonic-looking horned headdress. Flores's teeth flashed whitely in the firelight as he laughed. It was an eerie sound. The war chief grunted and considered how best to disarm his captive.

"This is for all my men, Flores!" Rafe sprang to his feet and dove toward the comanchero, knife outstretched. *If only I can take the bastard with me*, was his last thought before he felt shattering pain in his right arm. A Comanche war lance had smashed it. The knife flew from his numb hand. Still undefeated he rolled up and made a bare-handed lunge toward Flores, his eyes glowing with hate and desperation. It took four warriors to bring him down.

"Alive! I want him alive," came the war chief's command. Rafe recognized the first word. Joe had taught him a bit of the Snake language. Knowing what being taken alive meant, he fought with increased desperation while Enrique Flores watched like a bored spectator, as indifferent to his dead partner as he was to all the other dead men he had betrayed.

Finally one of the warriors twisted Rafe's broken arm. The bolt of searing, white-hot pain made him drop unconscious in shock. When he came to he was tied hand and foot, slung across a war pony. Every jarring hoofbeat caused another wave of agony to lance through his arm. He gritted his teeth and concentrated on the information Joe De Villiers had given him about the Comanche. They had gone to great trouble to keep him alive. Flores, like Joe, had said he had *puha*—the Snake word for power. He might survive, if he could keep his nerve—and stand the pain.

Chapter 20

I'm being saved for something special, that much is for sure. Whether or not it would be a blessing or a hideous nightmare remained to be seen, but Rafe figured on the latter. Only his hate for Flores kept him from going insane over the next three days. They rode at a brutal pace, stopping at night only to eat strips of dried meat, drink a few swallows of fetid water, and sleep an hour. All too soon they resumed the grueling return to their base camp deep in the heart of the southwest plains.

The men in the war party dressed in very little clothing, only breechclouts and blue-dyed leggings. Their hair was very long, braided, smeared with buffalo dung, and decorated with bones and feathers. Many wore the frightful war helmets, unique to the Comanche, great bison scalps with the horns attached. For war, their faces had been striped with black paint.

The first thing Rafe sensed when they arrived in the main camp was the overpowering stench of rotted meat and human and animal excrement. Crude brush arbors were strung out in no particular pattern, following the meandering course of a stream in a narrow, steep-sided ravine. Piles of bones and decomposing garbage littered the earth.

Women dressed in greasy yellow buffalo-hide tunics cheered as the captives and loot were brought home. Their faces were contorted as they cried fiercely, *"Yee-Yee-Yee!"* Gruesome circles of orange paint adorned their cheeks and ears. Their hair was hacked off short, and many were tattooed grotesquely with black dotted lines circling their breasts.

Rafe was hard put to say which was more intimidating—the warriors or their women. He had heard what the women could do to a male captive after the men broke his *puha* and made him scream. He vowed once more not to scream.

It was a night for celebration. There were two captives stripped naked, suspended between ash poles, bound hand and foot with leather thongs. With his arms and legs stretched tightly, Rafe fought pain with each breath. Stretching his broken arm had at least straightened the break, but if left this way for long, it would doubtless never mend. He laughed through his agony. *Mend! I'll be dead by morning, if I'm lucky!*

Sid Lattimer, the other captive, was a big burly teamster from Ohio who had arrived in Texas too late to serve in Houston's army, but still not too late to die in Texas. Rafe could see the man flinch and thrash, his eyes growing round with terror as two warriors approached him. Gritting his teeth, he rasped out, "Don't let them see fear! Taunt them so they kill you quick—otherwise they'll turn you over to the women!"

Even as he expended precious energy to speak, he knew it was useless. Lattimer no more than felt one knife slice across his bared chest than he was shrieking and babbling. Rafe let his head drop, unwilling to watch the systematic mutilation by knives and hot coals. Soon enough he'd know how it felt. After a few hours, Lattimer was cut down and thrown to a cluster of women at the edge of the fire. They eagerly took up their prize, dragging his mutilated body off to stake it to the ground. The pitiful devil might live for days before they were through with him.

Then Rafe heard voices speaking in a polyglot of Spanish and Snake. One was Flores, the other Iron Hand. Flores was telling the Comanche about Rafe's fight with Grazer back in Nacogdoches, describing how he withstood the beating and kept coming back for more. Something to the effect that Iron Hand could have the Creole's *puha* if he could break him. *The sadistic bastard wants to watch! It's a game to him.*

When Rafe sensed they had moved closer to him, he raised his head and stared into Flores's eyes. Using every last ounce of strength and what little moisture he had left in his mouth, he spat full in the comanchero's face. Flores lunged, but the chief caught his fist, stopping the wicked blow aimed at Rafe's groin.

Iron Hand issued a command and one young warrior went over to the fire. The crowd grew surprisingly still after all its chaotic chanting and yelling earlier. An air of expectancy fell over everyone as the brave returned with a pair of crude metal tongs, heated red-hot. He stood waiting for Iron Hand's command. The chief spoke to Rafe in his guttural but serviceable Spanish. "You understand me? The other white eyes says your medicine is strong. How strong, I wonder?" With that he took his knife from its sheath and cut a thin, elongated gash down Rafe's chest, leaving a bright ooze of red seeping through the dark pelt of his chest hair. When Rafe made no sound or movement, only stared impassively at him, he grunted in approval. "I think you could stand much," the chief said with deliberation as the youth with the glowing tongs stepped closer.

Rafe looked at the malevolent grin on the boy's face, then back at Iron Hand. "I know you will tell him to tear my manroot away with those," he said in flat, steady Spanish. "I laugh at you. You will never have my *puha*!" With that he smiled evilly at the boy, who blanched at his bizarre behavior. Then Rafe began to laugh, mustering all the contempt he could put into his performance. Let them think he was mad. There was magic in that, too. He fixed his eyes on Iron Hand and never let them waver.

Suddenly, with an abrupt shift in whim, Iron Hand dismissed the youth. Turning to Rafe, he said, "Your magic is strong this night. Maybe we will wait and see if it lasts." With that he gave a command and two other warriors cut the prisoner down. When the tension on his broken arm was released, the bones snapped back in place. Luckily one of the men grasped him just as he fainted.

Rafe awoke to bright sunlight and the screams of Lattimer. The women, he thought helplessly, squinting to see where he was. He lay on a crude pallet of lice-ridden skins beneath one of the open brush lean-tos. His feet were staked securely with rawhide loops attached to small pegs driven deep in the ground, but his arms were free. Indeed the broken one, still throbbing steadily, had been bound with willow strips and lashed firmly into a serviceable splint with pieces of rawhide. It was still agony to move it, but he had to try.

Despite the hammering pain, he could control the arm.

"The swelling is down. You are a strong man. The break was clean and pulled straight to mend well." A woman's voice spoke in clear Spanish. Rafe sat up slowly, feeling the sharp sting of the slash on his chest. He shaded his eyes and squinted at the small figure of a woman who stood before him dressed in the same greasy yellow buckskins he had observed the other women wearing. She was slight and small and her short, cropped hair had a slight curl to it.

"You're white," he said in Spanish. She shrugged. "I am Little Willow, wife to Iron Hand. Once I was Lucia Maria Gonzalez y Garcia, but that was long ago. I was taken by comancheros, just as you were," she replied.

His face darkened. "The one who betrayed me, is he still here?"

"No. He left this morning with many horses. The guns and bullets you had were worth much to Iron Hand."

"But he will return," Rafe said.

"He will return," she echoed, understanding.

Just then another woman rounded the corner of the shelter. She spoke sharply in their language to Little Willow, who quickly scurried away. Then she turned to Rafe and eyed him up and down with insolent slowness. She was tall for a Nerm and probably considered a handsome female by their standards with straight, unmarked features and large, upthrust breasts. However, like all the Comanche he had come in contact with, she stank. Joe had told him they only bathed for religious occasions. As Indians went, they were not very religious.

Her silent perusal began to make him uneasy. When she poked a heavy stick at him and pulled off the small robe covering his midsection, he knew his instinct was correct. She was inspecting him as if he were a stud horse! Or a slave on the auction block. The thought flashed into his mind as she grinned flirtatiously, revealing several blackened teeth.

"You strong—maybe too skinny, but good," she said in crude but intelligible Spanish.

Good for what? She bent over and cut the bonds on his ankles with a sharp knife. Then as several other women gathered around to watch, she tied a long, rawhide cord from his broken arm to her waist. Any time he dallied, a yank would quickly bring him to heel.

"Plenty work. Come." He was careful to keep up.

Rafe was forced to follow her down to the stream with a heavy iron cook pot; then she instructed him to fill it with water and lug it back uphill to her cook fire. He spent the day doing heavy chores at her beck and call with no rest and no food. As the sun arced high in the heavens, he knew his sunburn would hurt worse than the mortification of being paraded through the camp stark naked. Joe had told him all new captives were treated so in an attempt to break their spirit. He ignored the titters and stares of the pubescent girls as they viewed the tan marks at his waist. The lower half of his body was decidedly lighter than the upper.

Within two weeks his burned lower body had darkened and he forced himself to feel impervious to his nakedness. The grueling labor, dragging in firewood and pulling huge skin sacks of nuts and roots that the women had gathered, left him exhausted at night. He was given food at irregular intervals. It seemed the band members ate when they felt like it, at no set time. When his mistress sat down to eat she allowed him to do likewise. He thought it just as well not to know what was in the bowls of greasy, foul-smelling mush.

Sand Owl, his mistress, was the chief wife of Iron Hand, who had lent her the one-armed slave until he healed. Rafe was uncertain what Iron Hand planned for him then, but was positive it could be no worse than the squaw work he was given by Sand Owl. Working one-handed made him clumsy and Sand Owl would beat him with the large club she carried. The first time she did so, he made the mistake of trying to take it away from her. Three warriors with *his* new rifles materialized out of nowhere. One struck him from behind with a gun stock, knocking him unconscious.

Oddly, his defiance seemed to please Sand Owl. After that, whenever she clubbed him, she watched the fury blaze in his black eyes and seemed to feed on it like an aphrodisiac.

By the end of the month his arm was almost knitted and he could flex his hand and ball it up into a tight fist. He practiced each night when everyone was asleep. They tied him now, staked to the ground spread-eagled to ensure that he could not escape. But escape was all he thought of.

"Whatever happened to the other captive?" he asked Little Willow one night when she brought him food. It was late and few people were around. Soon they'd stake him.

She did not meet his eyes but said, "They did an evil thing. They strangled him after only a day."

Realizing the women could have kept him in agony for many more days, Rafe was relieved. "It's good he is no longer suffering," he replied simply.

"But they think he is. I—I do not know." At his puzzled look she explained. "The People believe if a man dies by strangulation, his soul rots with his corpse. It is trapped."

Obviously she remembered much of her white life. She spoke educated Spanish. "How long have you been here, Lucia?"

"Too long to ever go back. I have a son," she said quietly.

He understood. She could not leave her child and her Mexican family would never accept it, even if she were freed.

Changing the subject, she said, "Sand Owl wants to lie with you. The medicine man says she is barren, but she does not believe him. She blames Iron Hand and believes if you can get her with child, the chief will accept it as his."

Rafe blanched but was not really surprised at Sand Owl's lechery or her deviousness. "You said you had a son by Iron Hand. Why aren't you chief wife?"

She hung her head. "I was raped by many warriors when I was captured. Iron Hand married me when I gave birth because I was proven fertile. The People have few children and fewer still survive infancy. Most women have many miscarriages."

"So, he has no children and she figures this is the way to guarantee her position and give him one. Why use a white slave? Why not a warrior?" *I must figure a way out of this deadly tangle!*

She shook her head impatiently. "A wife can be killed or have her nose cut off for infidelity. No warrior would betray his chief this way."

"So, she figures to fool him with my get. Guess it'd for

sure have black hair," he said ruefully, but his stomach turned over in revulsion. "What happens if I refuse? Rape's pretty difficult in reverse."

"She will say you tried to escape and will have her sisters kill you," Little Willow replied simply.

He let out a deep, whistling breath. His life with the Nerms reminded him uncomfortably of that of a field slave on a Louisiana plantation. He'd heard rumors about the overseers and even some of their wives' appetites. Often he'd wondered idly if they were true.

For the past five weeks all Sand Owl had done was eye him lecherously and take him with her to the stream where she would occasionally disrobe and rinse off her tunic. He had known by the way she preened, thrusting out her tattooed breasts, that she was taunting him sexually.

Thinking of how she smelled, he knew he could be celibate indefinitely rather than touch her. But then looking down at his own sweaty, filthy body with shoulder-length matted hair and unkempt beard, he knew he must smell no better.

When Sand Owl came to tie him up that night he watched her closely. The looks she gave him in return made his flesh crawl. If only Iron Hand would notice that his arm was healed. He considered how to bring that fact to the chief's attention and thus escape Sand Owl. The next day he asked Little Willow to remove the splint.

"No. I cannot. It is for the medicine man to say," she replied.

He knew she was afraid and he could press her no more. That afternoon while carrying a basket of grapes back to camp, he spied an outcrop of sharp rocks. Feigning a slip, he dropped the basket. Sand Owl turned angrily and gave him several stout whacks with her club. His body was covered with lacerations and bruises from her beatings, but he had become inured to the blows. As he gathered the spilled fruit, he managed to slip a sharp piece of shale into the basket. Later, when they stopped to eat, he turned his back carefully and sawed doggedly at the splint's bindings until the leather gave way. Then he dropped it in a thicket of chokecherries.

No one noticed until they were back at camp. Sand Owl was furious and began to beat him. Seeing no men around, but wanting to attract their attention now, he made a light-ning lunge and caught her club, pulling her off balance. She fell at his feet. He stepped on her tunic, pinning her to the ground and used the club to knock her knife from her hand.

By the time the commotion brought several warriors running, it was apparent that Broken Arm, as he had been dubbed, had regained the use of his injured limb. That was how Iron Hand found him, standing over the thrashing, hate-crazed Sand Owl, her long, jagged pole in his hands fending off attackers on all sides.

Did the craggy, impassive face seem to smile? Rafe was not sure, but he knew his fate was now out of Sand Owl's hands and in her husband's.

"If you kill one of the People, you die," Iron Hand intoned.

"If I let your woman have this, I may die anyway," Rafe replied. He was certain then that Iron Hand did smile.

"Your arm has healed. You can leave woman's work now. Buffalo have been sighted. Or, would you rather gather wood?" It was the most contemptuous question a Nerm male could ever put to another man.

Rafe carefully sidestepped Sand Owl, pinning her to the ground with the pole until he stood before Iron Hand. He motioned to the long rope binding him to the woman. Iron Hand ordered one of the warriors to cut it. Following the chief, Rafe never looked back, but he knew he had made a dangerous enemy.

The next morning they left in search of buffalo. By midday the hunting party had found the vast herd, a brown-ish mass undulating against the horizon as far as the eye could see. Rafe was amazed at their numbers. The bison covered the deep grasses. He watched the other slaves dismount and followed suit. Most of the slaves were Caddoes or Shawnee with a smattering of Mexicans. He was the only American. Most of the captives had been castrated and were docile, beaten creatures who quickly leapt to do their masters' bidding.

The Comanche were the smallest in stature of all the

Horse Indians. But as Rafe watched the hunt, he realized why the Nerm were called Lords of the Plains. A Nerm warrior riding his pony at breakneck speed could put a flat-headed hunting arrow all the way through a large bull buffalo, just behind the short rib. Their saddles were no more than blankets and a few rawhide strips with stirrups attached. The riders hung at precarious angles, letting arrows fly while seemingly glued to the pounding backs of their horses. It looked like a magic act to Rafe as he followed the other slaves to gut and quarter the kills as they fell.

Women and children caught up with the men as the day wore on, eager to share in the delicacies of the hunt. After killing a large cow, one warrior slipped from his pony while the slaves butchered the buffalo. He then reached inside and extracted the warm liver, smeared it with the salty juices of the gall bladder, and devoured it hot from the body cavity. When women and children arrived, the favored sons and wives were allowed such treats as warm blood, brains, and sweet bone marrow.

Revolted by the smells and gore of the devourment, Rafe watched the slaves as they cried and pleaded for parts of the hot, vile-smelling entrails. When one warrior took a long strip of intestine and sucked the slimy green contents with his teeth, devouring the bison's predigested dinner, Rafe turned to keep from retching. He went to bed on a very empty stomach that night.

Winter came, bitter cold with deep snows, unusual in the sheltered ravines of central Texas. By the time the hunt had ended, Rafe had been blackened by the sun and his muscles had been honed to sinewy hardness. He could run alongside a horse until it dropped, do without food or water for days, and withstand heat or cold with the impervious calm of a Comanche.

He lived on his hate. Twice over the winter Enrique Flores came with another group of comancheros, but Rafe had no opportunity to get near Flores. He waited. Life had improved slightly since he had been a slave of the women.

Now he wore thick buffalo pelts and slept in Iron Hand's main tepee. For some perverse reason, Iron Hand had taken a liking to Broken Arm, now renamed Tall Stealer, because of his height and the fact that he had stolen Sand Owl's club. The men thought it highly amusing, but Rafe avoided Sand Owl and her sisters as much as possible.

Winter had been a time of quiescence and relative ease. After a plenteous fall hunt, the band had dried much meat. When the snows fell, they stayed in warm, bison-hide tepees in a sheltered river canyon far to the south, avoiding the winter winds. The men ate, slept, and worked on their sacred medicine shields and other war paraphernalia. The women did all the hard camp chores. Iron Hand did not let Sand Owl and her sisters take Rafe with them when they gathered wood, although most of the other captives were so assigned.

He knows she'll try to kill me, but why does he care? The mystery of the Nerm mind still eluded Rafe. After six months of living among them, he was mastering enough of their language to communicate easily. His stomach had long since quit rebelling at raw bison entrails. Hunger redefines even the most discerning palate. Iron Hand watched him learn and adapt with an interest that Rafe knew would eventually spell his freedom or his death.

One skill that he already possessed gave him an edge as a captive—his way with horses. Dozens of generations of Iberian horsemen were his Flamenco forebears. Even among his Creole racing companions, no mean riders any of them, he was an exceptional horseman. The Nermernuh were the horsebrokers of the plains, capturing wild mustangs, breaking them and selling them to all the other tribes, as well as to renegade whites like Flores's comancheros. Horses were Comanche money. And the great war chiefs like Iron Hand were rich. He possessed nearly three hundred horses and was always eager to acquire more.

Rafe watched the warriors breaking and training the tough, wiry little ponies; he admired their skill and was astonished at their patience. Although he tortured his captives and beat his women, no Nerm abused his horses unless in a life and death situation. Tall Stealer often assisted the warriors who broke newly captured mounts, holding and helping quiet the frantic beasts. His way with the animals was remarked on many times and finally an opportunity to elevate his lowly status presented itself.

Big Wing, another war chief and Iron Hand's friend, was breaking a white horse. That in itself was significant for white horses were the rarest and most prized of all mustangs. This one was particularly large and strong, as well as truculent. The chief was thrown repeatedly and doggedly rose from the hard earth to try again. A crowd of onlookers, including many women and slaves, had gathered to cheer him on. Rafe held the horse's rolling head while the banty-legged, barrel-chested man remounted. The horse possessed the dangerous cunning of a born man-killer. He looked for rocks and trees to roll against trying to crush the unwelcome burden on his back. Finally, he succeeded. Big Wing was struck by a sharp outcropping of shale, his body smashed between the jagged rock wall of the canyon and the powerful animal's body. He fell to the earth, bloodied and broken. The stallion trampled him before any of the warriors could come to his aid.

Rafe was the first one to reach the horse. Knowing Big Wing was dead and realizing that the chief's friends would want to kill the stallion, he caught the flying reins and pulled the horse away from the body. A plan formed in his mind. Heedless of the risk, he grabbed a fistful of the long, flying mane and vaulted onto the pitching white back, his feet digging frantically to find the rawhide stirrups while he pulled strongly and steadily on the reins to control the horse's head. He expected to feel a hail of bullets finish him as the Nerm killed the rogue, but he concentrated only on keeping his seat.

His father and most of his friends had laughed at the way he talked to horses, but Rafe knew he had what one old gypsy had called "the voice." He could make them respond with his low, silky commands. Now he combined that ability with sheer physical strength and a natural seat. Anticipating the horse's moves, he kept him away from the rocks and stands of trees. Twist and buck, circle and run, the white could not unseat the desperate Creole whose long legs and arms gave him an advantage as he held on tenaciously.

He kept up a steady stream of French words, alternately swearing and praying, as he let the horse move into the box canyon away from the noise and distraction of the crowd.

Gradually, the stallion slowed, exhausted but not beaten. It was a born rogue that should have been gelded. However, Big Wing had been taken with his size and the magic white color and had decided against the more sensible precaution.

Rafe finally subdued the stallion and began to urge it back to where the onlookers were waiting. No one had pursued him for they knew there was no escape in the blind canyon. Probably they expected the horse to kill him.

Shortly, Iron Hand and several warriors rode up, watching with the nearest thing to amazement that Rafe had ever seen register on impassive Nerm faces. Good. This might mean a change in his status, but volatile and erratic as they were, the warriors might just as soon kill him as reward him. He held the heaving, snorting white horse under firm control and waited for Iron Hand to speak.

"You have tamed a killer horse," he said, observing the way Rafe sat the horse.

"Only until this one gets another wind. He will never be broken," Rafe replied simply.

"Why did you do it?"

"I am tired of slave's work."

The chief laughed. "Even so, you are still my slave and I do not choose to free you. You would not stay with the People if you could leave."

"No," Rafe answered truthfully, "I would not." It would do no good to lie. Iron Hand was not stupid. Rafe was too old to adapt to Comanche life and become one of the People, although many white youths had done so over the years.

"Still, you have defeated the killer of Big Wing. Your skill with horses is great. Maybe I will give you another chance to break your arm." Iron Hand chuckled and the warriors with him joined in. "You shall tame my wild ponies."

As spring came over south central Texas, Rafe broke

fierce, swift mustangs and lived a unique existence among the slaves of the band. He was granted greater privilege and more respect than the other male captives because of his remarkable way with horses, yet he was still Iron Hand's slave, and Sand Owl's enemy.

As a rule, the uncastrated male slaves were not allowed privileges with Comanche women. But Iron Hand did Rafe the honor of offering him his choice among the female slaves. Most of them were Apache, Shawnee and Tonkawa with a smattering of young Mexican girls. After nearly a year of celibacy, Rafe was almost tempted, but they had all been pitifully abused and he was revolted at the thought of forcing his attentions on a cowering adolescent girl. Several were older and less fearful, but their stoic manner did little to stimulate him.

In truth, the only woman in the camp who appealed to him was Little Willow, Iron Hand's comely young wife, but he knew better than to dwell on that dangerous thought. During the winter her son had died of a fever. Iron Hand had no children now, and his attentions to Little Willow were jealously guarded.

When Rafe did not touch any of the slaves, Sand Owl began to spread rumors that he was impotent and had not feared her husband's threatened torture because he had nothing to lose. Rafe ignored her and applied himself to the same tasks he had set for himself since the previous fall— learning all he could of the band's language and location. If he were to escape, he must have some sense of direction.

Soon it would be the time of the Comanche Moon, the first full moon of spring when the grass was good for the horses and the light allowed the warriors to travel in speed and stealth. Slaves were never taken on raids. Many of the able-bodied men in the band would go, leaving fewer guards, more chances. He listened and he planned.

He also prayed that Flores would return one last time before he tried his escape. Now that he had achieved a quasi-free status he would have more chances to kill the comanchero than ever before. But Flores seemed to have vanished with the winter snows.

When Rafe had first overheard Iron Hand and his warriors

discussing a big raid against the Mescalero, he had secreted away a cache of dried meat and a water skin. He still puzzled over how to get one of his rifles. Perhaps he would simply have to take whatever he found on the body of the guard he killed when he fled.

"Deep in thought, Horse Tamer?" Little Willow came upon him as he sat by the cook fire in Iron Hand's campsite. The chief's four tepees were close together, linked by the rawhide pull rope, which went out from the main one where the chief slept to each of his wives' tepees. He summoned the favored wife by tugging on the rope to her tepee. Rafe knew Sand Owl's position as chief wife had been undermined since she alone of the three wives had never borne a child. Spotted Deer and Little Willow had, although the children were not their husband's. Of late, Iron Hand favored the slim Mexican girl over the squat Comanche Spotted Deer and bedded Lucia most nights. Rafe could see the circles beneath her eyes and pitied her.

He smiled. "Does everyone call me 'Horse Tamer' now?"

"Since you rode out the devil in the white horse, yes. It is a much bolder name than Tall Stealer." She returned his smile. "I gave you warning once before. Heed me now." Little Willow looked around to be certain they were not overheard. "I know you plan to escape when the war party leaves."

Rafe started to deny it, fearing for her to become embroiled in his dangerous attempt, but something in her eyes, a wild desperate pain, made him pause.

She continued, "You can take food and water, steal horses, and ride fast, but where will you go? What direction?"

He shrugged ruefully. She had hit on the one flaw in his plan. "I do not know, but I must try."

"I will help you. I know the way to a small settlement southeast of here. We have passed it many times in my travels with the Comanche. I can draw you a map."

Rafe looked at her closely. She was pale and haggard, taking a desperate chance for a complete stranger, yet not really a stranger, he realized. Since they first met there had been an odd, undefinable bond between them.

"Come with me, Lucia. You have no reason for staying now. You could begin again."

She regarded him with anguish. "Everyone would know I lived with them for eight years. I was a Comanche wife. My family thinks me dead and it is better that way."

"If you came with me I could send you east, or to Mexico, anywhere you wished, Lucia. You could escape your past. No one would know." What he did not offer lay as heavy between them as what he did and they both knew it.

"I—I will think on it, Rafe." It was the first time she had ever used his Christian name.

For two days, Rafe waited, wondering what Lucia would decide. When he found her alone by the fire the second night, he knew he must ask her. "The warriors leave tomorrow night. So do I. There will be a war dance and all those left in camp will sleep exhaustedly. It is dangerous, Lucia, but it is our only chance."

She nodded. "I will be ready."

The fires had died low and the silence was eerie after the noise of the war chants and the screaming of the women. The hoofbeats of fleet ponies had faded; the raiders had departed when the moon was high.

Once she was certain Sand Owl and Spotted Deer slept, the Mexicana cut Rafe free. Wordlessly she slipped off to retrieve their cache of food and water skins while he got their horses.

In the still darkness, Rafe crept near the corral where Iron Hand's ponies were kept. He had broken and trained two of the new, spotted horses that the chief had left behind. Everyone thought them too wild to ride on a raid, but Rafe knew better. They would take him and Lucia far.

Sentries were careless this deep in the vastness of Comancheria. All slaves were tied, and who would dare raid the Lords of the Plains? Rafe found one old warrior, Single Antler, sleeping near Iron Hand's horse corral. Like all the remaining Nermernuh, he was exhausted from the war dance and slept soundly. Near at hand lay a jug of mescal, no doubt a "gift" from Flores, Rafe thought with a ripple of hate. Single Antler had a good hunting knife at his belt and one of Rafe's Kentucky long rifles lay beside him. They would need the weapons. He hefted a heavy rock experimentally.

A hissing moan was the only sound breaking the stillness as he dispatched Single Antler. The horses moved in the corral, but because his scent was so familiar, none whickered. He secured hackamores on the two he singled out and led them silently from the corral to the edge of a thick copse of willows where he was to meet Lucia.

He tied the horses to a low, hanging branch and looked through the shifting shadows, straining his eyes in the darkness. They were not out of earshot of many of the sleepers, so he did not call but only watched and waited. Something was wrong.

Rafe could feel his skin crawl as he heard a hissing whisper and then a moan of pain. Lucia was pushed into the small clearing, collapsing at his feet. He stared at the hate-twisted face of Sand Owl as she walked out of the shadows, flanked by two warriors.

"I knew she betrayed Iron Hand with this slave! Now I have stopped their escape and my husband will listen to me. Little Willow will be killed and this one," she said, slithering up to Rafe and running her hand down his chest, "this one will have his manroot ripped off his body with fiery tongs and knives!"

She could not resist delivering the vicious taunt right in Rafe's face, and that was her undoing. Lucia, still sprawled in front of him, reached up and grabbed Sand Owl's tunic with clawing fingers made strong with desperate hate. The smaller woman pulled her tormenter down and they thrashed and rolled on the ground as Rafe dived past them at the older of the two startled warriors.

Landing on the man, he had his knife embedded in the Nerm's throat when they hit the ground. The other warrior, a green youth, turned to give a warning, but before he had run twenty yards through the root-gnarled, branch-infested willow copse, Rafe stopped the clear, shrill cries with his knife.

In seconds he was back in the clearing where Lucia was standing over Sand Owl. The small woman at last had revenge for the years of beatings and humiliations. She had killed the Comanche woman with her own knife. But not without cost. Her hands and upper body were covered with lacerations and a stab wound in her shoulder bled profusely.

Rafe scooped her up and placed her on the back of one of the horses. "Can you hang on?" At her affirmative nod, he said, "Ride down the stream bed. I'll catch up with you."

He ran toward camp on foot. Because of the liquor consumed and the frenzy of the war dance, the people in camp had not heard the commotion, but Rafe knew if even one gave the alarm, pursuit would be swift and relentless. He must give them something more pressing to do. Racing for the campfire in front of Iron Hand's lodge, he grabbed a dry piece of cloth. After tying it to Sand Owl's heinous club, he doused it in fat from a bowl kept near Lucia's cooking supplies. Then he stirred up the coals in the campfire and quickly had the makeshift torch blazing.

On his way to the corrals, he lit several fires. Many of the people had already rolled up their heavy skin lodges and were using brush arbors for sleeping. The spring had been dry so far and the twigs and branches flared easily. He stampeded the horses by setting fire to the dry grasses and waving the blazing torch in front of the terrified animals. Chaos reigned as they stampeded in all directions, trampling sleepy people and smashing shelters. Dogs yipped and barked furiously while warriors stumbled about searching through the leaping flames for sight of raiding Apaches or Rangers. Women and children screamed and fled.

He had almost made it clear of the pandemonium and back to his waiting horse when a shot whistled by his head. Then a hissing arrow found its mark. He felt the sickening impact in his side but grabbed the mane of the pony and swung up on it, sending it flying from the camp.

He rode west and then circled southeast once he was sure no one pursued him. He found Lucia waiting at a fork in the stream. Wordlessly she moved down the southeast branch of the creek. *If she can hold on, damn, so can I!*

Chapter 21

Deborah stood on the boardinghouse porch watching her son race across the backyard with fleet, long-legged strides. Considering how tall both she and his father were, it was scarcely surprising that Adam would be big for his age. "It's hard to believe he'll be six years old this fall," she mused to Obedience.

"He's a fine youngun all right. Shore could use a pa, though. Yew considerin' Whalen Simpson's offer? He's right taken with th' boy."

Deborah's eyes clouded with hurt, and she clenched her fists as she replied, "No, I'm not encouraging Mr. Simpson. I know he's fond of Adam and wants to marry me, but I can't do it, Obedience. I'm still married—at least as far as I know. If Rafael's gotten an annulment, that's his concern. There's no way I'll ever put myself under a man's thumb again."

Obedience snorted a solid Anglo-Saxon profanity. "We ain't talkin' 'bout thumbs 'n yew know it! They's bigger things ta consider." She watched the red creep across Deborah's face as she continued mercilessly. "Yew been without a man fer six years. Yer young, with all yer juices flowin'. Yew oughta be givin' thet boy some brothers 'n sisters ta play with and yerself some fun in th' doin' o' it."

"Well, let's just say Whalen tends to dry up my juices and leave it at that," Deborah replied testily.

"Yep, him, Mike Barberton, Malachi Foster, how many others over th' last years? It purely ain't natur'l fer a gal like yew ta live alone. I knew yew ain't one o' them cold-fish bluebloods whut don't enjoy it neither."

Deborah turned squarely on her antagonist. "Obedience, why are you dredging this up now? We talked the issue to

247

death five years ago. Might it have something to do with your new admirer, Mr. Oakley?''

For the first time in all the years she'd known Obedience Jones, Deborah actually watched her friend shuffle and fidget like a schoolgirl. ''Wal, Wash 'n me, we been considerin' gittin' hitched.'' She stopped and looked at Deborah with stricken guilt in her wide brown eyes.

''Why, Obedience, that's wonderful!'' Deborah exclaimed, reaching out to embrace her friend. ''Why shouldn't you be happy? Wash Oakley is a fine person and I'm sure man enough even for the likes of you!''

Still, Obedience was not mollified. She put one arm around Deborah and ushered her down the back steps. The two women walked slowly through the leafy bower of trees. ''We need ta palaver 'n they's always someone underfoot in th' house.''

Deborah smiled. ''I know. With twenty boarders the place is full to the brim.''

''Yep, thet's part o' th' problem.''

''But there'll be room for Wash, for heaven's sake! Surely you can't be worried about that,'' Deborah said incredulously.

Obedience shook her head. ''Naw, it ain't got ta do with room enough—it's got ta do with a vacancy. Yew see, honey, Wash's a mountain man. Spent him twenty years in th' Rockies afore he drifted down through them mountains in New Mexico and across th' Comancheria ta Santone.''

''And now he wants to go back up north, leave Texas, and take you with him,'' Deborah supplied for her friend.

''I put him off fer nigh onta a week now tryin' ta work up courage ta tell yew. Oh, Deborah, I don't want ta leave yew 'n Adam.''

Seeing the pain in the big woman's face, Deborah realized what she'd been going through. ''Remember when we talked about Adam growing up and you told me about your sons, Gabriel and Joseph? You said you raised them to let them go. Everyone's entitled to his own life and everyone is responsible for making his own happiness. It's not just true for our children. It's true for ourselves, too. You love Washington Oakley and your place is with him.''

"Yew are somethin', yew know thet? I reckon yew learned how ta take keer o' yerself real good, but I . . . aw, I jist wanted ta see yew settled with a good man afore I left," Obedience finished awkwardly.

By this time both women were crying and smiling at the same time, their overflowing hearts revealed in their faces and voices.

"Adam and I are going to miss you, but we'll get by. And without any help from Whalen Simpson. Adam has plenty of men in town who've adopted him—even Jim Slade rides in all the way from Bluebonnet to take him on outings."

"Jeehosaphet! With him 'n thet fancy widder lady fixin' ta git hitched, I 'spect he'll be too busy come fall," Obedience rejoined sourly.

"I admit, I was surprised to hear Jim was courting Tomasina again, after the way she jilted him six years ago to marry old Jake Carver, but I don't see how that will affect Jim's feelings for Adam."

"Harrumph! Thet one's cold as ice 'n mean clear through. She'll try her damblastedest ta git Jim away from yew 'n all his Texian friends, jist yew wait. Whut yew should do is—"

"Take Jim away from her," Deborah interrupted the familiar refrain. "Obedience, honestly, what do I have to do to convince you I'm not in love with Jim Slade, Whalen Simpson, or any man I've met in all of Texas. I can stand on my own two feet, run this boardinghouse, and raise Adam without a man to lean on. Lord knows, you've never needed a man for a crutch. Don't sell me short either."

What Deborah did not say was as significant as what she did say and both women knew it. *I do not love any man I've met in all of Texas.* But what of the man back in New Orleans, the one from whom she had fled?

"I'm goin' ta write yew 'n Adam. Shore am glad yew showed me letterin', even if I warn't th' best pupil."

The two women stood looking out over the large neatly planted garden remembering six years ago when they had begun their partnership with a half-finished house and weed-infested grounds.

A week later Obedience and Washington were married by a Methodist circuit rider who stopped in San Antonio on his preaching rounds. Because of the size of the crowd of well-wishers, the ceremony was held in the boardinghouse backyard.

"Whooie! Yew plumb take a feller's breath away, Obedience," Wash Oakley said, placing her on the back of a large tan gelding.

"Whut he means is liftin' a woman my size onta this pore critter plumb tuk his breath away," Obedience said to Deborah, Adam, and everyone gathered on the lawn.

Wash accepted their laughter in good spirits, just as he and his bride had accepted their congratulations at the wedding banquet Deborah had given them earlier in the day. "It be time ta move on, Mrs. Oakley, if'n we figger ta make a good camp on th' San Marcos by tonight."

Wash grinned as he swung into the saddle of his big bay. At six foot seven he was a giant of a man, with a barrel chest and a curly red beard streaked with gray. Even Obedience seemed dwarfed by his imposing bulk and booming voice.

"I got my writin' paper 'n pencils all packed. As soon as I git a minit's peace from this here rascal, I'll send yew a letter," Obedience's voice rang out gaily as they set out across the plaza at a brisk trot. Deborah held Adam in her arms so he could wave goodbye over the heads of the crowd.

"I wish I had a papa like Wash! He's fought Indians with his Bowie knife and even kilt buffalo with a long rifle," Adam said, looking down at his mother wistfully.

"Killed, not kilt, Adam," she corrected automatically. Then, as she slowly put him down she said measuringly, "Adam, would you like for Mr. Simpson to be your father?"

"Him? Naw. He's just a stable keeper. He don't—doesn't even carry a gun," he added dismissively.

Deborah grinned, both at his grammar correction and his evaluation of Whalen. Still, she felt compelled to say, "Mr. Simpson owns the largest livery in San Antonio. He's a successful businessman, Adam, not just a stable hand."

"I bet he don't—doesn't know which end of a gun the bullet comes out of." By this time, he was off and running around the side of the house before she had a chance to remind him to change out of his good clothes.

"Oh well, he already spilled ice cream on the pants," she said to herself, relieved to find she and her son agreed about Whalen. But the boy wanted a father, someone big and masculine, a real frontiersman like Wash Oakley, who had bounced Adam on his knee, tossed him in the air, and tickled him—not to mention telling the impressionable lad all sorts of hair-raising tales about wild Indians, outlaws, and grizzly bears. Deborah sighed, thinking of Rafael, wondering what her Texian son would think about his elegant, dandified father back in New Orleans.

However, Rafael was not in New Orleans. That very afternoon the bone-weary traveler arrived in Boston. As he struck the heavy brass knocker on the Manchester front door, Rafe Fleming laughed to himself. When he had come here six years ago he had been meticulously dressed as a Creole gentleman, quite different from how he looked now, after six weeks of grueling travel on horseback. The butler Ramsey's expression confirmed his surmise. His usually impassive face took on an affronted air. He could not believe the audacity of such a ruffian, coming to the front door!

"Sir?" The frigid tone of voice cast an aspersion on the polite form of address.

Rafe's unshaven face was slashed by a sharklike smile. "Don't you recognize me, Ramsey? I'm here to see my father-in-law. You do still work for Adam Manchester?"

Ramsey drew himself to stiff attention. "Mr. Flamenco? Of course, sir, come in." Despite years of Boston propriety he could not quite mask his incredulity.

Adam was expected home from the bank momentarily. Rafe paced impatiently after carelessly tossing his dusty, sweat-stained hat on a chair. The butler had been too shocked to take it when he ushered him into Adam's study.

Probably put me in here for fear I'd soil the velvet upholstery in the parlor, he thought with grim humor. Just then the door swung open and the tall, gray-haired figure of

Deborah's father stepped into the room. He paused in mid-stride, then reached back and closed the door.

"Well, Ramsey told me you'd changed, but I must confess my surprise at how much," Adam said as he stared at Rafe. His rough buckskin pants, homespun shirt, and scuffed, well-worn riding boots were a decided surprise, as was his unshaven face, which now bore several scars, giving his bronzed countenance a decidedly menacing air.

"My apologies for not taking time to change, but after so long on the trail, I was eager to talk with you," Rafe said, extending his hand.

Adam shook it, feeling the hardened calluses. "I assume you've come all the way from Texas, Rafael. Why?" His blue gaze was level and tentative.

"It's been a long time since anyone called me Rafael. I go by Rafe Fleming in Texas."

"You've lost your accent as well as your Creole name, I see. I repeat, why come all the way to Boston?"

Rafe smiled sadly. "A lot more has changed in the past six years than my outward appearance. I'm a rancher now. In fact, my partner Joe and I have one of the biggest spreads in north Texas. We built it from nothing but a crumbling stone house and a few hundred wild mustangs and long-horns. Now the house is restored, as grand as any built by my grandfather's people, with carpeted stone floors and whitewashed walls. We run over thirty thousand head of cattle and sell the best-trained saddle horses in the Republic." He paused for a minute, looking at Adam, who remained silent. "I guess what I'm trying to say is that I've cut my ties with my old way of life and built something on my own."

"And now you want Deborah to share it with you," Adam finished the thought for him. "I've followed your career, Rafe. My agents reported you killed by savages back in '37. You've got more lives than a cat, I'll grant you that—and I know about your success with Renacimiento."

Rafe's brows rose in surprise. "Even the name. If only your agents have done as well locating my wife."

Adam hesitated, measuring the man who stood before him. "No, they've found no trace of Deborah. That's the truth, but I have heard from her." He watched Rafe's body tense in anticipation.

"Is she well? What about the baby?" In his fear and excitement, he had almost grabbed Adam by the shoulders to shake him. Taking an iron grip on his emotions, Rafe let his hands drop, but he could not hide the naked anguish in his eyes.

Adam sighed and turned to his desk. He silently extracted a small leather stationery box from the top drawer and opened its lid. "You may read these. After all that you've gone through, it's your right," he said wearily, handing Rafe an untidy, water-stained bundle of correspondence.

The pages were obviously the worse for their long transit from Texas to Boston, stained, dog-eared, and tattered. "She sends them via Galveston, up through St. Louis, even one posted from New Orleans. My agents have tried every means of tracing them, but she's found ingenious ways to hide her whereabouts."

The letters were in chronological order. The one dated September 6, 1836 brought a brief blaze of joy to Rafe's face as he read that he had a son, but his elation was quickly overshadowed by bitter regret. His son was nearly six years old and he had never seen him. He read on, envisioning Deborah's sorrows and triumphs, seeing as the pages and the years unfolded, how she had matured and become a successful, independent businesswoman, asking help from no one, not even her father. How similar their situations were. They had each made a life in Texas, breaking traditions and family ties. *Does she ever think of me? I wonder. Has she taken a lover?* Rafe shifted uneasily in the chair.

Adam left him alone to read and ruminate. It was a very painful, private experience and watching the anguish and wistfulness on that hard ruffian's face touched a chord deep within him. *Damned if I don't hope he finds her after all these years*, he thought, amazed.

It was lonely with Obedience gone, but Deborah had to admit she seldom had time to brood over her friend's absence. "If only we could find someone to take over the kitchen," she muttered aloud to herself for the hundredth time. Since Obedience had left, Deborah had doubled as chief cook with only Sadie and one *Tejana* assisting. With all her other duties keeping books, ordering supplies, bartering and bargaining with tradespeople and Tonkawa hunters, Deborah felt she was neglecting Adam.

Just then the subject of her thoughts burst through the door of her office. "Mama, Jim's here to see you!" His shiny black hair hung in curly disarray, wet from the soft, misty rain that had begun to fall early that morning.

She stood up and tousled his damp head as he flew into her arms. "Please ask him to have a seat in the parlor and I'll be right out," Deborah said, then reached down to close her ledger and cork the ink bottle while Adam raced out to do as she asked.

When she reached the parlor door, she found an agitated Jim Slade pacing across the carpet. Despite the cool, steady rain he wore no coat and his shirt was decidedly wet. He was stalking around the room like a caged cougar.

"Take a seat, Jim, before you wear out my new rug," Deborah said, smiling in puzzlement. "It's awfully early for a ride into town. Something wrong at Bluebonnet?"

Slade stopped and nodded at her, then ran his fingers through his wet, dark gold hair as he answered distractedly. "No, nothing's wrong at the ranch. I've just been thinking . . . well, I heard you haven't been able to find a woman to take over the kitchen since Obedience left and I think I have the solution to your problem."

"Now why do I have the sudden intuition it might also be the solution to one of yours?"

"I've had this girl, er, young woman working at the ranch for a month or so. Her brother was Dick McAllister."

"You mean that cowhand of yours who drowned?" Deborah asked in puzzlement.

"Yeah—his orphaned sister. She's been helping Weevils with the cooking, but an eighteen-year-old girl working and living with a bunch of men—it isn't the best thing for her. Lee said he overheard you telling Paul Bainbridge that you still were looking for a cook. I thought maybe you might want to give her a chance.''

''I might at that,'' Deborah said, understanding a great deal from her friend's overwrought manner. So, Tomasina doesn't approve of an eighteen-year-old girl being under your roof. Small wonder! ''You say she can cook. Has she ever worked in a boardinghouse or restaurant?''

Jim shrugged helplessly. ''Charlee's rather, er, unusual. I don't think she's ever held a position like this before, but she's a marvelous cook!''

''Charley?'' Deborah's violet eyes widened.

Slade fidgeted, spelling out the name the way Charlee had for him.

Something was decidedly strange here, but if Jim vouched for the girl, Deborah was willing to try her. Lord knew she needed someone competent in the kitchen.

Even though it was still raining, Jim brought Charlee to town that night just after supper. Expecting a pretty, voluptuous creature bursting the seams of a tight calico dress and batting her eyes at Jim, Deborah was amazed at the forlorn, half-drowned waif and her scraggly cat.

One look at the wet little figure huddled pathetically on the saddle of her paint horse made Deborah's heart go out to Charlee. She clutched a scrofulous orange tom in a death grip, as if he were her talisman against life's cruelties. Her proud, stiff carriage and the pugnacious set of her chin as she brushed aside Jim's assistance in dismounting spoke volumes.

Deborah tried hard not to stare at the urchin's clothes. Charlee wore a pair of frazzled, baggy trousers and a man's oversize shirt. Although well mended and clean, they were decidedly the worse for wear and hung like sacking on her thin body. Her hair was knotted in a braided bun at the back of her head, covered against the evening rain with a battered felt hat.

Why, she's plain, Deborah thought as she shifted her evaluation quickly from the unsightly rags to the fiercely set little freckled face beneath the hat. The cat jumped free of her arms and scampered up onto the dryness of the porch. Deborah knelt and stroked him as he twined around her skirts, giving her time to recover from her shock and chagrin. She must make Charlee McAllister feel welcome. When the girl and Jim mounted the stairs and stepped beneath the shelter of the porch, she stood and extended her hand.

Although thin and tiny, Charlee had a firm grip and clear green eyes. She smiled hesitantly and said, "Hello, Mrs. Kensington. I'm pleased to meet you."

After Jim left, Deborah showed Charlee to her room where she deposited her meager belongings. Then Deborah introduced her to Sadie and Chester, as well as Racine Schwartz and Otis Bierbaum, two of the boarders who were still up playing checkers in the parlor. Mercifully none of the women boarders were about. She must get the girl into some decent clothes before anyone else saw her and was scandalized.

Like Celine and Claude were scandalized by you? The lonely misfit of a girl had struck a chord in her. She could not help but compare herself to Charlee. She had entered the alien and forbidding elegance of the Flamencos' home with the same trepidation the Missouri hill girl felt here in San Antonio. And, like Charlee, who was obviously smitten with Jim Slade, she had loved a man who did not return her affection either. She felt in her bones that she and Charlee would become fast friends.

It had been a long, hot trip from Boston to Renacimiento, Rafe thought as he walked to the corral. He was breaking a special new horse, a big, orangish sorrel with a white mane and tail, unusual both for its coloring and its size. The stallion had not been captured by his mustangers but rather purchased from an itinerant trader who said he had taken it off the high plains to the far north. Rafe suspected it had been stolen but could prove nothing. The magnificent animal had been mistreated, that much was clear, so he had rescued it from the brutal dealer, paying an exorbitant price. He wanted to gentle the stallion as his own saddle horse.

Admiring the beautiful animal's coat gleaming a pale

orange brown in the sunlight, he was reminded of the patina of the maple furniture Adam Manchester had sent to Renacimiento. The pieces were special favorites of Deborah's and her father had given them to Rafe as a parting gesture of goodwill.

The horse shied as the man approached him, then calmed at the sound of Rafe's voice, silky and whispering, hypnotic. "Yes, you shine like polished New England maple. When I finish, you'll have the manners of the most polished Bostonian, too." He thought a moment, then chuckled. "I've considered what to name you—how does Bostonian sound?" As he spoke he swung into the saddle and took the reins from the cowhand holding them, keeping up the low, musical conversation. He'd been gentling the horse since his return home. The stallion was smart and spirited. If only he could reclaim its affections, lost to some man's cruel and thoughtless actions in the past.

Joe De Villiers watched Rafe work the stallion, amazed as always by how his partner could communicate with horses. Once in the saddle, all Rafe's pain and sorrow seemed to evaporate as he became one with the animal. It was a good thing to have this new diversion. Ever since Rafe had returned from Boston, he had been morose and withdrawn.

The half-breed sighed, recalling Lucia's reaction when all Deborah's beautiful things had arrived. She had helped Rafe arrange the chairs and table in the big dining room and place the chest in the bedroom—his wife's bedroom.

"He's buildin' a shrine ta her, ya know," Joe had told the Mexican woman that morning after Rafe left the house.

Lucia had turned uneasily from his sad brown eyes. "What can we do? After all these years, he still searches."

"Do you want Rafe to find his wife, Lucia?" Joe had asked softly, knowing she had loved her boss in pained silence for all the years since Rafe had rescued her from the Comanche.

"I want him to be happy," she had said very carefully. "No one but Deborah can make him so."

Joe, who loved Lucia the same constrained way she loved Rafe, turned his thoughts back to the man in the corral. He had just received some news, news he was not eager to impart to his young friend and partner.

After Rafe finally dismounted, Joe took the sorrel's reins while the tall Creole strode over to the water trough and dipped his hat, replacing the sweat-soaked headgear and letting the cool water trickle down his bronzed temples and neck.

"Hottest August since I've been in Texas, I think," he said to Joe. "Who was the rider I saw you talking to earlier?"

The two men ambled leisurely toward the stables with Bostonian following sedately behind them. The silence lengthened as Joe pondered. Rafe knew his partner would tell him when he was ready. Over the years they had forged a unique friendship, sweating under the merciless sun, freezing in blue northers, laying stone for the house and running to ground the wild mustangs.

Finally Joe broke the silence. "Recall a drifter named Rameriz?"

Rafe's eyes bored into Joe's. "Yeah. He was also rumored to be a comanchero. Last I heard he was riding with some Mexican guerrillas, raiding Anglo settlers."

"Thet's him. He wuz ridin' with a feller named Perez. Big things in th' wind with th' Mexican army. Perez has hisself a real commission now. Him and his 'Defenders' wuz headin' to San Antonio. Rameriz split with 'em."

Rafe stood very still. There was more to this than Joe had indicated so far. "Why would I care where Perez and his banditti head?"

"Rameriz figgered ya might, since last time ya saw him, ya wuz askin' a lotta questions about his old sidekick Enrique Flores." Joe heard the intake of Rafe's breath.

If there was one thing that obsessed Rafe Fleming half as much as finding his wife, it was killing the comanchero who had sold him into slavery.

"Go on." Rafe's eyes were glowing black coals.

"Flores might be ridin' with Perez. Seems old Santy Anny's fixin' ta try 'n retake Texas, er so rumors go. Lots o' troops movin' south o' th' border, 'n th' irregulars sent ta raid in Texas er being organized real quiet like. Rameriz said he seen Flores with Perez's outfit the day he 'resigned.' "

"How much did that piece of information cost us?" Rafe inquired cynically.

Joe shrugged. "A few American banknotes and a pair o' half-broke mustangs. *Quien sabe?* Maybe he'll git throwed and break his neck." He grinned evilly and Rafe joined him.

Chapter 22

"Damned fog," Rafe muttered to Bostonian as he reined the big sorrel stallion to a slower pace. The peasoup fog followed a night of miserable drizzle, which had left the ground muddy and slick, treacherous for man and beast. Rafe was taking no chances that Bostonian might shy on the uneven morass that passed for a trail. This was the farthest southwest he had ever been in Texas. The muggy weather was unbearable. He would be glad never again to venture near San Antonio after his business with Flores was ended.

Rafe was trail-weary after the long, hot ride south. Traveling alone like this gave him too much time to think about Deborah and Adam. "Adam," he said aloud, letting his son's name roll off his tongue, finding he liked the New England simplicity of it. He brooded over the thought that he might never see the boy. "He's six years old now, nearly half his childhood gone and I've missed it."

By midday the fog lifted, replaced by blinding hot sunlight. The trail was well worn and easier to follow now as he neared the largest city in the Republic. Letting Bostonian have his head, Rafe suddenly heard the sound of hoofbeats coming much too fast. He scanned the horizon, his hand automatically going to the Hawken rifle on his saddle and pulling it free.

A big, thick-set rider with a drooping handlebar mustache was headed his way. By the look of his light brown hair and plaid cotton shirt, he was Anglo. Each man took the other's measure as they pulled up their horses.

Rafe, seeing no one but the lone rider, let the rifle drop back into its scabbard. Still he kept his right hand perched lightly over the Patterson Colt on his hip. "Afternoon," he said guardedly. "Someone on your trail?"

The Texian's expression became quizzical and his tenseness lessened a bit as he leaned forward. "You ain't Mex, are ya?" He sounded relieved at the softly accented Texian drawl Rafe had acquired over the years.

Sensing something was amiss, Rafe replied, "No. I own a ranch north of here. Name's Rafe Fleming. You coming from San Antonio?"

"Yep. I'm Whalen Simpson. Own a livery stable, or at least I did afore them Mex soldiers captured the city this mornin'," he added angrily.

So Rameriz's information was right! Rafe's pulse quickened in anticipation as he asked, "You say a whole Mexican army took San Antonio?"

"Yeah. We held 'em off at daybreak. Figgered there's only a few hunnert of 'em. When th' fog lifted, there was thousands o' them bastards, cannons 'n all. A few o' us escaped to spread th' alarm. Yew ain't fixin' to go to Santone, are ya? Real bad fer Texian health these days," Simpson added.

Rafe grinned evilly. "My going to San Antonio might just be bad for someone else's health, too. I'll take my chances." As he tipped his hat and pulled away, Rafe had to laugh at Simpson's yelled warnings. Little did the frightened stable keeper know that Rafe would revert to being Rafael Flamenco. Until he spoke, Simpson had thought he looked Mexican. His Spanish ancestry and fluency in the language should get him into the city. Rafe would just have to gamble that it would.

It was easier than he'd imagined. The youthful sentry who first challenged him outside of town looked to be a cadet scarcely out of knee breeches. The boy directed him to his lieutenant, an older soldier who questioned him cursorily and then ordered the private to escort him to the Mexican headquarters.

As they rode to General Woll's office, Rafe observed that this was indeed a city under martial law, occupied by a foreign invader. Few people were on the streets and those who ventured forth were subdued and watchful. He learned much of what was going on from his casual conversation with the soldier. Adrian Woll was a French mercenary in the pay of Santa Anna, a cultured European as well as a brilliant military tactician. *I can turn that to my advantage*. If Woll was like most Frenchmen abroad, he would be overjoyed to converse with someone fluent in his native language.

First Rafe must win over Woll, then find out about Perez. Once he located the captain and his irregulars, he could ferret out Flores. He had made up a story about searching for his runaway sister, enticed from her family's loving arms by a villainous Yankee. Now the aggrieved Flamencos planned to retrieve the disgraced young woman and place her in a convent. The tale hit close to home as he sadly remembered how poorly he and his parents had treated Lenore. Thank God she was well and happy now, with two children, according to the last letter he had received from her and Caleb. Stupid waste, he thought, then shook off the disquieting reminiscence as his escort dismounted in front of a large, whitewashed adobe building. The structure was an impressive private residence on the Main Plaza, obviously commandeered as Woll's headquarters. *I'll have to play my cards very carefully to get to Flores*.

After waiting the better part of an hour in a comfortably furnished anteroom, Rafe was shown in to see the general. Adrian Woll was a surprisingly young-looking man with rather blunt features and the pale complexion common among people from Alsace-Lorraine. Despite his reputation as a shrewd and skillful mercenary, his manner was flowery and gracious, doubtless the result of his long sojourn in Mexico.

"A thousand apologies for the delay in seeing you. I understand you have journeyed all the way from Nacogdoches in search of your wronged sister, Mr. Flamenco," the general said in Spanish, his tone solicitous as he reached out to shake Rafe's hand.

"I only hope to find her quickly and return her to the convent, General," Rafe replied in flawless French.

Woll's thick brows raised in surprise. "You are French, with a Spanish surname?" He was obviously intrigued.

"I am a New Orleans Creole." Rafe embroidered on the tale about a wronged sister hiding in San Antonio with a dastardly Yankee. "Her name is Rosa Louisa and she has long black hair and dark brown eyes. Quite a beautiful child, actually." That should be vague enough to fit at least a hundred girls living in the city, he thought.

Woll stroked his goatee and appeared to consider. "We captured the city only this morning, Mr. Flamenco, and I have a thousand details to attend to, not to mention reports to my superiors in Mexico. I will need time to make inquiries. If you would be so indulgent as to allow me a day or two?"

After agreeing to meet the general for luncheon the following day, Rafe left the harried conqueror to his reports. Carrying a safe conduct pass signed by Woll himself, he headed toward a cantina across the plaza to wash down the trail dust. Perhaps he might pick up some information about Flores in the bar.

The cantina was dark and smelled of the sweat of men and horses. The elderly *Tejano* behind the bar smiled nervously. Rafe ordered a whiskey and headed for a rickety table in one corner where he might eavesdrop on several small groups of Mexican soldiers. They were the only patrons except for a couple of elderly *Tejanos* and one wizened Anglo.

The soldiers discussed the long march from the Rio Grande that had started the twenty-fourth of August and the battle early that morning in which a number of their companions had been killed. Over fifty Texian men, including a number of the Republic's illustrious politicians, had surrendered when they saw the impossible odds.

"Where have they put the bastards?" one soldier who was not on the plaza during the fighting asked.

"They're under guard in a big house on the corner of

Commerce and Soledad Streets—the house they fired on us from.''

''I hope the general puts them on bread and water,'' a third said with a nasty oath. A small series of guffaws punctuated the remark.

Then the man who had described the battle said, ''I don't think they'll starve—after all, General Woll is a gentleman. When the women of the city offered to feed the prisoners, he could scarcely refuse. It saves our rations and keeps the civilians happy.''

''Yeah, and the general is also a Frenchman with an eye for beautiful women. That tall silverblond widow lady leading the delegation didn't exactly hurt their cause either.'' Everyone laughed and traded jocular comments about the tall blonde Yankee with strange colored eyes who had marched into the general's office earlier in the day demanding to care for the prisoners.

Rafe sat frozen in his chair, the drink in front of him forgotten as his heart hammered in his chest. He listened further. The widow ran a boardinghouse near the end of Commerce Street and she spoke to Woll in fluent French! It had to be Deborah! *I must have missed her in his office by a matter of an hour or less!*

It was nearing the dinner hour now. Would she be at her boardinghouse or on the plaza where the prisoners were? Unsteadily, Rafe got up and walked to the door on wooden legs. He would go to the prisoners' quarters directly across the square and see if she was there, then proceed down Commerce Street to her boardinghouse if she was not. His thoughts were jumbled and a part of his mind screamed at him to think this through before he blundered in on her. But he could not stop himself—not after six years.

Before he knew it he was nearing the large, low residence ringed with guards. Flashing the safe conduct with Woll's signature on it, he asked to see the officer in charge of the prisoners.

''Yes, sir, the captain is in the back, arguing with that widow who the general—''

The youth could say no more before Rafe spun on his heel and headed around the side of the building. He could hear the strident voices of his hated enemy Enrique Flores and Deborah raised in anger. Getting a hold on his emotions, he calmed himself before confronting them. *I can't kill Flores here and endanger Deborah and Adam. He's Woll's trusted officer.* Deborah and Enrique did not see him approach.

"I'd scarcely attempt to break fifty-three men out of your jail single-handed, Captain." Deborah's voice was scornful as she addressed Flores in Spanish tinged with a charming New England accent.

"Ah, but if you bring in such big pots and kettles, who knows what may be hidden in the bottom of them? Now, if you would only let me and my men watch the food being prepared in your kitchens, then we can be certain—"

"—of gaining entry to my house, which the general has already forbidden his soldiers to do," she interrupted fiercely.

"Such a beautiful face with such a suspicious mind," Flores scolded.

"A fault she's always possessed, I fear, Enrique," Rafe cut in smoothly. Every killing instinct he'd developed during six years of survival in the Texas wilderness took over now. He would protect his wife and deal with his enemy later.

Deborah froze, afraid to turn and face the owner of the low, silky voice addressing Flores in clipped Spanish. She watched the rapid play of emotions sweep over the captain's face as he turned to confront Rafael. Surprise, amazement, perhaps fear or anger—she could not tell which. Then he composed his features into an insolent mask.

"An incredible resurrection, but not without cost, I see," Enrique said to Rafe as he inspected Rafe's scarred, sun-darkened face.

"A cost you will pay dearly for when the time is right," Rafe replied evenly, one hand resting casually on the Patterson Colt at his side.

Flores smiled, glancing from Rafe to the woman. "You know the Widow Kensington?"

"We go back—all the way to Boston, but her name wasn't Kensington then," he replied carefully. "I haven't seen the lady in six years. You will forgive us if we request a private reunion?'' Rafe took a step forward casually, but his stance was menacing.

Flores shrugged indifferently. ''As you wish, Mr. Flamenco, Widow Kensington.'' He flashed Deborah a blinding smile and tipped his hat, then walked past Rafe, whispering as he departed, ''Until later, I presume?''

As Rafe watched him turn the corner and vanish with a cocky swagger, Deborah watched Rafael, her husband. He was the same arrogant man she'd left in New Orleans but so changed she would scarcely have recognized him but for the silky voice. He was dressed in dusty, trail-worn buckskin pants and scuffed leather boots. A low-slung gun rested negligently on one hip, a big, wicked-looking knife on the other. His black vest and flat-crowned hat were studded with silver conchos, giving him the rakish appearance of a Mexican *pistolero*.

But it was his face that was most dramatically changed. Always swarthy, he was now sun-blackened with small lines at the corners of his jet eyes. His left eyebrow was cut through with a thin, white scar that ran up toward his hairline. Another thicker scar was visible through the darkening shadow of his beard, running along the right side of his jaw. His curly black hair was badly in need of barbering.

A slash of white teeth showed as he smiled slowly, almost hesitantly and pushed the hat back on his head, revealing a few faint gray hairs at his temples. ''After all the years and places I searched . . . if I'd known you were here, I'd have dressed for the occasion,'' he said in English, noting the way she eyed his grizzly appearance.

''God, Moon Flower, you're more beautiful than ever, if that's possible.'' Her skin was no longer the porcelain white he remembered but a creamy pale gold now. Her figure, although still slim, was fuller. She stood facing him, posture ramrod stiff. He knew he must go slowly. ''Hadn't we better get to your boardinghouse so you can muster up the ladies to bring the food?''

Deborah's thoughts were in chaos and her knees felt like rubber, but she forced one foot steadily in front of the other, avoiding his touch, walking past him toward home. *He already knows where I live. I can't hide from him.* "How did you find me here, in the middle of an invading army?"

He walked beside her, drinking in the faint essence of lavender perfume, carefully choosing his words. "I lost your trail six years ago in the war. I've looked all over north and east Texas but I never came southwest. My finding you here was a blessed accident, I'm afraid."

She looked up at him in confusion. Do you live in Texas now?"

His eyes grew hard as he replied. "I left New Orleans for good in the autumn of 1836. I've never been back. I never intend to go back."

"But your family, your life—"

"—You and Adam are my family, and my life is here now," he interrupted.

She stopped short and said with a mutinous set of her jaw, "How did you know his name? Have you been to the boardinghouse and seen him?"

Unable to stop himself, he reached out and took one of her delicate hands in his, stroking the slim fingers as he drew her closer. "Your father told me." He could feel her stiffen.

"I don't believe you!" She jerked her hand away and began to walk briskly once more. *His fingers are callused! a part of her mind registered in amazement.*

"I went to Boston this spring. Your father had his agents following me as well as trying to locate you. He let me read your letters to him, Moon Flower," he replied softly, hearing her sudden intake of breath.

"Don't call me that," she said angrily.

"What do you want me to call you—wife?" he added with a taunt creeping into his voice now.

Panic flooded her. He could drag her and Adam back to New Orleans or take her son away from her.

As if reading her thoughts, he said earnestly, "The reason Adam Manchester wanted me to find you was because he believes I've changed, that I will be a good husband to you now. I have a ranch, Deborah. It's in wild, isolated country, but it's beautiful and successful, too. My partner and I run thirty thousand head of cattle and sell saddle horses."

"You look more like a border ruffian than a rancher," she said primly. When he threw back his head and laughed, the familiar sound gave her heart a fierce wrench. *I can't still love him! I can't!*

Sensing her weakening, he said, "Let's just give ourselves a little while to catch our breath, all right, Moon Flower? You can introduce me to Adam and send out your army of mercy to feed the brave defenders of San Antonio. Then we'll talk."

"What do you want of me, Rafael?" She had to get something straight before she turned her son's world upside down.

"Another chance—for me, for us, for our son. I was a spoiled boy when I left New Orleans. I've changed, Deborah. I want a chance to prove that to you both—at Renacimiento. My ranch—our ranch. I built it for you and our children. I always believed I'd find you one day, no matter how long it took. I've never given up."

"Then you don't plan to take Adam or me to New Orleans?" At least that was something for which to be grateful! She ignored his overture to renew their marriage and his reference to more children.

"When I broke with my father he disowned me just as he did Lenore. I'll never go back."

Deborah's eyes shadowed with pain and wistfulness. "I always wanted to write Lenore and Caleb and tell them about Adam, but I was so afraid . . ."

"That my sister might betray you to me?" he supplied for her. "In a way, she did. When I told her you were pregnant, she and Caleb told me all they knew. They were frightened for you, Deborah. They have two beautiful sons now, but our stupid father will never acknowledge them."

"But he'd acknowledge *your* son, wouldn't he, Rafael?" she accused.

"He'll never get the chance. Adam will grow up to run Renacimiento, not waste his life being a bored Creole dilettante," he replied with a hint of steel in his voice.

"I see you've made all the decisions about our future," she said stiffly. "What about my business and the life I've built here? I own a prosperous boardinghouse, Rafael."

Damn! "We'll figure out a way to handle it, Deborah. Just give it time," he evaded. "Is that the estimable establishment?" He pointed to the tall, whitewashed structure they were nearing. It was grand with a wide, cooling veranda circling it and tall oak and cypress trees shading the manicured yard and flower beds.

"My partner, Obedience Jones—Oakley now, inherited it from her brother. It was half-finished and shabby when we set to work," she said with pride in her voice.

"You've done wonders," he replied honestly. Now he knew what it meant to build something with his own sweat and backbreaking labor. "It must be the most prosperous boardinghouse in the city."

She looked at him in surprise. "You really mean that, don't you?"

Before he could reply, a set of determined women descended on them from the front door. "Your angels—or army of mercy, I believe?" he said with a grin.

"Oh, Mrs. Gardner, Mrs. Sandoval," Deborah exclaimed breathlessly, her mind going petrifyingly blank as the two ladies and their friends greeted her and looked questioningly at Rafael. *Ladies, may I present my dead husband. No, he doesn't look like a Boston Kensington, does he? He doesn't look bad for being exhumed either!*

Rafe took off his hat and made a courtly bow to the assembly. "Ladies, you must forgive my wife. She's just sustained a great shock; she had believed me dead. We've only this day found each other after six years of bitter separation."

For the rest of her life, Deborah would never remember how she dispatched the wonder-struck women on their mission, ushering them to the backyard where she and Rafael helped them load the boxes, kettles, and baskets of food into the wagon. Chester drove the whispering, tittering group to the Maverick House to feed the prisoners.

When Rafael addressed the women, Deborah's numb mind registered for the first time that he had lost his French accent. That silky, low voice spoke English with a faint Texas drawl! And the name—Fleming, Rafe Fleming. *I'm married to a total stranger.*

If Deborah felt confused and fearful, so did Rafe. He made up a ludicrous story about Deborah being so grief-stricken when she thought him drowned in Mobile that she had changed her name so as not to be reminded of her tragic loss. Oddly enough, most of the women thought it romantic and sighed over the lovers' reunion. But how did Deborah feel? She had grown remarkably independent, efficiently ordering the women to their various tasks and acting as unruffled as could be when she presented him to Sadie and Chester. He was Mr. Fleming, her husband. But her unspoken message to them and to him was that they still worked for *Mrs.* Fleming!

He was proud of her but afraid of letting her have too much head here in her own element. Before he bared his soul to her and let her know how desperately he needed her, he wanted to take her home—to Renacimiento, to his world. Then he would let down his defenses.

He stood on the porch watching her wave the ladies off, then walk toward the house. Just as he reached out his hand to assist her in climbing up the steps, a small bundle of squealing energy came thundering across the kitchen and out the backdoor.

Adam stopped short, eyeing the tall, dark gunman who had his hand clasped around his mama's arm. "Who are you, mister?" Protective and fascinated all at once, he strode manfully over and took Deborah's other hand.

Rafe looked at Deborah's stricken face. He desperately wanted to tell the boy the truth at once. Adam must learn sooner or later. What good would a lie do now? He settled for half the truth. "My name's Rafe Fleming and I own a big spread up north of here. I was just inviting your mother and you to come and see it."

"You a *pistolero*?" Adam asked with awe in his voice as he looked at Rafe's weapons.

Smiling, he knelt down beside the boy and said, "Not really. Oh, it's sometimes dangerous when we go mustanging or on roundup, so I have to know how to use a gun and knife, but mostly I'm a stockman."

"I got a friend named Wash Oakley who fought Comanche.

You ever fight Comanche?'' His big black eyes were aglow with excitement now.

Rafe smiled grimly. ''Yes, I fought Comanche a time or two.''

Deborah stood rooted to the porch, watching the scene unfold. How alike they were, with their glowing black eyes and curly black hair. Every aquiline, chiseled feature of Rafael's face was mirrored in Adam's boyish features.

Rafe's chest felt caught in a vise as he lifted his son and carried the delighted child back into the kitchen. *His son*, in his arms, after all the years of waiting! Choking down the lump in his throat, he turned back to his wife and whispered low in her ear, ''Thank you for Adam, Moon Flower, thank you.''

Chapter 23

''How long do you think it'll be before he learns for himself that I'm his father? Half of San Antonio probably knows by now.'' Rafe and Deborah sat closeted in her study.

''No one in San Antonio would know if you hadn't told Mrs. Garner and those other women,'' she said tightly.

''Considering the physical resemblance between us, how long do you think it would take those women to figure it out?'' he shot back. ''Sadie took one look at me and nodded as if she knew our whole history.''

Deborah rubbed her temples to soothe her pounding head. She had been up since the gunfire started at daybreak. ''You must forgive my deficient reasoning, Rafael. I guess an invasion and a resurrection in one day are a bit too much for a mere female.''

Rafe laughed softly. ''Nothing, as nearly as I can see, my love, will ever be too much for a strong-willed Yankee like you to handle.''

"I'm a Texian now," she said defensively.

"We have another thing in common," he replied with a lazy grin. Then he became earnest. "No matter how much you want to shield him, Deborah, Adam is my son. Even if I lost my right to claim him because of the past, he deserves a father. A boy shouldn't grow up alone."

She sighed and stood up, then began to pace. "So lots of folks have been telling me. Whalen, Obedience, even Sadie!"

"Whalen?" Rafe's brows rose.

"He owns a livery stable here in town. He's tried to court me," she replied distractedly.

"Big, beefy fellow with a mustache? Stoop shouldered?" He recalled the fearful man's flight on the road. At her puzzled nod, he scoffed, "Some great father he'd make for my son!"

"I am heartily sick of your jealousy and possessiveness! If you want heirs for your cattle kingdom, why not continue your usual habits—you could have dozens by now!" *Damn! I won't show him my pain—not after all these years!*

His eyes were shuttered as he replied, "I wouldn't even have to keep a mistress now, Deborah. No one in Texas knew I'd been married. I could have just taken another wife and had legal children—if that's all I cared about."

As she recalled Obedience's similar advice to her, Deborah crimsoned in mortification and turned away to gaze out the window. "Considering this accidental encounter, I guess it's a good thing neither of us did that, isn't it?" she whispered.

"My finding you is more than any accidental encounter, Deborah. I've searched for six years. I never gave up. But that Pettyjohn boy told me you and your spinster lady friend went north from Austin's colony. I was just looking in the wrong places."

Deborah whirled in amazement. "Thad Pettyjohn? He told you I'd gone north? And with a *spinster* lady?" She didn't know whether to laugh or cry over that spiteful boy's lies.

When her lips curled in a half wry smile, he felt a surge of anger. How could she think all these hellish, lonely years were anything to laugh about? "I fail to see the humor in six lost years," he said stiffly.

Deborah considered. "No, I guess since I had Adam and you . . . you didn't, that it was more difficult for you. But—"

"Maybe it was for the best?" he supplied. "It did give me time to grow up. But what about you, wife? Has any of that unbending Yankee stubbornness mellowed with age?" His black eyes searched her face.

What could she say? That she'd never stopped missing him? Thought of him every night in her big lonely bed? Loved him still? "Your idea of compromise seems rather one-sided. You plan to tell Adam you're his long-lost father and whisk us away to some wilderness ranch where you're in charge of everything."

"Even if we stayed here, people would know we're married. They can see Adam is my son. Your child and your property under Texas law, just like American law, would automatically go to me," he argued reasonably.

Deborah sighed, knowing it was true. At least she must spare their son the shock and hurt of learning the truth from outsiders. "Do you want to tell Adam or shall I?"

He walked over to her and put his arms around her gently, protectively, and stroked the long, silver hair falling down her back. "Let's tell him together, Moon Flower." He tipped her chin up and forced her to meet his eyes. She nodded in resignation.

"But where were you? Why wasn't—weren't you here with Mama 'n me?" Adam's small face was creased in puzzlement. Part of him was thrilled that the big *pistolero* was his papa, yet part of him was hurt for all the years of growing up knowing all the other kids had pas and he didn't.

Rafe knelt and reached out for Adam, who was regarding him warily. "Come here, son. It's a long story and maybe it'll be easier to tell if you sit on my lap while your mother and I explain." Rafe held his breath as the boy hesitated, then reached out and clasped the large brown hand in his small one. Adam allowed his father to lead him to a big leather chair across the room.

As Rafe met Deborah's eyes, a great deal was understood, and misunderstood as well. He began by telling the boy about what different worlds his parents grew up in and how hard it was for her to be happy in New Orleans where the customs and language were all foreign. "I couldn't live in Boston and your mama couldn't live in New Orleans. But Texas was a good place for us to start over—all new to both of us. But there was a revolution—a big war in 1836—"

"That's when I was born," Adam interjected excitedly.

Rafe nodded. "During that war and all its confusion your mother got lost from me. Neither of us knew where the other was. I've been searching all over Texas for you both ever since, and now I've found you. I'm only sorry it took so long, son. Will you forgive me?"

"Sure, Papa," Adam said, throwing his arms around Rafe's neck for a fierce hug.

As Rafe squeezed his eyes tightly shut and hugged the boy back, Deborah watched them. *How can I ever separate you two again? But how can I give our lives over to you, Rafael?*

Deborah dreaded dinner that night but knew she must face up to it. She had already told Sadie and Chester about Rafael. Now she would have to tell the boarders. If only Charlee were here, she thought forlornly, then reconsidered. She could not involve her friend in such a tangle.

Charlee had troubles enough of her own these days. A little over two weeks ago a deadly comanchero had nearly abducted the girl. Only Jim Slade's timely intervention had saved Charlee from an unthinkable fate. Something mysterious was going on between Slade and the gamin girl who had become such a close friend and confidant. Deborah could not get to the bottom of it and Jim had refused to explain, only saying that he was taking Charlee back to Bluebonnet where she'd be safe with him until matters were settled.

Deborah suspected the two had been lovers, despite Jim's engagement to Tomasina Carver, but Charlee had not confided this to her and she had felt too embarrassed to pry. *Now if I were Obedience, I'd have no qualms about meddling*, she thought wryly as she helped Sadie put the final touches on their dinner. Then she realized that she had never confessed her real feelings for Rafael to Obedience. A new wave of empathy for Charlee swept over her.

Miss Clemson nearly had the vapors when the darkly menacing stranger took his place at the head of the table with Adam that night. Deborah was thankful Rafael had at least shaven and shed his arsenal before coming to dinner. Most of the boarders were surprised but pleased at his improbably concocted tale about their separation and joyous reunion. By the end of the meal she was certain Kensington's was now Fleming's in everyone's mind.

Helping Sadie serve and clear the table gave her some chance to work off her tensions as she thought of the night ahead. *I'll put him in Charlee's room, that's what. No one need know we aren't sleeping together.*

"Doan be worryin' 'bout them dishes, Miz Deborah." Sadie shooed her from the kitchen. "Yo got yo *man* ta take ca'ah o' now!" She laughed as Deborah reddened and turned to leave the room.

"I'll go upstairs and see to Adam," Deborah said primly. But Rafael had already beaten her to it. She found father and son sitting on the bed. Rafael was telling Adam about being with the Comanches.

"And you were a horse trainer for Iron Hand?" His eyes were enormous.

Rafael made a scoffing noise. "I worked my way up— remember? First I was the water boy for his wife until I took a chance and jumped on that white stallion. Regardless, I was still only a slave until I escaped."

"Perhaps it served to give you some empathy for the runaways from the sugar plantations," Deborah said tartly from the door.

Rafe turned and looked up at her. "As a matter of fact, it did," was all he said before turning back to Adam. "Now under the covers for you, young man. It's past your bedtime."

Deborah stole from the room, deciding she would put fresh linens in Charlee's room for Rafael. She could scarcely ask Sadie to do so! *I could certainly use a nice, relaxing soak*, she thought as she headed to the opposite end of the hall where her big bedroom was situated. Earlier, she had asked Chester to bring bathwater for her tub. It was filled and steaming when she entered. She poured a generous amount of bath salts into the water and started to unbutton her basque, then stopped with a frown. Walking to the door, she slipped the bolt. *Surely Rafael wouldn't presume to come in here uninvited!*

Deborah finished undressing and then rummaged for a clean nightrail, which she slung across a chair next to the tub. Standing naked by her dressing table, she pinned her hair into a loose topknot. Once it was secured, she grabbed a chunk of soap and slid beneath the fragrant water with a sigh of bliss.

Rafe stood in the door that joined Adam's room to the master bedroom, staring transfixed at the glowing silvery beauty of his Moon Flower. She was facing away from him and her elegant head rested on the back of the tub as she closed her eyes and dozed. He could see two high-pointed breasts with pale pink nipples thrusting impudently in and out of the water with each breath she took. Stifling a groan of desire, he slipped into the room and closed the door to their sleeping son's room. Glancing over at the hall door, he smiled.

She has it bolted just as I knew she would, he thought in amusement. Then all humor fled as he considered how to proceed. Ever since he'd caught sight of her arguing with Flores this afternoon, he'd ached with wanting her, struggled mightily to keep from grabbing her and taking her in mindless need. What if she refused him? Could he force her? Even though it was his right as her husband, he didn't want her body that way. He wanted all of her, mind and soul as well.

There's only one way to find out, Rafe! He reached over for the towel slung on the chair and stepped nearer the tub. He could smell the lavender fragrance that blended so delightfully with her own unique essence and his heart began to hammer. He felt his desire rising as he draped the towel artlessly across his arm, holding it out in front of him. "You'll shrivel if you stay in that water any longer, Moon Flower."

Deborah's eyes flew open and she sat up in the tub with a

splash. "How dare you—" She stopped and slid beneath the water as a crimson flush stole across her naked breasts.

"Keep your voice down, you'll wake Adam," he said softly.

"How did you—oh!" Her eyes flew to her son's door. She'd completely overlooked that possibility!

"Here, stand up and let me dry you," he offered solicitously. She slipped lower in the tub. "No! I mean, I can dry myself. I made up your room at the end of the hall, where my assistant used to sleep." She eyed him warily to see what he'd do.

He smiled slowly, as if humoring a half-bright child. "Why should I take another room when my wife has this big, comfortable bed right here? Everyone will expect us to sleep together, Deborah. That is still my ring on your finger." He looked at the delicate, filigreed gold band she'd worn all these years—for convention, she had always told herself.

"What if I say I'm not ready to begin where we left off, Rafael?"

"This isn't where we left off. We're in Texas, in case you forgot. And we're both very different from the people we were six years ago," he argued persuasively.

"All the more reason to wait," she whispered as he knelt by the tub's edge.

"I've waited for six years, my love. I can't wait any longer," he said, his voice roughened in passion as he curved his dark hand around her pale arm. He could feel her trembling as he gently helped her stand up. When she did so, he wrapped the towel around her and massaged gently up and down her spine, across her shoulders, down to her breasts and belly.

Deborah stood still, shivering, but not from cold. His warm, callused fingers burned through the thin linen towel, working their old, familiar magic on her.

"I think you're dry enough," he said thickly, letting the towel drop as he scooped her from the tub. He set her down next to the bed but did not release her. Rather, he looked deeply into her eyes, willing her acquiescence until her arms came slowly up to touch his chest, then curve around his shoulders. Only then did he tighten his grasp and draw her to him for a savoring, devouring kiss.

His tongue raked across her lips until she gasped and opened to him. Moaning low in her throat, she reached one hand up and buried it in his long, curly hair, pulling his head down closer, deepening the hungry kiss. Slowly, laboring for breath, he broke off the kiss and once more slipped his arm beneath her knees to lift her and lay her gently on the bed. Then he silently began to strip off his clothes while she watched.

If he had looked dark and muscular before, he was sun-bronzed and sinewy now. As her eyes traveled over the familiar patterns of his body hair she saw the scars on his chest, arms, and even a wicked-looking one that slashed across his left thigh.

"A souvenir from an uncooperative mustang I was breaking," he said and smiled as he noted her staring at the long-healed tear.

"Did the Indians . . . ?" Her voice trailed away in horror as she imagined the pain some of the larger wounds must have caused. She reached up to run her fingers over the arrow scar on his side.

"Yes, the Comanche gave me that one and a few others," he whispered as he leaned down and ran his fingertips across her hips and up her belly, tracing the tiny white lines that radiated from her navel.

"I, too, have scars," she said, "stretch marks from your son. Do they displease you?"

He leaned down and traced the delicate patterns of the marks with his tongue, kissing her flat belly and nuzzling it. "No," he replied, "they don't displease me at all. Do mine displease you?"

Deborah pressed her lips to the whitened scar across his side, as her hand stroked downward to caress the slash on his thigh. "I think you're beautiful." She could feel his heart pounding as he pressed her down onto the bed. His hands stroked and teased her nipples to hard points until she arched up and cried his name.

"Rafael!"

"I never wanted anyone to use my old name because it

reminded me of who I used to be," he breathed. "But I love the sound of it on your lips, Moon Flower." He buried his face between her breasts now, using his lips and tongue to caress one, then the other. "Say it," he whispered against her neck, his breath warm, his lips searing.

"Rafael," she whispered in mindless compliance, "Rafael."

Feeling her buck and arch toward him, he groaned as he spread her legs and poised above her, gathering a small measure of control before he entered her. She was wet as she opened to him. He slowly penetrated her, gasping in surprise at how virginally tight she felt; he was afraid he would hurt her.

Far from feeling pain, Deborah felt only a consuming, desperate need. Tightening her legs around him, she arched up, drawing him deeply into her and whimpering in joy as he stroked her aching, hungry flesh with his own. They rode, letting the pleasure spiral up in ever-increasing waves. She clasped his back and buried her mouth where his neck and shoulder joined, muting her moans and gasps against his hot, sweat slicked skin. He whispered words in her ear, urging her on, telling her how beautiful she was, how much he wanted her, needed her, how good she felt to him, as no other woman ever had—and for the first time in six years, he unconsciously slipped back into his native language.

Deborah had been so long without his touch, without feeling the glorious pleasure that only this joining of flesh could give, that she did not consciously realize he spoke French. She sensed only that it was like going back so many years to the good part, the beautiful communion of their marriage in this wild, primitive joining. Soon, too soon, the rippling waves of orgasm gripped her, sweeter and stronger than any memory could ever recall. She gave in to them, letting the blissful fulfillment wash over her like a warm summer tide rushing over a Nantucket beach. When she felt him swell and stiffen she knew he, too, had joined her in the blinding surge of ecstasy.

With no other woman did this happen, this completeness, this tenderness fill every fiber of his being. Gradually, as his blood stilled its wild racing and his breathing slowed, Rafael gazed into Deborah's eyes, still darkened violet from passion. "Some things are too perfect to ever be merely remembered," he said, kissing her throat softly. Unconsciously, once more, he had reverted to English.

Even though he echoed her thoughts, Deborah felt herself growing fearful. For all he was changed into a Texian, he was still the wild, volatile Creole she had loved so helplessly in New Orleans. Part of him would always be *that* Rafael, arrogant and manipulative, using her, controlling her. Resentment welled up in her, but his soft, persuasive caresses as he cradled her against the heat of his body made her give in to an overwhelming satiety and exhaustion.

Daylight. The morning was bright and warm. Deborah awakened slowly, hearing sounds from downstairs and boarders walking in the hallway. She had overslept! Feeling the scratch of Rafael's beard and the warmth emanating from his long body, which was wrapped possessively around hers, Deborah tried to free herself without awakening him. Here they were, both naked in her bed, with half the boardinghouse right outside their door—and Adam! Oh, Lord. Her son always came in to wish her good morning as she was finishing dressing and putting up her hair.

Just then Adam's door opened slowly. The creaking noise apparently did what her squirming had not done, for Rafael was instantly awake and sitting up. Adam hesitated in the doorway, uncertain of what to do. His big black eyes were wide as he saw his mother still in bed—with his father. He had never considered his new papa would sleep with her! That was something reserved for him on nights when he had bad dreams or when it stormed.

Rafe looked at his son's face, which clearly mirrored surprise, embarrassment, and jealousy, all mixed in equal parts. Smiling, he patted the edge of the bed and said, "Morning, sleepyhead. Looks like we all overslept. Come here."

The smiling welcome was all he needed. The boy bounded across the floor and catapulted into his father's arms. He was still welcome. "I waited and waited, but I didn't hear you wake up, Mama. Are you all right?'' He looked questioningly at his mother who was huddled with the covers pulled up to her neck.

Suppressing a chuckle, Rafe answered for her. ''Your mother's fine, son, she's just been working too hard.''

Deborah reddened and sputtered but could say nothing in front of Adam to rebuke his father. ''Adam, why don't you get dressed and see if Sadie needs any help fixing breakfast? Tell her I'll be down shortly.''

''Since this is partly my fault, I'll go with you,'' Rafe added, hoisting the boy up and sitting him lightly on the floor. Throwing back his side of the covers, he slid from the bed and stood up, splendidly naked.

Adam stared enviously. ''How come you don't got any— have anything on? Mama makes me wear this ickey ole nightshirt.''

Reaching for his pants, Rafe smiled and replied, ''Well, several reasons. First of all, boys have to mind their mamas and wear what they're told. And, since papas sleep with mamas, that helps keep them warm.'' He winked at Deborah's scarlet face. ''Some day when you grow up and get married, you'll understand. Just wait.''

Adam digested this as Rafe rummaged through his saddlebags. He fished out a clean shirt and some toilet articles. ''Get dressed real quick and I'll meet you at the men's washroom so you can clean your teeth,'' he instructed.

''Can I watch you shave, too?'' Adam asked, eyeing the darkening growth across Rafe's face.

''Only if you hurry and dress.'' The boy vanished in a flash. Closing the door, Rafe looked over at his wife and said, grinning, ''You can come out from your burrow now, little mole.''

She responded by throwing a pillow at him. He ducked agilely. ''Watch so you don't break anything. How would you explain it to your son?''

''Why should I explain anything? You seem to have ample explanations for every situation that arises!'' she spat furiously. ''All you had to do was walk into his life and snap your fingers and he leapt into your arms.'' *All you had to do was touch me and I did the same.*

Rafe stopped buttoning his shirt and walked over to the bed. He sat down and pulled her resistingly into his arms. "Don't be angry. Adam was naturally jealous of my being in your bed—and it's time he began to understand the simpler facts of life. He needs a father as well as a mother, *cherie*."

She stiffened at the old French endearment. "Don't speak French!" she blurted out, then could have bitten her tongue.

Rafe looked puzzled. "*Cherie?* Calling you that is scarcely reverting to my old evil ways, Deborah..." His voice trailed off as he recalled how he had spoken French to her last night, revealing his need, his weakness. His face became shuttered. "So, you still choose to dig up the past and cling to it. It seems, wife, I'm damned for being a stranger and I'm damned for being the man you married. Maybe I'm both at once. You're still the same suspicious hardheaded Yankee—that's not changed." He sighed and stood up to button his shirt. As he glanced in the mirror, he could see Deborah's eyes following him avidly as she sat frozen on the bed. "Some other things don't change either, do they, Moon Flower?"

Rafe sauntered from the room after unbolting the door. Then he paused at the sill for an instant to whisper, "And don't ever lock a door against me again. Adam wouldn't like the explanation I'd give him for breaking it in!"

Rafe cajoled his son into cleaning his teeth and even washing his face, loathsome tasks for a six-year-old boy. As he combed Adam's unruly, black hair back and gave a mock inspection, he realized how much he had missed of his son's life. He could not bear to think of losing either the boy or his mother now.

Yet he knew he had handled things badly with Deborah this morning. He swore to himself, Adam needs a man's hand, dammit. She's coddling him. Only just now he had learned the boy had never been up on a pony! Every Creole boy received his first pony as soon as he could sit up and hold on, one of the few things they had in common with Texians. He would remedy that as soon as they arrived at Renacimiento.

"How would you like to go with me down to the stables

later this afternoon and meet Bostonian?'' Rafe asked the squirming child as he finished combing his hair.

Adam's eyes lit up. ''The big sorrel stallion you told me about! Oh, yessiree!''

Ignoring Sadie's smirking expression when she made her tardy appearance in the kitchen, Deborah began pulling tins of biscuits from the oven and piling links of browned sausage onto a large platter. As she took the food to the dining room, she noticed Rafael and Racine Schwartz lounging in the front hall, talking intently.

''You watch thet polecat, Mr. Fleming, mark me. No more'n Miz Deborah went out ta see thet General Woll, thet Flores feller come sniffin' back here right after her like a randy mustang. He's a rattler.''

''You say he was out back again this morning?'' Rafe asked casually.

''Yep. Askin' the hired man Chester if'n yew'n Miz Deborah wuz really married 'n where wuz yew now—real nosy like. 'Course, Chester didn't tell him nothin' 'n I come out fer my mornin' trip ta the jakes 'n run him off good 'n proper,'' the old man finished with glittering eyes. He patted an ancient flintlock pistol inside his coat pocket.

Rafe nodded, realizing that by acknowledging Deborah as his wife, he had put her and Adam in grave danger. Flores would not hesitate to use them as pawns to gain an advantage in killing the man who had sworn vengeance against him.

''I'm meeting the general today. Think I'll inquire about Enrique's job assignment while I'm there,'' he said to Schwartz.

Deborah overheard and felt a premonition of dread. She swept into the hall. ''Do you know this Captain Flores, Rafael?''

''Let's just say I bear him a grudge,'' he replied evenly.

''You're going to kill him, aren't you?'' Looking at his shuttered, hard features, she knew it was so.

Chapter 24

"I understand you have an Enrique Flores under your command?" Rafe said casually as he speared a piece of the excellent rare beef General Woll's cook had prepared for their noon meal.

The Frenchman paused to think for a moment as he sipped some wine. "Ah yes, a captain, one of the irregulars who volunteered under Colonel Antonio Perez. But of what interest is he to you?" Woll's gaze was keenly assessing.

Sidestepping the question, Rafe replied, "I told you that I have been reunited with my wife and son who were separated from me during the insurrection in 1836." He paused, then continued, "It was quite a surprise after six years to find them here."

"A joyous one, I am certain," Woll added. "Having met your lady, I can certainly attest to her beauty."

"That's part of the problem," Rafe said carefully. "You see, her beauty is what has drawn Flores to her."

"If Captain Flores's conduct toward your wife has been in any way improper, Mister Flamenco, I will take steps—"

"No, please, I assure you, General, I do not want any misunderstanding between the military and the citizenry during such a volatile time. The captain did not realize Madame Fleming was married when he paid her compliments. If you would be so kind as to explain to him that she is under your protection, I'm quite certain the matter need go no further." As the general nodded in understanding, Rafe breathed a sigh of relief. Such a reprimand would put Flores on guard against involving Deborah and Adam in his schemes. First Rafe must get his family to safety, then he'd deal with Enrique.

"I regret there is no word of your sister and that Anglo villain, Mister Fleming."

Rafe shrugged expressively. "So do I, but I have searched so many places, I was doubtless merely on another false trail this time. But it was a kind fate that brought me to San Antonio and reunited me with my wife and son."

As his orderly poured more wine and cleared the table, Adrian Woll thought it most odd that a man like Rafael Flamenco should have such difficulty keeping track of the female members of his family. But he forbore mentioning it.

"I have a responsibility to those prisoners and I won't shirk my duty because of some petty vendetta between you and Captain Flores," Deborah stormed at her husband that evening on the back porch of the boardinghouse.

"The man is a deadly killer, a comanchero. You've lived in Texas for six years. You know what that means," he replied levelly.

Remembering the big ugly brute who had abducted Charlee, Deborah shivered in revulsion. "I know what kind of men comancheros are, but I don't see that Flores fits the mold. You hate him for some other reason and I don't want to get involved in it."

He gritted his teeth in impatience. "You *are* involved in it simply because you're my wife. He'll use you and Adam to get at me. That's why you have to stay away from the prisoners. Flores is in charge of them."

"I can't hide in the house and hope they'll leave, Rafael. You've made friends with General Woll. Ask him to deal with the captain," she said, her voice laced with scorn.

"For what it's worth, I did tell Woll that Flores was enamored of you and the general said he'd reprimand him. But that doesn't mean it's safe for you to parade around the streets."

She put her hands on her hips. "Oh, so now we're down to it! Parade around the streets—unescorted. I've been on my own for the past six years, Rafael, making my own way, unescorted, unchaperoned. I'm not the twenty-year-old girl who fled New Orleans in tears six years ago."

He smiled crookedly and pulled her close to him as he said, "I know you've changed and I'm not trying to crush your Texas spirit, Deborah. I want you the way you are—but I want you safe, dammit," he rasped out as he bent his head to kiss her.

For a moment she struggled to resist the hard, warm demands of his mouth and hands, then she gave in, kissing him back fiercely. Only when she heard Sadie's arthritic shuffling across the kitchen floor did she pull herself free of his arms. "I have to prepare the food. I'll let Mrs. Parker and Mrs. Sandoval take it to the prisoners tonight."

By mid-morning of the next day their truce was broken. "What the hell do you mean, she went with Dr. Weidermann?" Rafe demanded of Racine Schwartz. "Can't I leave her unattended for an hour without her doing something crazy!"

"Tried my damndest ta stop her, but her 'n thet Rooshin doc, they skeedaddled out ta tend one 'o them fellers shot durin' th' fight ta take th' city. I come ta tell ya soon's they left," the old man said defensively. He'd hobbled fast as he could from the boardinghouse to the livery where Rafe was grooming Bostonian.

"Mama always goes with the doc. She's his best nurse," Adam piped up. He was clutching a curry comb in his hand, his small face creased in worried puzzlement at his father's anger.

"Please take Adam back to the boardinghouse, Racine. I'll see that his mother's all right," Rafe said, ignoring the boy's remarks as he turned and walked swiftly from the stable toward the Main Plaza.

The physician's brow was furrowed in concentration as he swabbed carefully around the stitches. The wounded man lay patiently on a kitchen table in the Maverick house, where the San Antonio defenders had been imprisoned.

"Ow, doc, that don't feel so good," Walt Mabry groused.

"But it heals cleanly. That is of utmost importance." Dr. Weidermann's English was precise and careful, tinged with a slight European accent of uncertain origin. "Mrs. Ken—Fleming, please give me the salve."

Deborah felt herself redden as she handed the doctor a vial of strong, smelly cream. *Everyone in town knows about*

Rafael and me. She swore to herself, looking nervously over her shoulder to watch for Captain Flores. She felt uneasy about slipping out to make these rounds with the doctor, but she was his only trained nurse. And in her heart of hearts, Deborah confessed that she had wanted to show her husband that she had a life of her own.

When they finished their rounds in the makeshift infirmary, she walked toward the boardinghouse. Deep in thought, Deborah did not hear the footsteps approaching until a whispery voice caused her to gasp and look up.

"So preoccupied, Mrs. Fleming. A lady requires an escort on the street, especially such a beautiful lady who does not look where she walks." Enrique Flores stared intently into her eyes as he reached out to take her arm proprietarily.

"My only requirement, Captain, is that you unhand me—at once," Deborah replied levelly.

Flores's black eyes danced, but their reflection was eerily cold and flat, like the sound of his laughter. "I do not think so. I always had a preference for blondes, but finding out you belong to Rafael Flamenco—well, that sweetens the bargain." Rather than releasing her, Flores's grip on her arm tightened as he began to shove her toward a ramshackle house whose door stood ajar.

Frantically Deborah looked around the deserted street. With the martial law, few people ventured abroad unless absolutely necessary. The neighborhood through which she was walking was empty and several houses stood vacant. Stupid fool, Rafael was right! she chastised herself as she tried to twist away from Flores's reptilian menace. Her shoes were hard leather, sensible for walking, and when she connected one foot squarely with his shin, he let out a grunt of surprised pain. Deborah raised her arm, hoping to rake her nails across his face, but the embattled pair was interrupted by a low, cutting voice that stilled their struggle.

"Let her go, Flores. I'd hate for you to die so quick and painless." The command was accompanied by a sharp jab from the barrel of a .36 caliber Patterson Colt pressing against Flores's neck.

Rafe had come upon them, silent as a Comanche. Every

nerve in his body screamed to kill his enemy, but he realized the folly of shooting one of Woll's captains in broad daylight. He'd stand before a firing squad within twenty-four hours for such a breach.

Flores grinned evilly as he released Deborah. "You ache to kill me, eh? I can tell. See, your hand shakes from holding back, but we must both respect our supreme commander, musn't we?"

"Don't push it, Flores," Rafe breathed, removing the cold steel barrel from the Mexican's neck.

Flores shrugged and backed off. "You can't shoot me in such a public place, my friend. Until a more opportune time, eh?" He tipped his hat to Deborah with mock politeness and ambled away.

As she faced her husband's anger, Deborah repressed a shudder.

"I asked you not to go out. Now perhaps you see why?" Rafe took her in his arms, but she pushed away angrily.

"You commanded me not to 'walk the streets unchaperoned'," she replied, feeling petty even as she spoke the words.

He leaned against the side of the building and pushed his hat back on his head. "He probably wouldn't have killed you—just roughed you up, maybe raped you, then sent you back to me with a message."

"If you're trying to frighten me, it's working," she answered, struggling to keep her voice level and to match his apparent calmness. "Why does he hate you so much?"

Rafe shrugged. "He stole my guns and supplies, killed my men, and sold me to the Comanche six years ago. He did it for money, but I don't think that was all. His kind likes to see people bleed. He stayed for the torture that night. He probably—" Seeing the look of dawning horror in her eyes, he stopped and reached out once more. "Let's just go back to the boardinghouse for now. You stay put and watch Adam closely." At her wide-eyed look of terror, he nodded. "Yes, he'd try to get to me through my son, too. You have to let me handle this, Deborah." When he put his arm around her this time, she did not resist. They walked quickly toward home.

As evening fell, Deborah's nervousness increased with the darkness. She must spend another night in Rafael's arms, drawn more closely to him, revealing all her want, loneliness, need, all the things she had buried for so long. *How can I trust him?* she cried to herself. And the night taunted in return, *How can you deny him?*

After the evening meal, Rafe went to check on Bostonian. Deborah busied herself with clearing the kitchen. When she and Sadie were through, she shooed the old woman off to bed and sat down to plan menus for the rest of the week. Finding it difficult to concentrate, she rubbed her temples and reapplied herself. Just then a small tap sounded on the backdoor and a familiar voice said, "Oh, thank heavens you're here and all right!"

"Charlee! How did you get into San Antonio?" Deborah rushed over to embrace her friend, who was dressed once more in the same scrofulous boy's clothing she'd given up months earlier.

"Sometimes it pays to dress like a boy, especially if you're an old squirrel hunter on a secret mission in the dead of night!" She hugged Deborah.

"But there are sentries posted everywhere and they have orders to shoot anyone out after curfew."

"They have to see you to shoot. Hell, Deborah, I could take any of those sappers into the best squirrel woods in St. Genevieve and they'd never bag a thing! Anyway, I'm real good at squeezing through small places."

"Still, it's dangerous. Now that you're here, you'll have to stay, unless Jim is—"

"Jim isn't with me," Charlee interrupted, dashing Deborah's hopes that they might flee to Bluebonnet and elude Rafael. "He'd skin me if he knew I sneaked in here. He and Lee are off chasing Comanches. We only got word today that the city was occupied. I came right away. Is Adam all right?"

"Yes, he's fine. Overjoyed, in fact." Her voice betrayed her agitation, as did the nervous lacing and unlacing of her fingers.

"Those Mexican soldiers really have you strung up tight, haven't they?"

"Oh, Charlee, it isn't that, it's—oh, you have to get out of here. It isn't safe. You'll be missed at Bluebonnet."

Rafe interrupted her, saying, "I second the motion." His eyes met Deborah's with a knowing glance. She'd run to her friend's ranch if she could! He looked at the slight girl dressed in baggy men's clothing. Observing them hug, he knew this must be Charlee. Grinning at the awestruck way she surveyed him, he put one arm around Deborah's waist.

"Who are you?" the girl asked in a small voice.

His eyes commanded Deborah to answer for him. *You must face reality, Deborah.* He could feel her take a deep breath as she replied, "Charlee, this is Rafael Beaurivage Flamenco, my husband."

"Also known as Rafe Fleming," he said, smiling.

"You're Adam's father! But how—why . . . ?"

"It's late and we have a long ride tomorrow, Miss—you never did introduce her to me, wife," he teased Deborah, knowing full well this girl's identity, wanting to let neither female off the hook.

"Charlee McAllister," the younger woman shot back forthrightly. "I used to work for Deborah. She and Adam are my friends."

There was a definite note of warning in her voice. Rafe respected such valor from one so tiny, but before he could frame a conciliatory reply, Adam came racing down the hall.

Catapulting into his father's arms, he cried, "Papa! You been gone!"

Deborah took Charlee's arm. "I'll explain it to you later, Charlee. Can you get her safely out of here, Rafael?"

"It'll be no problem. I have a safe conduct from the general. I should be able to escort an old family friend back to *his* parents," he said, teasing once more.

"How did you get a pass—oh!" Charlee flushed and stopped.

Rafe's answer was cold. "You're mistaken in your assumption, Miss McAllister. I'm not part of General Woll's army, regular or irregular, merely a Texian rancher from up north."

Bitterly, Deborah added, "What Rafael means is that he's from an old Creole family in New Orleans. As one of French and Spanish ancestry, he has no love for the Yankee usurpers in Texas."

290 / SHIRL HENKE

Rafe grunted in disgust, "At least that's what the general thinks, and I'd be a fool to disabuse him, wouldn't I, love?" He tousled Adam's hair and said, "Now why don't you see to getting your friend some food and a place to rest while I tuck this sleepy young rascal in?" As he turned to leave with Adam's head drooping on his shoulder, he couldn't resist one parting shot. "I'll be waiting for you in our bedroom."

He could just imagine the tale of betrayal and cruelty his wife would tell her friend. Forcing down the bitter lump in his throat, Rafe carried Adam up to bed and tucked him in. Already the boy was nodding off, but then he raised his head to ask, "Wasn't that Aunt Charlee or did I just dream her?"

Rafe smiled and said, "Yep, it was her, but she just came to see if you and your mother were all right. She's leaving in the morning, son. Now go to sleep."

He sat with Adam until the boy was soundly asleep. Then he went down the hall to the men's washroom and soaked his tired body in a hot tub. Damn, Flores was right. He had felt an aching sweat to kill the bastard this morning. He sighed and tried to relax. "And now my wife's blackening my already dubious name even more." He pondered how to handle tonight.

Deborah was considering the same thing while she gave Charlee an edited version of how she met and married Rafael. She simply told her friend that they disagreed over a wife's role. The fact that she was neither southern, Catholic, nor Creole had led to their separation.

Charlee tried to console her, contrasting Rafael's single-minded pursuit of his wife with Jim Slade's cavalier attitude toward her, but Deborah could not overcome her uneasiness about the night to come.

Just then, Rafael returned, obviously freshly bathed. Droplets of water clung to the gleaming black curls at his temples and nape where he had not toweled them dry. He wore soft moccasins and his shirt was unlaced. "Past time for bed, wife," he said in a whisper-soft voice, laden with insinuation.

Rafe reached out and put his hands on Deborah's shoulders, kneading softly, caressing across the delicate pattern of her collarbone, around the nape of her neck. Almost unconsciously, without willing it, she yielded to his soft, subtle pressure, savoring the stroking of his callused fingers.

"Adam's sound asleep and I'm sure after her adventure, Charlee here is tired. Better show her to *her* room." He smiled, sure it was the room Deborah had planned for him to occupy.

"I guess I am tired," Charlee ventured, aware of the tension between Rafe and Deborah. "I know the way to my old room and I can help myself to sheets and make up my bed."

Deborah felt she was being deserted, yet at the same time she wanted Rafael's hands on her, hypnotically weaving their spell. Just then, as Charlee left, Chester came into the kitchen. Nervously, he cleared his throat to get Mr. Fleming's attention. Rafe turned and asked, "What's wrong, Chester?"

It's as if he's in charge here, not me, Deborah thought resentfully. While he and Rafael discussed one of the wagon mares who was ailing, Deborah wandered off to the porch. *He has Adam, my employees, and my boarders on his side. Even Charlee backs off from him. Oh, damn him, why does he take over everything in my life? I never touched his life this way!*

Rafe could tell by the stiff set of her shoulders that she was tense and angry. He slipped silently from the kitchen and came up behind her, cupping her shoulders in his hands as he whispered into her neck, "Hiding out here won't solve anything, Deborah. If I have to, I'll carry you kicking and screaming to bed; boarders, neighbors, the whole Mexican army be damned."

She stiffened even more. "I am *not* hiding." She moved quickly from his embrace and turned to face him. "I just wanted a breath of fresh air before retiring."

He snorted in disbelief at her primly affected air. "Come here, wife," he commanded softly, seductively. Rafe held his breath and waited for her, willing her to make the first move, exerting iron will not to reach for her before she touched him first. *You want this as much as I, Moon Flower.*

As if in a drugged trance, Deborah complied, her steps

halting and slow until she stood very close to him, placing her trembling hands on his chest.

Unable to hold back any longer, he crushed her to him and swooped down to feast on her slender neck, raining kisses across her throat and up to her ears, temples, eyelids. Then, feeling her arms tighten around his neck and her fingers tangle in his hair, he growled low and ravaged her mouth. With a small whimper of surrender, she opened to his sensual onslaught and kissed him back. Their tongues dueled, twining together, probing and exploring until they were both trembling. Rafe tangled his hands in the long silvery skein of her hair, pulling on it, tipping her head back in submission. Their bodies pressed intimately one against the other. Finally, he broke the fierce kiss with a ragged sigh but still held Deborah tightly to him.

Sobbing, she choked out, "You may have taught me desire, but you care nothing for my spirit, my soul."

Her desolation tore at him and he gasped out in pain, "It is your spirit, your very soul that I wish to possess most of all, Deborah."

"Then you will leave me nothing," she whispered on the still night air, unable to relinquish the warmth of his embrace, holding fast to him.

"Then it's an even trade, for you have left me nothing, Moon Flower," he murmured against her throat as he swept her up and carried her into the house.

"Just because his wife is Anglo does not mean he is a spy, Captain," Adrian Woll said measuringly as he paced from behind the small desk in the sitting room converted into an office. Flores had been hounding him to arrest Rafael Flamenco for two days, just as Flamenco wanted him to arrest Flores. He sighed. "I know you and he have quarreled over the woman. Is there perhaps more to this feud than simple rivalry?"

Enrique Flores took a deep breath to calm himself. Woll had been a professional soldier for three countries. He did not get to the rank of general by being a fool or a poor judge of men. He had on several occasions made his distaste for the irregulars quite clear. If Woll knew Enrique was a comanchero, it might prove fatal. Flores must proceed very cautiously.

"My distrust of Flamenco, General, goes back many years to Nacogdoches. He and several of his friends picked a fight with me in a bar and beat me almost to death. He is a coward and a traitor."

"Odd, that a man of such obvious education and refinement should be living in this wilderness," Woll speculated aloud.

Flores pounced. "Yes, consider, if he is really from a distinguished New Orleans family, what is he doing here in San Antonio? And, why do all the Anglos in town call him Rafe Fleming, not Rafael Flamenco? His wife is a Yankee who consorts with prisoners and insurrectionists. I've had her boardinghouse watched. Late last night a messenger of some sort slipped in and met with Fleming and his wife."

At this, Woll's head jerked to attention. "Why wasn't I notified at once? I've left strict orders about curfews and men slipping in and out of the city."

Flores spread his hands in a placating gesture. "All I know so far is that one man on foot slipped through the guards and entered the boardinghouse. I have two of my best men watching this morning to see what they do next."

"Indeed. See to it that I'm informed of what transpires, Captain. Dismissed." Woll watched the guerilla salute and leave his presence. He sat on the large sofa in the corner of the room and rubbed the bridge of his nose. Christ! How he hated having scum like Flores in his command, but his orders had been explicit. He was to use the irregulars who raided along the border and dealt with the savages, but every professional instinct he possessed made him recoil from consorting with banditti who preyed on their own people.

He made a snap decision. Ringing for an orderly, he sent for one of his own trusted officers. "I want Mrs. Kensington or Fleming, whatever she calls herself now, watched. See who comes and goes and report everything to me, including

what Captain Flores and his agents do.'' Captain Rodriguez
saluted his general smartly and left to follow orders.

When Rafe awakened that morning he found Deborah
sleeping soundly by his side. He propped his head up on
one hand and watched her beautiful, expressive face. In
sleep it looked guileless and childlike, but he knew once she
awakened, her eyes would cloud with guilt and self-accusation.
*She comes to me in passion she can't deny, but I'm not
reaching her. She sees only a dangerous stranger and
remembers only a selfish boy.*

Praying that time together, spent building Renacimiento
and raising Adam, might allow her to love and trust without
reservation, Rafe quietly slipped from bed. He would let her
sleep a bit longer. There were purple shadows beneath her
eyes. Smiling, he recalled their loving of the night before.
She had good reason to be tired!

When he arrived in the dining room with Adam in tow,
breakfast was almost ready. Charlee McAllister had helped
Sadie prepare a feast. Watching Charlee's efficient movements, Rafe admired her grit. She had disguised herself as a
boy and slipped into town through Woll's lines. Still, he had
to get her out before she was discovered and jailed as a spy
or some such nonsense. He cursed the danger from Flores
and the ill-timing of Charlee's arrival.

As he listened to breakfast table conversation, it became
apparent that Charlee worked for a very prominent Texian, a
veteran of San Jacinto, who owned a large ranch nearby. If
only he could get his wife and son to Bluebonnet, they
would be safe from Flores until he could deal with him. He
would use his pass to get the ''boy'' out of town and return
her before anyone knew she'd slipped in. Then he'd also
know where the ranch was located. He only prayed he could
make arrangements with General Woll to move Deborah and
Adam as soon as he returned.

Planting a kiss on Deborah's brow and giving Adam a
hug, Rafe set out immediately after breakfast for the livery
to saddle Bostonian and rent a nag suitable for a ''boy'' he
was delivering to his cousin in Gonzales.

On the long ride to Bluebonnet, Charlee finally let her

suspicious reserve slip and questioned him about his past life and relationship with Deborah.

She's protective of her friend, he thought as he tried to frame a reply to her tentative query about his not looking like a Creole gentleman. Some gentleman! Scarred and callused, dressed in buckskins, living more like a wild Indian than a civilized Frenchman; he knew his family would cringe in mortification if they even recognized him in his present state.

"It's been so long ago I scarcely remember that life. I was a spoiled young fool, rich, bored . . ." Before he knew it, Rafe found himself unburdening a great deal to Charlee McAllister's sympathetic ears. His wife, it seemed, had confided little about their failed marriage to her friend other than saying that they wanted different things. Now, ironically, he wanted from Deborah the very same things she had asked of him seven years ago—and he wanted desperately to give them to her in return: complete fidelity and commitment, total trust and love.

By the time he had delivered Charlee to her big ranch house, he had made a friend. "I've seen the loneliness in Deborah's eyes ever since I met her. I think she loves you, Rafe. Be patient with her and don't force her. She's a strong-willed woman, but she's worth waiting for."

"After six years of searching, I figure we've got the rest of our lives," he replied with a sad smile. "Thank you, Charlee."

On the way back to town, Rafe pondered Charlee's words. He must curb his temper and sarcasm, stop teasing her, and try harder to see things from her viewpoint. After all, Deborah had made a new life for herself and her child without any help from him or any other man. Such an independent woman would have been alien and unappealing to Rafael Flamenco, but Rafe Fleming knew he could love no other.

"You are certain about this?" General Woll's keen gaze made Captain Rodriguez uncomfortable.

"Most certainly, Excellency. The 'boy' Fleming used his safe conduct to smuggle out of San Antonio is really a girl named Charlee McAllister, rather an infamous sort. She was involved in the shooting of a comanchero named Rufus Brady and lives with a Texian rancher who was one of Sam Houston's officers in the 1836 rebellion."

Woll looked across the office to Captain Flores, who had accompanied Rodriguez. "Well, it seems your suspicions may be justified. I want Flamenco taken into custody when he returns to San Antonio."

"What makes you certain he'll return?" Rodriguez asked.

Flores smirked evilly. "Oh, he'll return all right. His woman and his cub are here."

"I repeat, Captains, I want him taken alive for questioning—not shot!" Woll's voice scarcely changed pitch, but both men knew the danger in disobeying such a strongly worded order.

Enrique Flores planned to take his chances.

As Rafe neared the outskirts of San Antonio, he was deeply preoccupied with thoughts of what he would say to Deborah that night. Absently, he fished in his pocket for the safe conduct paper. Just as he began to pull it out he looked up and saw one of the guards at the roadside drawing a bead on him! The shot cracked over his head as he turned Bostonian, slid over one side of the horse, and drew his pistol, all in one continuous motion. Several shots whistled around him as he returned fire and beat a hasty retreat, zigzagging off the road into a copse of brushy shrubs and trees.

One of the soldiers crumpled and two others ducked for cover. Spurring Bostonian, Rafe cut down an arroyo and rode as fast as he dared over the rocky, uneven ground.

"You fools! Shitting ignorant whoresons!" Enrique Flores heard the report from the sergeant in charge of his hand-picked men. "After all the cautions I gave you about his cleverness—you're dealing with a man who escaped from Comanche, for God's sake!"

Sergeant Ortiz cringed under the tirade. "I have sent out two of my best men to search for him, Captain. They will surely capture him."

Flores snorted and swore again. "I can imagine! Capturing a man who lived with Comanche should be child's play for men too ignorant to hold their fire until he came into range!"

Flores's assessment was right. Rafe had no trouble shaking the two men on his trail. He doubled back and scouted the Mexican emplacements around the city. He might with luck get past them, but he was certain now that once inside he would face yet another ambush at the boardinghouse. *If only I knew someone in town I could trust.* But he didn't. *I'll just wait 'til nightfall and slip in. Something will turn up to help me.*

The something turned out to be none other than the very same nervous harbinger of disaster he'd met on the San Antonio road three days earlier. Knowing Whalen Simpson had courted Deborah did not endear him to Rafe. The very idea that the man might have become Deborah's husband or Adam's father appalled him, especially when he found Simpson sleeping beside a glowing campfire.

Even the click of his gun being cocked over Simpson's head didn't rouse him. Rafe had to resort to shaking the fool.

"Who—what in hell—you again!" The stable keeper sat up and shook his bearlike head. "I ain't had no sleep in days. Guess I took a chance fallin' off like thet." He looked sheepishly at Rafe's contemptuous expression.

"You're lucky I wasn't one of Woll's reconnaissance patrols," Rafe said levelly as he kicked dirt over the glowing coals. "What are you doing out here all alone?"

"I ain't alone. At least, when I meet up with 'Ole Paint' Caldwell I won't be."

Even in the wilds of north Texas, Rafe had heard of Matt Caldwell, a seasoned Indian fighter and veteran of the Revolution. "Caldwell figuring on rallying men to retake the city?"

"Got him near six hundred already, including a batch o' rangers under a young feller named Hays."

"Jack Hays?" At Simpson's affirmative nod, Rafe said, "I met him once a couple of years back. Good man to have on your side."

Simpson's eyes squinted measuringly. "You figger ta join up with us?"

"Seems General Woll's left me no choice," Rafe replied grimly.

Chapter 25

The smell of smoke was faint but Rafe's finely honed senses picked it up before he saw the sentry who challenged them in the still dawn air. The man was one of Jack Hays's rangers, a tough, wiry sort who nodded to Simpson, eyed Rafe up and down in one fast assessment, and then motioned them toward the camp. Men were rising from their bedrolls as the first faint streaks of pink light etched themselves across the stark landscape. Rafe estimated Caldwell had about one hundred fifty men. Long odds considering Woll had fourteen hundred.

Rafe's black eyes scanned the helter-skelter groups of men spread across the banks of the creek. He muttered to Simpson, "I'd be interested in seeing what Jack Hays has in mind. For sure not charging Woll's emplacements with a few hundred men. You say he's been stationed in the city this past year?"

"Yeah. Him 'n his men been scoutin' Woll's army even before they got near the city. His men are over there, near them willow thickets." He waved in the general direction of a large group of men, already up and eating their meager rations.

Dismounting, Rafe wended his way toward Hays's rangers. About midway there, he spied John Coffee Hays near one campfire, conferring with three other heavily armed men. Slightly built and quiet, Hays was underestimated by many people when they first met him, but Rafe had seen him back down a whole mob of drunken, dangerous Texians in Owl Creek a couple of years earlier. For cold nerve and common sense, Rafe had never met a better man.

Hearing Rafe's approach, Hays turned from his conversation and his expressive features split in a broad grin. "Rafe Fleming! You're a long way from Renacimiento."

As Rafe reached for his hand, he replied, "That I am, but who knows where our fortunes lead us? I'm here to join your fight. My wife and son are in San Antonio, Jack."

The younger man's expression registered amazement. "So you found her in San Antonio?" A look of incredulity spread across his face. "A blond woman, tall—Mrs. Kensington from the boardinghouse?"

Rafe smiled crookedly. "Yeah. She took on a whole new identity."

"I should have figured it out—her silver blond hair and Yankee accent—even her son's coloring. I never saw the boy, but several people told me he was dark."

"There's no way you could have known. She didn't want to be found, Jack." Rafe lapsed into silence.

Taking the cue, Hays quickly changed the subject. "You have plans to join our fight?"

Rafe nodded, then said, "I had a safe conduct from Woll. Seems someone rescinded it while I was out of town for a day. Ever hear of a comanchero named Enrique Flores? He's a captain with the invading army now."

"He have something personal against you?"

Rafe grinned darkly. "Let's just say I have something personal against him. How many men do you think Caldwell will muster, and how soon can we retake the city?"

Hays shrugged. "Ever since we got word of Woll's invasion on the tenth, I've been tracking the wily devil. He left the road and cut his own trail through impossible terrain. We never even found a trace of him until he'd taken the city on the eleventh. He's no one to underestimate. I imagine we can muster six to seven hundred men in a few more days."

"And in the meanwhile, Flores and his irregulars walk the streets of San Antonio," Rafe said grimly.

"We can move pretty quick to distract them, I think, even though we don't have enough men to risk an all-out fight.

Trick is to fool that Frenchman into thinking we have more men massed than we do. Not an easy thing to do—Woll's the best field tactician around since President Houston was a general.''

Rafe was impressed at the comparison, one that would not be made lightly by any Texian. ''You have any ideas on how we can fool a fellow as sharp as Woll?''

''Let me introduce you to some of my men and talk about our ideas over some hot coffee,'' Hays replied with a smile.

''Jist like yew said, Capt'n. They's all comin' out fer us,'' Jinx Ferguson said, lobbing a big wad of tobacco to the ground. The men under Hays's command were situated on a ridge around four hundred yards east of the Alamo. He had dispatched about twenty men with the fastest horses to ride around the city perimeter, rousing the sleepy soldiers with curses and insults, daring them to come out and fight.

Rafe had been one of the riders, drawing a good deal of fire as he hurled a series of particularly choice invectives at the Mexicans in their native language. As he trotted Bostonian up the ridge toward Hays, he grinned. ''I think they're taking the bait.''

''Yeah. If only they don't take it too good—and send more men than we can handle,'' Hays replied levelly. ''We need to lure them out a few hundred at a time and pick them off from ambush.''

''Speak of the devil, I think the first wave's coming,'' Rafe said as he watched the activity from the Alamo.

Hays swore as he assessed the number of cavalry heading their way. ''Let's rile them up and see how fast their horses are,'' he called down the line. Less than fifty seasoned fighting men under Hays formed up a loose line. Their leader spurred his big bay and headed down the hill pell-mell with his men close behind him, yelling bloodcurdling threats and insults at the column of cavalry, which immediately took up pursuit. Wheeling around in a broad arc, the rangers then headed north toward Salado Creek, where Caldwell's much larger force lay in wait.

Rafe flattened himself along Bostonian's neck and spurred the big sorrel forward as musket balls whistled and dropped all around him. Miraculously, none of the rangers was hit. It was almost five miles to their rendezvous point and Rafe hoped the Mexicans' aim would not improve with practice.

Just as the Texians' exhausted horses neared the brushy ravine where the militia lay in wait, Hays signaled the men to turn toward the creek. Their horses plunged into the icy water. The Mexican army was getting dangerously close and the Texian militia was nowhere in sight.

At once Rafe realized Hays's plan. Their only hope of escape was to ride back toward their camp, hoping to encounter the tardy militia. About a mile downstream the brushy thickets along the riverbank sprang to life with Texian riflemen, who set up a murderous fire against the Mexican cavalry. Colonel Carrasco's men quickly gave up the chase and retreated to take cover on the boulder-strewn ridge to the east of Caldwell's militiamen.

A withering fight ensued with the outnumbered Texians exacting fierce casualties from the Mexican cavalry, who possessed poorer arms and decidedly poorer marksmanship.

"We got them pinned down, Capt'n," Jinx said as he crawled up to where Hays and Fleming had taken cover.

"Don't be too sure who's got who pinned down," Hays said.

Grunting in agreement, Rafe swore. "Why the hell weren't those men ready by the ford? This is a piss poor place to fight. If Woll brings up his infantry and cannon, we're sitting ducks."

Jinx replied, "I palavered with one o' Ole Paint's men a minit ago. Seems a couple o' fellers wanted ta wait 'n th' volunteers had ta take a vote on backin' ya."

Rafe swore. "We took a vote on this plan last night, for Christ's sake!"

Hays only shrugged, used to the splintered loyalties and uncertain temperaments of Texian militia. "What we need to know now is just where the general is and what he's doing. Still got that Comanche instinct for slipping in and out of tight spots, Fleming?"

"Find Woll and check his strength," Rafe replied, anticiıg Hays's orders. With pantherlike grace, he vanished) the willows. He retrieved Bostonian from the shelter ere he was hidden and led him silently away from the ooting. Within an hour he had returned, reporting to Hays at Woll had just left the city with over two hundred infantry and two cannons.

"They should be here in a couple of hours," he finished.

Hays grunted, picking up a stick Rafe had used to draw a crude map in the dirt. "Never count on Woll taking that long. He marched with no roads and made it to San Antonio weeks sooner than we thought he could." He looked over to Matt Caldwell, who was present at the quick strategy session held during desultory firing.

Caldwell, thickset and stiff from multiple wounds accumulated in his years as an Indian fighter on the Texas frontier, sat back and rubbed his bristly mustache. "I expect he'll be along right soon. If the guns these boys got are any sample, we can take out a lot of them."

"Trick is avoiding the cannons while we're doing it," Hays added sourly.

"They know they outnumber us. Maybe if we fall back just as the general gets here, we can make him charge down that hill into a little crossfire," Rafe said. "Before he gets his artillery pieces sighted in."

"No, we'd have to move before that," Hays replied, turning an idea over in his mind.

By the time they heard the infantry rounding the curve of the ravine, the Texians' plans were in place. At the first sight of the Mexican column, the Texian officers began to yell in confusion, urging their men to retreat, leaving a handful of Hays's rangers in the willow thickets around the stream.

Holding his men in good order, Woll sounded the bugle and ordered a charge after firing several quick rounds from one of the cannons. The grapeshot missed its mark, but when the Mexican soldiers charged, the Texian long rifles did not miss theirs. The ground was quickly littered with Mexican dead and wounded as the Texian militia circled back and opened a killing fire.

Rafe had used his Hawken rifle several times but pre-